I0583526

PATH
OF THE
WOLF

PATH OF THE WOLF

Tony-Paul de Vissage

EPIC PUBLISHING

Love will find a way through paths where wolves fear to prey.

Lord Byron

Chapter One

IT WAS EARLY in the spring when Isabeau de Montaigne first met the man who would become her lover.

France was at war with Italy; that very day, the country had suffered another defeat in its continuing conflict begun by their king, Louis, the twelfth of that name. It was also the day when, after an absence of three months, Isabeau's husband returned to Aux-le-Piémont.

With her skirts skimming her ankles to avoid brushing the damp grass, which made up the untended meadow that called itself their front courtyard, she met François on the path connecting their cottage to the highroad. If the sluggishness of her movements was any indication, she was unenthused about welcoming him home.

The first time he went away, when she woke to find him throwing a change of clothing into his knapsack along with his sketchbooks and charcoals, she thought he was abandoning her.

He swore otherwise, that he would come back "when I've found what I'm seeking."

It had happened so many times since, she didn't worry if she awoke and her husband was gone, didn't wait in quiet distress for the sight of his silhouette on the highroad. Sometimes, she hoped he wouldn't come back.

Being an abandoned wife would've been sheer heaven.

Recently, he'd been approached by *le église de Rue Jean-Baptiste Amélioré* about painting a mural depicting their sainted namesake. François accepted and set off on a quest to find the man who'd be his subject.

This time, he'd been gone so overlong she wondered if perhaps *le bon Dieu* had finally granted her unspoken wish. Then she thought, *why should he? He never has before.*

Now, as if to underscore that belief, François was back, and this time, he wasn't alone.

There was a dog with him, restrained at the end of a length of rope; a big lumbering brute, loping clumsily behind him. Its gait was odd, as if its forelegs were shorter than the hind ones.

Merde, Isabeau thought resentfully. *Something else for me to tend after he loses interest.*

Like the bird he bought from a Spanish sailor off a ship, supposedly having sailed to the newly discovered land to the west. Or those exotic flowers that wilted and died as soon as the first cold wind blew off the mountains. Of course, he used the bird in several paintings, but after that, it sat in its cage, ignored. Isabeau was the one cleaning its droppings, taking it out and letting it fly around the cottage and sit on her shoulder, until one day it flew away, never to return.

She hoped it had made its way over the mountains into the warmer climes of Italy.

Now, her husband stood before her again, sweaty and travel-worn, the dust of the highroad surrounding him like a cloud, begrimed into the sleeves of his linen shirt and the shoulders of his doublet.

Briefly, she was tempted to stalk back to the house, refusing him the welcome he expected, he deserved, but, as usual, duty overcame anger. What would be the use of turning away? When she looked back, François would still be there, and so would that dog or whatever it was.

He stopped. So did she.

The creature dropped to its haunches.

Without preamble or greeting, she said, "Did you find what you sought?"

Not that she really cared.

"Yes," he answered. "I did. I found my *St. Jean.*"

"Where is he?" She looked past him down the track, expecting to see some beautiful boy on horseback, hurrying to catch up. It was usually the handsome son of a noble family whom he had entranced with promises of immortality on canvas.

She saw no one. The path was empty.

"Here." He held up the rope.

Her gaze traveled its length to where it wrapped around the animal's neck, only to have her attention caught and held by the oddest eyes she had ever seen. They were the color of molten copper, flecked with glints of bronze-patina-green, under heavy brows meeting in a single line, looking out of place in what she could see of the mud-bedaubed face.

Isabeau thought, *these are not the eyes of a beast.*

Frowning, she studied the creature's face. An odd countenance, no snout, no muzzle with a wet bulbous nose, though fur-covered and whiskery, as uncomfortably disturbing as its eyes.

She glanced at the creature's body, at the long, coarse hair growing in a tangled mane around its neck and down its back, spreading over dirty shoulders. A matted pelt encircled its hips, part of its texture and color like the skin of another creature, the rest its own flesh, and the legs ... hairy but relatively bare, as were the feet ... but so filthy.

With a start, she was certain she was looking not at an animal, but a man, a dirt-caked man, squatting at her husband's side, his fingers digging into the grass. A man, watching her with curious but intelligent eyes.

Oh, surely not.

As if sensing her unease, he growled, a rough, low grating, deep in the throat. Isabeau took a step backward.

"Steady," François said, but whether to her or the creature, she wasn't certain. "Don't be afraid. It's only that he doesn't know you. Hold out your hand."

When she didn't move, he repeated, "Hold out your hand. Let him get to know your scent."

As if he's a dog. She wanted to tell him she wasn't afraid, then thought, *Why bother?*

Her fear, or lack of it, didn't matter to François. Defiantly, as if she were dealing with one of her Uncle Étienne's hunting dogs, she offered her hand to the beast.

He sniffed at it, running his nose along her fingertips and against her palm, snuffling loudly. He barely touched her, a mere brush of flesh against flesh, but it made her skin chill slightly, though she managed to hide its shiver.

With a whimper, he thrust his head against her hand. Automatically, Isabeau's fingers stroked the filthy hair, creeping around the side of his head to one ear, over its slightly pointed tip, scratching behind it as she'd often done to her uncle's dogs. He grunted with pleasure, leaning against her palm.

His tongue shot out, brushing her wrist. She forced herself not to recoil, and made her fingers continue their scratching movement.

"He likes you. *Good*." François looked satisfied, as if *he* had something to do with the beast's acceptance of her.

She pulled her hand away. The creature stared at her. Reproachfully, she thought. He'd liked having his ear scratched.

Her hand felt greasy. She forced herself not to scrub her palm against her skirt. She hoped he didn't carry fleas or other vermin.

"I'm hungry." François's belly growled, underscoring his words. "For the past mile, all I could think of was a bowl of Mathilde's good lamb stew. Is supper ready?"

As if the cook had nothing more to do than prepare a meal to sit and spoil, waiting for his return.

"It should be soon." Isabeau put reproach into her next words. "We didn't expect you."

"No reason you should."

No apology for appearing with no warning. It wasn't in François's nature to think of others or show regret at their inconvenience.

"Tend to my pet." He tossed the rope to Isabeau. She nearly missed it, scrabbling to keep it in her hands.

"What shall I do with him?" She was resentful. As she had suspected, she was to assume care of the thing.

"Put him in the room inside my studio." His answer was offhanded, as if every day he appeared leading a creature that might or might not be a man masquerading as a beast. "There's some chain in there. Replace the rope, and fasten him to one of the window bars so he won't run away. He may be restless, being in a new place."

He took a key from his purse and lobbed it to her. François always kept the key to his studio with him. As if he didn't trust Isabeau not to snoop during his absence.

Isabeau caught the key more easily than she caught the rope.

He continued to the cottage.

"François, wait! Will he understand me?"

He didn't respond or look back.

"François?"

Together, she and the creature watched him walk away, studying the swagger of his body where the fabric of his doublet stretched across his broad shoulders.

"Come on, you." Isabeau tugged on the rope.

She started for the building that was her husband's studio. Rising from his haunches, François's new pet trotted behind her with that odd, clumsy gait.

Other than *le privé*, the studio was the only outbuilding on the property, situated to the side and behind the cottage but clearly visible from the path. Originally, it had been a stable. Shortly after they moved into the cottage, François converted it into the place where he created those paintings his patrons declared masterpieces.

Isabeau had no opinion on that score. She was rarely called upon to judge her husband's talent.

With his own hands, he'd toiled in the broiling sun, sawing, nailing, and hammering to make a home for his paintings. When it came to his art, François didn't stint.

Isabeau thought it was too bad he didn't do the same where his wife was concerned.

Refusing assistance from his in-laws, he and their one manservant tore out stalls and hayloft, using the boards to make a floor covering dirt and animal detritus. Part of the roof was removed, replaced with windows holding precious panes of clear glass, purchased from the glassblowers of Murano in Italy —this was before the war—and

brought to the cottage *via* ship through the port of Marseilles. They'd gone without meat for two months to pay for that glass, but François willingly suffered for his art and expected his household to do the same.

He also cut out most of two walls and replaced them with floor-to-ceiling windows.

It was fortunate the little building already faced north; else he probably would've shifted its foundation to catch that harsh, clear light so necessary for the artist's canvas.

The storage room was built into the back of the studio. Once a place where bags of grain and harnesses were kept, it was accessed only through an inner door. There was a single paneless and shuttered window François fitted with parallel iron bars, lest some miscreant attempt to break in, for that was where he now kept his canvases, finished paintings, and drawing supplies.

It also held a cot and blankets. When in a creative fervor, François worked late into the night, sleeping in the storeroom where he might awaken and immediately return to the canvas. Since those times generally coincided with his finding a new and pretty model, Isabeau didn't delude herself that he wasn't sleeping with her, too. She decided that was one of the reasons he didn't want her coming to the studio.

It was only with the pretty girls, however. François wasn't concerned with the equally pretty boys. He might paint them, but their bodies interested him only in the way they looked on his canvases.

Privately, Isabeau thought she would've been happier if François preferred boys, to the complete exclusion of his wife, but she couldn't be so fortunate.

* * *

WITH THE KEY, Isabeau opened the studio and went in, tugging on the rope as the creature hesitated at the threshold. He followed reluctantly. When she unlocked the storeroom and went inside, he stopped in the doorway, pulling back on the rope with a whimper.

That made Isabeau wonder if he'd ever been inside a building before.

Where did François find this creature?

Was he running wild in some wood, like a *loup-garou*? She had heard tales of abandoned children raised by wolves, but thought them merely fictions. Had he attacked her husband and been beaten into submission? Neither appeared injured in any way, but the creature's hair was so tangled and matted with dirt, he might have sustained a hidden wound.

How could she tell?

François seemed hale enough.

Just now, the beast didn't look ferocious. Squatting in the doorway, gazing about, then back at her with those unsettling eyes, he seemed more afraid. Cautiously, he stared at the wall, sniffing the boards.

Does he smell the long-ago scent of the horses once living here?

"Come in." She tugged on the rope, then thought better of it, for surely that must hurt his neck, perhaps make him resist more, even snap at her. Feeling a surge of shame, she spoke to him as she would to a dog. "Come. Good boy."

Is he a dog or a man? She assumed the creature was male. There simply was no feminine aspect about him. *How does one talk to a man who thinks he's a beast?*

He loped forward and stopped again, looking up at her, mouth hanging open. If he'd panted and tried to wag a nonexistent tail, she wouldn't have been surprised.

"There's the cot. You can sleep on it." She decided to speak to him as though he understood.

Perhaps he did. Her uncle's hounds learned commands. It

came to her that the creature was probably some poor half-brain turned out by his family and left to fend for himself. It was perhaps fortunate that François came upon him.

She gestured to the cot; a blanket folded neatly at its foot. He looked from her to it, cocking his head to one side.

"Sleep. Here." To emphasize her meaning, she patted the blanket.

Again, there was that unsettling stare. When he moved, it was so swiftly she startled, staggering backward.

Seizing the blanket in his teeth and dragging it to the floor, he pawed it into a rumpled heap, threw himself upon it, circled three times, and dropped with a grunt. He curled his legs against his chest, body twisting so his chin rested on crossed forearms in a pose so doglike she might've laughed if it hadn't been so bizarre.

"Not that way."

With both hands, she caught the edge of the blanket, pulling on it with such a heave that she jerked it from under him. With a yelp, he rolled over. Crouching, he cowered, arms over his head.

"Here now, I'm not going to hit you. Oh ..." Her voice rose in exasperation. Dropping the blanket onto the cot, she held out her hand.

He dodged, crouching lower.

"Shh, it's all right." She touched the tangled hair, feeling its gritty, greasy texture against her palm.

Whimpering, he flinched, arms wrapping tighter.

"There, there, I won't hurt you." She made her voice soothing, the way she might talk to a puppy someone had accidentally stepped on. "It's all right. Shh."

She continued caressing that filthy hair until the trembling ceased. He lowered his arms, peeping up at her fearfully. Again, she patted the blanket.

"Come now. Up. Here."

This time, he got onto the cot—actually leaping onto it, making it wobble precariously—tried to circle, lost his balance, and toppled over the side, crashing to the floor.

She was there before he could recover, catching an arm and pulling him upright, though it was more of a half-crouch, back curved in a hunch.

"Are you hurt?"

The oddest expression crossed that dirty, hairy face, what she could see of it.

Is this the first time anyone has asked that question, or shown concern?

Again, she patted the cot. Once more, he climbed back onto it. This time, he straddled it, a leg hanging over each side, watching her.

François had said to chain him.

She looked around, found the chain lying in a corner, and dragged it to the cot. It had a hook-and-clasp at each end.

She saw now that around his neck was a leather collar to which the rope was fastened. He didn't move as she untied the rope and let it fall. She used one of the hooks to fasten the chain to the collar. Other than a slight grunt, shoulders sagging under the weight, he didn't make a sound as Isabeau looped the other end around one of the window bars.

Without warning, he dropped onto his side, knees drawn up, head resting upon a bent arm.

"I'll see you in the morning."

Once again, she questioned speaking to the creature as if he could comprehend, but one talked to pets, even horses and cows, didn't one? She had chatted often with the bird, and it understood. At least, she thought it did, since it occasionally replied, making noises sounding like words. When it escaped, it had even sounded as though it called, "Goodbye," while soaring over the trees.

"Good night." She went to the door.

No answer, of course. What would she have done if he'd replied?

Isabeau shut the door and locked it.

By the time she entered the dining room, François was finishing a bowl of stew. From the spatters on the tabletop around his place, it wasn't his first. She thought of meals in her father's home, where no one raised a fork until all were present and seated. François never let his wife's absence keep him from a meal.

He no longer wore the same clothing. He'd exchanged his doublet and shirt for different ones, cleaner, much more elaborate, and newer in style. The shirt featured a wide, low neckline, its yoke decorated with smocking. The doublet was sewn tightly at the waist, its full sleeves slashed, and the fabric of his shirt pulled through the cuts, making linen puffs.

Richer clothing perhaps, but inside them was the same road-dusted man who greeted her on the path. A silent, deep inhalation told her François hadn't bothered to bathe or freshen up with a damp cloth before changing.

Isabeau didn't ask where he'd gotten the garments, which she was well aware he hadn't taken with him. Doubtless more hand-me-downs from the *marquis*, his friend and occasional patron.

It was a ploy of his to wear his poorest clothing when visiting His Lordship. Once, he'd actually torn a hole in the knee of his stock, having Isabeau darn it so he could appear before Alphonse du Maurier in patched stockings. When the *marquis* exclaimed over this, François explained he had yet to be paid for his last painting and "one needs to wear what one has, if the francs aren't forthcoming." He'd returned home with two barely worn outfits, taken from the nobleman's own wardrobe. His own clothing went into the rag basket, where torn garments were tossed to be resurrected as cleaning cloths. It had served its purpose and would now be used by Mathilde for dusting.

"Where did you find him?" Isabeau asked, taking her seat at the table.

Mathilde placed a bowl before her, setting it down so roughly the stew sloshed over the rim. Isabeau ignored her as she picked up her spoon.

Someday soon, I may reveal my true opinion of that fat sloven.

Until now, she'd forced herself to be civil to the cook, though the feeling wasn't returned. If anything, Mathilde was as openly insolent as possible without risking her place.

The manservant's attitude wasn't much better.

Mathilde and Maxime were both closer to François's age than Isabeau's. Living on the remnants of her late grandfather's estate, they were serfs trained to be house servants in the *château* where she was born.

In Isabeau's case, familiarity truly bred contempt. Unlike the feared reverence they gave Isabeau's mother, who ran her father's household, in their minds, they owed no homage to the young woman they'd watched grow from a colicky baby into a pretty but callow girlhood.

At her marriage, Isabeau received Mathilde and Maxime as part of her dowry. They accompanied her to her new home, where their status was as it had been before, receiving food and shelter in exchange for their labor. They called her *maîtresse*, but it meant nothing. As far as they were concerned, François was master of the house; he was the *artiste*, the one with God-given talent, and they immediately switched their loyalty to *him*.

Not that it mattered to François if either was blatantly

outright in their disrespect of his wife. As long as Mathilde continued cooking such excellent meals, and Maxime did as ordered, he didn't care how rude they acted.

His attitude was evident now, in fact. Ignoring the greasy stains on the tablecloth and the way the cook served Isabeau, he tore off a piece of bread, sopping up the last liquid from his own bowl before he spoke.

"I've had a long and arduous search," he said through the mouthful of bread, not really answering her question. The liquid caused his lips to smack unpleasantly.

Isabeau hid her distaste behind her table kerchief.

"I must have walked a hundred miles. I went to everyone I knew ... former patrons, friends, even searched among village streets, but I could find no man worthy to be my St. Jean."

Isabeau forced herself to remain silent. She might have questions, but she could see François was going to tell the story his own way, making his search seem more difficult and dramatic than it probably was.

"At last," he continued, "in my desperation, I found myself at the home of my old friend, Alphonse, *le Marquis* du Maurier ..."

* * *

"I HAVE FAILED, ALPHONSE." François moaned his lament over a goblet of the *marquis's* best vintage. "Nowhere have I found anyone who remotely resembles my St. Jean."

"Not even among my own sons?" Alphonse still smarted from François's rejection of any of his three children as his model. To the *marquis*, it seemed he was reveling in his unhappiness, though du Maurier was too polite to say so.

They were seated in the *marquis's* salon, enjoying some after-dinner wine. It was early in the evening, but Alphonse's lady wife and his sons had been given rather pointed permission to leave their presence so the two friends could speak of old times and escapades no spouse or offspring's ears should hear.

Some might have considered it odd for a noble to be friends with someone in whose veins no patrician blood flowed, but a chance meeting at a patron's home introduced the two, and they soon discovered mutual interests transcending lineage, namely, wine, women, and occasionally a somewhat discordant song. Alphonse also cultivated François so that he might claim the status of knowing someone on the way to becoming famous. François likewise ingratiated himself with the *marquis* for the other man's wealth and influence.

"Your sons are indeed handsome young men," François replied, raising the goblet and swilling down another swallow. "Even Aubert, who, I will admit, is so lean he appears to have spent at least forty days in the wilderness."

Aubert was currently fifteen and amid a gawky and rail-thin adolescence. Alphonse started to point out this fact.

"In spite of that," François didn't give him a chance to speak, "neither he nor his brothers have ever known hunger or privation. My St. Jean must be one who has starved in the desert, seen angels in his delirium, heard God speak ... his beauty should shine through his rags and filth."

"Have you looked among my servants?" his friend dared ask, somewhat mildly, but hopefully, after this grandiose speech.

"You feed your servants too well, *mon ami*." François emptied his cup and looked around at the wine steward, who didn't move.

"But of course. After all, I *am* a *marquis*." Alphonse gestured for the man to pour more wine. As the steward relayed the order to a footman who hurried to do so, he continued, a little defensively, "No one will ever say Alphonse du Maurier's servants have a lean or hungry look."

"I have failed then." François returned to his theme of self-pity, drawing the spotlight back to himself and away from his friend's self-praise. He took another loud swallow. "Now I must return to Aux-le-Piémont, inform the good fathers of *St. Jean-Baptiste Amélioré* of my defeat, and give back their retainer." He sighed heavily, declaring, "I'm a failure."

"Nonsense," Alphonse scoffed, slapping him on the shoulder and jarring his hand so the wine sloshed upon the tabletop. "You're François de Montaigne, the great *artiste*, creator of *Dove of the Annunciation, Travail of the Magi*, and other religious masterpieces."

François raised a brow. The gesture suggested that, being a minor noble, Alphonse didn't have to worry about such things as reputations or paying back money given in expectation of something in return.

The steward snapped his fingers, and a second waiting footman stepped forward. Over his forearm, he carried several spotless napkins and now used one to blot the spilled wine from the highly polished tabletop. As the servant hurried back to his place, folding the soiled and red-spotted cloth and placing it under the others he held, François resumed his lament.

"I've never failed to find my subject. The dove?" He refused to be consoled, waving a dismissive hand. "A simple task. It was one of a tame pair, living in a cote on the church grounds. The Magi?" He snapped his fingers. "Three priests who gladly posed for the glory of God. But this time? My reputation is ruined."

He shook his head and fell silent.

"Perhaps not," Alphonse encouraged. He took a sip of his own wine, marveling at how his friend could consume so much so quickly while his own goblet had been filled only once since they sat. "Take a different route as you return home," he suggested. "Why, you may meet your *St. Jean* begging along the highroad."

"Hm." François looked glum. His head drooped, chin resting against the smocked neckline showing through the front of his doublet.

Alphonse scowled at that. He'd made François a gift of the shirt during a recent visit, and already the white fabric was marred by several bright spots of wine and some older-looking grease smears. Apparently, the *artiste*'s manservant didn't know how to remove stains.

"In the meantime, forget your troubles for tonight and let's distract ourselves. My steward tells me a gypsy caravan has camped on the outskirts of my estate." Alphonse looked eager. "He says their *vaida*, their chief, has promised something extraordinary to entertain the *gadje* ... that's what they call us Christians."

"Gypsies?" François raised his head.

"Refugees, I don't doubt," Alphonse confirmed. "Escaping the ravages of that war King Louis is waging against Italy. I daresay our part of France may see a good many of their ilk, since we're so close to the mountains."

"But ... gypsies? The church fathers allow this?"

"I suppose it's our Christian duty to allow them shelter, though *I* certainly wouldn't," Alphonse answered. "So, we lock up our children and our valuables, and the town constable has his day *and* night watches on alert, in case they're to be routed immediately. They're no danger, and are entertaining, in their own heathenish way."

Setting down his goblet, Alphonse stood. He pulled François's cup from his hand and placed it on the table while he grasped his friend's elbow and hauled him to his feet.

"Come, we'll go there, see their dances, listen to their music, perhaps have our fortunes told by some toothless crone speaking our good French with a terrible accent. If we're lucky ..." He cocked his head to one side and winked. "I've heard those

Romany women make love like cats in heat. Perhaps we'll discover whether it's true. Maybe she'll even *transform* into a cat for us."

"That I'd like to see." François allowed himself to be persuaded. He retrieved the wine cup and gulped the remains, then set it down again, wiping his mouth with the back of his hand and adding more spatters to those on the smocking at his cuff. "Very well. Let's go."

Calling for their horses, they rode to where the caravan was camped.

* * *

"BUT WHERE DID YOU FIND *HIM*?" Isabeau persisted. "Who is he?"

"Must you be so impatient?" François asked. "I'm coming to that."

Isabeau forced herself not to answer as she'd like. With a sigh, she waited.

* * *

THE GLOW above the trees guided the two men to where the gypsies had set up camp. It was off the high road leading into the town of La Chapelle, in a nearby pine forest of Alphonse's *desmene*, far enough from the *château* that they had to ride for over two hours. Alphonse said the Rom were clever that way; if someone complained of being robbed or cheated, it would take the Watch so long to get there, the gypsies could have their teams harnessed and be gone before they arrived.

"They're wily as well as dishonest," he noted.

Leaving their horses tied to a rope stretched between two trees where the steeds of others, some of whom Alphonse said he recognized, already stood stamping their hooves and switching their tails, they walked toward the sound of voices and the crackle of campfires.

They found the camp a lively place, full of music and movement. At various spots within the fires's light, entertainments were being played out.

A dark man put a tame bear through its paces. Upon command, the creature balanced a ball on its nose, stood on its hind legs, and danced, crooning in a low growl to the accompaniment of the flute its master played. Those watching—only men, no women or children were allowed to visit a gypsy camp for fear of being carried off—laughed and clapped, as entertained as if they themselves were children.

Further on, two thick poles stood upright, driven into the ground. On a crossbar connecting them hung the gutted carcass of a deer. Poached from one of Alphonse's herds, no doubt.

We should set the magistrate on them, François thought, then added, *later, perhaps*, for he didn't wish to disrupt the fascination of all he saw ... yet.

In front of the deer carcass, two small stakes had been pounded into the dirt. Nearby, a mustachioed Romany played a violin.

Quite well, too. François approved, nodding. Amazing how one untutored could sound as good as a music master.

A gypsy woman whose weathered skin was the color of a roasted chestnut, ushered them to a row of stools already half-filled with an eager audience. She fit exactly Alphonse's description of a wrinkled crone.

"*Glasso* ... music ... you listen ...?"

They settled to be entertained.

While the musician made the instrument sing and wail in that melodious but haunting way only a member of a wandering people could, a heavy-bosomed, red-haired gypsy girl danced, striking a tambourine with elbows and knees. Faux *galbi*—gold coins awled and sewn into the bright shawl girding her skirted hips—jingled and jangled as she spun in a whirling tangle of colored cloth, lifting skirts to reveal naked legs and a thatch as coppery as the tangled curls bouncing about her shoulders.

François viewed that revelation with interest. Would such a burnished lady-nest make for more heated loving? He wondered if the girl could be enticed into letting him find out.

Caught up in the violin's mournful notes, the watching men swayed with the music. Someone began to clap, keeping time with the rhythm of the girl's movements. Others joined in.

She whirled, overblown breasts bouncing.

The violin moaned, and the men along with it. It skirled and sang a haunting, provocative tune. Sweat poured down the girl's face the faster she moved. Bright droplets of moisture struck the nearest men's faces as she spun.

She leaped into the air, shaking her skirts, darted here and there, teasing and taunting, close enough to be touched, then flitting away before eager hands could seize and hold. One or two rose from the stools on which they perched as if to follow her invitation, then sank back, pulled onto their seats by their companions as she continued dancing.

Abruptly, the fire seemed too hot, the spring night unseasonably warm. François swore he could feel a burning rivulet sliding between his shoulder blades, dampening his linen shirt and making it stick to his back. He glanced at Alphonse, then the others. All were oblivious to his discomfort or their own, the sheen of sweat upon their brows, the underarms of their doublets sodden.

The music became faster and faster, even more frantic and wild, the violin changing from a beautiful, if odd, melody into something bizarre and untamed, near frightening, like the shrieks of a lost soul. Several of the men leaned forward, their clapping intensifying to a thunderous din. Eyes widened, mouths hanging open.

The strings ended in a screaming crescendo, the dance in a swirl of fabric. Breasts heaving, the girl fell to the ground, full skirts spread, her head bowed, that glorious copper hair gleaming in the firelight.

"*Sacre!* What a performance!" Alphonse leaped to his feet, pounding his hands together so lustily it should've hurt.

The other men also stood, joining in the applause. The fiddler bowed, accepting their homage. The girl scrambled to her feet. She passed among them, holding out the tambourine for them to fill with their coins. The pieces of metal made a soft thumping as they struck the stretched-tight skin. Several whispered lewd suggestions. She smiled and winked. Clutching the tambourine, she retreated with her version of a curtsey, offering a good view of her bosom.

After that, the men got to their feet, milling about uncertainly. Some wandered to their horses, riding back to town. A few strolled through the caravans, seeking further pleasure, costing them more coins. The old woman worked her way among those remaining, telling fortunes.

Eventually, she came to Alphonse and François.

"*Drabasav, m'sieus*? Your fortune?" She gestured with one hand. "I read?"

Giving her a coin, Alphonse eagerly held out his own hand. She gave his palm a cursory glance.

"Not much to tell. You live long time in peaceful place. Nothing of note ever happen to you." Shaking her head in a parody of sadness, she gave his disappointment a sardonic smirk. "Apologies, my lord."

"Ah, well," Alphonse sighed. "Perhaps it's as well. Here ..." He gestured to François. "Read my friend's and make his better."

She turned to François. He tossed her a coin. She caught it and reached for the hand he held out, then recoiled.

"What is it?" Alphonse looked alarmed.

She had actually paled, coppery skin taking on a sickly hue.

"My friend's a famous *artiste*, but don't be afraid to touch him," he joked.

"Not afraid, good sir." The woman spoke to François, though she backed away as she spoke. "Don't need to take your hand to tell your future. You seek someone. Your quest, *and* your life, end soon."

"What?" François was more intrigued than startled. "What do you mean?"

Her dark gaze, remarkably bright for someone so ancient, met his before darting away. "You'll meet your death at the fangs of a *ruv*."

"*Ruv?*" he repeated. "What's that?"

"A wolf," she explained.

"Then I suppose I'd best stop gamboling in the meadows with the lambs." He laughed again, and Alphonse did, also, but this time his chuckle seemed slightly hollow.

"Laugh while you can," she warned, and bobbed a curtsey before scurrying into the shadows.

"Well." François watched her disappear. "That was a disappointment, and a waste of coin. I'd best be watching them from now on, if I don't find my St. Jean as she predicted."

"Aren't you worried?" Alphonse asked. "About the rest of it, I mean?"

"Why?" His bluster returned. "Because some ignorant gypsy hag says I'll die soon?" He struck his friend on the shoulder. "Hell, man, we're all in danger of that, what with plagues and wars, and such. Every day we live is a threat. As for wolves?"

He gave an incredulous sneer.

"There hasn't been a wolf around here in nearly fifty years. The huntsmen killed them all. If I listen to anything she said, it's that my search for my St. Jean will soon be over. Frankly, my friend, I'm disappointed."

Getting to his feet, François changed the subject.

"Where's this *something special* of which you were told?" He pulled Alphonse upright and took a step in the direction of the horses. "So far, I've seen nothing that can't be viewed at the most threadbare Romany caravan passing through—"

A ragged, bone-chilling howl rent the air.

A man who'd risen to leave stopped, looking around for the source of the sound.

From the shadows between two of the wagons, a gypsy stepped into view. Instead of a doublet, jacket, and stocks, he wore a deep-yoked, full-sleeved shirt bound at his waist by a colorful sash, its hem hanging over his thighs, and stocks stuffed into leather knee boots. There was a dagger tucked into the sash.

"Welcome, *mes maîtres*. I, Boamas, *vaida* of the Rom, invite you to a most remarkable event." He glanced at those walking to their horses. "So amazing, so unbelievable, I must wait until all leave who may be offended by what they see."

His gaze swept over them; hands raised eloquently as he gestured after those departing. A few heard and paused, looking back, listening. The man standing sat down again. So did several others.

"If there are those among you who are weak-hearted or easily distressed by the bizarre and grotesque, then go now, *please* ..." He paused, then added, softly, sardonically, no sneer in his expression but definitely one in his voice, "We will think no less of you."

Again, he paused. The seated men didn't move; a few of those leaving hurried to regain their places.

As he wanted them to, François thought. *What a showman. He's entrapped us using our own curiosity.*

What better way to get an eager audience to stay than by telling them to leave because what was to come was too horrendous for them to see?

"You will stay?" Again, the *vaida's* dark gaze swept the crowd as if challenging each one. "Very well ... I welcome you to something extraordinary."

From those same shadows came the mustachioed man who'd played the flute, leading an animal by a rope around its neck.

A wolf?

François started and half-rose, then tried to cover the movement by laughing slightly. After what the crone had said, that was a bit of a shock.

The beast truly looked lupine, then again, there was something grotesquely human about it, though it moved with a clumsy loping gait, as if it were lame or its legs were unequal in length. Barely out of the shadows, it paused, looking around, shaggy coat unkempt, eyes gleaming. Around its neck, in a travesty of a lady's choker, hung a wreath woven of leaves and flowers, each blossom bright as an amethyst among the greenery.

The creature growled and advanced a few more steps into the firelight, gazing at the crowd of men hurriedly taking their seats.

"*Besh!*" The *vaida* took the rope from the musician, jerking on it. "Sit."

It sank to its haunches.

François fell back onto the stool, legs abruptly weak. He tried to make it seem as though he sat of his own accord, was vaguely aware Alphonse edged his own stool a little closer as if for protection.

What could they do if the thing decided to attack?

For now, at least, the gypsy had it under control. When he pulled again on the rope and snapped a few words in his own language, the creature became docile ... surprisingly so for a beast so obviously untamed. He led it up and down in front of them, talking as he did so.

"This, *mes maîtres*, is Ruvo, found running wild in the Italian forests."

As if it knew he spoke of it, the beast paused. It seemed to acknowledge his introduction, casting that bright gaze over them, panting loudly.

"A creature, *messieurs*, that in our charity, we took in." Here, he bowed slightly, accepting homage for his goodwill with a hand over his heart, though his expression was ironic. "Ruvo is a mystery. Is he man ..."

Surely not. François refused to believe it.

"... or beast? *Le loup-garou* or *le homme*? We're unable to say. We can't tame him. He must be caged, for he has the appetites of a wolf."

Behind him, the old woman appeared. She carried a basket filled with flowers.

"But have no fear, *messieurs*, we offer you charmed herbs—wolfsbane—for protection."

The old woman moved among them, weaving between the rows, holding up the green sprigs with their purple blossoms, accepting coins in exchange. The men didn't hesitate, paying and clutching the long stems tightly. François shook his head, but Alphonse gestured frantically, holding out a coin. He plucked the herbs from her fingers, divided, and handed one to his friend.

"Better safe than sorry," he whispered.

François took the plant, twirling it between his fingers. A slender stem held trumpet-shaped, dark purple flowers, large leaves with deeply serrated edges at its base. It looked familiar.

Weren't these blossoms the same as those around the beast's neck? He tucked it into his belt, thinking he might later incorporate it into a painting.

Boamas moved again, drawing their attention. He walked to the scaffold where the deer's carcass swung, disturbed by a breeze wafting through the camp.

His audience was quiet, near enthralled.

Pulling the knife from his belt, he hacked off a chunk of meat from the carcass's hindquarter. He tossed it to the beast, who caught it in filthy paws that might've been hands beneath all that dirt and hair. It tore off a mouthful of flesh, snapping it down. As it chewed, blood drooled from the corners of its mouth, spotting the matted hair on its chest and dripping onto the dirt.

From somewhere in the audience, there was audible gagging. A figure rose and staggered to the back of the row, bent over, body heaving. There was a liquid splash into the grass.

The *vaida* smiled as if satisfied by that reaction.

"Yea, verily, *messieurs*, the appetites of a wolf ..." He raised a hand, gesturing at the sky.

Involuntarily, all looked up. Above the trees, a gibbous moon sailed through silvered clouds.

"... but also, the desires of a man!" He spun, holding up a finger in admonishment.

The men froze, all gazes riveted to that upright finger. Unnoticed, the man whose sensibilities had been defiled skulked back to his seat.

"The *wolf* has been fed," the *vaida* proclaimed with the bombast of the hero of a traveling mummer's show, his accent making their own language seem foreign as his voice floated over them. "Now the *man* must be."

Two more gypsies appeared, dragging a struggling female by

the wrists. They recognized the red-haired dancer. Instead of smiling enticingly, she now looked stricken with fear.

A murmur arose. *What's about to happen? What are they going to do?*

They understood the purpose of the second upright pole as the men holding the girl tied her to it, arms above her head. One caught a bare foot. She kicked at him. He swatted her with an open palm and, as she stilled, looped a leather thong around her ankle, tying it to one of the stakes. Her other ankle was fastened to the second.

The girl twisted ineffectually, revealing to all she was now helpless, arms secured and legs spread wide.

Looping the end of the rope around Ruvo's neck to the base of the pole, the mustachioed man secured it in a knot.

Spinning, he pulled a knife from his belt. The onlookers gasped, shrinking back. With a single movement, he slid the blade under the wreath around the creature's neck, slicing through the woven stems. He caught the wreath as it fell, tossing it away.

The beast shook his head and shoulders as if casting off a heavy weight. He grunted in relief.

Boamas said, "You've dined, Ruvo. Your dessert awaits."

All three men backed into the shadows.

No one spoke from that moment on.

With a growl, the creature approached the pole and its terrified occupant. It nosed the hem of her skirt, face brushing against the fabric, sniffing loudly up the cloth from hem to waist.

With a feeble whimper, the girl cringed and turned her head.

The creature rose to its hind legs.

A ragged murmur rippled through the crowd as it dragged a tongue across her cheek. It sniffed at her bosom, lapping at it before burrowing briefly between her breasts.

In the audience, someone groaned.

She flinched and shrank away, but there was nowhere to go. She was held securely by her bonds and could only cower against the pole, helpless as the creature again dropped to all fours, seizing the hem of her skirt in its teeth. Shaking its head, it ripped away the cloth.

With a collective gasp, everyone jumped.

The tatters fell to the ground. The girl was bare from the waist down, her splayed thighs and tied ankles displaying her female parts for all to see. She trembled as the beast licked across her bare belly, then drew back its head, looking up at her.

It growled.

François would have sworn the sound held a note of anticipation, even pleasure.

She shuddered and closed her eyes. With a lunge, it buried its face in that coppery thatch.

The girl screamed. The men winced.

They could see that red tongue moving back and forth, lapping and laving. The girl continued trembling, the movement becoming more and more visible as the brute drove its face deeper between her thighs. Abruptly, her cries changed to moans, rising and falling, getting softer and quieter until they sounded almost like sounds of pleasure. She stopped struggling and cried out. Her entire body quaked as if in a fit.

She went limp.

Ahhh ... the men in the audience echoed her cry. One or two swiped at their brows, flinging away sweat.

"*Dieu*," Alphonse whispered, fingers digging into François's arm. "Did I actually see what I think I saw?"

François didn't answer but simply sighed, feeling as wrung as if he, too, had pronged the wench.

The creature sat back on its haunches and howled, the hair

on its upturned face wet with female juices. Its tongue swiped out, licking around its mouth.

"The Lord have mercy." One of the men crossed himself.

"We've just witnessed an abomination of Nature," another muttered. "God forgive us."

"*Mon Dieu*," a third gritted between clenched teeth. It was the one who'd emptied his belly. He now placed a hand over a damp spot on his codpiece. "How will I ever be able to face the priest after seeing that?"

The beast looked out over the audience. Its gaze met François's.

Holy Mother. He was shaken as with a stab of recognition. *It can't be.*

Those eyes were definitely not an unthinking beast's. There was intelligence behind them.

It's a man, a man who's seen absolute misery and something more.

In the next breath came the thought: *It's my St. Jean.* Merci, le bon Dieu. *I've found him, as she said.*

He was so astounded he didn't think about the rest of her prediction. Instead, he continued studying his discovery, enthralled.

The *vaida* and the second gypsy reappeared from the shadows. One cut the girl's bonds, catching her as she fell into his arms, as limp as a woman sated with lovemaking.

He carried her away.

The *vaida* stood before them, bowing. "Noble gentlemen, our show is concluded. Of course, we rely on your discretion in not telling anyone what you've witnessed tonight."

A good way to ensure a full audience for as long as they're here. François's thoughts were cynical. *Not if I can help it.*

If he had his way, there would be no repeat performance.

In the meantime, a hail of coins met the *vaida's* statement, the men tossing them and hurrying away, ashamed of their voyeurism, hoping their money would buy forgiveness for participating, even as an audience, in that outrage.

With practiced ease, the *vaida* scooped up the money, dropping the handful of coins into a small iron pot near the campfire. They made a sharp metallic clash as they struck those already inside. He picked up the wreath of flowers, unwinding the rope from the post. Jerking it roughly, he led the creature away.

"Well, that was invigorating, wasn't it?" Alphonse also made ready to go. He placed a hand over his codpiece, pressing in slightly. "Perhaps a little too much so. Still, I'm disappointed."

"Why?" François asked. He continued looking in the direction the *vaida* had taken the brute.

"Damn it, François." Alphonse's reply was that of a petulant boy cheated of a treat. "I'd hoped to buy that wench for an hour's pleasure, but I could see she's in no condition for any more groaning tonight, nor perhaps for some time to come. Damn, if I could make a woman scream that way ... François?"

He stopped as he realized his friend wasn't listening.

"I must speak to that gypsy." François pushed past Alphonse. Not waiting to see if his friend followed, he started through the space between the caravans.

Alphonse ran after him, protesting, "Why? What could you possibly have to say to ..."

"It's my St. Jean." François turned so quickly that Alphonse staggered against him.

"What's your St. Jean? That gypsy?" He grasped him by the shoulder. "Surely

not. I don't think Our Lord's cousin would've sported such a mustache."

"Not the gypsy ... The ... that *thing* ..."

They were in the shadows now, could see both the *vaida* and the creature, standing near a large wooden cage on wheels, an enclosure made of sturdy, rough-cut branches held together with wrapped bonds of thick rope. Words and designs were painted in bright red on their bark. Nailed to the branches were the same long-stemmed herbs and deep purple flowers, like the ones the old woman had sold them, like those in the wreath the creature had worn.

Charms and herbs to keep it quiet? François wondered.

The *vaida* set down the pot containing the money, placing the now-tattered wreath atop the cage. He unfastened the padlock on the cage door.

"You did well, my Ruvo," he said to the creature. "An extra piece of meat for you tonight."

"You, there! Boamas." François rushed toward him.

"Me, good sir?" The *vaida* turned a masterly, innocent expression on him.

"I want to talk to you."

The man immediately said, "Any money you paid tonight won't be returned. We never guarantee a customer will be satisfied by what he sees or does here."

"It's not that," François denied, shaking a hand as if to dismiss what had been said. "I want to talk to you about the wolf ... or whatever it is."

"What about him?" The answer came with practiced suspicion.

"Where did you get him?"

The guarded expression relaxed. "It's as I said. We found him running—"

"*Non,*" François interrupted. "Don't give me that story you told the others. Running wild in the forests, indeed. What is he? Some poor mentally deficient abandoned on a mountaintop, and you came along and, with your great sense of charity, rescued him?"

He gave the man a sneering glance. If there was any charity in the fellow's heart, it was encircled with the sign of the franc.

"For *this*?" He waved a hand in the direction of the post.

"You wish the truth?" The gypsy seemed surprised.

"Didn't I say so?" François's answer was curt.

"Very well." The gypsy didn't hesitate. "I bought him."

"*Bought?*" François repeated.

The gypsy nodded.

"How? Where?"

"You see ..." Boamas looked around. Though no one was close enough to hear, he lowered his voice. "Ruvo had the bad manners to be born on your god's day. You *gadje* Christians have an interesting belief when that happens."

François nodded. Anyone unfortunate enough to be born on Christmas Day was automatically cursed for having the audacity of attempting to share the glory of the Savior's birth. He was destined to lead a most unhappy life, and had a good chance of becoming a *loup-garou* or, at his death, a revenant, destined forever to walk the night and prey on the living.

"In our travels, we passed through a little town called Casa di Lupo—the Wolf's Home—fitting, don't you think? A most interesting infant had been born there some years before. The priest had already told the parents they must rid themselves of the child. He offered to take it to a monastery where pious prayer and daily scourges would tame the beast they knew to be within, but they hesitated. It was only after a series of misfortunes that they agreed the little creature had to go. Then, our caravan arrived."

He paused.

"Yes?" prompted François. "And?"

"I suppose they thought they deserved a little recompense for being good, pious people cursed with such an offspring.

They offered to sell him to *me* instead." He shrugged. "I know a profit when I see one. I agreed."

"And brought him back to your camp and put him in a cage," François finished.

"He was destined to become a wolf." There was another shrug, this one more eloquent. "I simply helped. What else could I do? You saw what he did to poor Mariah. Our womenfolk—indeed, *no* female—would be safe otherwise."

By now, François was beginning to wonder how much of Mariah's defilement had been real and how much a well-rehearsed theatricality.

"Why the interest, *messieur?*" the gypsy asked. With a smirk, he looked François up and down, then glanced at the creature, now sitting docilely at his feet. "Do you wish to be pleasured as he did the girl?"

Briefly, François had forgotten he was standing so close to what might or might not be a wild animal, if not a bestial human. He took a step away.

With another of those shrugs, the gypsy continued, "I suppose sucking a rod is no different from licking a cunt."

"Don't be absurd." François snapped, forcing anger to overcome his embarrassment. "I wish to buy him."

Alphonse, silent until that moment, gaped. "François?"

Even the gypsy looked surprised. "I assure you, *maître*, it can be done in private *here*, just as good as elsewhere ..."

François shook his head impatiently as if the man were too stupid to continue existing. "I don't want him for *that*. I want to *paint* him."

"Paint?" The *vaida* looked as if he'd never heard the word.

"I'm an artist and I want him as my subject. I want to *buy* him." To François, the matter was simple. "How much?"

"He's not for sale." The gypsy made his refusal a flat statement.

"Anything can be bought," François argued.

"You *gadje* always think that," the gypsy replied. "I keep him; he brings me more money wherever we stop. I sell him; I have coins lasting a few days. Why would I wish that?"

"Because if you don't, I'll report you to the priests—tell them you give shows of bestiality—and they'll take your precious Ruvo, and that wench, and you, and burn all three of you at the stake for promoting carnal congress with a beast ... perhaps everyone within your camp, for tempting good Christians with your heathenish ways."

"Do you threaten me?" The man's hand went to his dagger.

Alphonse flinched, grasping François's arm, whispering, "François, what are you saying?"

Only he seemed aware the other men had ridden away, and they were alone in a gypsy camp where his friend was threatening a man holding a knife, with a ferocious beast crouching at the end of a rope. His own sword, hanging at his side, would be of little use if they were set upon.

"Of course not." François smiled, but it was more a baring of teeth. "Merely a warning of what might happen if someone who was here spoke out of turn, or several someones, perhaps." He looked pointedly at the hand touching the knife. "Don't think to kill us, for my friend here is an important noble, and many are aware of where he went tonight."

Alphonse conveyed confirmation of this with a nod, though he'd told no one where they were going.

"It seems I have no choice." Surprisingly, the man didn't argue, deciding capitulation was the better form of valor.

"You can always find some other halfwit to train." François was unsympathetic. "I'll give you two coins. Gold ones. No haggling," he continued as the man started to speak. "Three, if you include the rope."

It was the final bit of money from his last commission, all

he'd brought with him, but he *had* to have the creature. Considering what the church fathers were offering for the painting, three coins seemed a pittance to pay for its subject.

Glancing from François to the beast and back, Boamas thought that over.

"Done."

He spat on his hand and held it out. François looked at the hand, dug into his purse, and slapped the named amount onto his palm. He waited while Boamas carefully bit each coin, assuring himself he wasn't being cheated and they were genuine. He handed the length of rope to François. Bowing, he picked up the money pot, dropped the coins into it, and walked away.

"François, let's go." Alphonse tugged at his friend's sleeve. "Please. Before he changes his mind and comes back with his *compagnons* and some sharp knives."

It took some doing to get the creature to go with them. It growled and fought the rope, not wanting to leave its former master.

Even François's command, "Shut up, you misbegotten cur. You're mine now," did nothing but urge it into louder cries of protest, with never an intelligible word in the mix, as it half-stood and tried to follow in the direction the *vaida* had gone.

Digging in its heels, it was dragged several feet until at last, seeing the gypsy wasn't going to return, it gave up, dropped to all fours again, and gave François a defeated look. He thought he read in it a question, as well as a grudging realization that this stranger was now his only hope of survival.

"Come along." This time, when he tugged on the rope, it followed docilely with that hunched-over, shambling gait, though it continued whimpering.

Alphonse carefully stepped to his other side, making François's body a barrier between them.

"Relax," François told him, pulling the sprig of herb from his belt. He held it out.

The creature immediately quieted.

Alphonse snatched the sprig, clutching the long stems with his own.

"Now you have double the protection," François told him.

After they calmed the horses and were mounted, the beast trotted silently behind François's steed. Ruvo might not be frightened of *them*, but they were upset by *his* presence. They danced and neighed all the way to the *château*.

His goal now achieved, François decided he'd leave for home in the morning.

That night, he slept in one of Alphonse's guest rooms. Ruvo lay in the kennel with the dogs who, after some sniffing and barking, accepted him. In the morning, with the herb Alphonse insisted on returning to him tucked into his purse, François began the walk back to Aux-le-Piémont, taking his prize with him.

* * *

"You BOUGHT HIM?" Isabeau was aghast. "Like a horse or a cow? Surely, François, that's most un-Christian."

"But not unheard of," her husband replied, slurping another spoonful of stew. "Don't discompose yourself, wife. It's done every day in the southern countries. When I lived in Italy, many of my patrons had slaves ... blackamores, even some Egyptians and Turks."

"That's different," she answered. "Blackamores, Egyptians, and Turks aren't Christians."

"Neither is that poor brute." François chuckled at his own joke and swallowed another mouthful. "I daresay he's more animal than human, anyway."

"But to sell a person as if he were chattel," Isabeau protested. "Surely, the church would protest."

It occurred to her this was exactly what her parents had done in giving her to François as his wife, and the church hadn't disapproved of that with a single word.

"Let me worry about the church," François answered. He picked up his wine glass. "For now, I have my St. Jean." He paused, goblet halfway to his mouth as a thought occurred. "You'll not be mentioning to anyone how I came to get him, or what he is, either—if you know what's good for you."

Isabeau didn't answer. She knew that wasn't an idle threat.

"He'll need to be fattened up a bit," François continued, thinking ahead. "But only a little. Right now, he's too thin, even for a fasting St. Jean. In the meantime, I'll paint him as something else to get him accustomed to being around people ... a mendicant or such ... yes, *The Beggar and the Nobles* ... a good title..."

"Is it safe?" Isabeau had visions of the creature attacking François's models and devouring them. She didn't worry so much about François, but some noble's innocent child...

"As long as I have this herb." François patted his purse.

"What will you do with him once you've completed your great work?" Isabeau dared to be sarcastic as she also looked ahead. "When he's fulfilled his purpose?"

"I've no doubt he's simple-minded, as well as dangerous." François set down his goblet, surprising Isabeau by waving Maxime away as the servant stepped forward to refill it. "I doubt he could fend for himself. Perhaps I'll simply take him to the woods and put him out of his misery. A good clout to the head with a stone should serve."

"François, you wouldn't." She blanched at the cavalier way he spoke of disposing of the creature.

"Of course not." He touched her cheek, patting it in that

maddeningly patronizing way he had, revealing he was silently teasing her with a cruel jest. "Don't know why I even said such a thing. I'm aware how softhearted you are, my dear, and how that would distress you. Didn't I let you keep that parrot when you stopped me from wringing its neck?"

Looking away, Isabeau forced herself to accept her husband's caress. She didn't want to meet his eyes and see the cruelty in them. She was well aware that François would do exactly as he threatened without hesitation, then toss the bloodied stone aside and return to the cottage and demand his supper.

"I imagine *Pére* Ambroise would take him. After all, that priest did say contemplation might help overcome his bestial tendencies." He repeated what Boamas had said about the priest offering to take the child away. "I'd be lauded for my charity in rescuing the creature, no doubt. I imagine the sanctity of the church would keep the priests safe from harm. Don't worry about it. There's plenty of time to think of that later. In the meantime ..."

He ate another piece of bread, belched loudly, and slammed the hand holding the spoon against the tabletop. Reaching for the little bell by his plate, he rang it impatiently.

"Matilde! Bring me some more of that stew. I vow it's better than any of the fare I've eaten for these three months." He didn't mention the pheasant he'd devoured at Alphonse's. "Maxime, more wine!"

He looked back at Isabeau, pinching her cheek.

"And then, my lovely spouse, we'll go to bed. I've also missed your wifely duties during my search."

Cheek stinging, Isabeau silently doubted that.

While the cook hurried from the kitchen, ladling more into her master's bowl from the stew pot she carried, and Maxime filled the goblet to the rim, Isabeau simply sat, thinking frantically. She worried about the future of the creature her husband had brought into their home, as well as their own well-being.

* * *

Isabeau Lascaux de Montaigne might've repeated those vows of honor and obedience, but no mention was made of love, and indeed she had none for her husband. She'd been given no choice in the matter of marrying him, and no feelings, even the slightest fondness, were involved.

François de Montaigne was an artist of no small repute, and soon, many thought he would be even more well-known. At this moment, his name was already recognized in the Mediterranean kingdoms and was slowly becoming notable throughout southern France.

He was from a well-to-do, though not noble, family and had studied with those in Rome, Florence, and the surroundings already known as masters of their arts. He'd begun in a workshop along with other apprentice painters, but while they worked in various media, creating jewelry, birth trays, frescoes, or decorative papier-mâché, François concentrated solely on painting. Though he swore landscapes were his *métier*, he'd soon been commissioned by various well-known Italian families to do their portraits, and that was how his fame spread.

Then, he returned to France, intent on going to Paris.

On the way, he stopped in Aux-le-Piémont. Distracted from the City of Lights by the town's bucolic scenery, majestic mountains, and the Rhône River meandering nearby, he claimed he would settle there and make it his home.

To do that, he needed a place to live and was thus introduced to Pierre Lascaux.

Though a member of the town's small upper class, Pierre was a man tottering on its periphery. He offered François rooms in the overly large *château* that his family could no longer afford. The rental fees kept him from losing it and enabled the family to live in the manner they'd always done. Renting a small studio in Aux-le-Piémont, François set about practicing his talent on higher-class French families, painting landscapes and still lifes, with an occasional portrait by special commission. He entertained them with tales of Italy and the opulence of his patrons there, tossing about the names Michelangelo, Botticelli, and others as offhandedly as he would speak of his host's.

Fifteen-year-old Isabeau's parents were charmed, but not their daughter.

She thought François a boor. He was handsome, to be sure, with his blue eyes and chestnut hair, in a florid, over-exaggerated way. Talented, certainly, but loutish in his manners. He drank too much and caroused and wasn't quiet when he returned home, though her father made excuses for the late-night disturbances, and what he called his tenant's *eccentricities*.

Isabeau didn't think drinking too much was an eccentricity. Neither was whoring, for it was rumored François slept with his models, who were no better than they should be. After all, what decent female would undress for a man day after day, allow him to look on her naked form, and not expect that sooner or later, she'd find herself in his bed?

Everyone made excuses for François. Even *Père* Ambroise. When François frankly stated he had no time for attending church services, the priest absolved him by saying that since he did a great many religious-themed paintings, the Lord would understand.

Isabeau was even more disturbed when she realized *she* had caught François's attention, especially when he spoke to her father about paying court to her. Nothing she could do discouraged him. Neither did her pointing out his very bad habits have any effect. Eventually, to her dismay and then horror, François asked for her hand.

Pierre was a social climber with no ladder to climb until François came along. He perceived quickly enough that being the father-in-law of a famous *artiste* would have its advantages, both status-wise as well as financially.

He agreed to François's request.

No amount of pleading could change Pierre's mind. He was brutally frank in his reply to his daughter:

You've no other suitors, ma petite, *and since we're too poor to supply you a dowry, probably won't have any. It's through M. de Montaigne's generosity that we're able to keep our fine home. Accepting him as your husband is the best way to show your gratitude.*

Isabeau replied that she had never wanted to live in such a grand house, that it was her father and mother's desire to be thought of as higher than they should be, which had caused them to move from the estate inherited from her grandfather to a home demanding more upkeep than they possessed. As with her other arguments, this one was also ignored, and Isabeau exchanged her snood and braids for the wimple and veil of a married woman.

With a disastrous wedding night in which François proved he had no care for the sensibilities of an ignorant virgin, except how quickly he could deflower her, thus earning his bride's eternal hatred, Isabeau found herself married to a man marginally famous, one who painted beautiful landscapes as well as beautiful women and men. A man who drank generally became desirous while in his cups and demanding, sometimes violently so. He continued bedding his models, whether those he hired or those who hired him.

When Isabeau complained to her mother about this unfaithfulness, she was informed that François was an *artiste*, a man set apart from mere mortals, blessed by *le bon Dieu* with a talent few possessed. Therefore, one must allow him leeway to act as he would. If one of those lovely creatures he painted caught his eye, it was his right and privilege to indulge himself, and a wife must understand and forgive his unfaithfulness.

Though she deplored those seductions, Isabeau eventually was grateful, for that meant he'd ignored her while otherwise occupied. Indeed, when François was painting, he ignored almost all the necessities—eating, sleeping, drinking—except his work and whoever was his subject.

When not painting, he was gone often, in search of some idealized model ...

... and Isabeau rejoiced in those times, as she had when he left to find his St. Jean.

He decided the forests and meadows of Aux-le-Piémont would be appropriate for the background. What did it matter if they might be out of place since the personage who was the subject had lived in the arid wilderness of the Holy Land? Transporting John the Baptist to the green meadows of France was artistic license, which *le bon Dieu* would forgive. After all, wasn't the church for which the painting was destined also in France? Therefore, shouldn't the portrait of its namesake be in the same setting?

With his usual fervor, François claimed he was inspired, but he always did that, so Isabeau thought it was more for his patrons' benefit than not. It would not be a mural, *non, non* ... but *a painting*, life-size and large enough to fit the space where the proposed mural would have been. He made preliminary sketches, setting down on the thick, cheap sheets of coarse-rag paper in his sketchpad his idea of how the saint should be depicted. He roamed the countryside, drawing various scenes of forest and meadow until he found the perfect setting.

Once that was done, he began the arduous task of selecting a model to portray his subject.

Isabeau, who'd never seen him this involved with a painting before, was surprised. Could it be her husband was as enthusiastic as he appeared? If so, it might take him from her for a *very* extended period.

She hoped.

When a month passed, then two, then a third, she began to wonder. François had never been away for more than five days. Had he met with an accident, was he even now lying in a ditch somewhere, recognized as a famous artist by robbers, thinking fame equated wealth, and killed when they discovered otherwise?

Perhaps he'd realized his ideals were too lofty and abandoned what he sought. With that shortness of attention, he sometimes displayed when he became bored, had he at last decided to seek other scenery and better vistas to paint? Could he simply have abandoned both Aux-le-Piémont and his wife for other climes?

Isabeau waited with concern mingled with dread. She truly had no wish for misfortune to befall her husband. She simply wanted to be in his company no longer than necessary.

Now, however, he was back, as obnoxious as ever, bringing that benighted *thing* with him, a creature frightening Isabeau while at the same time fascinating her.

Chapter Two

AFTER HE'D EATEN his fill, which included two more bowls of Mathilde's stew and four slices of bread plus a third goblet of wine, François set down his spoon, yawned, then patted his belly.

"I vow, now I want nothing more than to go to bed." Clutching at the table and revealing the third goblet had been a bit too much, he stood, wiping his bread-greasy fingers against his doublet.

Isabeau watched that action with dismay, setting down her own spoon.

A table kerchief lay near his bowl, a twenty-four-inch square of embroidered linen matching her own. All François had to do was drape it over his shoulder, where it was within easy reach for wiping his fingers or his mouth, but no ... he preferred to ignore the niceties of table manners and use his doublet or his shirt instead, usually ruining the fabric and causing more work for Mathilde when she did the laundry.

Not that Isabeau minded if Mathilde had more work to do, but there was such a thing as good manners. Her husband was from a well-to-do family, or so he said. Had his parents not thought to have him instructed in proper table etiquette?

She didn't say anything. If she had, François would simply look at her, then at the napkin, and walk away without speaking.

"I also wish you to join me there, wife," he continued. "Finish that bowl of stew you've dawdled over the past hour." He walked to the door as he spoke. "Make haste. I wish you in my bed sooner rather than later."

Isabeau dipped her spoon into the remnants of her only bowl of the night. She generally ate lightly when François was home, her husband's presence killing all but the faintest appetite.

"I suppose Ruvo should be fed, also." He spoke as if it were an afterthought, pausing at the door. "Tend to that, then come along to bed."

"Why should I feed your new pet?" She looked up, indignant. "You bought him. Why can't you ...?"

"Because I've been wandering the south of France for three months searching for him." The rise of his voice meant *no argument*. "I walked most of the way, except when my friend Alphonse was gracious enough to loan me a horse, and I now need rest."

"Is it my fault you don't have a horse?" she retorted. "I'm not the one who could've bought several if he didn't give his money to the physician for paints and charcoal sticks."

François always chose to buy artist supplies instead of things others considered *necessities*, and he insisted on obtaining them from the local leech who never hesitated to take the money.

"Those the physician mixes stay brighter and last longer," he replied. "I need those colors."

The leech was always finding new herbs and minerals during his roaming in the hills. Since many could be compounded into painting media as well as medicines, the physician sold those to his friend, the *artiste*. He also had some fine grape vines which, when treated properly, made the finest charcoal sticks available.

He shrugged. "Why am I defending myself to *you*? You can't possibly understand. Go. Do as I say, then hurry back."

"Is it safe?" she persisted. "François, is he really a *loup-garou*?"

"Yes. No. Who can say? Who cares?" His answer held scorn. "*Sacre*, Isabeau, you're as superstitious as a peasant. Do as I say."

He spun and went out, staggering slightly.

Sighing, Isabeau set down her spoon. The prospect of feeding that dirty creature challenged her appetite; the thought of submitting to François in his current unwashed and wine-soaked state sent it fleeing. Wiping her hands on her kerchief, she patted her lips before dropping it to the table. Pushing back her chair, she got to her feet, thinking resentfully that Maxime should be there to assist her, but he was who knew where, having disappeared the moment the master indicated his meal was over.

"By the way ..." François reappeared in the doorway so abruptly that she jumped, gripping the chair arms. Hands on the door frame, he leaned in. "No table scraps. Only raw meat."

Then he was gone again, bellowing for Maxime: "Bring bath water."

At least he's going to bathe.

Frequent baths were a subject over which she and her husband were always at loggerheads. François stubbornly clung to the belief set forth by *Pére* Ambroise and most of the towns-folk, that too much bathing diluted the body's humors and made one ill. Once a month was enough, the priest opined, and even that could possibly be too much.

Isabeau resigned herself to gratitude for the smallest of favors, which, at that moment, was a husband freshly bathed.

* * *

WITH A LANTERN in one hand and balancing in the other a trencher of scraps trimmed from the mutton that provided tonight's stew and rescued before being tossed in the *puit de cess*, she went down the steps.

By now, it was twilight. Isabeau walked slowly, in no hurry to reach her destination. The walkway was dark, and she didn't want to trip and fall. It was a planked platform accessed by a side door at the end of the corridor running the length of the cottage, leading to a built-on porch at the studio door, covered with a protective tiled roof. The cottage's previous occupant, a member of the gentry, had built it so he could reach the stable and not be out in the elements when it rained or snowed.

Too soon, her destination loomed ahead. Setting down the lantern, Isabeau unlocked the studio. François hadn't asked for the return of the key, and that made her think he'd planned all along for her to feed the creature. Going inside, she was grateful the fat candle housed in the lantern made a wide beam, guiding her across the former stable's darkened expanse.

At the storeroom door, she hesitated as a muffled but very human-like snore came from inside. Putting the key into the lock, she pushed the door open. The next moment, she staggered backward, gasping for breath as a wave of stale air, redolent with a putrid mix of sweat, dirt, and the scent of an animal locked in an unventilated space, rushed out.

The lantern's wavering beam showed Ruvo on the floor, sprawled on his back on the blanket, arms flung wide, knees bent. Loud snores issued from his open mouth.

Fighting the desire to gag, Isabeau turned her head, breathing deeply and slowly.

With her first gasp, he awoke with a snort, rolling over and crouching. Isabeau recovered and stepped inside the storeroom.

A second smell, this one even more malodorous, assailed her. She pointed the lantern downward.

A few feet in front of the door, barely an inch from her slippered foot, was a pile of what could only be human excrement.

"Oh!" She cringed in disgust.

Surprisingly, she wasn't angry with Ruvo. Neither she nor François had thought the creature might need to be allowed a call of nature, so it simply acted as any animal locked up would, and now, the result must be disposed of.

The injustice of it all was what roused her anger. *Why must I have to clean up after this ... thing?*

Would she have to train it, too, as she'd done her mother's lapdog, who would've piddled everywhere if she hadn't taken the little beast in hand because *Mamére* had no idea what to do? François should be the one ... but François would never do anything, she knew. The creature could fill the storeroom with its droppings, and he'd simply open the window and the door, pray for a strong wind, and go about his business.

Ruvo whimpered, as if he sensed her dismay. Perhaps it was also an apology.

Whirling, she set the trencher on one of the studio tables near the door, the beam wavering as the lantern swung from her hand. With great care, she stepped around the filth on the floor, hurrying to a small chest near the window where a double candleholder sat. Ruvo watched her intently as she opened the little door on the lantern's side, removing each candle from the candelabrum and touching their wicks to the one inside. Brightness lit the room as she replaced them in the holder.

Ruvo continued watching her.

At least he isn't afraid of fire.

She stamped over to where he crouched.

"Bad." She raised her voice, making it firm, and shook her finger. He had to learn. "Bad ... dog ... uh ... boy ..." She pointed to the floor. "No. No."

He cocked his head, gave a questioning sound, but not a growl.

Isabeau tensed. *Don't show fear. Animals can sense that. Anger, too. Don't be either.* She forced herself to relax.

Walking to the door, she pointed again. "No. Bad."

While he watched, she went back into the studio. François had hired a brick mason to build a small fireplace so he could work in winter, and his naked models wouldn't freeze. Picking up the ash shovel, she returned to the storeroom, scooped the vile stuff from the floor, and walked to a corner of the room where a chamber pot rested. Like the cot, it was placed there for François's convenience.

Isabeau tapped the shovel against the rim, depositing its contents inside. Picking up the chamber pot, she walked to where Ruvo hunched upon his blanket. He straightened, looking up at her.

Again, she pointed to the spot on the floor: "No," then at the pot: "Yes." She held it down so he could see inside.

He peered in, grunted, then looked up at her. She repeated her gestures, saying, "No, bad boy," and "Yes, good boy," hoping he'd get the idea. His gaze went back and forth, following her finger before he looked up at her, again cocking his head.

She'd swear his forehead creased in confusion.

"Now, I have to clean up what you've done, you *stupid créature.*"

With that, she carried the chamber pot through the door, tossing the shovel against the hearth. She went outside and around the studio, to the spot where someone had dug a large pit behind the *privé*, a *puit de cess* for chamber pots to be emptied and any leftover or spoiled food tossed. A worse smell yet emanated from it, and she held her breath as she emptied the pot, setting it beside the studio door.

She stalked back to the kitchen.

"What are you doing here?" Mathilde, busy washing dishes, showed her surprise at seeing Isabeau. "I thought you and the *maître* had retired."

"I won't be doing that for some time," Isabeau snapped. "Where's the kitchen pail and scrub brush?"

"Why do you want it?"

"That creature has made a mess in the storeroom."

"Don't expect me to clean it. I've dishes to wash." Mathilde gestured to where the pail and brush sat in a corner.

Isabeau didn't answer. She picked them up, going outside to the well. It took several minutes to lower the well bucket, fill it, and retrieve it. Carrying a pail of water, cursing silently as it sloshed and spattered the path in front of her as well as her shoes and the hem of her gown, she returned to the studio.

Ruvo hadn't moved. As she appeared in the doorway, he made a sound she'd swear was a greeting.

"Quiet. I should be angry with you, you know." Pouring some of the water onto the damp splotch on the floor, she knelt, scrubbing at it with the brush.

It took some time to get the spot clean.

I shouldn't be doing this. It should be Mathilde on her knees, scrubbing the floor, Isabeau thought.

She had a sudden memory of overhearing the cook bragging to someone in the marketplace, *I'm servant to the artiste François de Montaigne. He never requires me to do menial tasks. Such a good master.*

Her lips curled in anger.

I'm the wife of the artiste François de Montaigne, mentally mimicking what the cook had said. *I do my own darning, my own laundry, because my servants are too lazy, and I clean up the messes made by strays he brings home. Such a good husband.*

She poured the rest of the water over the spot and set brush and bucket aside.

"I pray you understood what I said, for I don't want to repeat this." Taking the trencher from the table, she came inside.

He perked up as he saw the platter, raising his head and sniffing loudly. He began to bounce around on the blanket, making little high-pitched whimpers.

"Yes, this is for you." She hesitated, then set the platter on the floor.

He threw himself upon the wooden plate, grabbing the bits of meat and stuffing them into his mouth, gobbling loudly. Blood dripped from his fingers, spattering the blanket.

Isabeau turned her head before nausea set in. She couldn't bear seeing those raw pieces being shoved into that hungry maw. She only looked around when the sounds of chewing ceased, in time to see Ruvo lick the blood from his hands, then wipe them on his chest.

"You've no better manners than your master," she muttered. Stooping to retrieve the trencher, she went on, "I think there are going to be some changes in your dining habits, and soon." She took a deep breath and turned her gag into a cough. "Also a few other things."

Ruvo's only answer was a deep sigh as he collapsed onto the blanket and closed his eyes. Like any dog when well-fed, he fell asleep.

"You're welcome." Isabeau replaced the chamber pot, picked up the lantern, collected brush and pail, and, stepping over the damp spot before the door, went out.

As she pulled the door shut, she heard a loud snore.

* * *

"Wʜᴀᴛ ᴛᴏᴏᴋ ʏᴏᴜ ѕᴏ ʟᴏɴɢ?" François asked.

Though there was no fire, he stood naked before the hearth, only a large piece of flannel towel wrapped around his hips. A few feet away sat the bathing tub. His body was still damp, and his shape, both fore and aft, was well-defined by the clinging cloth.

Isabeau looked away, not wanting to see any appendage or body part before she had to.

"I asked you to feed the creature. Did you have to find a lamb and slaughter and dress it, too?"

"That thing relieved himself in the storeroom," she snapped, for once unable to contain her anger. "Besides feeding him, I had to clean the floor."

Worry flashed across his face, but what he said wasn't sympathy for the unpleasant task she'd had to perform. "He didn't get at my paintings, did he? None of them were harmed? Or my canvases?"

"Not that I could see." Isabeau hadn't thought of the paintings stacked around the walls or the unused canvases, and apparently, neither had François. It would've served him right, had they been ripped to shreds, for locking an animal in with them.

His expression changed, relieved. "*Merci, bon Dieu.* I suppose you'll have to housebreak him, then, won't you?"

Isabeau stared at him. For a moment, she truly couldn't speak. Instead, she looked at the tub.

"You've bathed?" Best to divert her anger before she threw something at him.

"Obviously. Do you think I plan to wear this towel to bed?"

Answering his own question, he slid it off his hips. Propping one large foot on a nearby stool, he leaned forward to wipe it dry, giving her a good view of his dangling privates.

Once more, Isabeau averted her gaze. Another woman might've been aroused by the sight of her husband's member and stones so enticingly free, but to her, it was merely a reminder of what was coming.

François dropped the towel onto a chair. He turned to face her. "You can't imagine how I've longed for you, Isabeau."

"Oh?" Still resentful, she dared sound doubtful, keeping her face turned away, refusing to look at his nakedness.

If she did, François would preen. He was proud of his body, and he had a right, she'd admit that, even if she didn't want it. He looked better than most of the men in the town. François had a soldier's body, muscular chest and arms, narrow waist, and flat belly. His hair was dark chestnut, the color of an old coin, his eyes sky-blue. Many times, Isabeau told herself she should be proud to have such a man as her husband. She'd often wished that the sight of his body aroused her.

It never had.

"You didn't find someone to slake your thirst while you were gone?"

"How can you say that?"

He didn't deny it, she noticed.

"I was on business. I had no time for women."

"Except your wife, you mean."

"Exactly. If only you'd come with me."

"I've no desire to tread the countryside like an itinerant peddler." She didn't remind him he'd left in the middle of the night while she slept.

His member rose slightly. "See my desire for you, wife?" He spread his arms as if offering himself to her.

Isabeau flicked her gaze across his body, felt nothing at the sight of the stiffening organ, and looked away.

"I even bathed to please you."

Liar, it was merely to make me come more quietly to your bed, she silently corrected.

"Here, let's get you out of that gown." He reached for her.

"Perhaps I should bathe, too." Her dodge was barely noticeable, just enough to elude his hands. *Anything to delay.*

"That would mean having Mathilde heat more water. I've dismissed her and Maxime. Your bathing can wait until tomorrow. I want you now."

He caught her around the waist, pulling her against his body. She kept her face turned away. He grasped her chin, turning her head. Isabeau didn't respond, but he didn't seem to notice as he pressed his mouth against hers, forcing his tongue between her clenched teeth. His kiss was loud and moist.

She wished she had the courage to bite him.

Releasing her, he spun her around so quickly she staggered. He began working the laces on the back of her gown.

Too soon, he got them open and pulled the gown over her head, taking wimple and veil with it. Kirtle and chemise followed, landing in a limp heap on the floor as he picked her up and carried her to bed. He was fully aroused now; undressing her had been enough foreplay. When he pushed into her, with no warning, doing nothing to prepare her, she bit her lip and closed her eyes.

As François's thrusts began, she swore she heard a mournful howl coming from the direction of the studio.

Chapter Three

At breakfast, François said, "Today I will begin preparations for *The Beggar and the Nobles*. I've decided Alphonse's sons will be my nobles, as a consolation for disappointing him. Therefore, I must return to La Chapelle and let him know."

Good, thought Isabeau. *That means I'll be without your presence.*

Her body still ached from last night's too-vigorous joining. If she'd been caressed a bit beforehand, she told herself, perhaps she might've enjoyed it as much as François apparently had.

Wishful thinking on her part.

He rose from his chair, using the back of his hand to wipe the grease from his mouth, then scrubbed it against his thigh, ignoring the table kerchief still neatly folded by his plate.

As usual.

"Since I've no horse and thus must use shanks's mare unless I can thumb my way on a passing cart, I must leave *now*. Of course." He looked from her to the door and back.

Isabeau started to speak.

"Was there something?"

"The storage room. It needs to be aired. I must open the window and the door."

"What do you expect if the creature shites in it? Train him, Isabeau."

"It's not that," she denied. "I scrubbed the floor ..."

Though that should've been Mathilde's job. She paused slightly, waiting for him to say that.

When he didn't, she went on, "It's clean. It's the creature himself. If you're to begin painting, and others are involved, something must be done. No one can come close to him without losing their belly. He's filthy. He *reeks*, François."

She made it a plea, emphasizing her words by pressing the table kerchief against her nose.

"So did I, last night." François's answer indicated this was a mere inconvenience. "Yet you didn't deny me." He smirked. "We were *very* close."

"You bathed first," Isabeau pointed out. She'd prefer not to think of last night's coming-together.

"Do you mean if I hadn't splashed in that tub, you might've rejected me?" François looked startled at the idea of such a thing, as if he'd never thought of it before.

"Since you did, we'll never know, will we?" Isabeau surprised herself by that glib retort.

"There's your answer then. Bathe the beast." To François, solutions were so simple. "Have Maxime take the tub to the studio."

"I? Bathe that creature?" The thought made her shudder.

"Have Mathilde do it if you've not the stomach." He couched his insult as a suggestion.

"I imagine she'd swoon the first time he growled." Isabeau doubted Mathilde would come within a mile of the beast. She never did anything outside her narrow view of household duties. Bathing a man disguised as a wolf didn't fit within her purview.

"Then *you'll* do it." François made that announcement like a royal decree.

"But, François, won't it be unseemly for your wife to see the creature naked?"

"Come, wife, with all that heavy fur, he's already naked. It'll be no more than sluicing down a hound. Anyway, surely you helped your mother care for your brothers when they were babes?"

"Yes," Isabeau admitted, "but my brothers were, as you say, infants. Ruvo is ... older." That was the only way she could answer without going into intimate detail. She wasn't certain what might lurk beneath that matted fur.

"Not that much." François brushed away her protest. "He's probably barely into adolescence, perhaps thirteen or fourteen ..." He was clearly tired of the argument. "I gave him into your care, wife. Tend to him."

A flick of his hand concluded their conversation.

"Very well, I will."

If he noticed the grim tone in Isabeau's reply, he didn't show it.

* * *

AFTER SEEING François on his way, this time with an ambiguous sensation of wishing he'd stay while wanting him gone as quickly as possible, Isabeau put a bibbed apron over her gown and removed her wimple, pinning up her hair and wrapping it in a length of fabric to protect it. Remembering seeing her uncle's servants struggle with his hounds, she expected bathing Ruvo to be dirty, wet work. Who knows, he might never have had a bath before and would fight it.

That made her shudder as she rummaged through the rag basket.

Once he was clean, he'd need something to wear, too. She'd have no naked boy running around her home, no matter how much body hair he had. François's cast-offs would cover him.

Before he left, François insisted she pack his shabbiest-appearing garments, even worse than those he'd worn on his last trip.

Isabeau wanted to ask what excuse he would use this time, since the *marquis* knew he had already been paid part of his fee for the St. Jean. As always, her husband had a ready answer: *one can't spend money when the work hasn't yet been done.* She wished he'd enquire if Alphonse's lady wife might have a gown or two; she would contribute to the *artiste's* spouse.

Isabeau had brought several gowns with her as part of her *trousseau.* With no new ones forthcoming, they were becoming worn and, as she could tell by seeing the other goodwives in town, already outdated. She had heard that in Italy, necklines were now in a V-shape and so low the kirtle showed, and a partlet was used to fill the space. *Robes déguisées,* they were called.

Isabeau truly wished she owned a couple of those.

If I only had some fabric, she thought, *I could sew myself a new gown.*

François never thought about how his wife might wish for new clothing, however. His only concern was his own appearance. After all, an *artiste* must appear well-to-do before his patrons, unless it was one as easily gulled as the *Marquis* du Maurier happened to be.

She wondered how he would react when her gowns were reduced to mere tatters. Perhaps no better. At that point, she would have to appeal to her parents for clothing; she didn't doubt.

Could they spare a franc or two for their daughter, the wife of the *artiste*? Or would her father give her his usual excuse that the *château* had gobbled up all the extra money?

Whatever her clothing problems, François had gone on his way, pack slung over his shoulder, hurrying to the high road in the hopes of meeting someone going in La Chapelle's direction.

* * *

WITH THE GARMENTS and some other items tucked into a small shopping basket, Isabeau sought out Mathilde.

The cook was in the kitchen, busily scrubbing the inner walls and ceiling of the brick oven built into the wall next to the cooking hearth. Her upper body was completely inside, one arm moving vigorously while the other hand clutched the outer edge, maintaining her balance.

For several seconds, Isabeau waited for the servant to emerge and acknowledge her mistress. She hadn't been quiet as she entered, so she knew Mathilde had heard her coming down the kitchen stairs.

Mathilde continued working.

Wretch. Isabeau's hands clenched. She'd like to push her fully inside the cavernous oven and light a fire under it.

After several minutes, she said, "Mathilde."

The servant ignored her for a few more moments while Isabeau waited, impatiently fuming. Then she pulled her head out of the oven.

"What do you want?"

If a servant had spoken to her mother that way, her father would've backhanded him to the floor. François had heard Mathilde address his wife thus many times and never batted an eye.

"Food for the creature."

"It's there." With the hand holding a cleaning scrubber made from the dried inner fibers of a gourd grown in the garden, she gestured to a platter on the center table where she prepared food before carrying it to the hearth or oven. It held several strips of meat bits trimmed from that morning's breakfast. "Raw. As *le maître* ordered."

"Not anymore," Isabeau said. "I want it cooked."

"*Le maître* said—"

"*Le maître's* not here. *I* am." Again, Isabeau was surprised by her own effrontery. "From now on, the creature eats cooked food."

"Who are you to give me orders?" Mathilde dared ask.

"I'm your *maîtresse*, and when my husband is absent, I'm in charge of this household," Isabeau snapped.

Grumbling, Mathilde picked up the trencher.

"Will stewing be acceptable?" she sneered, as if daring Isabeau to disagree. "I've water boiling."

"Yes." Isabeau didn't care, as long as the meat wasn't red and bloody.

Taking a pothook from those leaning against the hearth, Mathilde swung the black stew pot hanging over the fire toward her. The water inside was bubbling and hot, perhaps ready to wash the breakfast dishes. She dumped the meat inside, then pushed the pot back over the fire, dropping the pothook atop the others. Without looking, she tossed the platter back onto the table.

It landed with a loud clatter. Isabeau was thankful it was made of wood. Mathilde's carelessness had already broken several pieces of the dishware she brought with her.

"While the meat cooks, I want Maxime to bring the bathing tub to the storage room. Also, buckets of hot water and cold, bathing cloths, and a bar of that soap you use for the laundry."

If she were to get the filth off that creature, she'd need strong soap, none of the gentle olive oil milled cakes used for her own bathing, and François's occasional ablutions.

"Maxime is busy chopping firewood," Mathilde replied. "Besides, the tub's heavy."

"In that case, you'll help him carry it."

"I? I've more important things to do." She sniffed. "Who's going to bathe that thing anyway? I hope you're not expecting me to."

"You will, if I say so."

"Hardly. I haven't seen the creature, and I don't intend to." She hesitated. "Is it a dog or not? Maxime said he heard the master say it's a *loup-garou*. Is that true?"

"Of course not," Isabeau denied.

"It kept Maxime and me awake half the night with its howls. It certainly sounds like a wolf, and that makes it dangerous."

Isabeau remembered that single howl she'd heard. The room where Mathilde and her husband slept was a small one off the kitchen, behind the creamery, closest to the converted stable. It had originally been the scullery. Since François didn't have to pay the two servants, he realized he'd have even more money for his supplies if he didn't add on a room for them. Instead, he converted the scullery into a small bedchamber. Now, all work, from preparing meals to washing dishes and other dirty chores, was done in the kitchen.

They would've heard any sounds coming from the studio, even if muffled. It gave Isabeau some small gratification that the cook and her husband might've been kept awake by Ruvo's cries.

"Is there anything else? I've work to do." Mathilde turned her back, bending to dip the gourd's innards in the bucket of water at her feet.

"Don't turn away from me." Isabeau's voice was so sharp it surprised even herself. She seized the cook's wrist, jerking her upright despite her bulk. "You'll do what I say."

Mathilde goggled at her, mouth open, expression saying, *Since when did you grow a bit of backbone?*

"I'm *Maître* François's servant," Mathilde answered. "He hired me, and—"

She broke off with a gasp as Isabeau tightened her grip, fingers squeezing.

"My husband did *not* hire you," she corrected, teeth clenched.

Mathilde had circulated the myth that she and Maxime were *paid* servants and not serfs.

"Tell yourself that lie if you wish, but you were given to me by my father, and therefore, if you owe allegiance to anyone in this household, it should be me. Such insolence could get you turned out ..."

"*Le maître* would never—"

"He will if I tell him the jewelry I brought with me is missing, and I found it under your mattress. You know what they do to thieves."

Isabeau had only one set of jewels, a freshwater pearl necklace with a single small garnet and matching eardrops, given to her on the morning of her first communion. Most of her mother's jewelry was disappearing, piece by piece, sold for the upkeep of the *château*, with a few pieces saved to keep up the pretense of wealth.

"You wouldn't."

"Try me and see what I will or won't do."

Mathilde winced. Isabeau flung her hand away.

"Now then, I think the mutton's cooked enough. Dish it up. Put it in a bowl."

Rubbing her wrist, Mathilde obediently seized a ladle and

took a wooden bowl from a stack on the center table. She swung the cook pot from the fire, filling the bowl and casting sullen looks in Isabeau's direction.

Indeed, Isabeau felt a bit gratified—as well as astounded—by her sudden show of authority.

When Mathilde thrust the bowl at her, she studied its contents. The meat was barely parboiled, but at least its color was no longer bright red, and the juice running from it was a clear amber.

She forced herself to say, mildly, with no visible show of her triumph over the cook, "Thank you, Mathilde. Now, if you'll have Maxime bring the tub and the other things ..." She paused.

"I'll tell him," Mathilde said, adding grudgingly, "It may take a bit for fresh water to boil."

"That'll be fine, send it along when it's ready."

Reaching for a pitcher on the table, she poured water into a pottery cup. Balancing bowl and cup, Isabeau left the kitchen.

At the storage room door, she paused, wondering what malodorous horrors awaited her this time. She inclined her head, not quite pressing her ear to the wood, listening.

No sound. Not even a snore.

It was too quiet.

What had happened? Had the creature died during the night? Did the weight of the chain break his neck? Or was he even now crouched, waiting to pounce once the door opened?

The beast was chained. He couldn't harm her as long as she stayed out of reach. Telling herself she was being fanciful, Isabeau unlocked the door.

* * *

THE STENCH WAS as bad as the night before, if not worse. Holding her breath, she hurried to the window, ignoring Ruvo,

62

who greeted her with what might've been a yelp of welcome. Fumbling through the bars, she opened the latch and pushed the shutters outward, letting sunlight and fresh air stream into the room.

Behind her, she heard a gusty sigh. Turning, she saw Ruvo had risen into his usual half-crouch, the chain around his neck scraping the floor as he moved. Her gaze swept the room, with relief finding nothing on the floor that shouldn't be there, except ...

... the chamber pot was gone from its place in the corner.

She looked around, not finding it. *Where ...?*

Ruvo shifted. She looked back at him.

He held something in his hands, raised it, offering it to her.

The chamber pot.

Isabeau took two very slow steps toward him, glancing inside the vessel. Yellowish liquid, something dark and semi-solid floated ...

He made a questioning whimper.

"Yes, yes ..." She dared place a hand against that filthy head, giving it a pat before taking the pot from him. "Good boy. Yes."

She thought he might've looked pleased, but with that hair falling over his face and the matted beard, she couldn't be certain. Awkwardly juggling cup and bowl in one hand, holding the basket, she set the chamber pot aside, saying, "I've brought your breakfast."

He dropped to all fours, tongue lolling, looking eager.

Instead of placing the bowl on the floor, she took the garments from the basket and dropped them on the cot's end. His gaze followed her, disappointment in his eyes as she sat upon it, placing the cup of water near her feet.

"You won't be eating off the floor anymore," she continued, keeping her tone conversational, as if she were speaking to

Mathilde or Maxime. No, not as she would speak to them. To Ruvo, Isabeau made her tone gentle and friendly. "You will sit *here*,"—she patted a space beside her—"and eat your breakfast." She added, "Even if you insist on sleeping on the floor."

He stared, making no sound. Isabeau hoped he was trying to reason out what she'd said.

"Come, now." She patted the cot again, tone coaxing. "Come sit."

Slowly, he rose, not upright, though in less of a crouch, and lumbered toward the cot—and her. He looked at her hand, still resting on the spot she'd touched, then at the bowl. His own paw-like hand, dirty and clawed, tentatively reached for it.

"No." Isabeau moved it away.

The hand stopped.

"Not until you sit." For the third time, she touched the cot.

There was a rumble of a growl, holding slight exasperation and puzzlement. He took a step toward her, then another, then climbed upon the cot as he had the night before.

It was awkward, encumbered as he was by the chain. The cot teetered as he balanced. Isabeau wavered, then caught the edge, righting herself. Ruvo squatted beside her. She thought he looked pleased. Again, he reached for the bowl.

A wave of stench floated toward her.

"Not that way. Feet on the floor." She gasped, fighting the gag rising from the vile smell his nearness brought. *Oh, Maxime, hurry with the tub.*

She flicked her fingers at one ankle, pointing at the floor. With a look of resignation, he thrust one foot, then the other, over the side of the cot. They struck the floor with dull thuds.

With a grunt, Ruvo slumped.

"Good boy. That's the way you must sit from now on when you eat." She wondered how much he understood, or if he was simply obeying her gestures, as the dogs did. "Here."

She held out the bowl.

He took it eagerly, scooping out a handful of meat, cramming it into his mouth. He chewed ... once ... stopped, made a sound she interpreted as holding disgust, then spat. With a sickening *splat*, the mouthful of meat struck the floor. Growling, he thrust the bowl at her, releasing it.

Isabeau caught it before it fell.

"Stupid of me," she muttered. "Of course you don't like cooked food."

She wondered if he'd ever before tasted anything not raw.

"However ..." She caught his hand, replaced the bowl in it, then wrapped the other around its curve. "That's the way it'll be from now on, so"—she gestured at the floor—"put that back in the bowl and finish your breakfast."

He didn't move.

"*Now.*" She made her voice harsh.

There was a moment more of silence, as he looked from bowl to floor to her. Slowly, grudgingly, he slid from cot to wood, scraped the meat back into the bowl, and returned to sit, a little awkwardly, beside her.

"Go on."

After another long hesitation, Ruvo began to eat. Ravenously. So swiftly, Isabeau was certain he didn't taste the meat at all. At last, he made a final swallow and held out the empty bowl. Isabeau took it ...

... as Maxime came through the door with the tub.

With a growl, Ruvo spun on the cot.

Maxime froze at his first sight of his master's acquisition.

The tub, balanced on his shoulder, slid from his grasp, crashing to the floor. Splinters flew upward. Snarling, Ruvo leaped to his feet, throwing himself between Isabeau and the servant.

Mon Dieu, he's protecting me, came her astonished thought.

In the next moment, there was chaos, with Ruvo snarling and lunging at Maxime, Isabeau trying to restrain him by hauling back on the chain around his neck, and Maxime, crying out, "*Mére Sainte!* What is this demon? Where's the master's dog?"

She managed to quiet Ruvo, patting his head, saying, "It's all right. Shh. Shh, now. This is just Maxime."

With a guttural rumble, he quieted.

To the servant, she ordered, "Come, Maxime, let him get to know you," as François had said to her. "Hold out your hand."

"*Madame*, I'm fond of my fingers." He put his hands behind his back. "I'd rather not."

"And I'd rather you did," Isabeau replied, hardening her voice. "Hold out your hand, Maxime."

With obvious reluctance, Maxime obeyed. Perhaps he'd spoken with Mathilde and learned of the incident in the kitchen. With the expression of someone sticking his fingers into a roaring fire, he extended his hand.

It secretly amused her to see the servant so cowed. Maxime wasn't as tall as François, but he was almost as muscular, years of chopping wood and hauling buckets of water giving him a strong physique. At the moment, his robust complexion was pale, and his eyes were wide with fear.

Isabeau loosened her hold on the chain. "Go ahead, Ruvo."

Maxime's fingers trembled as Ruvo sniffed at them, then up the sleeve, dusted with wood chips. When he leaned back and snorted as if to clear the servant's scent from his nostrils, then squatted by Isabeau's side, Maxime retreated quickly.

"This is to be the master's model?" he exclaimed. "How can he expect to paint such a wild beast?"

"That's the master's concern," Isabeau retorted. "See to the tub. I hope you didn't damage it."

Maxime scrambled to obey. He righted the tub, dragging it

to the spot Isabeau indicated. There was a deep dent in the floor where the metal edge struck, but thankfully, the plank wasn't cracked. Once that was done, he backed out of the room, returning surprisingly soon with buckets of hot water, pouring them inside. Next, he brought the cold water, splashing some into the tub to cool it to a bearable temperature, and set the other nearby. He made three trips in all, bringing the cloths and soap last.

All the while, he kept a wary eye on Ruvo, who growled low and deep every time the servant looked his way.

When Isabeau said, "*Merci*, Maxime. Now empty the chamber pot and you may go back to your chores," she managed to wait until he was out of sight before she laughed at the way he ran from the storage room as fast as he could.

"Oh, Ruvo, thank you!" Still laughing, she acted before she thought, kneeling and throwing her arms around his neck as she often had with her favorite of her uncle's dogs.

When he stiffened, making a sound not quite a growl but not exactly his usual inquiring whimper either, then rubbed his head against her cheek, her laughter stopped. Realizing she was hugging someone believing himself not human, though she knew under all that hide and hair must undoubtedly be a fellow being, she quickly pulled away, scrambling to her feet.

"But you mustn't do that again," she continued, smoothing her skirts as well as her composure, and picking up the bowl. She placed it on the cot. "Though I appreciate the gesture."

Ruvo cocked his head, watching her. *He has no idea what I'm saying*, she thought. *No more than the hounds do*. It was only her tone of voice he responded to, she was certain.

"Now then ..." Isabeau straightened and took a deep breath. Either she was becoming accustomed to the smell, or the open window and door had considerably aired the room. "It's time for your bath."

She wondered exactly how *that* would fare.

Where to start?

With his hair, she supposed. First, she tested the water. She wouldn't put it past Maxime to not add enough cold, so Ruvo might be scalded, thus paying him back for that sleepless night and today's fright.

Deciding it wasn't too hot, she pointed to the tub. "Come now, get in."

There were more glances from her to the tub and back. He shambled over, peering in, before giving her one more questioning look. When she nodded encouragingly, he cupped his hands, dipped them into the water, and raised them. He slurped the water dripping from his hands.

"No, no." Isabeau laughed. "I want you *in* the water. If you're thirsty ..." She glanced at the cup of water.

Surprisingly, it sat unharmed on the floor, not kicked over by Ruvo's reaction to Maxime's arrival.

Just then, the servant reappeared with the emptied chamber pot. Without speaking, he set it just inside the door.

"Thank you, Maxime."

With a bare nod, Maxime disappeared again.

She picked up the cup, offering it to Ruvo. "Here."

He took it awkwardly in both hands. Sticking out his tongue, he attempted to lap the water.

"Oh, that's not the way. No." Isabeau pulled it from his hand. "Let me show you." She raised the cup to her own mouth, mimed drinking, then held it out again.

He refused to take it, just stood there.

"Very well." She put a hand under his chin. Placing the cup's rim against his lips, she tilted it.

Water splashed his face. Involuntarily, his mouth opened. The rest of the cup's contents ran inside, filling it, overflowing, dripping down his chin and beard onto his chest. He swallowed, choked, and coughed convulsively, spraying. As Isabeau dodged, he pulled the cup from her hand, took a deep breath, then continued drinking in loud gulps until it was empty. Lowering the cup, he thrust it at her with a grunt.

"Good boy." She patted his shoulder this time, thinking how stiff and wiry the hair there felt, then gestured again to the tub. "Get in."

It took two more gestures, ending with Isabeau lifting her skirts to clear her ankles and pretending to place one foot, slipper and all, into the water before he understood. When he copied her movement, balancing on one foot and stepping into the tub with the other, the chain around his neck clanking and clanging as it struck the rim, she applauded.

"Yes, that's it."

Once inside, he looked as if he enjoyed the sensation of water around his feet. He moved back and forth, raising one foot, then the other, then stamped back into the water. He slapped the water. It splashed his calves. He bent, dipping both hands, moving them in a circle, then raising them to watch droplets fall from them back into the tub.

A child, playing in his bath.

"Before we go any further, let's tend to your hair." From the basket, she took a pair of shears.

Ruvo recoiled. Obviously, he recognized the twin blades as some kind of knife. When she approached him, shears upraised, his hands clasped his nethers, fingers spread protectively. He backed away, struck the side of the tub, and nearly fell.

"It's all right." She put a hand on his shoulder as he clutched the high rim for support. "I'm not going to hurt you."

As she slid fingers under the hip-length fall of hair hanging over his shoulder and down his back, he calmed, but warily watched the hand holding the shears. Isabeau eased the blades around a single lock and pressed them shut.

His hair was thick and tough. The blades chewed and pulled. Ruvo rolled his eyes and whimpered. She shushed and soothed as she continued sawing and hacking until the handful was severed.

Isabeau dropped it to the floor.

She continued across his back and to his other side, until all the hair had been trimmed to a ragged imitation of the style favored by the young men of the town, a bowl-shape covering forehead and ears, and brushing the nape. It would never approximate that smooth style, however, for his hair was very curly; the reason it was so matted.

She continued her barbering by next attacking his beard. Seizing the wiry length in her fist, she wrapped it around her hand, wondering how François could think someone with so much facial hair could be only thirteen or so. Ruvo unconsciously cooperated by trying to raise his head, pulling the hair taut. With a loud *snip,* the shears cut through the outer edges. There was more sawing and hacking as she trimmed it as close as she could, the nearly three-foot length coming off in her hand.

It joined the rest of the hair on the floor.

She again circled the tub, snipping here and there to even the cut-off locks. All this time, the chain hung over his shoulder, dipping into the water. Isabeau decided to risk removing it, and that was when she discovered something she hadn't noticed the night before.

Under the leather collar, the nape of his neck was bare, the hair on his back beginning inches below it. When she looked closer, she saw that what she'd thought was hair was instead a garment of some kind, fashioned of an animal's hide, holes cut for his arms, and a leather thong inserted into the neck opening, drawn tight and knotted under his chin.

She got the chain out of the way, dropping it to the floor.

The sound he made seemed to be a sigh of relief, welcoming the lack of weight around his neck. He shook slightly, flexing his neck and shoulders.

Clipping the leather string, she slid a hand inside the garment and began to cut, splitting the hide down the back from neck to waist. It fell into two pieces, dropping on top of the pile of hair.

Next time Mathilde does laundry, I'll have her toss it into the fire. The hair was too filthy to use, even for stuffing a pillow or plumping a mattress. Besides, it probably held vermin of some kind.

Through it all, Ruvo barely moved, but whether from fright or simply trusting her when she promised he wouldn't be harmed, she couldn't tell. Occasionally, he whimpered, moving his arms slightly and shivering as if distressed. She wondered how long it had been since he was without that heavy, disguising animal skin. He was now bare from the waist up, his skin darkened by a crusted coating of dirt and bits of loose hair sloughed from the hide. It was remarkable how hairless his body was. He now had the odd appearance of a man who'd fallen into a mud puddle and emerged covered with shed dog hair and debris.

What François had said about fattening him up was true. His ribs were thin and prominent. She could count each one. Why had the gypsies starved him so? There was barely any spare flesh on him anywhere, and that made him look smaller than ever, slender, fragile ... surely, he weighed no more than she.

Isabeau felt a rush of pity. Poor child—so young to be treated in such a way ...

Around his waist, she found a second knotted strip of leather. Attached to it were two wide pieces of pelt, one in front and one in back, like a breech clout. Lean, narrow flanks were visible between them. Ignoring his sounds of protest, Isabeau used the shears to clip through the strip, catching the pieces as they fell away. She studied them for a moment, turning the two segments over in her hands. Then she looked up ...

"Oh, *mon Dieu* ..." She swallowed, took a deep breath, stammered out, "You're ... you're ..." and didn't finish.

This was no child standing before her, up to his knees in bath water. Not even an adolescent. Even if her horrified eyes hadn't told her this was a man, full-grown and an adult, the now exposed *organe d'amour* nestled against his thighs did.

She found herself staring, unable to look away. Surely that member rivaled François's in size, and yet ... There was something wrong with it.

It took her a moment to realize part of it was missing. The enveloping flesh had been cut away, the crown and half the shaft bare.

Why? She was shocked by what was obviously a wanton mutilation. Why did they do that? To make him appear more of a beast, to keep him from seeming human? She remembered the protective gesture he'd made when he saw the shears, his hand shielding his crotch. An image flashed through her mind, men holding a screaming child while another wielded a gigantic pair of shears, seizing that small, tender member, and slicing ...

Ruvo's eyes met hers. Not ashamed, not asking for pity, neither preening, yet with no pretense of modesty, simply a copper-colored gaze looking into her own.

She dropped the breech clout atop the others. "Sit down."

He didn't move.

She later told herself it was her shock making her act so roughly. She plunged a hand into the water, caught an ankle, and hauled upward. He was pulled off his feet, striking the back of the tub and grasping it as he fell. The tub lurched and water surged upward, splashing Isabeau and the floor.

She was glad she'd worn an apron.

Before he could recover, she released his ankle, draping it over the side of the tub, and seized the other one, pulling it from the water. Picking up the laundry soap, she knelt, rubbing the bar against his sole.

Vigorously.

He protested with a high-pitched cry that rose and fell in an oddly familiar pattern while he wriggled the ankle, body twisting. It took her a moment to realize he was laughing—his version, at least. She trailed a fingertip across the bottom of his foot. With something like a giggle, he kicked slightly and tried to pull away.

"So, you're ticklish, are you? Then be still or I'll tickle you until you scream for mercy." She remembered how her youngest brother, Antoine, had been so sensitive that her mother could barely dress him sometimes, and how she used to tease him the same way.

Whether Ruvo understood or not, he stilled, allowing her to scrub his legs and feet with the brush. His toenails were long and thick. She tackled them with the shears, causing several whimpers of protest but no attempt to shy away. She did the same to his fingers, shortening the untended claws to an acceptable length, then scrubbed both toes and fingers, removing the dirt under them.

Isabeau worked silently and swiftly, not giving herself time to think of who she was bathing, just that he needed to be *clean*.

She finished by rubbing the bar of soap through his hair, raising a thick lather and taking the drinking cup to scoop water and pour it over his head. He didn't like that, snorting and swiping at his eyes as some of the suds dripped into them.

A minor surprise: at some point during the inundations of water and soap, that single brow disappeared. Now, heavy but separate crescents rested above each eye. The bit of hair connecting his brows was false, glued to his forehead, to enhance that *loup-garou* image, she didn't doubt.

After that, only one thing was left—the remnants of the beard.

He didn't protest as she patted lather onto his cheeks and chin, nor when she drew François's razor from the basket. Obviously, he'd seen someone shave. The gypsy Boamas, perhaps?

Nevertheless, his eyes rolled frantically as Isabeau touched the razor to his jaw. She was careful not to cut him, wiping the blade against her apron skirt to remove the clinging hair after each stroke. The shaving went remarkably quickly. Isabeau swished the blade back and forth in the water, then dried it on her apron. She replaced it in the basket and turned to look at her handiwork ...

... and gasped.

She couldn't help it. The face hidden by all that hair ...

Oh, mon Dieu.

Though narrow to the point of thinness, cheekbones prominent and sharp, it held an ascetic beauty. She could see how François might believe Ruvo his St. Jean, the face of a man who'd experienced the extreme of poverty combined with religious fervor. At the same time, it was the face of an angel, skin translucent, those dark eyes filled with an inner glow, one Botticelli or the great Raphael might've chosen. The slight point to the tips of the ears showing through his curls only added to his otherworldly appearance.

Briefly, Isabeau felt as if she'd been admitted into the presence of something holy. She was shaken. It was only as she saw small patches of drying suds clinging to his chest and in his hair that she was reminded this was merely the most pitiable of humans.

She glanced down, unable to meet that stare, and looked

into the tub. The once-clean bathwater was now mud-colored, bits of hair floating on its surface like pond scum.

"And now for the finishing touch." She got very busy again, reaching for the last bucket of water. "Stand up."

Without protest, he rose into that usual crouch, dripping water back into the tub.

"No," she said. "Stand up. Straight. You're no longer a beast, Ruvo. You're a man, and men stand upright."

Setting down the bucket, she placed a hand against the small of his back, and the other against his chest, and pushed.

Ruvo straightened.

Isabeau stared up at him. He wasn't quite François's height, but much, much taller than she, so tall she couldn't pour the water over him. There was a stool in a corner. She dragged it over, climbed upon it, and upended the bucket over his head, washing away the sudsy remnants.

He shook, dog-like, head, shoulders, that prominent member, and waited for whatever came next.

Seizing a wrist, she dragged him from the tub, using a towel to rub him dry. She was rough, her movements hasty, but he submitted with no outcry. Pulling François's cast-off shirt from the basket, she threw it over his head before he could protest. It was too big, hung past his knees, but would do, she supposed. As for the stocks...

Isabeau was grateful they were an old-fashioned pair, another reason François rid himself of them. The *marquis* gave him some in the latest style, one piece with points tying them to his shirt, and a codpiece attached with little bows. She doubted Ruvo had any idea how to tie a bow or unravel a knot, but the old style consisted of separate legs with a wide top, tied around the opposite hip. The pieces of cloth girded the hips in a criss-cross that could be pulled apart for necessary actions. Once tied, they needn't be unfastened again.

She had a moment of panic when he jerked away, scrambling out of reach. With an expression much like a pout, showing quite plainly he didn't want to wear them, he began kicking and moving his legs about, just as Antoine did when *Mamére* tried to dress him.

"Stop it!"

That one command brought an immediate cessation of movement. Isabeau gritted her teeth and seized an ankle, holding tight. She twisted his leg, making him lose his balance and fall onto the cot, where he stayed still as she knelt and worked the stocking over his foot and up his leg, biting her lip and trying not to blush as she made certain his rod was cupped inside the wider, upper part. She crossed and tied the stock, and then the other, feeling a bit of relief when that poor, maimed member was safely nestled inside and hidden from her sight.

She was thankful that particular pair of stocks had leather soles, so she didn't have to worry about forcing shoes onto his feet. She had an idea he wouldn't like that any better than he liked the stocks.

As she brushed back a stray lock of hair that escaped the kerchief she'd tied over it, she was startled to feel the back of her gown sticking to her shoulders, wet with sweat.

With a sigh, Isabeau straightened and sat back on her heels, surveying the result of her toil. What she saw told her she'd wrought a miracle. In place of a hairy, dirty beast crouching like a skulking wolf, sat a young man in a worn shirt and stocks.

"Oh, Ruvo." She caught his face in her hands, staring into his eyes. "You're beautiful."

He blinked. His mouth opened. For a moment, she thought he was going to speak. Instead, he raised his hands, copying her gesture and rubbing them against her cheeks in an awkward, if startlingly gentle caress before dropping them again to his sides.

That movement broke the spell. Who would ever believe this transformation? She wondered what François would say.

"What do you think of all this, Ruvo? If only you could speak ..."

Then the second miracle happened.

Again, Ruvo opened his mouth. He coughed, swallowed loudly, and with a great effort, said, "I ... can ..."

Chapter Four

His voice was grating and raspy, like a rusted gate forced open after long inactivity. The harshness of it sent a thrill through Isabeau, tunneling deep inside. She was startled as she realized the feeling wasn't fear.

For three heartbeats, she stared at him in stunned silence before demanding, "Why haven't you spoken before?"

"*Vaida* Boamas ... not ... like. He say I ... *loup-garou*." There were long pauses between his words, as if he searched his memory for each before he spoke. "*Gadje* ... not want hear man sound like man ... want ... man sound like wolf. He beat ... if I talk."

"How cruel." She seized his hands, clasping them tightly, feeling a flaring of hate for the gypsy chief she'd never felt for anyone, not even François. "Ruvo, I'm sorry you've been treated so badly," she said and meant it.

"Not call me that." He shook his head vigorously, making his curls bounce in disarray.

Even in her surprise, Isabeau thought how unruly but beautiful they were in their glossy darkness.

"Ruvo not my name."

"What shall I call you?" she asked, confused. "What is your name?"

There was a long pause. He glanced around furtively, as if making certain there was no one nearby to hear.

Isabeau thought that odd. Had Boamas done that? Let him think no one was around, tricked him into speaking, then revealed he had an audience and beat him for his lapse in obedience?

At last, he said, very softly, in a hoarse whisper, "Giovanni ... Giovanni di Casalupo."

"Giovanni?"

That was an Italian name. In the tale he'd told her, hadn't François said his family was from Italy? It sounded as if it should've been the name of a scion of a great family. And his surname ...

"Giovanni of the House of the Wolf?"

There was a twist to his mouth that might've been a rueful smile. "Boamas say ... that good jest ... call me 'Ruvo' ... that mean 'wolf' in Rom because I *loup-garou*."

"You aren't a *loup-garou*, Ru ... Giovanni," she corrected. "Don't say that anymore." Realizing she still held his hands, she released them, placing her own tightly in her lap. "You're a man, not an animal."

"*Oui*," he agreed, nodding. "You ... make me a man." He ducked his head in such an exact imitation of Maxime's bow she nearly laughed. "Thank you, *Maîtresse* Isabeau."

He'd listened well to the people who came to jeer and gape. Nevertheless, his broken French, spoken with that gravelly accent, sent shivers through her, not frightened ones but more like a caress of sound, like the brush of a finger against the spine.

"Now I look like a man, not wolf." His words came quicker, as if with each he spoke, his tongue more easily formed them. "How *Maître* François explain that to *gadje*?" He waved a hand as if gesturing to something. "Here, *loup-garou*, but he not look it?"

Mon Dieu, he thinks François bought him to show him as the gypsies did. Isabeau hurried to explain, "He's not going to exhibit you, Giovanni."

"No? What then?"

His eyes widened. Was that fear she saw in their depths?

"He want me like men do, Mariah? Pay coin, have me bed him in wagon back?"

Heavenly Father, did they do that to him, too? She was shocked and silent.

When she didn't answer, he continued, "Maybe he want me for you? Want me tongue cunny? Make mistress moan?"

"N-no. H-he..." Face burning, Isabeau stared at him, stuttering stupidly. He hadn't moved, made no gesture of threat, but the thought flashed through her mind, *Am I in danger of being ravished?*

When he leaned forward, towering over her, she became aware that she was sitting on the floor before him. She scrambled to her feet.

"Mistress?" That one word held concern. "Your face ... what ...?"

He raised a hand as if to touch the blush on her cheek.

She backed away, dismissing from her mind the thoughts making her flush, explaining,

"He's going to *paint* you."

"Paint?" His brow wrinkled. He frowned, trying to grasp that concept. "Like Rom paint on wagon to chase evil spirits?"

"Not exactly." She forced herself not to laugh at his misunderstanding, relief flooding through her at his distraction.

Of course, raised with those pagans, he'd think that. She relaxed, realizing he'd probably never had a truly lascivious thought about a woman in his life, in spite of that gypsy girl. He simply did what he was told.

"Here, let me show you."

Taking his hand, she pulled him to the nearest stack of canvases. They were close enough he could've touched them at any time if he'd wished. She remembered François's distress as he asked about their safety.

"My husband is an *artiste*," she explained, as she pulled the first from where it leaned against the wall. "These are his paintings."

It was large, almost four feet high, and unwieldy. She glanced at him as if expecting him to help her. He didn't move.

What does he know of gallantry? A thought occurred, and it startled her. *I'll make him aware.*

Aloud, she said, "This is heavy. Help me."

As if only waiting for her order, he seized the other side and helped her turn the picture around.

It was a landscape—*Mountain Meadow at Sunrise*—a beautiful scene, the sun just peeking between the mountaintops, touching the meadow below it with gold. Dew glistened on the grass and the meadow blossoms, reflecting back the sun. It looked so real that if one touched it, one would expect one's fingers to come away damp.

Giovanni stared, silent. She wondered what he was thinking.

Can he appreciate the beauty of this scene?

She showed him another. *Madonna of the Grotto*. Isabeau had posed for that one, but reluctantly. She hadn't felt worthy to be François's model, not for something so reverent, but after he said he'd asked one of the women he paid to sit for him, she thought perhaps she was better to serve as his Madonna than any of those sluts.

She'd accompanied her husband to a place he found during

one of his jaunts. She posed there for weeks, high rock surrounding her, greenness masking the gray cliffs, amidst fern, wildflowers, and moss, she in a grass-colored gown, cradling the Blessed Child in her arms.

Giovanni studied the painting. "You have a little one?" His fingers touched the canvas face, stroking gently.

She should've told him not to touch it. François said a finger's touch could corrupt the paint and make it change color. Thinking of the dirty claws his hands had been and that now they were slender and clean, seeing them brush against her painted image made her wonder how it would feel to be touched so gently, to have those unsullied fingers caress her body.

"*Maîtresse?*"

His voice plucked her from that untoward fancy.

"No." There had been no real babe, only a doll François borrowed from the town toymaker and afterward returned. He'd instructed her to embrace it as she would a real child.

She had, lovingly, briefly wished it *were* a real child, *her* child, ignoring who would be its father. In the Madonna's image, François definitely captured her wish for maternity.

"Why not?"

That angered her. She told herself it shouldn't. It was the question a child might ask, not the probing one of her parents with their desire for a grandson, nor the accusing one from François when he wondered aloud why she didn't conceive. *Perhaps I should send you back to your parents and get myself a fertile wife.* He never thought to question his own virility. Not that he would care for a child, it would be merely a manifestation of his masculinity. He would make a son into an image of himself, a boorish, selfish, occasionally drunken, womanizing lout. Isabeau would merely be the vessel of its creation.

Perhaps that was why it was better that there was no child.

"I don't know." She forced the anger away and pointed out a third painting, a portrait of a young noble soon to be delivered to its owner.

"I like this," he decided and looked interested. Perhaps the bright colors and the jewels attracted him, the way shiny baubles did a magpie. "He paint me this way?"

"I doubt it." She explained about the *St. Jean.* "He wants you for your suffering, but first, he will do other paintings to get you accustomed to posing."

A sound at the door made both whirl, Isabeau guiltily, though there was no reason, and Giovanni protectively.

Maxime stood there. Giovanni growled low in his throat. He took a step, beginning a crouch, a wolf preparing to spring. Isabeau put a hand on his arm. It wouldn't have stopped him as fast as he could move, but he halted.

"What is it, Maxime?" She made her voice brusque, angry that the servant was intruding.

"Mathilde sent me to see about you, mistress," he said, not looking away from Giovanni, with evident surprise at his change in appearance. "You've been out here overlong, and she wanted to make certain you were ... safe."

Giovanni growled again.

"Quiet." She patted his arm and assured Maxime, "I'm fine, as you can see. It's good of Mathilde to worry about me." She filled her voice with irony.

If she's worried, it's the first time.

Early in her marriage, Isabeau had decided to take a stroll in the forest behind the cottage. She'd fallen and sprained her ankle, unable to walk; it hurt so badly. She wasn't missed until evening fell and François came in from his studio, demanding to know why his wife wasn't at table. That brought on a frantic search until they found her, nearly hysterical and hoarse from calling for help.

François carried her back to the cottage, cursing at her for wandering away so carelessly. Not a word to the servants about ignoring her absence. Not a concern that she might've been harmed by a wild animal or some marauding human. The local leech was summoned, and Isabeau was confined to bed until she could walk again. Mathilde complained the entire time she had to bring her meals to the bedside.

Now, she worries about me? Had her show of spirit wrought this change?

"You may take the tub away."

Without looking away from Giovanni, Maxime advanced into the room. Giovanni also took a step, still growling. Maxime tugged at the tub. Filled with water, it was too heavy to lift. He picked up one of the buckets, scooped water, and hurried to the window, where he sloshed it through. He repeated that, urged on by sporadic growls, until the tub was empty enough for him to lift.

As he hoisted it, leaving a damp outline on the floor, Giovanni made a mock lunge. When Maxime started and dashed for the door as fast as the weight of the tub would allow, Giovanni began to bark, the sound following the servant.

He stopped as Maxime disappeared.

"Why did you do that?" Isabeau stifled her own laughter, making the question a reprimand.

"He fear me even if I not look like wolf." His explanation was delivered with contempt. "Like to see him run."

"Nevertheless, you mustn't do that," she said.

"If you wish it, *maîtresse*." The look he gave her was as slavishly adoring as a hound's.

"I do." She replaced the painting and moved away.

He followed.

"Now I must go back to the house. Mathilde's right. I've been here too long and I've other chores to tend."

Like doing her husband's darning and making the beds because that lazy creature wouldn't.

She picked up the chain, reattaching it to his collar. He looked sad at that, but didn't say anything.

"I'm sorry," she apologized.

All he said was, "I'm thirsty."

"Next time, I'll bring a pitcher so you'll have water during the day," she promised.

She looked at the blanket on the floor. Luckily, it hadn't been dampened by any of the water splashed from the tub. Most of that had dripped through the planks and onto the dirt beneath. Picking it up, she dropped it onto the cot.

"You'll sleep here from now on."

"Not comfortable," he protested. He pointed to the floor. "That better."

"Nevertheless, you're a man now, and men sleep in beds."

He didn't answer, simply dropped onto the cot, on top of the blanket, much as a reprimanded hound would do.

She had no doubt the moment the door was shut, he'd have the blanket on the floor again.

* * *

THE NEXT MORNING, her women's time came upon her, and Isabeau stayed abed. It never bothered her; it was simply a relieved indication she wasn't about to carry François's child, but Isabeau pretended otherwise, asking for compresses of heated rice to lay on her belly, chamomile tea, and other remedies for female complaints. That was mainly to keep François away and perhaps gain a little sympathy from Mathilde, though that never happened.

The only response she got this time was a refusal to feed Giovanni.

"Maxime won't do it," Mathilde informed her. "He growls."

"He won't bite." At least, she hoped not.

"He won't do it, and neither will I," Mathilde added as if she thought Isabeau was about to say that.

"Then, when *Maître* François returns—whenever that is— you must be the one explaining why his precious St. Jean has starved to death," Isabeau retorted.

Fear of François's temper sent Maxime to the storage room twice a day until Isabeau pronounced herself able again. Her time generally lasted only four days, and this once she was impatient for it to be over.

Chapter Five

SHE HURRIED to the storage room, anxious to see Giovanni, worried as to how he might look, for she didn't doubt he'd been fed, but how much she couldn't be certain.

There was a rustling inside as she unlocked the door. As it swung open, she saw Giovanni sitting demurely on the cot, hands clasped in his lap. She was certain he'd scooped the blanket off the floor and crawled onto the cot as he heard the key in the lock.

"Good morning." She made her voice bright, for she was glad to see him.

"*Maîtresse.*" He inclined his head, surprising Isabeau with the movement just short of being a courtly nod.

He didn't look as if he'd been starved, so perhaps Mathilde had fed him well. In fact, except for the mop of wild curls, he looked very tidy, shirt and stocks still clean and unstained except for a few grease spots on the shirt's front. The air in the room smelled better, also.

She held out the platter. He took it and began to shovel the meat scraps into his mouth. Isabeau found herself wondering if he could be taught to use a fork, but no ... giving him something sharp wouldn't be a good idea. Not yet. Perhaps she should add some bread and vegetables, proper human food.

He swallowed the last morsel and handed back the platter. As she took it, he started to wipe his hands on his shirttail.

"Here." She fished her handkerchief out of her bosom, handing it to him.

He took it, holding it awkwardly. He opened it, studied the lacy edging, then sniffed at it.

"Wipe your hands."

He obeyed and handed it back.

She tucked it back into the neck of her gown between her houppelande and chemise. Was it actually warm from his touch, or did she imagine it?

Setting down the platter, she said, "I'll show you François's studio today. It's where he'll paint you."

He didn't answer, simply sat still as she unclasped the chain. When he got to his feet, the crouch was back, as if he'd forgotten in the past four days how to stand upright.

"Up." She poked him in the chest, not very gently.

He straightened without a word. Still not speaking, he followed her through the door, only to stop, looking around in wonder. She showed him the easel where the canvas would rest, the little platform on which the model stood, sat, or lay, as François ordered.

"I stay on this?" That was his first question as he stepped onto the platform and looked back at her. He bounced slightly as if testing its strength. "What I do?"

"All you have to do is stay where he puts you and be still. I'm afraid it's going to be very tedious."

He shrugged. "I good at staying still."

She supposed he was, lying in a cage day after day.

Then, he smiled, though it was more a baring of teeth with the corners of his lips curling. With practice, it might become genuine.

"Perhaps I sleep with eyes open so *Maître* not know."

She thought she saw a twinkle in those eyes.

She returned him to the storeroom. As she started to reattach the chain to his collar, he said, "Chain heavy. Don't," and before she could protest, as if he knew the argument she'd give: "I not run away. Where I go, locked in here?"

She dropped the chain to the floor. "I'm trusting you. Don't let me make a mistake."

In answer, he lay on the cot, awkwardly, on his belly, chin resting on his crossed forearms, so much like the way the hounds slept on the hearth, she was shocked. She didn't say anything.

Why should I think one bath and a few kind words will make him forget the way he's lived for so many years?

Retrieving the platter, she left without a word.

* * *

The next day, she heard a mad scrambling as she opened the door and came in to find Giovanni standing by the cot, shirtless, frantically tugging the top of his stocks. It was obvious he'd taken them off, for they now barely covered his belly, though thankfully they were pulled high enough to hide his nethers.

"What are you doing?" she asked. "Why did you take off your clothing?"

"Can't sleep." He avoided her gaze. "Not like."

"You will not do that again," she ordered, setting down the platter and pushing his hands away. "Do you understand? You may have slept your entire life with nothing but those hides covering you, but now, you're a man. You'll sleep as men do."

She ignored the image of François's naked slumbers springing into her head.

"*Oui, maîtresse*," he responded obediently, like a schoolboy replying to his tutor.

"If you have need to take them off, however," she went on, knowing full well he would again attempt to remove them at night, "do it like this."

Starting at his ankles, she worked the fabric upward, smoothing the wrinkles and adjusting the waist-ties, which he hadn't opened but simply slid over his hips. She made certain the pieces at the crotch were securely crossing each other.

"Do you understand?"

"*Oui, maîtresse*." Reluctantly, he picked up the shirt and pulled it over his head, then waited for whatever she would say next.

She handed him the platter. She had also brought him a table kerchief and showed him how to drape it over his shoulder, stressing that he wipe his hands on it as well as his mouth after he'd finished eating. He obeyed without argument, though the hand and mouth-wiping were little more than a clumsy swipe. Accepting the attempt, she folded and placed it on the windowsill to await his next meal.

She looked back to find him studying the floor.

He did that a great deal, she noticed—looked down, avoiding people's eyes. The few times he'd looked into hers, it had been unavoidable. Her uncle's dogs did the same, she remembered. The only time they met someone's eyes was when they were reprimanded, and then, only fleetingly.

Something else to work on.

Isabeau showed him where the *puits de cess* was located. Because Maxime refused to come into Giovanni's presence, though there had been no more growling or barking incidents, she told him from then on, he'd empty the chamber pot himself.

Then, she said, "I'm sure you must be bored."

"What is 'bored?'"

Having never known anything else, would he think of all the time he spent sleeping or simply lying around as boredom?

She ignored his question, saying instead, "I thought you might like to go outside."

"I go outside when you show me *puits de cess*," he pointed out, sounding as if he were protesting.

"True," she agreed. "However, I meant for a much longer time."

The first eager expression she'd seen came over his face. He got to his feet, straightening without her reminding him. Isabeau considered that a minor victory.

"You aren't chained," she pointed out. "Promise you won't run away?"

Would he know what a promise was?

"Not run away," he answered, solemnly. Then he did a curious thing: he spat in his hand and held it out.

She stared at the gleaming streak across his palm, forcing herself not to make a *moue* of disgust. "Why did you do that?"

"Make oath." He gestured. "You spit in hand. Shake mine. Seal promise. I not leave you, *maîtresse*."

She shook her head. "I'm sorry. I won't touch your hand while it's..." She didn't finish.

He looked at his hand, frowned, then started to wipe it against his shirt, where it covered his thigh. At the last minute, he stopped, and to Isabeau's amazement, pulled the table kerchief from the sill and wiped his hand on it. He replaced the kerchief and held out his hand again. Isabeau placed her own within it. His fingers closed around hers in a gentle grasp.

The tremor coursing through her made her want to shiver.

Pulling her hand away, she led him out of the storeroom to the studio's door, and from there, into the sunlight. She'd already warned Mathilde and Maxime so they wouldn't panic if they saw Giovanni outside.

"Ahhh." He stopped beside her.

Raising his head, he took a deep breath, inhaling the fresh air, perhaps the scent of the flowers in the overgrown courtyard. He looked out over the meadow-like expanse in front of the cottage, then at the walkway, and the path leading to the high road, the trees ...

In a rush so swift Isabeau couldn't have stopped him even if she'd been forewarned, he dashed past her, leaping off the porch into the waist-high grass. Trampling the meadow flowers, he began to run.

"Giovanni!" she screamed. "No, you promised," then fell silent as she saw he wasn't running *away*.

He was simply *running*.

He skidded to a stop, spinning in a circle, stamping the grass, and jumping up and down. He began running again, sprinting toward the path, then veered away, galloping in a curve, around and around, making circles in the grass, crushing it into narrow paths, all the time barking and yelping, making sounds like the foxes she had seen in the woods one spring, when they leaped and played their mating games. Abruptly, he dropped to his knees and disappeared into the grass, leaving it swaying and rippling.

"Giovanni? Where are you?" Isabeau ventured into the field, running until she found him.

He lay on his back, rolling in the grass, giving little grunts of pleasure. Without warning, he rose to his knees, giving what could only be a mock growl.

Remembering playing this way with her mother's little pet, she began to run. With a *yip* of delight, he pursued.

She didn't get far. Weeds wrapped themselves about her ankles, her skirts tangled around her knees. She hesitated, not wanting to trip. Giovanni overtook her. He stepped on the hem of her gown, and she fell backward against him. With a playful growl, he seized her about the waist and flung them both into the grass. His arms went around her as he rolled her over and over among the daisies and lupines. She began to laugh, and his own hoarse laughter encircled hers.

Movement came to a halt, with him on top, her pressed into the crushed grass. His eyes met hers, glowing as if reflecting the sun itself. She thought she had read a question in them. Isabeau's laughter ceased. The pressure of his body against hers wasn't unpleasant, but it was disturbing. Something rigid pressed against her belly.

With a grunt, he slid off her, getting to his knees and then his feet. He pulled her upright, releasing her hand.

With what dignity she could muster after such behavior, she walked past him, back to the walkway's porch, where she seated herself upon it.

After a moment's hesitation, Giovanni followed, falling to his knees, then lying at her feet. She caught his arm and tugged.

"Get up. Sit beside me."

He obeyed, though he looked ill at ease, as if lying prone were more comfortable.

"This beautiful." His gesture covered the entire scene before him. "Want to run through it forever."

"Why didn't you? Why didn't you run away?"

He gave her a look she thought held reproach. "I promise I not leave you, *maîtresse*." There was rebuke in his tone, as if the answer should've been obvious.

Something stabbed through her, as piercing and sharp as a white-hot blade. François had never said such a thing to her. Whenever she protested something he did, he let her know quickly enough that there were many women who'd be glad to take her place. Each time he left the cottage, she always had some doubt he might not return. Never had he told her in any way that she was *loved*.

From far away, a bell began to toll. Isabeau slid from the walkway to her knees, crossing herself. Hands clasped to her breast, she murmured a prayer.

"*Maîtresse*, what you do?" Giovanni asked.

"It's the Angelus." She broke off long enough to answer.

The excitement of his arrival had made her forget. Today was Sunday.

Their cottage was far from town, and François used that excuse for not coming to services in winter, since they would have to walk, though a good many did exactly that. In summer, he managed to get by with the defense that he couldn't interrupt his work. He'd also decreed that if he didn't attend services, neither would his wife or servants. Maxime and Mathilde accepted that well enough. Neither had liked to get up so early to attend, anyway, but this dereliction worried Isabeau to that day.

Père Ambroise, tolerant as always, didn't complain.

Privately, François admitted to Isabeau he didn't believe in God, and anyway, the church was too far to walk to listen to a sermon on something he didn't think existed.

When she asked how he could, in all good conscience, take the money from so many churches if he felt that way, he replied, "They are playing for my talent, not my belief."

She'd countered with the fact that God had given him that talent, to which François declared, "Really? I thought the masters in Italy taught me." He then told her she'd best never repeat to anyone what he'd said.

Nevertheless, on Sundays, she tried to observe the Angelus, saying her prayers, and again when the Matins bells rang, including within them the impious hope that her husband would make a slip some day and find himself on the way to Hell for his disbelief, by way of a heretic's fire.

So far, it hadn't happened. That was simply another instance of François's talent saving him. Another instance of God not answering her prayers.

"What is this, Angelus?" Giovanni asked.

"When the bell rings, we must stop and celebrate in prayer the incarnation of Our Lord." She refused to think about how she'd ignored the bells since Giovanni's appearance. Distracted by him, she might forget them completely.

He cocked his head, listening. "Bells not ringing now. You stop."

"It isn't that simple."

"Why?" Apparently, to Giovanni, it was.

"Because ..." She didn't wish to get into a theological debate with this wolf-newly-turned-into-man. "Don't the, uh, the Rom have prayers in their religion?"

"Don't know they have religion," he said. "Never tell me."

She had no answer for that, so she simply crossed herself again and slid back to sit beside him. She thought about what he'd said. Perhaps the gypsies had no religion. Perhaps they didn't stay in one place long enough to formulate a belief in deities, but he'd said they painted charms on their wagons to keep away evil spirits.

If they believed in evil spirits, they must also believe in good ones.

That made her ask, "How long were you with the gypsies, Giovanni?"

"Not know ... can't count. Many summers. Many winters."

"Do you remember anything about your family?" What kind of people would sell their child?

He thought for a moment, plucking the stalk of a wilted

blossom growing near the porch, twirling it between his fingers. He appeared fascinated by the movement.

He didn't answer for so long, she thought he hadn't understood what she had asked. Finally, he said, "Nothing. Always been with Rom."

"I'm sure that's not so." Not to have other memories, he must have been very young. "How old were you when you came to them?" she persisted.

"Not know." He frowned as if her continued interrogation was becoming annoying.

"How tall were you?" She was determined to learn his age.

He thought, then gestured. "Like this." His hand struck somewhere between his hip and knee.

About the height of a small child. Five, perhaps, or six? Old enough to remember his name. That would make him about her own age, or a little older, perhaps. She studied his face. It didn't yet have the hardened tone of masculine maturity but still held some of the unformed softness of late adolescence in spite of a fresh bristle of beard. She reminded herself to see if he knew how to use a razor. If she dared trust him with a blade.

Giovanni spoke again, face screwed up as if squinting into the sun.

"Remember ... holding hand, walking. Legs too short, had to run to keep up. Then someone else take my hand, big man. Boamas. He take my clothes, put animal skin on me. Look more like *loup-garou*, he say."

"And he put you in that cage?"

"He say *gadje* expect *loup-garou* in cage."

Where else would a wolf be?

"Do you really think you're a wolf?" she demanded.

"Of course."

"Why?"

He shrugged. "Boamas say so. If I not, why he lie?"

He made it sound so simple.

She became aware that the sun was directly overhead. Isabeau scrambled to her feet.

"It's time for you to go in."

He held back. "Not want to."

"You must," she said firmly, determined to quell this minor rebellion. "I have other things to do, and I can't let you run loose."

She raised a hand, intending to point to the studio. He dodged and cowered, arms raised protectively.

"Giovanni ..." She touched his arm.

He fell to his knees. "Don't beat me, mistress."

She pulled him to his feet. He straightened, towering over her, yet in that moment she felt as if he were shorter than she, the size of that child who'd been sold by his parents, of a height between hip and knee.

"Giovanni, I'll never hit you."

"Promise?" He held out his hand.

"Promise." She clasped it. "Now, go inside."

Once he was again sitting on the cot, she said, "You said you don't know how old you are because you can't count. Would you like to learn?"

"How?"

"I could instruct you."

She'd teach him his numbers and sums, instruct him in letters, and educate every ounce of the wolf out of him.

"Why you do that?" He looked doubtful.

"Because you need to know. So you can read the wisdom of your fellow men. Don't you want to be able to read and write?"

She thought he looked as if he didn't care how intelligent his fellow men were. Perhaps he doubted it, considering how he'd been treated so far.

"Boamas reward me when I good. If I learn, you not feed me bad-tasting food?"

"We'll have to talk about that," she hedged. She was certain eating raw meat was one way to keep the belief of the wolf in him alive, but she wanted to starve to death that part of Giovanni without harming his human side.

"We bargain," he decided, sensing her hesitancy. "I learn, you give me something."

"What?" Realizing he'd probably watched the Rom barter, Isabeau wondered what he'd ask for. "I can't let you go."

"Not want that," he denied.

"What, then?"

"Bring back big bowl."

"*Big bowl?*" She shook her head.

"Big bowl," he repeated impatiently. "Frightened servant fill with water."

"The tub?"

He nodded.

"Why do you want the tub?" She struggled not to laugh at his description of Maxime.

"I like. Feel good." He stamped his feet as he had while in the water.

So. Even a beast likes to be clean. What do you think of that, François? Isabeau felt as if she'd somehow won a major victory over her absent husband.

On the way back to the cottage, Isabeau began to doubt her own plan.

Who am I to dare presume to teach one God has cursed to be a beast? Yet it isn't his fault he was born on the Lord's Day. Why should he suffer for it? If anyone is guilty, it's his parents for coupling so their child would be born on that holy day. Immediately, she defended herself as well as Giovanni to the Heavenly Father. *Punish me as you will, Lord, but I'm going to do it.*

She could already hear what François would say. *By my vow, Isabeau, have you lost your senses? Trying to teach that halfwit to read? He's a* beast, *wife, a* loup-garou. *You'll be fortunate if he doesn't kill you instead. Non, I forbid it. I won't have you alone with him.*

I've already been alone with him; she silently answered that imaginary argument. *If I can do it before François returns, teach Giovanni enough that he can read a few sentences, write his name, have him able to sit at table, then he can't argue.*

Chapter Six

IN THE KITCHEN, Mathilde greeted her with a sneer. "I saw you from the kitchen window. I wonder what the master would say if he knew his wife was publicly disporting with that beast."

Isabeau turned a frosty gaze on her. "We weren't *disporting*," she corrected, giving the word as much disdain as possible. "He was playing, and I joined in."

"Playing." The cook smirked. "Is that what they're calling it nowadays? With him lying atop you and your skirts up to your knees?"

Isabeau was momentarily silenced. Had her skirts hiked that high? Well, what did it matter? Giovanni hadn't tried to put his hand under them. Indeed, she doubted he'd ever had a lewd thought. She truly believed that, in spite of the corruption of his life, he was an innocent. Any immorality was forced on him by the gypsies.

"How dare you spy on me?" Isabeau was outraged. "If you were doing your work properly, you'd have no time to tend to others' business."

"When the master's not here, someone has to," answered the cook, pertly.

"You'll watch that tongue of yours, Mathilde, or—"

"Or what, mistress?" The cook dared raise her brows in a leer. "I swear, I'm glad we have no close neighbors, else I'd be mightily shamed to know someone else might've seen my dear master's wife rolling in the grass like a common trollop—ow!"

She reeled as Isabeau slapped her.

It happened before Isabeau realized. Her arm seemed to swing of its own accord, open palm making a loud smacking against Mathilde's plump cheek. Red finger marks appeared as the blood rushed back under the cook's freckled skin.

Giving Isabeau a murderous glare, Mathilde rubbed her smarting cheek. Isabeau bit back the apology, rushing to her lips. *Bitch, you deserved that.*

"You'll keep quiet," Isabeau gritted through clenched teeth. "Do you understand me?"

"Y-yes, mistress." Mathilde waited until Isabeau walked out before she muttered, "You'll regret that, I swear."

* * *

THE NEXT DAY, Isabeau brought a slate and chalk to the storeroom. Giovanni sat straight and attentive as she wrote his name upon the gray surface.

"There." She tapped it with the chalk. "That's your name. *Giovanni.*"

He brushed his fingers over the word. It immediately blurred. He looked distressed.

"Gone ..."

"You must be careful. Chalk smears." She rewrote his name and held out the chalk. "Now, you try."

It was a disaster. He didn't know how to hold the chalk, pressing it firmly against the slate and making the soft end crumble. It tumbled from his fingers, impacting the floor, cracking a piece off the side.

"Be careful!" Isabeau exclaimed. "Chalk is expensive, and I don't have enough household money left to purchase more."

François certainly wouldn't give her one of his pastels, not even a worn-down stub.

Giovanni immediately looked as chastened as a dog caught in some misdeed. She ignored that. At least he didn't cower.

"Try again." She placed her hand over his to show how much pressure to apply.

The squiggly design he made on the slate might, with a squint and a vivid imagination, be his name. Nevertheless, he looked proud as she released his hand.

"Giovanni," he proclaimed, and tapped the slate as she had. "Me." He handed her back the chalk. "More."

He was a remarkably quick study. By the end of the session, she had written out the entire alphabet and he could repeat it back to her, recognizing each letter and not merely parroting the sound, even if he didn't know how they made up other words. He also managed to scribble his name legibly.

The following day, she began with numbers.

"This is *one*." She held up her forefinger, pointed to the cot. "One cot." And then to a painting. "One painting."

He nodded, repeating what she'd said.

"This is *two*." She held up two fingers. "Two"—pointing to herself and him, then to the platter and water pitcher.

Again, he repeated her words.

And so it went. She quizzed him, holding up three fingers, putting together four items, patting him on the shoulder, repeating, "Good boy," when he got the answer correct. They went over the alphabet again. Once more, he wrote his name.

"Now then, look at this." She wrote "Isabeau" on the slate under his name.

He stared, shook his head.

"This is *my* name," she explained.

"Isabeau?" He whispered it like a prayer. Reverently. He stretched out a hand, didn't touch the slate, but let it hover over the letters. "Isabeau ..."

Isabeau shivered. If only François would say her name in that tone.

"You cold?" Before she knew what he intended, he began pulling his shirt over his head.

She stopped him, pushing it back onto his shoulders, smoothing the sleeves. "Thank you, Giovanni, but you mustn't take your clothes off like that."

"Not mind," he protested. "Not like clothes." He gave her a look that in someone else she might've called flirtatious. "No feel good."

"I'm not cold, and men don't run around naked."

"*I* did."

"You're not a wolf," she snapped abruptly, angry at him for continuing to refer to his former life, at Boamas who'd put him in a cage, and at his unknown parents who'd been so cruel as to sell their child. "I don't want to hear you say that again."

He hung his head, a dog who'd misbehaved.

Still angry, Isabeau wiped away the word on the slate with a single swipe. "I think that's enough lessons for today."

Getting up, she walked out, back stiff, clutching the slate to her breast.

"*Maîtresse—*"

She didn't look back, but locked the door and returned to the cottage. Behind her, she heard the mournful howl of a punished hound.

Later, when Maxime brought the tub, she stood in the doorway, not speaking.

Giovanni looked at the tub and then at her, not moving. Waiting.

Nursing her anger, thinking to punish him with her absence, Isabeau said, "I think you remember how to bathe. You have half an hour."

She walked out, pulling the door shut. Later, she sent Maxime to remove the tub. When asked, the servant reported Giovanni's hair was damp and the bathwater filled with suds.

The next day, François returned.

Chapter Seven

Isabeau thought him a stranger, riding down the path on a blood bay whose coat gleamed in the late afternoon sun, his own clothing as bright and sumptuous. Because of that, she didn't go to meet him. Instead, she waited at the entrance to the cottage, wondering why someone would be coming to their home. From the looks of the fine animal he rode, she thought him perhaps a prospective patron, a noble wishing his portrait painted. No one else ever came to visit, not her parents, not even François's drinking companions, whom he always met at the taverns and inns.

Yes, it had to be a probable customer.

As he pulled the horse to a halt before her, she saw, to her astonishment, that it was her husband.

"Well, wife." As usual, his tone was ironic. "Do you no longer come to greet me?"

"François ... it's you?" How idiotic that sounded.

"None other." He slid from the horse's back. "Have I been gone so long that you no longer recognize me?"

"I-I ..." What could she say but the truth? "You left here

walking. Where did you get the horse?" A horrid thought intruded. "You didn't *steal* it?"

Famous *artiste* or not, he'd face a reckoning for that crime.

"Don't be stupid," he answered. "I had no idea your imagination was so outrageous. From my good friend, Alphonse, of course." His reply indicated it should've been obvious. "He was appalled that I, such a talented *artiste*, should have to walk all the way from Aux-le-Piémont and back."

"That was generous of him." Isabeau didn't point out that Alphonse was aware of how he traveled all those other times he went to La Chapelle.

She ignored his clothing, refused to comment on yet another new suit, courtesy of *le marquis*.

"The *marquis* is a generous man." François simpered.

"And now you will paint his sons? Where are they?" Isabeau looked back along the path, expecting to see three young horsemen or perhaps a coach.

"They'll be here soon," he said.

Moving away from her, he led the horse to a large oak at the cottage's side. He tied the reins to a low-hanging limb so the horse could graze.

"That'll do for now. I'll tend to him later." He spun, facing Isabeau. "I'm famished. Does Mathilde have the evening meal ready? Today's Thursday ... roast goose, isn't it?"

"She should be dishing up the vegetables momentarily," Isabeau replied and couldn't resist adding, "You seem to have a knack for arriving home by mealtime."

"My belly has an unerring sense of timing," François agreed, unperturbed. He left her standing there, going into the cottage and directly to the kitchen.

Isabeau followed.

* * *

MATHILDE WAS bent over the hearth, basting a goose purchased that morning from the butcher.

It had already been killed and dressed, for Mathilde didn't like the mess of doing that herself. She'd had a long conference with the butcher on how her master liked his birds prepared. Flattered that the *grande artiste* would be his customer, he gladly had one ready and waiting every Thursday when Mathilde walked to town and brought it home. All she had to do was spit it and swing it over the fire.

Lazy creature, Isabeau thought resentfully. The butcher and then the fire did most of her work for her, and yet François would praise her as if she were King Louis's own chef.

"Ah, Mathilde, preparing my homecoming feast?"

"*Maître!*" She spun, bobbing a curtsey. The basting spoon tilted, spilling juices into the fire, where they spat and sizzled. "Welcome back."

"*Merci.*" He dipped a mock bow. "Have you kept yourself busy while I was gone?"

"Oh, *oui, maître.*" Mathilde's plump hands fluttered. "Cleaning, doing the laundry, so many chores ..."

Liar, thought Isabeau. *You wouldn't even do the laundry if François hadn't told you to. You've never touched our bed or changed its sheets. I do that myself.*

"Has anything of import happened while I was gone?"

Isabeau's anger flared brighter. Surely, he should be asking that of his wife, not the cook, unless...

Did he tell Mathilde to spy on me?

Surely not. That implied jealousy. François couldn't be bothered to be jealous.

The anger stifled to a twist of fear as Mathilde answered coyly, "I'm sure the mistress would know more about that than I, sir." Eyes brimming with malice, she cast a sideways glance at Isabeau.

Isabeau glared a threat, thankful that François's back was to her and he didn't see. Her hands closed into fists. Heart abruptly pounding, she waited for what the cook would say next.

Mathilde merely looked directly into her eyes and smiled, an expression completely without humor. "Supper should be ready soon," she told François.

"In that case, I'll take myself to the dining room to wait." He did so.

Isabeau trailed behind, wondering frantically how she could answer if Mathilde told him of her letting Giovanni run through the grass, coloring it with her own lewd interpretation.

* * *

THE COTTAGE FELT CROWDED.

With François's return, its solitude was shattered, the air loud with his voice. In his absence, it had seemed so quiet and peaceful, she thought.

It was only as he began to eat that François remembered his question had never been answered.

"Well? Has anything noticeable happened during my absence?" Without giving her time to answer, he continued, "How is my St. Jean?" He asked around a big bite from a drumstick he'd wrenched from the goose. "You haven't mentioned him. He still lives, doesn't he?"

His tone implied woe be to Isabeau if he didn't.

"Of course," she replied calmly, refusing to let him shake her from the happiness Giovanni's presence gave her. "Why shouldn't he?"

"I don't know. Sometimes wild creatures don't fare well in captivity."

108

She didn't remind him that Giovanni had been in captivity almost all his life and had survived in spite of that.

"I thought perhaps he … what did that gypsy call him? Ruvo? I thought perhaps Ruvo might be one of those unfortunates."

"You mustn't call him Ruvo," she told him, wondering how he would react to her news. She toyed with the meagre two slices of meat he'd placed on her plate. He always seemed to begrudge carving any portions for her. It was cut from the back, the toughest part of the bird.

"Eh?" He picked up the carving knife and fork again, slicing from the bird's breast this time, putting it on his own plate though he hadn't yet finished the drumstick. "Why not?"

"Because that isn't his name."

"Oh?" He gave her a bemused look as he set down the carving set and reached for his wine goblet. "Who says so?"

"*He* does," she answered, and wanted to laugh at the surprise in his expression.

"*He*? The creature can *talk*?"

"Yes. Though broken, his French is very understandable."

"*Sacre!* That's something I didn't expect. I knew the beast could understand simple commands, but to speak …" He paused. "Very well. What does he call himself?"

"Giovanni," she said. "Giovanni di Casalupo."

"Giovanni." François took another bite, considering. He swallowed and shook his head. "That'll never do. Too civilized. *Non.* He'll stay Ruvo."

"I think you'll find him much changed," Isabeau said.

"You've piqued my curiosity." He dropped the half-eaten drumstick onto his plate, reaching for the usually ignored kerchief. Wiping his hands, he tossed it back to the table. "Perhaps I'd best see my property now rather than later." He got to his feet. "Maxime, bring me a lantern."

* * *

IT HAD DARKENED QUICKLY, and the walkway was dim in the twilight. Isabeau trotted behind her husband, who followed Maxime. She kept her skirts lifted past her ankles so she could move quickly to keep up with his long strides.

"Open the door, Isabeau," François ordered. "You do still have the key?"

She did, in her pocket, but as usual, she'd left the door unlocked. Moving past him, she fumbled with the handle, blocking it with her body so he wouldn't be able to see she didn't use the key. She pushed the door open.

"Well?" François waited for the servant to step ahead of them and light the way.

"This is as far as I go, master," Maxime said.

"What's this?" François scowled.

"Maxime's afraid of Giovanni," Isabeau put in, relishing the fear flitting across the servant's face. In the lantern's flickering, François might've mistaken it for a shadow from the flame, but she knew better.

"Afraid?" François was disbelieving. "Of a half-starved gypsy boy?"

"He's more than that and you know it, master," Maxime dared defend himself. He bent, setting the lantern on the floor. "Punish me if you will but I'll go no further."

With that, he spun and ran into the darkness. They heard his feet slapping on the planks of the walkway.

François retrieved the lantern.

"What has Ruvo done to make Maxime so afraid?" Holding up the lantern, he went inside, through the studio to the storage room door, with Isabeau following. "You're certain he's harmed none of my paintings?" he questioned, as if remembering asking that before. "I've several items I must deliver this week."

"He's harmed nothing," Isabeau assured him, forcing aside that bit of satisfaction Maxime's discomfort gave her. "He's very well-behaved."

"That doesn't sound like the creature I saw at the gypsy camp nor the one I brought home. I remember he growled at several travelers we passed. A carter offered me a ride but changed his mind and drove away when he saw Ruvo, though I told him the creature could run behind the cart." He frowned, inclining his head as if listening. "It's very quiet."

"I told you, François, he's different now," she repeated. "I bathed him and kept him fed as you wished." She added, "That changed him."

"Then open the door and let me see for myself."

"The door's not locked," she said.

"You've left it open?" He looked angry. "Stupid! He's probably gotten out and run away. I give my treasure into your care, and ..." He raised a hand, looking upward to ask the God whom he didn't believe in, "How could I have such a fool for a wife?"

Isabeau closed her eyes, forcing herself not to respond, not to tell François he was the one who was stupid—stupid *and* cruel—for treating a fellow human like an animal.

Swallowing her anger, she pushed open the door with a defiant shove. Still grumbling, François didn't move, except to hold up the lantern so they could see inside.

Chapter Eight

GIOVANNI HAD HEARD them and was on his feet. He was fully dressed, *merci Dieu*, and stood near the cot, waiting.

"Giovanni, your master's here," she called. "Come out."

"*Oui, maîtresse.*" His voice was still a rasp but welcome to Isabeau's ears.

As he heard it, François stopped his ranting. He raised the lantern higher.

"You, wolf," he called. "Come here."

Giovanni came through the doorway. His glance at Isabeau held something she interpreted as devotion. Taking two steps to her side, he turned directly to face François. There was nothing slavish or adoring in the look he bestowed upon his master.

"*Maître.*" He bowed.

Isabeau struggled to keep her astonishment from showing. She'd once witnessed a noble give the same greeting to her father, a brusque, short inclination of the body while speaking only his name as if he didn't wish to have it in his mouth any longer than necessary. Its very brevity was an insult.

How had he known to do that? *Why* did he do it? *Oh, Giovanni, why?*

She looked at her husband, hoping he didn't realize what Giovanni had done, praying to see surprise, perhaps pride on his face, for the transformation she'd wrought in the beast he'd given into her care.

Instead, she saw only fury, but not for his "pet's" action.

"You idiot! You stupid bitch." Face suffused crimson, he shook with rage.

Why is he angry?

"I said *tend* him, not ruin him."

Before Isabeau could move, he started toward her, arm raised.

With a growl, Giovanni flung himself between them. He caught François's arm as it swung down, sinking his teeth into the wrist.

Cloth tore. Isabeau swore she heard flesh do the same. François howled in pain. He dropped the lantern. Miraculously, it landed right-side-up, sending the shapes of their bodies onto the walls in a nightmarish shadow show.

François struggled to pull his wrist from Giovanni's grasp. He beat against the boy's shoulder with his fist. The studio was filled with a terrifying chorus of cries and howls. Blood dripped from between Giovanni's teeth, soaking François's sleeve. Snarling, he shook the arm as a wolf might a rabbit.

Sweet Heaven. Isabeau cowered against the storage room door. *He* is *a beast.*

He was shorter than François; he was no match in weight and bulk. As Giovanni loosened his hold to get a better grip, François's fist collided with his jaw, sending his slender body flying across the studio against a stack of blank canvases. He crashed to the floor, canvas frames toppling over him.

"François, you've killed him," Isabeau spoke before she thought.

"I may as well," François snapped. "He's no good to me as he is."

She looked at him in horror. "You wouldn't."

Across the room, Giovanni sat up, pushing aside the frames.

"See? He's not dead." François gestured, slinging blood. "I'll have to find some use for him. To pay me back for what I spent."

In the fluttery lamplight, his expression looked demonic. He clasped his bitten wrist.

"Damnation, that hurts! You cursed beast, if you've injured my hand ..."

Giovanni struggled to his feet, shaking himself. He took a step.

There was a tack hammer lying on the table, used to nail canvases to the stretchers. François picked it up. "Stay where you are."

Giovanni stopped.

Holding out his bleeding wrist, François glanced at Isabeau. "Quit worrying over that creature and tend my arm."

Pulling her handkerchief from her bosom, she rushed to his side, blotting the blood and pressing the little square against the wound. She was appalled at the gash in his flesh, a perfect crescent, the mark of eyeteeth especially deep.

"François, I'm sorry—" She began an apology.

"Well, you should be, you fool wench. Now he looks like everyone else." As she ministered to his wound, François continued raving, though more out of anger than pain. "How can I paint him as my St. Jean, as a beggar, even, when he's clean ... fat ... How will anyone believe he's suffered when he looks like a young lord stepping out of a dining hall? Where's all that hair ... the dirt ... the beard ... Ow! That hurt," he flung at her as she knotted the handkerchief. "I'll probably have a scar, damn it."

Giovanni's hands curled into claws, his body crouching,

ready to attack again. Isabeau stopped him with a frantic glance and a shake of her head. He stood still, but continued growling low in his throat, barely audible, eyes flicking from Isabeau to François and back.

"Lock him away." François jerked his wrist from her grasp, turning his back. Dramatically, he flung away the hammer without seeing where it landed, putting his uninjured hand to his eyes. "I can't look at him."

Silently, Isabeau took Giovanni's arm and led him back into the storage room.

"Make sure he's chained," François called after her. "I'll have him bite no one else."

"He wouldn't have done that if you hadn't tried to strike me," she dared say.

She picked up the chain from where it lay still attached to the window bars. Giovanni turned his head away as she attached it to his collar.

He snarled, baring his teeth, as he looked through the doorway at François, who was clutching his injured arm and muttering under his breath.

Isabeau startled. His eyeteeth ... surely, they looked longer than before, curved, more like ... fangs. Red-stained, they sparkled in the moonlight coming through the window.

"Quiet," she whispered.

Surprisingly, he subsided.

There was blood at the corner of his mouth. She caught at her sleeve, pulled it over her hand, and pressed it against his mouth. When she backed away, the red smear was gone.

She returned to the studio.

"Give me the key," François said. As she handed it to him, he slammed the storage door, then locked it. Dropping the key into his purse, he stalked out.

Head down, Isabeau followed.

Behind her, she heard a long howl, muffled by the closed door.

François said, "He bit me. You know what they say about a *loup-garou's* bite."

"There's a full moon." She could barely keep the irritation out of her voice, wanting to remind him he'd said *loup-garou* didn't exist. Also, he didn't sound too worried. "You're unchanged. So is Giovanni, for that matter. You're in no danger."

"But if I were," he persisted. "Would you kill me, with a weapon made of silver?"

She didn't hesitate as she said, "Of course," and added as if in afterthought, "to save your soul." Her answer was sardonic.

He laughed, his tone mirroring her own. "*Merci*, wife. It gratifies me to know I can count on you to save that which I don't possess."

Back in the dining room, Mathilde and Maxime waited. Neither looked as if they were aware the master had been in a bloody attack by his pet, though both gave the torn, red-bespattered sleeve startled looks. Maxime abruptly relaxed, his anxiety over any punishment he might receive for his disobedience forgotten at this new development.

Isabeau wasn't so confident.

François dropped into his chair, gesturing to his plate. "Take this away and bring me hot food. Maxime, wine!"

Maxime hastened to fill his goblet. Mathilde hurried to remove the plate.

When she reached for Isabeau's as well, he went on, "None for Mistress Isabeau. She'll eat what she has."

Is that my punishment? Cold food? Isabeau would've felt relief if she thought that was all he would do. She had a feeling further punishment would come when they were abed.

Mathilde took away the platter holding the remnants of the goose.

"That reminds me ... that hair he was covered in, was that his?"

"No."

There was a moment's silence.

"None of it?"

"The beard, the hair on his head." Memory of Giovanni's naked body flickered into her mind. She thought of the tangle of curls around his *organe*.

"Well? What was it?"

"A hide," Isabeau answered reluctantly. "The rest of it was all animal hides."

"Animal hides," he repeated as if thinking that over. "What did you do with them?"

"I gave them to Mathilde to burn."

"Mathilde?"

She paused in the doorway, balancing a platter and a plate.

"Have you done that yet?"

"No, master. I thought to put them in the fire next time I boil water for laundry."

"Maxime, get them."

"Sir?"

"You heard me, fetch the hides."

Maxime whirled and ran from the room. Mathilde followed at a slower pace.

François didn't speak. He sat looking at the door, ignoring Isabeau as if she weren't there.

Abruptly, he pushed back the cuff of his shirt, untying Isabeau's handkerchief from his wrist. He unwound it and dropped it to the table. Picking up his table kerchief, he folded and dipped it into the wine goblet, then patted the soaked fabric against the wound, muttering all the while of "... killing any noxious humors floating about ..."

The bite was raw and angry-looking, and the red of the wine made it appear more so. It stung, if the grimaces and quick inhalations he made were any indication.

Afterward, he tore a strip from a clean edge of the napkin, wrapping it around the wound and tying it by looping and pulling it tight with his teeth.

As he did this, Isabeau attempted to continue eating, but the food was now cold. The goose had a greasy, unpleasant taste. When she swallowed, it seemed to expand, clogging her throat. She clutched knife and fork, and didn't move.

"Something for your rag bag." François wadded the remains of the napkin and her handkerchief and tossed them at her.

They landed on her plate, spattering grease onto her hand. Silently, Isabeau removed the two pieces of cloth and laid them aside. She used her own table kerchief to blot the grease from the back of her fingers.

Maxime returned, holding a smelly, hairy mass as far away as he could.

"Come." François got to his feet. "I'll carry the lantern this time."

"What are you going to do, master?" Maxime turned to follow.

"I'm putting those hides back on the creature, and you're going to help," was François's reply. "No argument."

Isabeau listened to their footsteps disappear in the direction of the walkway. Setting down knife and fork, she sat in silence. Mathilde did not return, and she was grateful for that. She had no desire to either see or hear the cook.

The silence lengthened. She wondered what was happening in the storeroom. Before she realized it, her hands clasped each other. Unconsciously, she began to pray.

Please don't let him hurt Giovanni. Don't let Giovanni do anything to anger François.

A muffled yelp broke the quiet. A man's voice raised in a shout. There was a series of barks and growls, and then ... nothing. No sounds. No voices.

Heavy stamps in the hall. François appeared in the doorway. Maxime took his place beside the door. He was pale. His master was red-faced. Neither seemed injured.

"Hurry up with that plate, Mathilde." François settled in his place, resuming the conversation as if he'd never left at all. "By the way, Maxime. There's a horse tied to the oak in the courtyard. See that it's taken to the old paddock behind my studio."

"If you've now a horse, he'll need—" Isabeau began, only to have him continue smoothly, "In the morning, you'll go to the livery stable in town and buy whatever feed he needs."

He fished in his purse and brought out a coin, tossing it to the servant.

Isabeau didn't ask where he got the money. A bit pilfered from his fee for the St. Jean? A gift from Alphonse?

"A horse needs shelter, master," Maxime pointed out. "When winter comes."

"Then you'll build one," François replied. "I imagine there's enough leftover lumber stacked behind the studio." Obviously, he wasn't about to expend his own energy on a horse as he would for his precious canvases.

"Yes, sir." Maxime looked a little unhappy at the prospect of such heavy labor. He didn't add that the lumber was probably warped by rain and sun.

"Otherwise,"—François glanced at Isabeau—"Ruvo will share his accommodations."

"François, you'd put the horse in the storage room?" Isabeau wasn't certain if that was a jest or not.

"Why not?" He looked surprised she'd protest. "It's a

blooded animal, very valuable." He paused before adding, "At the moment of more value to me than what's already living there."

"Won't you fear it might damage your canvases?" She reminded him of what he'd said about Giovanni.

"I'll move the canvases to the studio, and"—he hurried on, as he saw her about to say something else—"if Ruvo protests, *he* can stay outside in the paddock."

Isabeau didn't answer. She was certain he'd calmly turn Giovanni out into a snowy winter if she showed too much concern. She remembered how the boy had said he hoped his life would be better now. She was beginning to wonder if he'd be better off with the gypsies.

Mathilde returned with a platter of steaming food.

"Has the beast been fed tonight?" François asked of her, now ignoring Isabeau.

"It's ready, master," she replied. "Cooked, as the mistress ordered." Mathilde shot her a glance. "But as cold as that on her plate."

"Toss it out."

"Sir?" Mathilde looked startled. François wasn't one to waste food.

"Throw it into the *puits de cess*," he continued. "Ruvo won't be fed tonight. It's a good time to start his fast, since tomorrow's Friday. He'll have no meat, along with the rest of us."

"What about the baths, sir?" Maxime spoke up.

"Baths?" François glanced at him.

"The creature seems to have a fondness for bathing, sir." Maxime's expression showed an espousal of the priest's opinion. "*Madame* Isabeau said I was to supply him with bath water."

"None of that, either. If he's to look like a beggar, he must be neither fed nor clean," François answered, then muttered under his breath, "though a day probably won't make much difference."

"That's when the *marquis's* sons will arrive?" Isabeau asked. "That doesn't give me much time to open and air the bedrooms." A thought intruded. "But we've only two guest rooms and you said there are three ..."

"Yes, that's when they'll arrive." His answer held irritation, as if she criticized the time of their arrival. "They're noble. They can't simply pick up and go like the gypsies can. As to their accommodations, they'll be staying with your father."

"When did you see—"

"I stopped by the *château* before I came here."

"I see."

While it was true the cottage was small, it was finely, if sparsely, furnished, with furniture given to them by her parents as well as various clients. If he went to a noble's home to do a portrait and saw something he liked, François might ask for the item along with his fee. It was surprising how often they would give him what he wanted. His patrons were so pleased with his work that he'd acquired several well-crafted pieces of furniture and some fairly expensive sculptures that way.

"I'm sure you do," he said, his tone sarcastic. "He was most delighted to play host to the *Marquis* du Maurier's sons."

François was well aware of Pierre's social aspirations, always had been, and was equally scornful of them when not in his father-in-law's presence. Isabeau imagined her father would be ecstatic at being able to boast of housing nobility in his home, no matter how many of his wife's jewels or furniture they had to sell to feed them.

"It's been some time since visitors have come here," Mathilde said. She shot Isabeau a mean glance. "I'm certain the mistress will be pleased. I know how she likes to entertain. Don't you, mistress?"

"Really, my dear?" François turned to Isabeau.

Isabeau remembered that confrontation in the kitchen, the little dig before they left for the studio.

She's going to tell him. She looked up, her eyes meeting Mathilde's. Her hand tightened around the handle of her knife. *Don't say it, wench, or I swear I'll kill you. I'll drive this knife into your fat gut.*

She didn't think of the consequences of such an act, merely of François's wrath.

"Mathilde is mistaken," she replied calmly. "I believe she's remembering a remark I once made about how my mother enjoyed playing hostess to my father's guests and that I found our home so different in that respect. I quite enjoy the quiet but will gladly welcome the *marquis's* sons when they appear, be assured."

As she spoke, she kept her gaze locked with the cook's.

Mathilde must've seen the threat in her gaze, for she merely said, "You're correct, mistress. I misremembered."

Calmly, Isabeau raised her fork to her lips. It shook slightly as she bit the cold meat from its tines. Mathilde might not have spoken, but the threat was still there, hovering. She was certain some day the cook would speak up. She dreaded when that time came.

"See that you do." François finished his meal and rose. Giving her what she thought was a sarcastic bow, he offered his arm ... his uninjured one. Listlessly, Isabeau got to her feet and placed her fingertips upon his wrist.

As he led her up the stairs, she asked timidly, "François, tell me, what did you do to him?"

He didn't ask of whom she spoke. He said simply, "I made him into a wolf again."

* * *

THAT NIGHT, François swore his wrist pained him so much that he needed the local leech.

Isabeau thought it a ploy for sympathy. She suggested instead that he take some of the potion Dr. Rambeau prescribed when she sprained her ankle.

"Tincture of valerian. That will help you sleep."

Perhaps the wound really did hurt. He accepted the two drops in a glass of wine eagerly and soon was snoring.

Assuring herself he was too deep in sleep to awaken, Isabeau crept from the bed. Wrapping a dressing-gown around herself, she found his purse and took out the storeroom key, making her way in the dark to the walkway. She didn't dare light a candle, but the moon was still up, near full and glowing, so she could clearly see the way to the studio.

Once there, she opened the door, calling out, "Giovanni?"

"*Maîtresse?*"

The hairy mound on the floor raised its head.

She ran to him, falling to her knees. François had double-wrapped the chain, looping it through the window bars and attaching both ends to the neck-collar so Giovanni was unable to move away from the window. Moonlight fell full upon his face. She could see a black and ugly bruise swelling his jaw and spreading onto his cheek. A larger, redder mark on his forehead extending across his right eye to the cheek was no doubt the one that had wrenched the cry Isabeau had heard from him.

She thought he looked like an abused angel.

The water pitcher sat nearby on the floor. She caught a piece of the blanket and dipped it into the water, pressing the wet fabric against the bruise.

It hurt; he winced and jerked away, snarling softly. She made a soothing sound, brushing the hair back from his forehead. She thought it already looked shaggier and more tangled, as if wearing animal hides again made it grow faster.

"You shouldn't have done it," she whispered.

"Not let him hurt you," he muttered.

He bared his teeth, moonlight gleaming against them. The bloodstains were now gone, but they looked as large and wicked as before.

"Shh." Impulsively, she caught his face in her hands and kissed his cheek. "I'm so sorry." Ignoring the smell of the hides and their filth, she cradled his head against her breast.

He subsided, relaxing against her.

Frightened by her audacity, she jerked back, heart pounding.

His hands clasped briefly at her waist, then fell away. That was all. Turning his back, he settled himself on the blanket, head resting on his forearms.

Isabeau got to her feet, stood a moment longer looking down at him. When he didn't move, she spun and hurried out. Locking the door, she hastened along the walkway.

She was able to return the key to François's purse and get back into bed without her slumbering husband being aware.

Chapter Nine

IT WAS past midnight when a pounding on the door jolted them from sleep.

"*Maître ... maître!*"

"What the hell?" François came awake with a curse, then winced as movement sent sharp pain through his wrist. "What's that? I need my sleep."

Again, a frantic fist struck the door.

"*Sacre.*" He rolled over, pressing his face into the pillow. "Tend to it, Isabeau."

Struggling out of bed, Isabeau threw on her dressing-gown and staggered to the door, becoming more awake as she moved. She pulled the door open, peering out.

Mathilde's face, shadowed grotesquely by the candle she held, stared back at her. Behind her, Maxime hovered. Both servants were in nightclothes.

"What is it?" she asked sharply.

"Mistress, the creature. It howls so we can't sleep."

"Shutter your window," she snapped, the lateness of the hour making her voice sharp, irritated they'd been awakened for such a trivial matter.

"I did," Maxime replied. "It does no good. The sound comes through. The beast's rabid, mistress."

"That's absurd …" Isabeau's voice trailed away as she thought she heard something: several short, sharp barks, then a long, drawn-out howl.

It floated through the hallway and up the stairs, directly to where they stood, sounding as if it began inside the cottage instead of the storeroom. A loud crash followed.

"*Merde!* Can no one stop that noise?" came from the bed.

"Master, I don't know how," Maxime answered. "I went to the storage room window and pounded on the wall, yelled at the creature to shut up. All that did was make him howl more loudly. I think he threw something at the window. It's as if he's tearing up the storeroom."

François rolled over and sat up. "If that beast's harmed my paintings …" He didn't move, however. Nor did he bother to replace the bedclothes falling to his waist, revealing his naked chest.

Mathilde blushed and averted her gaze.

"It's the moon," she said, voice quavering. "It's full. Master, that thing's a *loup-garou*, isn't he? Wolves always howl at the moon, and—"

"Stop that foolish talk," Isabeau said. "Giovanni's nothing but a frightened boy who's been mistreated …"

"… and is keeping his master from sleep," François finished.

Another howl resounded, followed by a ragged scraping, like claws being dragged across wood.

"Master, do something," Mathilde begged.

He won't do anything, Isabeau thought. *He hasn't moved, because he's more afraid of what's in the storeroom than he is of what may happen to his beloved paintings.*

Abruptly, François spoke.

"Maxime, take my pistol and shoot the beast."

"François, no!" Isabeau whirled to stare at him.

Even Mathilde looked shocked.

"Have you a better way to silence him?" he demanded.

"I..."

"Well? Speak up!" He seemed to enjoy her fear.

"The valerian." She waved a hand at the small, dark bottle sitting on the lamp table by the bed. "It'll make him sleep."

Surely, he wouldn't kill Giovanni. He mustn't.

François glanced where she pointed. "Who will give it to him?" He laughed at her expression of dismay. "Maxime's too cowardly to do it."

"That's true," Maxime verified, unashamedly.

"And I'm too injured." François raised his wrapped wrist. A few blood spots had seeped through. "Thanks to that thing."

Irrelevantly, Isabeau wondered if her handkerchief was ruined, if the blood would wash out.

"Shooting him is the best way for me to get back to sleep."

"What about your St. Jean?" Isabeau asked acidly.

"I'll find another. Somewhere. After I've had a good night's sleep." He reached for the covers, drawing them up.

"Oh, for the good Lord's sake!" Stamping to the lamp table, Isabeau picked up the bottle. She returned to the door.

"Where are you going?" François demanded.

"To give the *loup-garou* a sleeping potion so you may sleep, my dear husband," she hurled over her shoulder and snatched the candle from Mathilde's hand, sweeping past the startled servants.

Halfway there, she realized what she'd said.

He is not *a* loup-garou. She reminded herself. *I said that in anger.*

Hearing footsteps behind her, she became aware that the servants were following.

She ignored them, going to the kitchen. Setting down the

candle, she got a small tin cup from the cupboard, filling it with water from one of the buckets on the hearth. As she uncorked the little bottle, however, she thought, *how much should I use? The leech said two drops, but will it be the same for someone so agitated?*

Maxime and Mathilde stood in the doorway, watching. She would swear she felt their gazes upon her.

At last, she let four dark drops fall into the cup, then watched them disperse and discolor the liquid with a faint, yellowish tint.

Picking up the candle again, she marched out.

"Don't worry. I won't ask you to accompany me," she muttered as she passed Maxime.

He had the good grace to look ashamed.

Isabeau was halfway to the studio before the thought came, *What if I'm wrong? What if Giovanni is truly a* loup-garou? *If he's transformed, he won't know me. He could kill me, or worse ... if I'm bitten ...*

She knew the legend. Everyone did.

Wait. He bit François. Would her husband now change into a wolf, too, when the moon was full? Well, the moon was full now, and François was still his obnoxious self, demanding nothing more than a wish for silence so he could go back to sleep.

Small comfort, that. Better consolation: didn't it mean Giovanni was simply a man, if a very confused and savage one?

She reached the studio. She could hear the howls and cries clearly, frightening but at the same time heart-rending. In her haste, she hadn't thought of the key, and the only way to see inside the storeroom was to do as Maxime had. Go to the window.

Walking carefully, she went around the side of the studio to where she saw the open shutters pressed back against the wall of the building. She approached quietly. Her bare feet scarcely made a sound in the grass.

He won't hear me. He's making too much noise.

She was wrong.

In the midst of a bloodcurdling howl, the sound stopped.

Total silence.

He recognized my step. He won't harm me.

Setting the candleholder in the grass, she approached the window, peering into the darkness past the bars. She could see the chain wrapped around them. They moved slightly as whatever was on the other side pulled against them.

"Giovanni?"

Something large and heavy threw itself against the bars.

With a cry, Isabeau leaped back, nearly dropping the cup. As she clutched it tighter, the thing slid off the sill and back into the shadows. There was a clanking as the chain struck the floor.

"Mistress?"

His voice was so harsh it was nearly a croak, as if being forced back into that animal hide made him forget how to speak.

"I'm here, Giovanni." She wanted to rush to the window, hold out her hand, have him grasp it as he had when they made their bargain, but she feared what touched her fingers might not be human.

"Help me, mistress." His plea was a rumbling growl.

"How? What must I do?"

"Thirsty ..."

"I've brought you something to drink." She offered the tin cup. "It'll help you sleep, too." She pushed it against the bars. It was almost too wide. It barely slid through, scraping against them.

His fingers wrapped around the cup. In the moonlight, the nails looked longer, curved. Did she really see that, or was it merely suggested by the shadows?

The cup disappeared into the dark. She heard noisy gulping. He thrust the tin back through the bars.

"*Merci, maîtresse.*"

She took back the cup. He sank into the darkness again. Harsh panting accompanied the movement. She wished she could see his face.

"Is there anything else I can do?" *Free you? Open the door and let you escape?* She was too cowardly to do that.

"Make moonlight ... go away ..." His whisper dissolved into soft breathing.

He's sleepy. The potion's working.

Isabeau picked up the candle and stepped to the window. Holding it as close to the bars as possible, she peered inside. Its gleam spread a feeble light onto the floor, revealing a furry clump sprawled awkwardly below the frame. The soft whisper of breath assured her he merely slept, and she hadn't given him too much of the potion.

Silently, she pushed the shutters closed, blocking out the moonlight. From within came a soft moan, then silence.

Clutching a candle and a cup, she hurried back to the cottage.

* * *

As SHE SETTLED herself once more in bed, François awoke.

"Did you quiet the beast?" he asked, sluggishly.

"Do you hear anything?" She was too tired and upset to speak prudently.

He listened. "No."

"Well, then?"

He shrugged and rolled over, then looked back over his shoulder. "Did he harm you?"

130

"Of course not." No need to tell him how frightened she'd been.

He was silent.

"Would you really have shot him?"

"How could I? I don't have any silver bullets." He rolled over. "There's not enough of that precious metal in the house to make even one."

Liar. There was that silver tray some *comte* had given him, and a set of goblets from the *marquis*, and ... *Nothing he wishes to part with,* she amended.

Before he went back to sleep, she said, "François, don't hurt him."

"What?" He roused slightly.

"Don't harm Giovanni. Promise me."

He rolled over. "Keep him obedient and quiet, and I won't. Can *you* promise that?"

"Yes, I will." She'd speak to Giovanni, impress on him how his safety depended on doing what he was told.

"Then he's in no danger." He raised himself slightly, pounded his pillow, then lay down again.

In a few moments he was snoring once more, while Isabeau lay unsleeping, thinking of that hand with the perhaps imagined claws as it accepted the cup from her. If she could've really seen into the storeroom, what would she have observed sleeping upon the floor?

Chapter Ten

IN THE MORNING, at breakfast, Isabeau asked, "How is your wrist?" She couldn't resist adding, in irony, "Are you going to be permanently damaged?"

"It's in remarkably good condition." François missed her sarcasm altogether. "I slept well after you quieted the wolf. What did you do?" He stabbed a spoon into the bowl of coddled eggs Mathilde had set before him.

"Don't speak of him that way."

Isabeau grimaced, partly because she didn't like him saying that, partly for the unappetizing appearance of the eggs. She always demanded hers be hard-boiled, shelled, and sliced, then basted with butter. She couldn't abide eating anything that looked as if it were still in its natural state. She thought of the bloody strips of meat Giovanni ate with such relish.

"He's a man, as you are."

"Not as *I* am, dear wife," François corrected, thrusting the spoon into his mouth. He swallowed. "But as you wish ... How did you calm the *man?*"

"I gave him the potion." That should've been explanation enough, but she had to add, "He was thirsty. He really must have water, François." To keep from sounding as if she begged, she continued, "Then I pushed the shutters closed, keeping out the moonlight. Between the two, he quieted immediately."

"Hmm." He looked thoughtful when she mentioned the moon, a little perturbed, as if that somehow refuted his disbelief.

"You can't keep him drugged." She tried to sound matter-of-fact and not as if she were concerned for Giovanni's well-being. "Is there nothing else that can be done to quieten him?"

"Nothing I know of." His answer was reluctant, delayed as he bit off a hunk of bread, chewed, and swallowed. It was obvious that François hated admitting his ignorance of controlling *loup-garou* or even pseudo *loup-garou*.

"How did the gypsies subdue him?"

"How should I know?" He dropped the bread onto his plate, the movement angry. "Why do you persist in asking these questions?" Looking at her, he spoke in a studied monotone as if to a stubborn child, "I don't know if the gypsies did anything. I ... no, wait."

His expression changed.

"What is it?" Isabeau asked, uneasy.

"That gypsy, he sold us an herb he said was a protection against harm. Wolfsbane ... yes, that was it. Charged an outrageous price for that useless sprig."

"Why did you buy it if you thought it was useless?"

"*I* didn't buy it. Alphonse did," he retorted. "I remember now, the wolf wore a necklace made of the same blossoms. It was removed before he ... never mind about that."

He laid down his fork. "I gave mine to Alphonse because he feared the creature might attack us. Before I left, he returned it. I'd thought I might sketch it and use it in a painting sometime."

Pushing back his chair, he stood and slid his purse from his belt. Tugging on the drawstring, he upended the little bag, shaking its contents upon the tabletop. Coins and what looked like a handful of leaf fragments scattered.

"Here it is." What he held up wasn't much to look at. The leaves had been crushed by the coins. "I doubt this will be much good, a stem and one desiccated leaf. Still ..." With his forefinger, François poked the pieces. "I suppose I could disperse these about the room."

"Perhaps the leech would have some?" Isabeau suggested. "He must have a knowledge of all the herbs hereabouts." *Anything to prevent another occurrence of last night and the threat to Giovanni.* "Or he might tell you where to find some. Surely in the forests ..."

"I can't ask the leech," he interrupted. "The fewer people who know I have a supposed *loup-garou*, the better. If word got back to *Pére* Ambroise, you know what they'd do to him." He added, "I paid too much to lose him that way."

Isabeau had no idea as to the punishment for being a *loup-garou*, but she was certain it wasn't a thing she'd wish to see. She thought François had been fairly imprudent in mentioning Giovanni as much as he already had.

"In that case, you'd better tell Maxime and Mathilde also," she cautioned. Like most men with servants, François spoke in front of them as if they weren't there, and he'd indiscreetly said a great deal within their hearing. "That one chatters like a magpie to anyone who'll listen."

A stab of fear shot through her. Who knew whom the cook might've already spoken to?

"A good idea." François looked surprised she'd had it. He picked up the stem. "In the meantime, you'll take Ru—Giovanni some water and pin this to that hide he's wearing."

"I? Why do I have to do it?" Though she didn't mind, Isabeau was angered because François once again foisted his responsibilities onto someone else. She pretended reluctance so he wouldn't sense how concerned she was. "You bought him. Why don't you—"

"Because at the moment, he doesn't like me very much," he said, in a tone implying he couldn't understand that. "You seem to have found yourself a champion, lady, so you'll be the one doing the honors, and shielding the rest of us from your protector's wrath." He shrugged. "I doubt he'll harm you."

"And if he does?" she dared ask. "What if he were to kill me?"

"In that case, I suppose I should have to find myself another wife."

"François!" He'd said many cruel things to her, but this callousness shocked Isabeau. More than that, she was inwardly shaken by his insensitivity. "How can you be so cavalier about my fate?"

"My dear Isabeau." He picked up his wine goblet, dabbing at his mouth with the kerchief in an exaggeratedly delicate movement, as if mocking its use. "There are many marriageable women in the world, but few *artistes*. It's easier to find a wife than a man of my talent."

He drank from the goblet, then wiped wine from his lips.

"You should consider yourself honored, my dear. You've tamed a *loup-garou*, much as the maiden conquers the unicorn, though the wolf apparently has the better taste, since he's subdued by a non-virgin."

Isabeau clutched her napkin in silent rage at this insult.

"Keep him that way, with his head in your lap, else you may find it on a pike—"

At that moment, Mathilde appeared, bearing a trencher of pork cutlets. Behind her, Maxime followed with a platter holding two more loaves of freshly baked bread and a bowl of oatmeal.

François broke off his insults, making appreciative noises as the cook set the trencher before him. With his fork, he stabbed two cutlets and transferred them to his plate. Three slices of bread followed, and while Isabeau watched, he reached for the bowl of butter already on the table, picking up the little silver butter knife and cutting a swathe through its contents.

Their conversation of the night before came back to her, his question as to whether she would kill him with a silver weapon.

Yes, François. I'd do it. Her eyes closed. For a moment, she envisioned herself seizing the butter knife, raising it and slamming it against her husband's chest, slicing through fabric and flesh as easily as he cut through the butter in the bowl, crimson blood gushing out and mixing with that yellow creaminess.

Her hand closed around her fork; she raised it ...

"Isabeau! Watch what you're doing."

François's exclamation brought her back from that vision.

Isabeau stared. He had been reaching for a third cutlet. Her fork was poised above it. Another inch and she'd have driven it into the back of his hand.

"If you're that hungry, wife, please, be my guest." He withdrew his hand, gesturing at the remaining cuts.

A little shocked by what she'd nearly done, Isabeau quickly slid a smaller slice from the platter and timidly reached for some bread, keeping her gaze on her plate.

François had already lost interest. He looked up at Mathilde as the cook turned to leave.

"By the by, Mathilde. You're aware of how things stand now. With the boy, and his nature, I mean. I don't wish it bandied about. There's a *loup-garou* under my roof. You mustn't say anything."

She stopped, looking back, guiltily. "I'm afraid I may already have, sir."

"To whom?" He stopped eating to scowl.

It was so seldom he bestowed such a glance upon Mathilde that she paled slightly.

"The dairy herder's boy, when he brought yesterday's eggs."

Jean-Henri, supplying eggs and milk to those of the townspeople who didn't own cattle or chickens, usually sent his son Robert to make his rounds while he tended his livestock. Isabeau rather liked the youngster, but Robert and Mathilde never got along. He had an impertinent tongue, the cook said.

"He tried to tell me there were twelve eggs in the basket when I could see there were only ten," Mathilde defended herself, preening a little because she could count enough to know how many eggs were in a dozen.

Isabeau thought a little knowledge could indeed be dangerous, for she'd several times noticed the cook miscounted things.

"The creature began to howl and he asked me if we now had a dog. I wanted to frighten him, so I told him my master had a *loup-garou* locked in the storage room and I'd set it on him unless he gave up the other two eggs."

"Then you must let him know you were joking," François ordered. "Say it was a stray dog I'd penned up to make certain it wasn't diseased, that it died and I burned the body. And don't say another word to anyone." He shook his fork at her. "We must all now exert caution where the creature's identity is concerned."

"*Oui, maître.*" Her answer was both humble and obedient. She relaxed visibly as she saw he wasn't angry.

When he dismissed them with a nod, she and Maxime left.

François went back to his meal. After a few bites, he pushed the leaf toward Isabeau, using the handle of his knife.

She didn't look at it, keeping her attention on her food.

"Would you truly risk all of us to paint that creature?"

"*St. Jean dans la Région Sauvage* will be a masterpiece,"

François declared. "What are a few lives compared to the magnificence my talent will create?"

* * *

After breakfast was over, while Mathilde cleared the table, placing the dishes on a tray to carry them to the kitchen, Isabeau prepared to take the herbs to the storeroom.

She didn't ask if Giovanni was to be fed, for she knew what the answer would be. The bread hadn't yet been removed from the table. As Mathilde reached for the platter on which the last two slices remained, Isabeau snatched the platter from the cook's hand.

"I vow, Mathilde." She took one of the slices. "The bread was so good today, I must have another slice." She nibbled at the crust.

Mathilde stared, probably because Isabeau had never complimented her on any of her meals before. That was François's duty, to bestow praise upon the servants.

She handed the goggling cook the platter, picked up the sprig of wolfsbane that had lain on the table during the meal, and reached for the pitcher of water sitting near her place. Balancing the herb and the pitcher handle in one hand, she walked out, still pretending to eat the bread.

As soon as she was out of sight, she ran for the walkway.

Where was François? If he were in the studio ...

He was nowhere to be seen but she heard movement behind the building, and his voice, though she couldn't understand his words. He was with the horse, possibly saddling it, to ride into town. If so, she wished he'd get on with it and be gone.

In a moment, he appeared, riding the animal. He pulled the horse to a halt before Isabeau. She put the hand holding the bread behind her back, clutching the pitcher against her chest.

"I'm going into town," he informed her. "Some of my paints need replenishing and I must get some new brushes, too. I also must arrange to have that portrait picked up."

"When will you be back?"

"Later."

That meant he would also stop at a tavern and show off his blooded steed, possibly brag a bit about his friendship with the *marquis*. So, he'd be out of the way until late afternoon, at least.

She nodded.

"You've the herb, I see."

"Yes." She looked at it. "I thought to go ahead and get it done." Sliding the bread into her pocket, she shifted the sprig to her free hand. "I'll need the key."

Without a word, he pulled it from his purse and tossed it to her. Hands full, she attempted to catch it. It fell short, landing in the grass.

"Clumsy," he said. "Pick it up before it gets lost." He turned the horse's head.

She waited until he had ridden to the spot where the lane joined the highroad before she set down the pitcher, parting the grass to find the key. Once she had it, she ran to the studio door.

She'd been expecting a rush of rank air, filled with that vile animal smell. The air in the storeroom was close, but as yet not ill-smelling.

Giovanni lay on the floor. He appeared none the worse for being dosed with valerian, springing to his feet as he saw who stood there. He'd pushed the shutter open, letting in sunshine and fresh air.

"I brought you this." She held out the bread.

He snatched it from her hand, gobbling it down, and not making any remark about "bad-tasting food."

She thought he already looked thinner, his hair longer. A thick shadow hid the high curve of his cheeks. Because his hair was so thick and dark, in a few more days, Botticelli's angel would again be lost inside it.

As he finished, he asked, "More?"

She shook her head. "I'm fortunate I managed to sneak that one slice."

"Thirsty, too." He looked at the pitcher she held.

She offered it. He snatched it from her hands, tilting the pitcher, gulping down water in loud slurps and spilling it on himself. Water dripped from his mouth into his beard, dribbling onto the hide covering his chest. It splashed the floor, wetting the toes of his stocks.

Isabeau thought he'd never stop drinking. *I'll have to refill it or bring him a bucketful.*

He raised his head, setting the pitcher on the floor, then leaned against the wall by the window, slowly sliding down it, head lolling. He gave a long, satisfied sigh.

"Heard someone moving outside in big room."

"It was probably François, readying the studio for his other models to arrive."

"Models? Like me?" His eyebrows rose.

"Models," she agreed, "but definitely not like you." As he looked disappointed, she explained, "These are a noble's sons." Her tone turned earnest. "Giovanni, promise me you'll behave. You won't harm them."

He didn't answer, simply stared at her, as if considering that.

"I mean it," she persisted.

"Full moon gone." He nodded to the window. "No danger now."

Somehow, that didn't reassure her. Unconsciously, she'd begun twirling the sprig between her fingers. Around and around, the single leaf spinning.

He looked at her hands. "What you have?"

She held it up.

He half-rose, glanced at it, scowling. "Wolf herb."

"You know of it?" Why was she surprised? Of course, he did.

"Boamas sell to men before I perform." He snorted. "Say keep them safe."

"Does it?" She wanted him to say it didn't. That Boamas was merely playing on their fear. That there was nothing for them to be protected from.

"Truly."

That wasn't what she wanted to hear. His frown mirrored her own, and he hurried to explain.

"Boamas make me wear around my neck. He take off when show me to *gadje*. When I pretend attack Mariah, it excite them. Make blood pump fast, sometime so loud I hear. Blood rush bring wolf to surface." Getting to his feet, he gestured to the sprig. "Wolf herb keep him from attacking."

"If Boamas knew that, why didn't he give some to my husband when he sold you?" Isabeau asked, appalled that it might possibly be true. "Why did he leave him unprotected?"

He shrugged, looking ignorant of his former master's motives. "Perhaps Boamas think it amusing what I might do when full moon come?" His expression was belied by a sudden brush of slyness.

Isabeau didn't want to think of that. She hurried to him, seizing the leather collar and twisting the stem of the herb around and around it.

Immediately, a change came over him. He paled slightly, falling against the wall as if his legs had lost their strength.

"Are you all right?" She knelt beside him, hand on his shoulder.

"Herb strong, even this little bit." His gasp was oddly like a breathless laugh.

"Would it have quieted you last night?"

His eyes met hers. "What you put in water do better."

It shook her that he'd known there was something in the water but still drank it. She'd heard that if a man were thirsty enough, he'd drink water he'd been told was poisoned.

"Wait few minutes, I overcome this twig." He flicked a finger at the one remaining leaf. It crackled, and the tip dropped away, floating to the floor. With the heel of his hand, Giovanni ground it into the boards.

"François wants to get more," Isabeau said. "So do I."

He shot her a startled glance.

"We must have it, for I don't want you harming anyone." As his expression changed to a deep scowl as if he couldn't under-stand her concern, she added, "Nor do I want you harmed."

That pleased him.

"We don't know where to find it. François doesn't dare ask the town physician for fear he'll tell someone about you."

"What matter if people know? Boamas say it loud and clear."

"I can't speak for Boamas, but François says if the church finds out, they'll kill you."

"That true?" He didn't look particularly frightened.

"I'm afraid so, if they think you can change into a wolf. A *loup-garou* is a cursed creature. You know that."

"Why the master not afraid of me, then?" He nodded to the door, then added, "Not much, anyway."

"My husband is a brave man." That was a lie. As far as Isabeau was concerned, François was as cowardly as they came. "Anyway, he doesn't believe in *loup-garou*."

Another lie, she was certain.

He thought that over. "What you believe?"

"He hopes the herb may grow wild in the woods." She

avoided answering, for if she did, she might tell the truth. *Yes, I think you are, but I don't care.*

"He right," he said.

"You sound certain."

"I am."

"Do you think you could find it?" If he could, it would save their roaming the forest searching for it. "Can you tell me where it is?"

"Why I want find herb making me like baby can't walk?"

She put her hands on his shoulders, clutching them tightly. Through the animal hide, she could feel how thin they were, bones hard under the thick hair.

"Because I don't want you hurt," she repeated, shaking him slightly.

"Take me into forest." He met her gaze steadily. She looked away. "I find for you, mistress."

"Thank you, Giovanni." Realizing how tightly she held him, Isabeau released his shoulders. She got to her feet. "I'll tell François."

"When we go?"

He sounded eager. She hoped this wasn't merely a ploy to get outside again.

"Perhaps tomorrow. I'll speak to François tonight," she promised, not looking back, not wanting to see him crouched on the floor, wearing that ugly hide, the chain around his neck.

He didn't answer.

She hurried out, locking the door behind her.

Chapter Eleven

WHEN FRANÇOIS RETURNED, she thought he looked angry, so she delayed telling him what Giovanni had said.

Without a greeting, he dismounted, bellowing, "Maxime! Did you buy the grain?"

Maxime appeared, puffing as if he'd run. "*Oui, maître.* It's under the eaves at the back of the studio."

"See to my horse." Tossing him the reins, François dismissed him with a gesture, then glanced at Isabeau as if expecting her to speak.

"You look worried." She couldn't think of anything else to say.

"And you look smug," he replied. "Does my distress please you? Best hope it doesn't, since it's your wolf who caused it."

He walked into the cottage, stamping his way to the salon, calling to Maxime for wine.

"Maxime's caring for your horse," Isabeau reminded him.

"He should work faster. *You* serve me, then." Throwing himself into one of the chairs before the hearth, he gestured.

She took a decanter from the fireplace mantel. Pouring red wine into a goblet, she presented it to him.

"I stopped at Dr. Rambeau's." He drank deeply, then leaned back, staring into the cold hearth moodily.

Isabeau sank into another chair, waiting.

At last, he said, "I couldn't think of a way to ask about the herb without arousing his suspicion."

She wasn't certain what to say to that and remained silent.

"I tried to open a conversation about various herbs he used, and attempted to steer the subject to some that might also be poisons if misused. He answered at first, then seemed to become suspicious and gave me such a stare as if he thought I wished to poison someone. He was already surprised because I came to see him and wasn't ill." He shrugged, defeated. "So, I changed the subject."

Francois raised the goblet, drinking again.

"I must have more of the herb. I don't dare risk the *marquis's* sons."

"The full moon's past," Isabeau reminded him. "Surely there's no danger."

"True," he agreed morosely, "but it's going to take more than a month to finish a painting. And the full moon will shine again. Who knows what mischief the creature can do under his own power in between?" He set the goblet down with such violence that wine splashed onto the tabletop. "I vow, Isabeau, I can't afford to lose the *marquis's* patronage and having that *bête* make a meal of his sons might do that."

Isabeau wanted to say that if the marquis lost his sons to a *loup-garou*, François would definitely have more to worry about than losing a patron. She also wished she dared remind François that his friend was already aware of the nature of the beast before he consented to placing his offspring in danger. She prudently kept quiet.

"I must have something to ensure his obedience."

"I spoke to him," she said. "He promised ..."

"What are promises to something like that?" He looked up. "Perhaps the valerian ..."

"You can't keep drugging him." She thought about how fast Giovanni had fallen asleep after drinking the water. "He won't be conscious enough to pose."

"I suppose you're right," he conceded reluctantly. "If I hadn't had such a difficult time finding him ..." Abruptly, he seemed to remember commenting on her expression. "Why did you look so smug, Isabeau?"

"Because," she took a deep breath, "I spoke to Giovanni ..."

"You've already said that."

"He says the herb is here. In the forest. He knows where to find it."

"He's lying. How could he?"

"He sounded very certain."

He sat up. "Did he say where?" Without waiting for an answer, François sprang from his chair. "I'll talk to the creature."

He was out of the door before Isabeau could get to her feet. Gathering her skirts, she hurried after him, running to keep up.

At the studio, however, François refused to go into the storage room.

"Bring him out," he ordered.

He's afraid, she thought. *He thinks I can control the beast in Giovanni. Can I? Would he heed me if the wolf broke free?*

Obediently, she went inside.

Giovanni was lying where she'd left him, turned so he could look out the window at what sky was visible past the kitchen roof. He rolled over, getting to his feet with some difficulty, holding onto the doubled-over chain and sliding it up the window bar.

"François wishes to speak to you."

"About wolf herb?" He didn't move.

She nodded and unwrapped the chain from the window. When she tugged on it, he followed her passively enough, stopping when he saw François standing with his body tense, hammer in his hand as if prepared to meet an attack.

Giovanni also stiffened. His throat tightened, preparing to growl.

"Don't," she whispered.

He relaxed. His body dropped into that familiar crouch.

"*Maître*." The word came out as a low rumble.

"You say that herb the gypsies use against you is in the forests on my property?" François didn't waste time.

"*Oui, maître*." Giovanni kept his head down, hands curved together, pressed against his chest.

"The gypsy caravan has never been through my land. How can you say the herb grows here? Where is it?"

Giovanni turned his head so he was looking up at François. Bent as he was, it gave his body a more grotesque stance, as if he were preparing to leap.

"I not know your land. Can't say."

"So you were lying." François shot Isabeau a satisfied glance. *See? I knew it wasn't so.*

"Didn't say that," Giovanni contradicted.

"In that case, what *did* you say?" François ordered. "Explain."

"I do better," Giovanni answered. "I show you. Take me into forest."

"Oh, no." François shook his head. "I'm not letting you into the woods to run away. You'll tell me." His voice rose, becoming firmer, grip tightening on the hammer. "Where does the wolfsbane grow?" When Giovanni didn't answer, he continued, "You don't know, do you?"

"I know," Giovanni repeated stubbornly.

François's face reddened. Isabeau tightened her grasp on

the chain, ready to jerk Giovanni backward out of reach if her husband attempted to strike him.

"Prove it." Those two words were forced through gritted teeth.

"They in painting." Giovanni straightened, gesturing at the stacked canvases by the door.

"What?"

Giovanni took a step forward. François jumped back, then stepped aside when he realized the boy wasn't looking at him. Instead, he went to the paintings so quickly that the chain was nearly pulled from Isabeau's hands. She hurried behind him, clutching at it.

He reached for the top painting in the stack, flipping it around awkwardly so he could see it.

"Be careful with those, you dumb *bête*," Francois shouted. He ran to them, hovering protectively as Giovanni set the painting aside and reached for the next.

"What are you looking for?" Isabeau asked.

"Madonna in forest," he muttered.

"It's here." She indicated the fifth painting in the stack, and he pulled it out, turning it around, holding it up for François to see.

"My *Madonna of the Grotto*?" He looked surprised.

"Flowers." Giovanni's slender forefinger indicated the green plants growing out of niches in the rocks, in the grass around the painted Isabeau's feet, green plants with dark purple blossoms.

Isabeau remembered the flowers. How she'd thought they were pretty, and was glad François included them in the painting. She'd wanted to pick some and bring them back to the cottage, but he wouldn't allow it. Everything had to stay as it was for the duration of the sitting. Afterward, when he finally finished, she was too tired to pick anything. After coming back day after day, she only wanted to get away.

"Those?" François was disbelieving, then suspicious. "How did you know they were in this painting?"

"*Maîtresse* show me painting, I see wolf herb. Wonder why you worry about it when it grows so plentiful."

François ignored him, turning to Isabeau. "Tomorrow, you'll go to that spot and pick all the flowers you can find."

"François, I'll never locate it," she protested. She hadn't paid attention to which way they'd walked.

"That's true." He regarded her scornfully. "You've no sense of direction. You'd get lost going to town if Mathilde didn't accompany you."

Isabeau took a deep breath. She'd never gotten lost going to town. The road was straight with but one turn. Mathilde only went with her because she was ordered, and then with loud complaints. Nevertheless, she silently agreed, because the thought of walking with Giovanni in the forest, of being alone with him away from the sight and sound of the cottage, the servants, and François, was so tempting.

François decided. Tossing aside the hammer, he spun to look at the boy who was silently regarding the painting. He wrenched the canvas from his hands, setting it atop the others.

"You'll go with your mistress."

Giovanni bobbed a bow, silent, subservient.

"Where's that sprig?" François asked.

Isabeau indicated the collar around Giovanni's neck. There was barely any of that one leaf left. His movements had crushed most of it.

"I suppose that's enough to ensure your safety," François grunted. He stalked back to the door. "If he can truly lead you there ... if this isn't some kind of trick. Pick all you can." He went through the door. "Put back my paintings."

Chapter Twelve

"Come, Giovanni, let's go." Isabeau tugged on the chain.

She was as excited as someone going to a fair. Clutching a basket in which lay her shears and a length of twine for tying the herbs, she prepared to follow the path behind the studio into the forest.

For a few hours ... escape.

Before she left, François did an odd thing.

"Use this to cut the plants." He held out a dagger.

"I have my shears," Isabeau protested, indicating the large garden shears she'd used to cut Giovanni's hair.

"Use this," he repeated, and caught her hand, slapping the handle onto her palm so soundly it stung. "To cut the flowers, and for any other reason."

That made her look at the knife more closely. It was a *miséricorde*, an *arma insidiosa* François brought with him from Italy. With a richly engraved handle and a cross hilt, the blade was slender, tapering to a needle-thin point. It was double-edged, each side of the blade covered with a thin sheet of gleaming silver, a gift from one of his patrons, he'd said. He carried it with him wherever he went, tucked into a small scabbard sewn into the top of his boot.

He'd bragged about the knife, told her it was favored by assassins because of its slender blade that could penetrate chain mail and plate armor.

"It's banned by the authorities, so I must keep it hidden."

Isabeau had wondered if François was capable of fighting with such a weapon, but never voiced that because she knew he would consider her question an affront, and his answer would undoubtedly be the back of his hand against her cheek.

Accepting the dagger, she said, "*Merci*, husband."

"It's silver, you understand," he went on.

Realizing what that meant, if she had to use it, she was both touched and surprised. "Thank you for your concern for my welfare."

At that, François laughed, bursting the little bubble of warmth she abruptly felt. "Your welfare is of no concern to me, wife. I merely wish you to realize the value of this blade and remind you not to lose it. If you do have to use it against the beast, I wish it returned clean of blood."

Without another word, Isabeau dropped it into the basket atop the shears. *How can he say such a thing with Giovanni standing here?* Immediately she asked herself why she was surprised. When did François care for anyone's feelings but his own? She'd not use the knife at all, not to cut plants or to do anything else, she decided.

Wrapping Giovanni's chain around her hand, she walked away without another word.

* * *

GIOVANNI LOPED ALONG BESIDE HER, his long legs soon outdistancing hers. When the chain pulled taut, he had to slow his steps so she could keep up. Isabeau loosened her hold on the chain, allowing him to run ahead. It slid from her fingers. Before she could stoop to retrieve it, he began to run.

In dismay, she watched him disappear into the trees.

"Giovanni. Wait up." Gathering her skirts in one hand, she tightened her hold on the basket and ran, too, fearing this time he was actually going to escape, leaving her to face François's wrath that his prized possession had gotten away.

To her surprise, Giovanni turned and galloped back. He circled around her, chain dragging. Slowing his pace, he came to her side, trotting beside her as she picked up the chain.

"You frightened me. I thought you'd run away."

He gave her a chiding glance. "Never leave you, *maîtresse*. I say that. Why you not believe?"

"I do. Now," she answered. In that moment, she realized he really meant it.

They walked along in silence for a while, Isabeau enjoying the fresh air and the stillness broken only by an occasional bird tweet or the rustle of some small creature in the undergrowth. She wondered what Giovanni was thinking. If he was enjoying the forest in the same way as she, or did he simply appreciate the fact that momentarily, he was free of his storeroom prison?

As free as I am. For now.

When he stumbled slightly and stopped, she looked at him in concern. "What is it?"

His head came up, nostrils flaring as he drew in a sharp, deep breath, then began to sniff loudly.

"What do you smell?"

"Herb here." He nodded to his right.

Through the trees, she saw it. The little cave and the outcropping of rock surrounding the clearing that François had used in the painting. Behind it, the foothills of the mountains rose, the gathering of boulders and loose rock their beginnings.

It looked as it had when she was there before, and was so close to the path she should've been able to find it by herself. Nevertheless, Isabeau was certain she'd have walked past it, probably searched for hours if Giovanni hadn't stopped. She might have circled around it without ever discovering it was there.

How had he found it? Did he smell the blossoms? Did the scent as well as their actual presence affect him?

She walked toward it. It was only when the chain stretched tight, and she looked back to see Giovanni standing at the end of its length, that she realized he hadn't moved.

"What is it?"

"Not go there. Too many plants." He backed away, shaking his head, pulling on the chain and making it slide from her hands. "I stay here."

"I can't leave you," she argued.

"I not move," he promised. "You pick. I wait."

Frowning, Isabeau dropped her end of the chain to the ground. He stayed where he was. As she turned away, he said, "Mistress, cut plant close to dirt. Not get sap on hands. Poison."

She nodded and made her way through the trees to the high shelf of rock, cautiously, as if approaching a darkling shrine where evil spirits might lurk.

There was a stream nearby, an offshoot of the Rhône, gurgling gently as it sped past. She remembered it fell from inside the rock, a waterfall forming a small pool before flowing onward; somewhere along the way becoming the pond and feeding the spring in the well behind the cottage.

The plants grew everywhere. They had definitely multiplied since she'd been there. Thick green stems and long slender leaves, with bright purple trumpet-shaped flowers at the top twelve inches of the stalk. They hung high in the rock's crevices, stood tall in the grass, gathered around the bases of the trees, their tops waving gently in the wake of a breeze sweeping through the forest.

Setting down the basket, she reached inside. Her fingers first touched the stiletto, so she drew it out. In a split-second thought, she decided: *Why not use the thing, dulling its gleaming blade instead of her shears?* Gingerly seizing a plant, she pulled it sideways, slashing at the stalk just above the soil. It separated with a wet sigh, and she held it up, sap weeping to the grass. Keeping it carefully away from her body, she shook it, slinging more sap to the ground, then laid it in her basket. She turned to the next plant, the first now a low nest of leaves, looking shorn and naked without its long stalk.

It took her almost an hour to gather them. During that time, Giovanni didn't move except to drop into the grass and sit with arms wrapped around his knees. He was so quiet she kept glancing at him, making certain he hadn't crept away while she was busy. Whenever she looked up, however, he was still there, silently watching, waiting for her to finish.

When she placed the last stalk into the basket and looked up, she found him on his feet, halfway to where she stood.

He moves so silently. He could've leaped upon me, and I wouldn't have known until it was too late.

She envisioned a wolf creeping through the grass, preparing to pounce on its prey, some unwary rabbit or a straying lamb. That startled her, though she tried not to show it. She was certain he sensed it, however, for he looked directly at her and scowled.

She dropped the knife atop the flowers. Already, they were beginning to droop, looking wrinkled and brittle.

"You wash away sap." He gestured at the blade. "Not use again until then." His fingers tapped the basket's handle. "Basket, too."

"Is it that deadly?"

"Sap not know difference between wolf and human."

She shivered and picked up the stiletto. "I'll wash it in the stream."

"No. Poison water. Soak in wine, then pour into *puits de cess.*"

"Very well." She dropped the dagger back into the basket.

What would happen if I gave the dagger to Mathilde and she used it to cut the meat for our next meal? What if François ate that meat? Would it kill him? No doubt if that happened, the Watch would accuse the wife first of all. Poison was always a woman's weapon. Anyway, she'd have to give the knife back to François. He'd ask for it since it was a precious possession. *He wanted it returned clean.*

"Well, mistress." Giovanni spun, regarding her. "I do what *le maître* want. You reward me?"

"A reward?" When he nodded, those copper eyes bright, she was startled to feel her heart beat faster. "What do you wish?"

"To run." He didn't hesitate.

The downward rush she experienced could only be disappointment. What did she expect him to ask for? Silently, she unsnapped the chain from his neck.

He stepped away, shook, spun into a crouch, and sped away into the forest, then whirled and galloped back, dodging trees, going around them, back and forth, until Isabeau thought he surely should become so dizzy he couldn't stand.

Giovanni seemed unbothered. Indeed, it was she who felt giddy from watching him, though the joy with which he moved made her smile, also.

There was a rustling, a squirrel running from one tree to another. He looked up, watching it scamper to safety.

Isabeau laughed at his expression. Shaking his head, he seemed to be debating whether to pursue the little animal into the branches.

Don't be silly. Wolves don't climb trees. In spite of her many denials, her own mind betrayed her. Mentally, she sighed in defeat.

After a moment, he moved again, but slower this time, more cautious, as if ...

... as if he's stalking something.

He stopped, head snapping around, tensing. There was a rustling. Something running. Giovanni burst into movement, dashed after it, bent, leaped, landing in the midst of many somethings that tried to escape, darting this way and that. He growled, reaching, catching. There were squeaks and squeals, shrill screams, quickly broken off.

Isabeau's hand went to her mouth, stifling her own gasp.

He raised something feebly kicking, carried it to his mouth, and crouched. There was ripping, a liquid tearing. Teeth ground and bones crunched.

Isabeau turned away, fighting rising nausea.

The sounds continued for several minutes. When she looked back, he was upright, kicking at the leaves, scooping handfuls of grass and dirt, sprinkling it over whatever lay on the ground. Straightening, he returned to her.

His mouth was wet, with spatters on his chin and cheeks. Something clung to the corner of his mouth, a tuft of fur, dark gray tipped with brown, still attached to a bit of skin. Isabeau plucked it away and flicked it off her fingers, rubbing her hands together in disgust. He swiped a hand over his mouth, making a smear; under his fingernails was stained dark red.

"I was hungry."

She didn't answer.

He saw the stream and ran to it, scooped water, splashing his face. When he looked back at her, his mouth was clean. Before she realized his intent, he began pulling off the hides, tugging one over his head, struggling out of it.

At the first sight of bare flesh, she called out, "Giovanni, wait. What are you doing?"

"Want bath." Stripping off the hide around his hips, he tossed it aside and waded into the stream, toward the waterfall.

I must look away. Isabeau didn't move.

With a thrill of the forbidden, she continued watching as Giovanni cupped his hands, catching the falling water. He drank, then splashed the rest onto his face. Stepping directly under the falling water, he raised his face to its clear cascade.

It's not wrong, she told herself. *It's as if I'm watching an animal bathe.*

Water dripped from the curling locks, rolling off his shoulders, cascading down his bare skin, and falling back into the water.

He's so beautiful and unashamed. Like a woodland creature, innocent in his nakedness ... a woodland creature who just tore another to pieces and ate it ...

She didn't care.

Her hands tightened into fists. She wanted to rush to the stream, reach out and run her hands over his shoulders, stroke that wet, gleaming flesh, feel its warmth through the chill of the water.

He fell forward and began to swim, an awkward paddling like the hounds made when fording a stream during a hunt, making those little yips she's now come to recognize as his version of laughter, while she stood, entranced, watching ...

"*Maîtresse,* come." He rose to his feet, water waist-deep spilling around him. He extended a hand, beckoning. "Bathe with me."

"No ..." Now, she did turn away, hand to her mouth. Oh, how she wanted to be immoral yet innocent, like Adam and Eve, the forest their Eden, before the Serpent came ... but in this case, Giovanni himself was the serpent, both innocence and beguiler, calling to the wanton stirring within her, tempting her. If he called to her once more, she'd cast all caution aside, tear away her garments, and leap into his arms ...

Do it, Giovanni. Ask me again. Invite me into the water with you. Isabeau closed her eyes, waiting. Hoping.

There was splashing, movement, then footsteps behind her. She turned. He'd redressed in his animal hides.

"I did wrong?" He looked uncertain.

She nodded. "It isn't proper for me to see you unclothed."

"Why?" He cocked his head to the side, a dog contemplating something puzzling. "You put me in big bowl, no clothes, touch me—"

"I only touched you to bathe you," she interrupted, defending her actions. "That was different."

"How?" He wasn't arguing. He truly wished to know.

"It's difficult to explain." She couldn't tell him how he'd stirred something inside her, something she'd never felt for François, or any other man for that matter. "Just believe me when I say you mustn't do that again."

"How I bathe then?" He gave her a look as teasing as a precocious child, so charming Isabeau held her breath.

"Except when you bathe," she amended.

He nodded, then caught her hands. "Play with me?"

Before she could answer, he swung her around and around. Spinning, he again ran through the trees, pulling her with him, moving so quickly her feet occasionally left the ground. She laughed until she gasped for breath and pulled away.

"Oh, stop. I ... I must rest ..."

"Yes." He pulled her to the grotto, the little clumps of leaves with their bare stumps no longer affecting him. "Sit, mistress ... like in painting ... be *Madonna of Wolfsbane.*"

"But I have no baby to hold," she protested, allowing him to push her onto a hillock of grass.

"Not hold baby." He stretched full-length beside her, placing his head in her lap. "Hold me."

He closed his eyes and lay still.

Isabeau didn't move, aware of how warm he felt, the heat of his cheek seeping through the light wool of her gown. She swore she could feel the beating of his heart. Its pulse was visible in his throat, a gentle thumping echoing through his body. There was an answering throb of warmth between her thighs, becoming stronger with each beat.

She studied his face, the thick curve of dark brows, the way his lashes made fringed shadows upon his cheeks. After a moment, Isabeau dared stroke his hair, brushing back the damp curls. The bruise where François struck him was fading. Only a slight bluish area remained, blending into the dark tangle of shadow that would soon be a heavy beard, transforming the angel once more into the beast.

In the meantime, he sleeps with his head in my lap, like the unicorn does with the virgin. She remembered François's threat. *I've truly tamed the beast and he trusts me. No matter how terrible he may become when the moon is full, I must keep him safe, for his sake as well as mine.*

"Oh, *mon ange.*" Impulsively, Isabeau leaned forward, brushing her lips against the bruise.

He didn't move.

She continued stroking his hair, running her fingers down his cheek, brushing fingertips against his throat and across one shoulder where the hide slipped and it was bared slightly, wishing he were once more as naked as when he stood in the stream, that she lay the same way beside him, and he wasn't sleeping ...

What would he do if it were so? Would he pull her again into a childish dance, or would it be an old and different one, that dance of the ages between man and woman?

The sun moved to high overhead, then began to sink into the trees. When shadows lengthened around them, she said, "Giovanni, you must wake up. It's getting dark. We have to go home."

He opened his eyes, looking up at her, blinking as he came awake.

Oh, to see that face in the morning instead of François's.

"Home. *Oui, maîtresse.*"

Getting to his feet, he found the chain and presented it to her, waiting patiently as she reattached it to his collar. She picked up the basket.

On the way back, he walked far enough behind her that the herbs didn't affect him, or so he said, but she thought once or twice he faltered, as if very tired. She wondered if it was exhaustion or the wafting of the wolf herb's spell.

* * *

FRANÇOIS WAS IN THE STUDIO, carefully placing the little pottery jars containing his new paints on the shelves. A wide-mouthed urn held his new brushes. They looked pristine and out of place next to those used so much their threadbare bristles were clotted with dried paint, not even turpentine could clean away.

The model's platform, which had been propped against the back wall, now rested in the center of the studio floor, between François's easel and the hearth. Isabeau imagined Maxime had helped his master drag it to its current position. The portrait was missing. Its owner had come and gone, taking it away with him.

"Well?" He gave her a glance, ignored Giovanni, then went back to what he was doing.

There were a great many jars. The physician had obviously

found numerous sources for new colors on his last expedition into the hills.

"Did you find the plants?"

Isabeau answered by holding up her basket. She ignored the way Giovanni cringed and turned his head as she did so. He bolted to the closed door, making her follow or have the chain pulled from her hand.

"You'd best teach him to heel," François muttered, just loud enough for her to hear.

She set the basket on a nearby table and opened the door to the storage room. Giovanni was pathetically eager to get inside.

Once there, she unhooked the chain from his collar, putting a finger to her lips. Their eyes met. He caught her hand, pressing it against his forehead, then dropped to the floor in front of the window. Isabeau walked out, locking the door behind her.

"What shall I do with them?" She had some vague idea that François was going to ask her to weave them into wreaths to be worn about the boys' necks. She wondered what they would say to that and how he'd justify it.

"Spread them upon the table to dry."

"On this table?" Isabeau glanced from it to the door. The table was directly beside it.

"Is there some problem with that?" He was irritable, not wanting to be distracted from his preparations.

"It's so close to the storeroom. Giovanni will be affected by the nearness of the flowers."

"Good. That's exactly what I want. There must be no way he can offer harm to *le marquis's* sons."

"But ... so close to the door?"

"Heed me, Isabeau, and listen well." He whirled, catching her by the shoulders and staring into her eyes. "I don't care what happens to the *bête*. As long as he's able to stand where I say and doesn't harm anyone. He's only important to me as far as my paintings are concerned. Do you understand?"

Silently, she nodded.

He released her, going to the door and flicking a hand in the direction of the table where the basket sat. "Put them there. Spread them over the table, so they can dry as quickly as possible. Later, you will scatter them around the room."

Isabeau knew better than to argue, but she had to make one last effort. She decided to try a different argument.

"You say you don't wish anyone to know you've a suspected *loup-garou* here. If you have the herb in plain sight, anyone seeing it will wonder. What will you tell them when they ask why you have such a thing if it isn't needed?"

He didn't answer. Obviously, he hadn't thought of that.

"I'll leave them in the basket," she suggested when his silence continued. "If you insist on them being here, I'll set them on a shelf. If anyone asks, you can say it was a flower arrangement you used in a painting." As she spoke, she picked up the basket, looked around, and dropped it onto the shelf of an open cabinet on the wall behind the easel. That was close enough to the platform to be effective. "If someone is so learned he recognizes what they are, you can pretend surprise and avow ignorance."

He didn't argue. "As long as it's within easy reach should I need it. If the *bête* misbehaves."

Isabeau relaxed.

He went back to his task.

Without looking around, he finished with the paints and turned to the empty canvases, searching through them. "Damn, I don't have one big enough. That means I must make another trip to town tomorrow, to the carpenter for a specially made frame." As if in afterthought, he added, "Reward the *bête*. Give him some food tonight, but not much. A couple of slivers."

"Yes, François."

She decided she wouldn't tell him about the poisonous nature of the sap. Perhaps, if she were fortunate, he'd accidentally learn for himself. She wished he'd asked for his dagger back. She could say he didn't give her time to clean it, or avow ignorance of the poisonous nature of the sap. So far, he hadn't remembered that he gave it to her.

Immediately, she was shocked by the thought, reproaching herself for even daring to think of her husband coming to harm.

I'm truly a wayward wife. She was unable to argue with that.

Chapter Thirteen

THE NEXT DAY, her father's footman rode to the cottage on one of the horses still remaining in the Lascaux stables.

Isabeau came down the stairs. Hearing voices from the salon, she went there, finding the footman standing in the door-way, and Maxime waiting a few feet behind him.

"Gervais?" She recognized him immediately.

He was the same age as she, had been promoted from being a mere errand boy to footman the year she married François. Isabeau had never considered Gervais particularly ambitious, since he seemed happy enough in his position of delivering messages, chopping wood, and performing other menial tasks. She always suspected he'd been given the promotion because of his looks.

Pierre liked his footmen of a standard height, slim of build, and comely of countenance. Gervais fit all requirements.

At the moment, he appeared to be back to his original status: delivering messages.

"Why are you here? Has something happened at the *château*?"

Turning slightly, Gervais swept her a bow, his rolled-brim

bag hat pressed against his heart. He gave her that shy smile she remembered, and Isabeau smiled back. She noted that his livery was threadbare and there was a mended place in the seam at the waist of his doublet.

Instead of answering her question, however, he simply said, "I've brought a message to *Monsieur* François, *Madame*."

He looked back at François.

"Indeed, he has." François's reply came from the chair where he half-reclined, looking, to his wife's mind, both the indulgent lord as well as a slovenly lout. A flick of irritation touched his face.

Isabeau knew immediately why. The footman had called him *monsieur,* the designation for someone from the *bourgeoisie,* the rapidly rising merchant middle class, instead of the more formal *seigneur*, indicating a gentleman or someone of the same class as his master.

"Well?" Isabeau wanted to grind her teeth. *Am I supposed to beg to know what you were told? I won't do it.*

François ignored her question, directing his next words to Gervais. "Thank my father-in-law for the gracious invitation. You may go." He punctuated the order with an imperious wave of his hand.

Surprise flickered over Gervais's face. Ever the good servant, he quelled it as he bowed again.

"*Oui, monsieur,*" he replied, as he'd been taught, and disappeared into the hallway.

Maxime gestured to the entrance and led him back there.

"I don't like that footman." François reached for an apple from the compote he'd ordered Mathilde to make certain nearby when he was at home.

He liked to eat fresh fruit during the day and wanted it within easy reach. A bowl, filled with apples and pears, and occasionally grapes, sat by his chair in the salon, as well as in the studio while he worked.

Isabeau liked fresh fruit also, but she'd been told by Mathilde in no uncertain terms she wasn't to bother the master's. Ignoring the cook's warning, she'd gotten stinging fingers from having them slapped by François himself when she once helped herself to a couple of grapes.

"Gervais? Whyever not?" Isabeau came into the salon. "I find him most polite."

She ignored the fruit bowl but simply watched silently as her husband enjoyed its contents.

"You would." François sneered, biting into a grape and spitting seeds into the fireplace.

What that meant, she didn't divine, for Isabeau had no more acquaintance with the young servant than she had any of the others when she'd lived in her father's house, which was to say enough to give orders and exchange a few simple pleasantries. She'd never found any problem with his manner.

"I find him discourteous and insolent. Do you refuse to see that simply because he may remind you of your former home, run-down as it is?"

He never ignored a chance to deliver an insult outside of his father-in-law's hearing.

"Or is it because he has a pretty face and a well-formed calf?"

"Insolent?" she repeated, ignoring the insult he'd given her. "How? What did he do?"

"Did you not see the way he looked when I dismissed him?" He waved a hand at the doorway as though Gervais still stood there. "As if he couldn't believe it. Did he expect I'd invite him in to sit and share a goblet?"

"I expect he thought you'd at least offer him some water

from the kitchen and perhaps let his horse drink from that trough Maxime built for the one *le marquis* gave you."

Maxime had labored long and loudly over having to repair the bottomless water trough in the paddock behind the studio. Using some of the lumber from the interior of the stable, he fashioned a clumsy but utilitarian box into which he poured fresh water from the well every three days because that was how long it took for the water to leak out if the horse didn't empty it first.

"Why should I do that?"

"Because it's the proper thing," Isabeau explained, with a patience she didn't feel. "It's common courtesy to provide a servant and his horse water before sending them on their way again." She couldn't resist adding, "Some households even furnish a meal before they go."

"For merely riding across town and relaying a one-sentence message? I doubt that." François looked surprised that he might be expected to do such a thing, that he thought Isabeau was jesting. There was a slight pause before he said, "You smiled at him. Quite familiarly."

He sounded jealous, and that surprised Isabeau. She'd thought François didn't care enough about her, except as a glorified housemaid and satisfier of his lust, to be jealous. It gave her an odd feeling, and it wasn't a pleasant one.

She didn't answer, but instead seated herself in her chair and opened the sewing basket she held. She took out one of Francois's blouses. The sleeve had been ripped, but he could continue wearing it once it was reattached. Knowing his disdain for patched clothing, she had hoped to do so before he could return and toss it into the rag basket. Instead, she'd allowed Giovanni to monopolize her time. She hoped he wouldn't be too curious about what she was working on.

After a moment, however, he said, "You're repairing that

shirt I tore when I carried those canvases into the studio several months ago."

She nodded, keeping her attention on the raw edges of the seams as she pressed them together, watching the needle pierce the wash-worn cloth. Briefly, she wondered how it would feel to push a needle into François's chest. Not a needle, but a knife, with a point as thin and sharp as a needle, like the *miséricorde*, Mathilde was even then washing in wine to remove the poisonous sap, as Isabeau had repeated to the cook following Giovanni's instruction.

She waited for him to tell her to throw it out. With as few garments as he had, François refused to wear any obviously mended ones, except when he visited Alphonse.

"Make certain the repairs don't show. It's a comfortable one. I can get more wear out of it." He paused before rushing on, "Put that aside for now, Isabeau. We must get ready."

That surprised her so much that her fingers stilled, needle half-thrust into the fabric.

"Ready for what?" She didn't look at him.

"The du Maurier youngsters have arrived. Your father has invited us to supper in their honor." He got to his feet, tossing the apple core into the fire. "Come."

Obediently, she stuck the needle into the sleeve near the top of the yoke and stood, laying the blouse and sewing basket in the chair.

François was already out the door and halfway to the stairs. Isabeau followed him, mentally mulling over the gowns in her wardrobe, wondering which might still be in good enough condition to wear when greeting the sons of a *marquis*.

In response to the bellows, François aimed in the direction of the kitchen, Maxime hastened up the backstairs and was waiting at the bedchamber door. Bowing, he opened the door, and after François entered, he followed him, neatly stepping in front of Isabeau and impeding her entrance into the room.

She jumped back to avoid being knocked down, wearily thinking once again how Maxime would've suffered if he'd been in her father's home and dared do that. Fuming, she went inside where her husband and servant were already deep in conversation.

"I'll wear the new outfit *le marquis* gave me."

Now in the role of valet, Maxime pulled open a drawer of the shirt press.

"That shirt."

François pointed to a linen blouse with applied braid and embroidery around the low neck as well as the yoke, cuffs, and hem; the brilliant blue of both contrasting with the white fabric. Since shirts usually had one or the other as decoration, *le marquis* was obviously a bit of a fashion iconoclast.

Maxime took it out of the drawer, draping it reverently over his arm.

François opened the double doors of the clothing armoire against the wall across from the bed. "With that new suit he presented me on my last visit."

When Maxime's hand hovered over the indicated garment, as if uncertain which part to remove, he continued, "Yes, the entire thing."

"And your chausses, *maître?*" The doublet followed the blouse over Maxime's arm.

"The ones with the codpiece, of course," François snapped. "This suit is all of a piece. One can't wear those old-fashioned double-crossed kind with a doublet like that."

Despite her anger, Isabeau managed to stifle a giggle as she thought of François wearing a pair of hose like those she'd put on Giovanni. In spite of their overlapping top constructed in a way to conceal a man's privates, she'd often overheard her father laughing as he related a fashion *faux pas* when the pieces parted as a man sat or bowed, displaying his prized possessions fore and aft for all to see. Imagining such a thing happening to her pompous husband in his gifted second-hand finery made her bite her lip.

"What about this, sir?" Maxime tapped a finger against an elaborately embroidered *journade*, the short, tabard-like cape worn as an outer garment.

François considered, then rejected it. "Not tonight. I wish nothing to hide this fine doublet. I'll go without it, a fashion to the moment as it is."

"Will you wear a *chaperon*, sir?"

"Of course." He acted as if Maxime had insulted him. "How would it look if I go out in such splendor and don't have a head covering?"

Maxime didn't answer, merely bowed.

"Now, then, let's ..."

François turned, hands going to the doublet he wore, preparing to pull it from his shoulders. He saw Isabeau standing in front of the wardrobe, studying her own meager garments.

"Why are you standing there? Why aren't you changing out of that shapeless gown?"

Because I've nothing more fashionable to wear, and how dare you insult my gown when you won't buy me others? Isabeau didn't say that aloud, of course. Instead, she said, "I was trying to decide which set of sleeves I could change to which gown to make it look newer."

"You won't need to."

"No?"

"I forgot." Reaching into the top of the armoire to a shelf above the hanging garments, he took down a large, bulky package wrapped in coarsely woven hemp. "Here."

He tossed it to her.

Isabeau caught it awkwardly, staring at it.

"A gift from *la marquise*," François went on. "When she heard His Lordship had presented me with a gift, she very generously sent one to you also." He shrugged. "Can't imagine why. Didn't want you jealous, I suppose."

"Oh." Isabeau ripped apart the twine holding the bundle together, pushing aside the hemp. A flood of colored fabric spilled out.

"You must remember to write Her Ladyship and thank her for her generosity," François continued, as if she were a schoolgirl needing reminders of social graces.

He turned back to Maxime, hovering with his own garments in his arms.

"Now, then, my dear, since you can't put on that garment in the presence of my man here ..."

Isabeau stiffened at that proprietary statement.

"... I suggest you retire to one of the other bedchambers to change. And hurry, the hour is getting late and it'll soon be time to go."

"Are we walking? Won't I be dusty when we arrive? Or am I to ride pillion and get horse sweat on this finery?" she asked, clasping the garments against her breast as if he might take them from her.

"Don't fret on that point, my dear. Your father is sending his coach for us." He paused, then added, "He knows how things are done."

Implying his wife obviously didn't.

"I need Mathilde to assist me."

"Mathilde is busy in the kitchen. Surely you're not so helpless you can't prepare yourself?" François obviously saw no parallel between his being dressed by his valet and his wife being assisted by the cook.

He turned his back on her. She was dismissed.

Isabeau didn't argue. Clutching the bundle, she fled to the bedchamber next door, letting her excitement over the gown overcome her husband's rudeness. She was anxious to see the gift in its entirety.

* * *

FRANÇOIS VIEWED her finery with a bare nod. "You'll do, I suppose." His disinterest quelled what excitement Isabeau felt in the wearing of these new garments. New to her, anyway. Even his "I vow, they make you look quite comely, wife," didn't bolster her esteem, for once deflated, the joy couldn't be rekindled.

Isabeau merely remained grateful she wouldn't embarrass her parents by wearing one of her patched and repaired gowns.

Chapter Fourteen

THE COACH ARRIVED PROMPTLY. It looked dreadfully out of place as it stopped before the cottage, in its worn finery, appearing as if it were somehow lost and had merely halted to ask directions. Though the groom kept the horses' harnesses polished and the hardware on the coach itself was gleaming, it was still obvious the vehicle was of an older vintage and not one of the more modern designs.

Unassisted by François but with the footman offering his hand, Isabeau climbed in, followed by her husband. Again, it was Gervais doing the honors, making Isabeau certain her father had been forced to release the other two footmen from service.

They didn't speak during the ride across the length of Aux-la-Piémont; not until they arrived did François say a word. It was as if he couldn't think of an insult worthy of the indignity caused by his having to ride in such an ancient vehicle. It was only after the footman leaped down and opened the coach door that he spoke.

As François alighted and Gervais offered Isabeau his hand—a gloved hand in which a resewn seam was clearly visible on one finger—her husband elbowed him out of the way so violently the footman stumbled backward, leaving Isabeau with her hand extended to empty air.

"I can assist my wife." He caught her fingers, nearly jerking her from the coach.

Once she was standing beside him, he firmly affixed her hand to his forearm and strode toward the entrance to the *château*, where her father and mother waited. He moved so quickly that Isabeau had to run to keep from being dragged.

"François, what ails you?" she whispered.

"I won't have that impertinent footman touching my wife."

This display of jealousy, directed toward someone she had rarely seen since leaving her parents' home, puzzled Isabeau, while frightening her a little. François had never acted like that before. Of course, there were rarely any young and obviously good-looking men near her.

He saw her frown. "Appear pleased, my dear, that your husband is looking out for you."

Looking out for your wife, or simply for one of your possessions?

Out of the corner of her eye, she saw Gervais, white-faced with affront, climb back onto the coach. The driver shook the reins, and the horses galloped away in the direction of the stables.

They reached the *château's* entrance.

There was a flurry of greetings. Isabeau's mother hugged her, kissing her on both cheeks in a semblance of affection while her father took her hand, accepting her curtsey before pulling her into his arms for a brief embrace.

"Are you well, daughter?"

As she assured him she was, thinking it an odd question, he greeted François more effusively, while Madame Lascaux enviously admired her daughter's gown. Isabeau recognized her own as one she'd worn to her daughter's commencement, though still in very good condition, if now out of style, with a wide, scooped neck and a long-waisted body. It was as obviously not a *robe déguisée* as her daughter's apparel was, thanks to *la Marquise* du Maurier.

Pierre gave his son-in-law covetous glances but didn't mention his attire, which piqued François no end if his scowl was any indication. Isabeau noted her father's garments were of a later, more up-to-date style than her mother's and in much better condition. Inwardly, she sighed. Once again, the men in the family saw to their own clothing rather than their wives.

They were escorted to the salon where the young nobles waited.

As they were introduced, all three nodded familiarly to François, whom they knew from his visits to their father, then each took Isabeau's hand, bowing over it with some murmured phrase of compliment.

Isabeau was charmed by all three. It was obvious they were related, for all had the same blond hair, not the pale ash color of those from the frost-ridden countries of Norway or Sweden, but a darker wheaten gold. They also had dark blue eyes dancing with mischief. André, the eldest, was twenty, a few months older than Isabeau; Auguste was seventeen, and Aubert, the youngest, fifteen.

They reminded her very much of her own three brothers, who were now away at school. Pierre was determined his sons would marry well and bring in plentiful dowries for him to squander, since having a semi-famous son-in-law had so far brought in no coin, though it did afford him credit to get himself more into debt. Now, it was up to his sons to ease their father's old age, and to do so, they needed to be educated. Besides, being enrolled with other noblemen's sons would give them chances to make influential friends.

The young du Mauriers were dressed in the height of

masculine fashion, similar to François's own garments. André was wearing a *jourdance* over his doublet, and the others had considerable dagging on their sleeves and doublet fronts. Auguste was clothed in blue watered silk and Aubert in green, with contrasting hues of yellow showing through the carefully made rents in their clothing.

Isabeau thought they might comment on her gown, note how much it resembled one their mother had worn, perhaps with a sly innuendo or a sideways glance saying they knew to whom it had formerly belonged, just as they were aware François now wore one of their father's cast-off suits. The boys were either too polite or not yet versed enough in subtle insults. Perhaps they simply didn't know. Unless it was that, like most men, they never noticed what a woman wore but only how they could get her out of it. If it was the latter, she thought that a bit sad.

After her introduction, no one spoke to Isabeau, though she thought her parents gave her several anxious glances.

Supper was as elaborate as she expected it to be, making her wonder which room was now partially emptied of its contents to pay for the meal. She supposed she should be thankful the *château* had so many chambers. Gervais, acting as both footman and server, was presided over by Gaston, her father's butler, who had been with them so long he'd probably die in their service whether he was paid or not.

Plates were brought out and placed before each. Except for the meat, or in this case, the meat substitute, since it was a Friday, portions were already served on each plate. After those were eaten, the diners would pass around the platters and bowls now upon the table. Compared to their own plainer fare, the meal was much too rich, making Isabeau decide she'd best eat slowly and sparingly, not because François's uncouth manners chased away her appetite as happened at home, but she didn't wish the heavily seasoned and somewhat greasy foods to make her stomach rebel.

Because no red meat was served, Pierre made an elaborate show of apologizing for that.

"It's a mercy you scheduled your arrival on Thursday, my young lords. Otherwise, you would've been met with this poor fare then, instead of the feast as was served last night."

Surveying what now filled the table, Isabeau wondered what Thursday's meal had contained.

To her mind, the dishes upon the table held a wondrous display of foods. There might not be as much as generally graced a noble's table, but what was there was rich enough to make one ignore its paucity. If she wasn't mistaken, the cabbage pie sitting directly before her, with a crust so fluffy and light she knew it would be like tasting a cloud, was prepared with the green and leafy vegetable from Senlis, purported to be the most delicious in the world.

Surely Pierre had paid a pretty *sou*, and more, to have those brought all the way from the farming community in Hauts-de-France. It had been done very quickly, also, for the visible leaves appeared remarkably unwilted, even after being boiled. The cook had layered them between crisp dough filled with onions and garlic, over which a creamed sauce made from almond milk and eggs had been poured before the latticed crust was placed atop the mixture.

Another platter held row after row of eggshells, sliced in half and stuffed with boiled fish roe beaten with almond milk, dill, and anise. There were also boiled turnips, buttered and creamed with almond milk, and two salads. One was a delightful combination of shredded raw cabbage, lettuce, dandelion, and radish greens over which was drizzled a verjuice mixture of pressed green grapes, crabapples, and unripe gooseberries, stirred with sorrel extract and cinnamon. The other contained only fruit, both fresh and dried—apples, quince, wild cherries, and pears, sliced and soaked in a honey glaze.

There were several loaves of bread on their own platters, accompanied by plain and garlic-flavored butters.

When it was brought out, the meat substitute was so large that it took both Gervais and Gaston to carry the platter. In case anyone didn't notice, Pierre was quick to draw all attention to it.

"I was in a quandary as to whether to serve beaver tail or oysters instead of the usual fish today. I hope I wasn't amiss in making such a choice."

"Beaver tail?"

He got no further as André interrupted with a near-whoop of joy.

"Monsieur Lascaux, you truly work miracles." The boy glanced from Pierre to his siblings. "My brothers and I tire of fish on Fridays, but Papa's so custom-bound. He never thinks to look for anything else acceptable to serve. I vow I think he's charged the cook to turn her head where beaver, squid, or even lamprey are displayed."

Auguste and Aubert nodded, making sounds of agreement while eyeing the platter eagerly. The tail had been skinned, marinated in red wine and garlic, sprinkled with paprika butter, and broiled over an open flame. Grilled lemon slices had been added as a garnish.

"You flatter me, Your Lordship." Pierre placed a hand over his heart, bowing. "I'm grateful I chose so well."

Isabeau managed to hide her smirk at her father's false modesty, since the boys' praise was exactly what he wished. She could almost hear his thoughts as he imagined the youngsters reporting this luxury to their father.

"Now then." He raised his hands as if in benediction. "Since the Good Lord has blessed this food for today's meal, we thank Him and now receive His bounty." Pierre picked up the carving knife and fork, placed horizontally on the top rim of his plate. "I'll carve. How many slices would you like, Your Lordship?"

André's plate was held out and waiting before he finished speaking.

The boys ate with the hearty appetite of the young, unaffected by spices, herbs, or fat. After all, they were accustomed to such meals.

As was inevitable, the table talk turned to the painting and how they were to be depicted.

"It's to be called *The Beggar and The Nobles*," François explained, going over the basics again because they hadn't been present when he spoke to their father. "You'll be depicted standing together while a beggar kneels in the dirt, asking for alms. He's thin, starving, but you ignore him while one of you munches on a piece of fruit and another eats a pastry."

"It sounds interesting," André said. He raised his head, squinting at the ceiling as if envisioning the scene.

"But, of course, we'd never do that," Auguste put in, hastily, as if he thought François was making an accusation. "At home, we give daily to the poor, and our kitchen puts out any leftover food from our meals for them to eat."

"No one goes hungry in La Chapelle," Aubert added. "We also have an almshouse." His voice squeaked when he said that, and he reached for his goblet, drinking quickly.

Isabeau hid a smile behind her table kerchief. As the candlelight struck his face, it created a gingery sheen along his jaw, the shadow of a beard, barely noticeable before. Aubert was growing into the handsomeness his brothers already possessed.

He caught her glance and flushed, perhaps thinking she was laughing at him for the sudden change in the timbre of his voice. She wished she could reassure him, but was aware that would only add to his discomfort and bring him more attention. She was certain he didn't want that.

The conversation continued for a few moments more in that vein, then André, who led the talk for his brothers, said, "What of your other model, *Monsieur* François? Your beggar? You haven't mentioned him."

He already knew the answer, Isabeau could tell, by the way he looked at François. She also saw the flick of irritation touching her husband's face as the boy used that title, the same expression as when Gervais had spoken to him earlier. Only now, he couldn't retaliate with a sharp word. Not to the son of his friend and patron.

Before her husband could swallow the food he'd just stuffed into his mouth, André continued, "Is it true what my father told us? That you bought a *loup-garou* from those gypsies who camped in the woods? And he's to be your beggar?"

"Your noble father's mistaken, Your Lordship." François managed a laugh that to Isabeau sounded false as well as panic-stricken. He couldn't very well call Alphonse a liar since he was present when he purchased Giovanni.

"But wasn't he kept in a cage?" André persisted. "Brought out and paraded before you at the end of a chain, and forced to" —he hesitated, giving both *Madame* Lascaux and Isabeau quick glances—"perform most unsavory acts?"

"Yes, he was kept in a cage," François admitted, clearly uncomfortable by how verbally lax Alphonse had been to his sons about their visit to the gypsy camp. Why forbid them from going there if he was going to tell them about it? "But he's no unnatural being. Giovanni's merely a poor half-wit they found and took advantage of."

"Giovanni? That's his name?"

François nodded, as if giving his purchase a name lent him more authenticity as a normal being.

"He's Italian, then?" André looked surprised. There was no way his father could've known that.

"That's what he says," François confirmed, and went on before the boy asked more questions. "To be truthful, he's a rather docile soul." He nodded to Isabeau. "My wife can vouch for that."

Everyone looked at Isabeau.

"That's true."

She cleared her throat, thinking of how Giovanni had looked as he romped in the grass, of the beauty of his wet flesh when he stood under the waterfall. That made her flush slightly, and she hoped everyone thought it merely because she was now the focus of attention. Into her mind came Giovanni's image as he defended her from François's wrath. Not so docile then.

"He's a little rough but harmless."

She told the lie without a quiver, though her hands tightened slightly around her knife and fork. François gave her a conspiratorial look as if to say they were now fellow liars.

"Of course, I didn't think he'd be otherwise," André went on, laughing. "Papa would never have allowed us to come if there had been any danger."

"Of course not," François agreed, looking relieved.

"Well, if there had been ..." Aubert spoke up. He'd been steadily eating his way through his meal with the appetite of a growing adolescent. "... none of us would be imperiled."

"What do you mean, brother?" Auguste was the quietest of the three and sat silently while André and François spoke.

At a signal from Gaston, Gervais began to clear away the supper plates.

"You're aware I've occasionally assisted the apothecary in gathering his herbs?" Aubert asked his brother.

Auguste nodded.

"He's also let me read his *Herbiary*. Besides being a

compendium of all herbs propitious for saving lives and ensuring good health, it also lists various plants that can be used as protection against unnatural beasts and vile creatures of the dark, so"—laying down his knife and fork, he reached into the breast of his doublet and brought out something wrapped in tissue-paper—"when Papa mentioned the *loup-garou*, I went to the woods and picked these."

Placing the paper on the table, he opened it, displaying some long, leafy stems with bright purple flowers. Isabeau barely managed to keep from dropping her fork.

"Wolfsbane," he explained, and looked around the table.

François appeared disturbed. Auguste and André were fascinated. Isabeau's mother and father were merely confused.

"Just in case," Aubert added, pleased with their reactions. He touched one of the sprigs.

"Oh, be careful with that," Isabeau spoke before she thought. "The sap is poisonous."

"Eh?" François looked startled. "What's that?"

"Don't worry, *Madame*," Aubert assured her. "I dried the tips, then sealed them with a flame."

He held up the sprig so she could see its charred end.

"No poison can escape." Pushing back his chair, he stood, leaning over to offer one to André, who took it gingerly, then to Auguste, who accepted his, studying it with curiosity. He laid one by François's plate, and held up the last one, "For myself," then smiled. "Now we're fully protected."

Isabeau didn't bother asking why he hadn't one for her.

"There's no full moon, also," Auguste chimed in. "So we're doubly safe."

"I assure you, young Aubert." François injected a patronizing tone into his voice, the wise adult calming a much younger person. "There's nothing to fear. No *loup-garou* resides in my home, and these herbs are unnecessary." As if he realized he might be insulting the boy, he added, "However, your concern for your brothers' welfare and my own is appreciated."

He dipped his head in a bow, to which Aubert gave one in answer.

"I hope your father hasn't bandied that thought about," François went on, as if just thinking of it. "That there's a *loup-garou* in the vicinity, I mean. It could cause an unnecessary panic, you know."

"Don't worry, *seigneur*."

François beamed at his use of that last word.

"Papa spoke to us discreetly. He laughed as he did so, assuring us he knew the gypsy lied to merely frighten his audience. *A theatricality*, he said." Aubert lowered his voice, nodding wisely, man to man. "He didn't even tell *Maman*. A woman's frail sensibilities, you know."

Surprisingly, Isabeau felt no anger at that remark, but merely a bit of amusement at the boy's naïveté. *Oh, my dear Aubert, you have so much to learn about women.*

"I suppose I really should be upset with both you and Papa." Shaking a finger, André directed his words to François as silence settled over the table.

"Why's that, Your Lordship?"

"Because you didn't take me with you. Saying I was too young." He pouted slightly, pursing his lips in an expression Isabeau imagined would win many a maiden's heart in a year or two more.

"I might say the same thing," Auguste put in.

Gervais came in with *pomme caramel*, two plates at a time, setting them before Pierre and Marie and leaving to fetch two more.

"Well ..." François was clearly at a loss as to how to reply to that. "One must go by what one's parent decrees," he finished, looking as if he hoped that was a safe answer.

"I believe I'm old enough to know what goes on in gypsy camps. He told me about how the *loup* ... I mean, your Giovanni mouth-serviced that girl, making her scream with passion. I'd like to have seen that. I've known women, so has Auguste."

He glanced at his brother, who began frantically shaking his head. André ignored him.

"So I don't see why I wasn't permitted to accompany you. Now, Aubert, I can understand his exclusion. He has yet to get even a hand under a wench's skirts—Ow!"

He broke off, glaring at Auguste.

"Why did you kick me?"

Auguste jerked his head in Isabeau's direction, then shook it. "The ladies ..." He spoke between gritted teeth.

Abruptly, his brother looked stricken, as if he'd been caught in some embarrassing behavior.

"Oh ... uh ..." André coughed, flushed slightly, and pushed back his chair, getting to his feet. "*Madame* Lascaux, *Madame* Isabeau, I apologize. That was an inappropriate subject matter to be spoken of before gently bred females. I hope you can forgive me for my lapse in manners."

"These things happen." Marie smoothly accepted his apology, gesturing for him to be seated. "It's only when the young don't learn from their mistakes that a problem occurs."

Properly chastised, André dropped into his chair, picked up his fork, and attacked his *pomme*.

"What shall we wear tomorrow, *Maître* François?" Auguste spoke into the ensuing silence, changing the subject.

The rest of the evening was uneventful. Isabeau spoke little, as did her mother, her father, and François, dominating the conversation. When she did speak, she thought her mother and father both gave her rather assessing looks. Her mother seemed particularly worried, she thought. Nevertheless, the evening went well. When they left, returning to the cottage by coach, Francois looked very satisfied.

As they arrived home to a dark and sleeping house, he said, "You'll go to the wolf."

"He's not a wolf," Isabeau reminded him. "You said so yourself."

"That was to calm a curious boy," he retorted. "We both know what he is, and we'll all be wearing that herb whenever we're in his company, thanks to young Aubert. Now then, you'll go to him and tell him about the boys and impress upon him how he must behave."

"May I take him some food? A well-fed wolf is less apt to look on those around him as a meal." She spoke sardonically.

His expression said he hadn't thought of that, in his desperation to make Giovanni's gaunt and half-starved appearance return. He made a permissive gesture. "See if Mathilde has any scraps. I'm going to bed."

* * *

MATHILDE AND MAXIME were already asleep, and Isabeau wasn't about to awaken them. She found some slices of fat with streaks of meat running through them, set aside by the cook to render into cooking oil for preparing some foods in a new way she'd heard about—immersing battered pieces in hot fat and frying them. She picked up the entire plate, carrying it with her without so much as a qualm of conscience for thwarting Mathilde's culinary plans.

Giovanni might've been asleep, but by the time she got the door open, he was on his feet.

"I've brought you some food," she greeted him, holding out the platter.

He snatched it from her hands, reached for a strip, then

185

hesitated. Whirling, he dropped onto the cot as she'd taught him.

She was glad he remembered. She held up the lantern so he could see, then looked away as he thrust a hand into the strips, shoveling them into his mouth.

She kept her head turned away until the sound of chewing ceased, and he asked, "*Maîtresse*, did you bring me a kerchief?"

She looked back. His mouth was smeared with a greasy sheen blending into a red stain.

"The frightened servant took my other away." As he spoke, bits of fat slid from his lower lip, dripping back onto the plate.

"His name is Maxime." Isabeau swallowed, feeling her gorge rise slightly.

He shrugged. "He's still frightened, whatever his name."

"I'm sorry. I didn't bring a table kerchief." She pulled her handkerchief from her sleeve. "Here, use this."

Bandages, table kerchiefs ... her poor handkerchiefs were being used for everything except their true function. She thought of the bloodstained one now stuffed in the rag basket.

He accepted it, scrubbing at his mouth, then his hands, wiping each finger carefully until no evidence of his bloody meal remained. When he held out a plate and a handkerchief, she accepted them back, taking the square of muslin gingerly between thumb and forefinger and dropping it onto the greasy surface.

"Twice now he feeds me," he said, holding up his hand, with thumb and fore fingers raised. "See, I count them ... one, last night, for being good wolf and bringing herb." His lips twisted sardonically. "And two, tonight, for ... doing what?"

"I'm glad you've remembered your lessons," she said. "The boys will be here tomorrow, and François will begin his preliminary sketches. He wants you to behave. He ..." She hesitated, then decided to simply say it. "He thinks to keep you well-fed and that, plus the wolfsbane will prevent you from harming anyone."

"I not harm anyone as long as moon not full." He shrugged. "When that happen, can't promise." He shook a finger, giving her a surprisingly teasing look. "Best keep wolf herb nearby then."

"I suppose that's all I can ask," Isabeau muttered, startled by his manner and how it was slowly changing. Where did the cowering creature go? "Just behave yourself. Please."

"These are the boys you tell me about? Those not like me?"

She nodded. He also seemed to have very good recall of their conversations.

"How do I act around them?"

His diction was changing; also, sentences were more fluid, and his French was not as broken.

She set the plate on the end of the cot, preparing to explain.

"Don't speak unless spoken to. Be polite—that means saying 'yes' and 'thank you' and such. When you're introduced, simply bow and say, 'Your Lordship' ... no, wait ... that's not right."

"I not say 'Your Lordship?'" He looked puzzled.

"No, I mean ..." She remembered only André had a title. "André is the oldest. He's a *vicomte*, so you say '*Vicomte* la Chapelle' to him. To Auguste and Aubert, you simply bow, say 'Lord' and use their names."

He got to his feet, dipping his head slightly, "*Vicomte* la Chapelle." Then again, "Lord Auguste. Lord Aubert. Like that?"

"That's perfect. Do it that way and François will have no complaint."

"What I do if I introduced to woman?" he wondered.

"I doubt if that's going to happen." Surely, François wouldn't think of pairing him with one of his female models for another painting. Would he? Isabeau realized she didn't like that thought.

"But if it did?" he persisted.

"Then, say '*Madame*' or 'My Lady'." She spoke reluctantly. "If she's an unmarried woman, you take her hand and bow over it."

"How I know that?"

"She won't be wearing a ring." She held out her hand, tapping her finger. "Here."

"Bow. Like this?" He caught her hand, dark head hovering.

He cradled her fingers gently. She thought of how roughly François had seized her hand as he shouldered Gervais out of the way and pulled her from the coach.

Giovanni glanced up at her. "And if she married?"

"In that case, y-you ..." Abruptly, she couldn't concentrate. He was so close, she could've placed her hand on those unkempt curls, touched his whiskered cheek. She forced her thoughts into order. "You take her hand and kiss it."

"Kiss," he repeated. "How?"

"You touch your mouth to the back of her hand."

"Bite? That allowed?"

"No, you don't bite." Of course, he might think that. She hurried to correct what she'd said. "You simply ..."

"Lick? Use my tongue like I did with Mariah?" he suggested, frowning.

"Merciful God, no!" Isabeau let her shock show. "*Never* do that."

"Then, how ..."

"Like this." Desperately, she caught his face in her hands and pressed her mouth to his, briefly, only a peck of a kiss, but enough.

Heat surged through her. Giovanni didn't move. She

wanted to stay that way forever, but forced herself to release him and pull away.

She straightened. They stared at each other. He looked startled and confused.

"But on the hand, not the mouth," she added weakly. She released him.

He immediately raised her hand and brushed his lips across her fingers, a little awkwardly, but properly. She closed her eyes, drew in a long, slow breath, and held it. When he didn't release her hand, she pulled it reluctantly from his grasp.

"You do that to me before." His voice was filled with sudden wonder, as if he'd just understood something that until that moment had been a mystery. "You kiss me."

"No," she denied. "I never ..."

"Twice," he argued, shaking his head and holding up two fingers. "The night *Maître* François strike you. Then, when I sleep in the forest. Why you do that, mistress?"

"I don't know!" She backed away, leaving him staring at her, startled by her response. "I don't know and don't ask me again."

Grabbing the plate, she spun and ran for the door, slamming it and locking it behind her.

Under the shelter of the walkway roof, Isabeau paused.

Dear Lord, I love him. The admission shocked and frightened her. *How could this happen? What must I do?*

Leaning against one of the roof supports, she began to sob, very quietly.

From inside the studio came a low growl and a single harsh ripping, as of a claw being dragged across a wooden surface. Giovanni had heard her despair and responded with his own confusion.

Chapter Fifteen

THE BOYS ARRIVED PROMPTLY the next morning. Isabeau greeted them in the hallway as Maxime ushered them inside while the coach rattled on its way back to the *château*.

"*Madame* de Montaigne." André took her hand, bowing and kissing her fingers.

Immediately, she was reminded of Giovanni's gesture the night before. She made her hand lie still in André's.

Auguste and Aubert did the same. Though it was a courtesy she deserved, even coming from well-mannered strangers and not her husband, it made her feel awkward. To cover that sensation, she forced herself to smile at the three.

All three youngsters were again dressed in the height of fashion, in finery so rich she was dazzled. In her homely, everyday gown and not her fine hand-me-down, she felt drab in comparison. She was also a little disturbed that each had the wolfsbane pinned to the chest of his doublet.

"Where is *Maître* François?" Auguste asked, looking around.

"He's in his studio setting up," Isabeau replied. "Come, I'll take you there, but first …"

She placed a hand on André's arm, detaining him. "A word, Your Lordship."

"What is it, *Madame*?" He looked down at her.

She drew him away from his brothers, who were momentarily distracted by examining a statuette on the hall credenza. "Surely you aren't going to be painted wearing that ridiculous herb?"

"I was of the opinion we shouldn't, especially after our discussion with *Maître* François last night, but Aubert was insistent." Immediately, André affected a superior, older brother's attitude, laying the blame on his youngest sibling. "You know how children are. It was the only way to quiet him, so ..."

"Aubert's young and I'm certain still believes in goblins and fairies." She lowered her voice as she'd heard her mother do, ridiculing some idea of her brothers' while appearing not to. "However, it isn't good for him to have you always give in to his whims, you know."

"You're right." His expression changed to a decisive one. Seizing the sprig, he pulled it from his doublet, ripping off most of the leaves in the process. They fell to the floor. Luckily, they were now so dry that no sap leaked out.

Before the others knew what he intended, he reached over and removed their herbs, also.

"Here now, what are you doing?" Aubert demanded, trying to take it from his hand.

"I'm getting rid of this show of childish superstition," André declared in his most adult-sounding tone. "It's an embarrassment to those of us who are now man-grown." He included Auguste in that statement.

There was a salver resting on a credenza by the door. He dropped the herbs into it.

"*Madame* François, would you see that these are disposed of and save us from further humiliation?" He glanced at Aubert, whose lower lip thrust itself into a pout. "No argument."

The boy stayed silent.

Relieved that she'd successfully rid them of the wolfsbane and therefore saved Giovanni from potential harm, if at the cost of Aubert's good nature, Isabeau led them through the house to the back walkway and the studio where François waited.

He was impatient to get to work. With a greeting effusive but bordering on curt, he immediately gestured to the model's platform, explaining how they were to stand, and the effect he wished to achieve.

Though she was ignored and effectively dismissed, Isabeau lagged behind. She'd never seen François at work and was curious.

"Where is your fourth model?" André asked, stepping onto the platform and immediately off again.

"Yes," Auguste chimed in, looking around. "Where is your beggar?"

François stopped his explanations. It was plain the boys were eager to meet Giovanni, and just as obvious, he was delaying bringing him out as long as possible. He glanced at Isabeau, seeming surprised she was still there.

"Fetch him."

François had given her a duplicate key, made during one of his trips to town. She saw how all three watched as she went to the storage room door and unlocked it, and could almost feel the question, *He keeps him locked away?*

Inside, Giovanni looked shockingly eager. "I heard them. They sound young."

"They are," she answered, lowering her voice so they wouldn't hear. "André is about your age, and the other two are younger. They mustn't see this." She reached up, removing the collar from around his neck and dropping it on the cot. "Giovanni, please be good."

He didn't answer but followed her into the studio.

There was a moment of complete silence as he emerged into their sight. The three stared. Giovanni returned their startled looks boldly, making Isabeau hope that wasn't going to anger François. It definitely wasn't the proper servile attitude. The silence lengthened, as each studied the other, weighing and deciding.

Their differences were such a disturbing contrast, it was a shock to the eye: the boys' beautiful clothing, their carefully trimmed locks and smooth cheeks, Giovanni's animal hide, his tangled curls and bearded face.

"*Maître* François, *this* is your beggar?" André's question came out slightly stifled.

François didn't answer. Instead, he glared at Isabeau, as if the question were her fault, somehow.

Raising her chin, Isabeau said, "Giovanni, this is his lordship, André du Maurier, *Vicomte* la Chapelle."

Giovanni didn't move. Isabeau dared place her hand against his back, prompting him with a slight shove.

"*Vicomte* La Chapelle." His bow was a little jerky and stiff, but good enough, she supposed.

"My lord, this is Giovanni di Casalupo."

André hesitated, then seemed to recover, replying with a sharp bow. "Is this your usual clothing?" He indicated the animal hides.

"Uh ..."

To Isabeau, Giovanni's expression said plainly he wasn't certain how to answer. Not giving him a chance to say more, she repeated the introduction to Auguste, and this time, Giovanni gave his own name as he bowed. At his supply table, she saw François lift an eyebrow, saying, *Who taught him to do that?*

As if he didn't know.

Aubert bowed also but then said, "*Il suo vestito è più elegante, signore.*"

Giovanni looked even more puzzled. "I'm sorry, I ..."

"*Maître* François told us you were from Italy, but you don't understand Italian?"

Giovanni glanced at Isabeau.

She had no idea what he was going to say and tensed.

He shook his head. "I left there very young. No longer remember the language."

"Then I apologize for being so officious." Aubert was very serious. "I merely wished to display my proficiency in your language. Excuse my pride."

"What did you say?" Giovanni dismissed his apology with a wave of his hand.

Poor ignorant, he doesn't know he should be begging Aubert's forgiveness for not remembering his former language, for making him explain, Isabeau thought with tolerant fondness. She was well aware that if someone other than one of the *marquis's* sons were present, Giovanni would've been lying on the floor, sent there by François's fist, while he railed at him for daring to be so impudent as to have a faulty memory.

"I merely complimented you on your quite stylish outfit." Aubert gestured at the animal hide. When Giovanni scowled and touched the loincloth, he added, "A jest," and smiled. "Though I'm surprised you're allowed to dress so ... oddly."

At the easel, François, busy with the canvas, his back to them, stiffened. Isabeau saw and tensed, too.

"Jest?" Giovanni gave Isabeau a sideways look. His expression cleared. He looked back at Aubert. "*Oui,* jest. A good one, no?"

She nodded, thankful there was a bare smell coming from

the hide now. The time spent away from Giovanni's body had given it a chance to air, and his baths had helped.

He glanced at François. "You must thank *Maître* François for that."

"Oh, it's your costume for the painting." Aubert laughed as he understood. He touched his *journade*, "As this is mine."

Isabeau was relieved to see François's posture relax.

There was a pause before Auguste spoke up, as if trying to prevent it from becoming awkward.

"Giovanni di Casalupo—a fine-sounding name, but too much to use among friends. Would you permit us to shorten it?" He looked slightly anxious as if about to say something impertinent, wondering if he was stretching the boundaries between his status and whichever Giovanni belonged to.

Giovanni frowned. He glanced sideways at Isabeau as if asking her what he should say. She raised her brows and gave a slight shrug. *Wait.*

"To call you ... Gio?"

"As you wish, *maîtres*." Giovanni bowed again.

"Good, then." August returned the bow. "From now on, we're merely Gio, Auguste, Aubert, and André. No titles."

"Aubert ... Your names all start with 'A,'" Giovanni noted.

"Yes," André agreed. "Our father's name also starts with that letter. Alphonse. It seems he was caught on the first letter of the alphabet when it came to naming his offspring." He laughed. "I suppose if we had a sister, she'd be called Annette or Alicia or something."

"Well and good." François's words cut impatiently into their laughter. It had been some time since he'd spoken, and his impatience to begin painting, as well as at not being the center of attention, was evident. "Introductions have been made. Let's get to work. Giovanni." Ignoring Isabeau, he jerked his head in a nod. "Get on the platform."

Giovanni obeyed. The other three crowded behind him. The brothers jostled each other, making remarks while Giovanni stood silently to one side, waiting to be told what to do.

François set about posing each one. He pushed the boys around, positioned them here, moved an arm there, but he simply spoke to Giovanni, directing him verbally and curtly. If the others noticed how he never came near or touched him unless he had to, they didn't comment. They were too busy being caught up in the wonder and excitement of *being painted*.

François had set a stack of baskets and hemp bags on the back edge of the platform. It was to be a marketplace scene, he explained, and should look as if the beggar had slept amidst them and knocked some over. He would fill in the rest of the background from his imagination.

With relief, Isabeau noted the basket of wolfsbane wasn't among them.

André, Auguste, and Aubert stood on the opposite corner. André and Auguste faced Giovanni, while Aubert had his back to him. He held a bunch of grapes that François handed him from the ever-present fruit compote. Aubert held it aloft while André was ordered to reach for it, playfully teasing his brother that he'd take his prize. Meanwhile, Auguste watched and bit into a croissant, which he did with relish, chewing enjoyably.

"My compliments to your cook, *Maître* François. This is quite tasty."

"Don't eat it all, dunce," André cautioned. "It has to last the life of our posing."

Behind them, Giovanni raised his arms in supplication, wielding a begging bowl. François had to touch him for that, and he did it quickly.

Isabeau was thankful the boy grasped what he was to do, so François didn't have to linger near him.

"Look hungry. They're enjoying food you wish you had," François told him, "but will never get."

Giovanni had only been fed twice since François returned from his second trip to La Chapelle. *How much of that hungry, beseeching look on his face was real, and how much pretense?* she wondered.

Once he had the scene set, François retrieved his sketch pad and charcoal. It was only then he realized Isabeau still stood in the doorway. "Why are you still here? Go, so I can begin work."

Reluctantly, she went out.

"Shut the door," he called, so she pushed it closed.

Isabeau went back into the cottage, where she would spend the rest of the day anxiously hoping everything went well.

With his audience absent, François made several sketches, getting various aspects of the same scene by moving about the room and viewing them from different angles.

That went on for some time while the sun climbed overhead toward noon. Several times, the boys fidgeted. Once or twice, they spoke, complaining of boredom. Each time, François politely reminded them they had to be quiet and still. Giovanni didn't move, not once, making a sound.

At last, François moved back to the easel, saying, "While I look over these and decide on the one giving the best view of what I wish to portray, you may rest a few moments."

He laid the sketch pad upon the table.

"*Merci, Jesu,*" André gasped, lowering his hand from its reach for the grapes. He flexed his fingers and rubbed his biceps through his sleeve. "I vow my arm was beginning to go numb, being held over my head like that."

"I'm afraid I took several bites out of my pastry," Auguste confessed, chewing and swallowing. He laid the remnant of the croissant on the table beside the compote and gave the fruit a longing look. "I fear hunger got the best of me."

"Mathilde will be bringing more pastry and fruit," François replied, not looking up from his sketches. "We will have a light repast before we start up again."

"While we wait, may we go outside and get some fresh air?" Aubert asked.

At an absent nod from François, they trooped out. Giovanni stayed where he was. Aubert looked back.

"Gio? Aren't you coming?"

"Master?" He didn't move, looking at François.

"Go ahead, I suppose." François didn't look up.

Scrambling to his feet, he ran to follow.

Chapter Sixteen

Outside, Aubert dropped to the porch's ledge, sitting in much the same spot Isabeau had the day she let Giovanni run through the grass. Auguste leaned against a roof support and looked across the unkempt field of grass and flowers. André paced back and forth, flexing his arms as if he feared they might grow stiff if he didn't keep moving. Giovanni hovered behind them, uncertain what to do.

"Here." Aubert looked up and gestured, slapping the plank beside him. "Sit with me."

He dropped gingerly onto the boardwalk.

"Let me apologize again for committing such a *gaffe*," the boy said.

"It was nothing." Giovanni felt that it was safe enough.

"No, it wasn't," Aubert insisted. "It made me appear I was aiming for superiority, and that wasn't my intent." He looked curious. "Do you truly not remember your own language?"

"Not a word." As far as Giovanni knew, that was the truth.

No one in the gypsy camp had ever spoken Italian to him. While they roamed through the country before traveling into France, none of the curious ever got close enough for him to hear the language. It was only the French who'd been brave enough to let him hear their speech.

There was a slight pause, broken when Auguste, who'd wandered nearer and heard Giovanni's last remark, asked, in a jocular tone, "How did you come to be with the gypsies? Did they steal you from your parents?"

He shook his head. "My parents sold me."

"What?" Aubert was aghast. He actually went pale. "You're joking."

"*Sacre*," Auguste said. "Why?"

Giovanni shrugged. He had enough caution not to tell them more of the truth, wondering if even saying this much might anger François if he heard. "I suppose they needed the money."

"That's atrocious." Aubert was incensed. "Reprehensible."

"I knew gypsies stole children, but ..." André began to laugh. "Best watch it, Aubert. If they buy children, Papa might decide to rid himself of a certain pesky younger son." He shook a finger. "Think of that next time you anger him."

Glaring at his brother, who was always gibing at him and telling him such things, Aubert changed the subject. "I'm glad there are large windows letting in the sunshine. Is a glass ceiling a usual thing in a studio?"

"An artist needs all the light he can get," André, the know-it-all, answered.

"Be that as it may, it's good to get outside into *real* sunlight." Aubert ignored him.

"Perhaps we should suggest *Maître* François move his studio outside," Auguste spoke up. "Then he'd get all the sunlight he needs and so would we."

"As well as plenty of pesky insects." André swatted at a horsefly as it flew around his head, then buzzed away. "I think we'd best not say anything. We don't want to appear as if we're telling him how to paint."

"*Le bon Dieu* forbid," Auguste murmured. "Since none of us know anything about being an *artiste*."

"We'll have to return to posing soon, so we should make the best of this leisure time and not simply sit here," Aubert said. "We should do something. What's your pleasure, Gio?"

"My pleasure?" Giovanni looked puzzled. "When I'm outside?"

Aubert nodded.

He had no idea. Being in a cage most of his life, unsheltered as it was from sun and the weather, he was *always* outside. Since leaving the gypsies, he still wasn't free. He was still imprisoned, only now inside the storage room.

What would you like to do if you were really free? Is that what Aubert means? He thought it over, remembering how good it felt as he galloped through the grass. "I like to run."

"Run?" Aubert repeated. "You mean, as in foot races?"

"Yes." Giovanni hoped he was answering properly. He had no idea what a *foot race* was.

"Are you very fast?"

"I think so." He knew he was faster than Isabeau. Her skirts made her slow and clumsy. He was also certain he could outrun François if he had to. *The master is big, and that makes him lumbering, like a trained bear.*

"Aubert's fast, too," Auguste put in. "When we have outdoor *fêtes* and include athletic games, he always wins."

"Why don't we have a race now?" Aubert got to his feet. "Between you and me?"

"Oh, I ..." Giovanni wasn't certain that it would be a good idea.

Aubert ignored his protest. "I'll race you to the turnoff to the highroad and back." As he spoke, he stripped off his doublet, dropping it to the porch, then rolled up his sleeves.

"I'll call," André offered.

"Very well." Giovanni's answer was unenthusiastic.

He walked over to where Aubert stood, and they aligned themselves. André crossed before them, dragging one foot, digging a small trench in the dirt.

"That's the finish line." He stepped aside.

At his "Ready, set, go!" they raced to the turn and back. Aubert was a good runner, starting off with a burst of speed. His legs were as long as Giovanni's, and at the start they ran evenly together, but before they reached the turnoff, Giovanni was in the lead. As they spun and started back, he raced ahead by a length, then two. When they arrived back at the porch, Giovanni was ahead by five lengths.

"That was amazing," André gasped as he brought down his hand behind Giovanni, signaling he'd crossed the dirt furrow first.

"And looked like fun," Auguste added, staring at his puffing younger brother, who slowed and simply walked the rest of the way. Now he was bent over, hands resting on his knees. "Can you survive a second go-round, Aubert? I'd like a try. Gio, how about it?"

Still attempting to be affable, Giovanni nodded. Auguste took off his doublet also, dropping it atop Aubert's.

As the three lined up before the porch, André said, "Wait. I want in on this, too."

He struggled with the buttons on his doublet, added it to the others, then positioned himself beside Giovanni. "Ready? One … two …"

Giovanni won that round as well. He was barely winded. The others huffed and puffed.

While they were congratulating him with a pounding of shoulders and shouts, François came onto the porch.

"If you young gentlemen are finished with your display of speed …?"

* * *

WHILE THEY WERE OUTSIDE, Mathilde brought in a tray of fresh fruit, cheese, bread, and wine.

They fell upon it, eating as if they were starving. Seeing several replacements for his croissant, Auguste devoured the pastry he'd sneaked nibbles from the entire morning. When Aubert saw Giovanni holding back and not partaking, he tossed him an apple.

Neither saw François's grimace that the boys were including the *loup-garou* in their luncheon.

As if sensing François's disapproval, Giovanni retreated to the storage room door with the apple. He ate slowly, merely smiling when Aubert urged him to join them, shaking his head and staying where he was.

Auguste teased him about biting into the apple as if he'd never tasted the fruit before. He wasn't about to say he hadn't. When André poured the wine, then noted there were only four cups, Aubert piped up, "Gio needs one. Do you have a cup, Gio? Is there one in your room?"

When the boy disappeared inside and returned holding the tin cup, Isabeau left with the water pitcher; François's scowl deepened.

André filled the cup. Giovanni accepted it, then abruptly saw his master's expression. Waiting until none of the three were looking, he sniffed at the liquid. It stung his nose, but pleasantly, and he'd like to taste it, but the look on his master's face suggested it would be well if he didn't.

Judiciously, Giovanni set the cup upon the table, leaving it untouched. When he finished the apple, he placed the core beside the grape stems, cherry pits, and breadcrumbs decorating the tabletop next to the compote.

Having by this time finished his own repast, opened new

pots of paint, and cleaned his brushes, François called an end to their feast.

Like children returning to class, they muttered under their breaths as they arranged themselves again in their poses. François made a few changes and corrections, raising an arm a little higher, turning a head a bit more.

He worked until André called plaintively, "*Maître* François, I fear I must request a brief respite. I swear my bladder's bursting."

"My apologies, Your Lordship." François's gesture was brusque. He didn't want to stop, his enthusiasm and single-mindedness setting in, but for a necessity like this ... "The *privé* is behind the studio next to the paddock."

"I suggest we all go." With that, André ran out, and his brothers trooped after him.

Again, Giovanni stayed behind, holding his pose. François gave him a hard stare.

"What about you? I don't want you pissing on my studio floor."

Silently, the boy rose from his crouch and ran after the others in time to hear André gasp, "I can't make it to the *privé*."

His brothers agreed. At the edge of the *puit de cess*, they untied their codpieces and extracted their rods, pale and slender in the noon sun, aiming golden streams at the pit's stinking contents. A cloud of flies floated over the surface in a dark mass, buzzing loudly. Struck by the liquid, they fluttered into the air.

As Giovanni joined them, pushing the hide loincloth aside and adding his own contribution to the flow, Aubert glanced idly in his direction.

"*Sacre nom!*" His exclamation caused the others to jump. "Your rod. It's disfigured." He was so shaken, he didn't think to be discreet. "What happened?"

His cry startled Giovanni so much that the stream

slackened. With a shake, he started the flow again. Otherwise, he didn't react.

"What do you mean?" André asked. From where he stood, he couldn't see.

"His rod-sheath." Aubert's voice shook slightly. Now, he thought to whisper. "It's missing."

"For the Lord's sake!" Now it was André who was startled. "Gio, was it some accident at your birth?"

"The gypsies did it."

Giovanni's careless explanation shook them.

"Why?" André demanded, voice quivering.

"I not know. They simply get knife, hold me down and ..." Giovanni left the rest unsaid.

"That's monstrous. Barbaric," Aubert burst out. "I'm telling Papa to have the Watch hunt down those bastards and kill them."

"For a crime happening probably a long time ago?" André was a little more clear-headed. "You'll do no such thing." He looked at Giovanni. "It *was* long ago, wasn't it?"

"I barely remember now," Giovanni affirmed.

"Like you don't remember Italian?" He sounded as if he wished to be reassured of that.

Giovanni nodded, looking as if he didn't understand their reaction. He finished and tucked everything away, pulling the animal hide back into place.

"Why did they do it?" André wondered. "The only people I've ever heard of who do such a thing are the Jews. Are the gypsies Jews?"

"Gypsies are Rom." Giovanni had no idea what a *Jew* was. "I never heard of these Jews."

"Perhaps it was for the same reason they put you in a cage?" The boy struggled to find some cause for what he and his brothers considered an atrocity. "To make you more of an oddity for people to gawk at?"

"Perhaps." Giovanni shrugged.

"Tell me ..." André's tone changed, curiosity now getting the better of outrage. "Does it make a difference when you lie with a woman?" He lowered his voice. "Do wenches like *that*?" He nodded at the loincloth, then glanced away, as if uncertain he should even be looking in Giovanni's direction.

This time, the answer came slowly, as if he were thinking about it. In fact, Giovanni had no idea what a woman would've thought of his lack of foreskin. He gave what he hoped was a *safe* answer. "They ... they not complain."

An embarrassed silence settled, broken only by the buzzing of flies hovering over the pit.

"We should go back," Aubert spoke up. "The sunlight's going. I don't think *Maître* François will appreciate us standing here conversing about Giovanni's rod and its differences while we waste the daylight." He shook, lifted his codpiece and began to retie it.

As they returned, around the studio to the front, Aubert asked, timidly, "Did it hurt?"

Giovanni gave him a steady stare. "Truly, I don't remember."

"I suppose that's a small mercy then." The boy spun, running ahead. "Come on, the others are already inside."

Chapter Seventeen

At last, the light waned and François called the first session to an end.

"May we see?" André asked as he stretched and stepped from the platform.

"Yes, I'd like to see how I look in paint. Papa's not commissioned anyone to make our portraits yet." Auguste brightened. "Perhaps if this goes well, you could do that also, *maître*."

"I'm afraid you can't view the painting until it's finished." Surprisingly, François sounded sincerely apologetic. "It's bad luck to look upon an unfinished painting," he explained to Auguste's *moue* of disappointment. Carefully arranging a length of muslin over the easel's frame so the cloth didn't touch the surface, he continued, "I doubt supper is quite ready yet, so you've some time to relax before we eat."

"I've a wonderful idea what we can do to while the time," André said. "If you permit, *maître*?"

"What's that?" François asked.

"When we were at the *puits de cess*, I noticed you've a small lake with a stream running into it."

"Yes, I suppose." François wasn't about to show his ignorance of his own property by admitting he had no idea there was a lake or any kind of waterway, other than the spring filling the well.

"Stream run through woods," Giovanni put in, as if in reminder. "Make waterfall at grotto where you paint picture of Madonna."

"Is that so?" François gave him a glance, accusing him of showing off his knowledge. He didn't like the creature pointing out his master's unfamiliarity with the land around the cottage. Swallowing whatever emotion he was feeling, he looked back at André. "What is it you wish to ask about the lake, Your Lordship?"

"Would you give us permission to swim there and bathe away the sweat we worked up with our athletics earlier?"

"So, we won't offend *Madame* François?" Aubert added.

"The lake looks fairly sheltered by trees. I doubt anyone will see," André added.

François gave his permission. What else could he do? When Aubert said, "Giovanni, come on," however, he balked.

"Giovanni doesn't need—"

"He ran faster than any of us," the boy interrupted. "He won every race."

"Sir?" Giovanni looked at him hopefully. He bowed his head. In an undertone, so the others wouldn't hear, he said, "Please? I've been good."

"So you have." With a gesture, François sent him after the others. Going back into the cottage, he ordered Maxime to take four towels to the lake.

"Towels?" Isabeau asked. She came to the head of the stairs when she heard his voice. She watched the servant disappear down the hall to the laundry room, where cupboards held clean towels and linens. "Whatever for?"

"Our young guests are freshening themselves for dinner."

François's mouth twisted as if he couldn't understand the thought processes of the young, voluntarily wishing to *bathe*.

"You said *four* towels," she persisted.

"They insist the wolf bathes with them."

"François." Her voice was a sharp whisper. "Don't call him that."

"I suppose I shouldn't, since he's acting very human just now, but those youngsters are treating him too familiarly. I must remember to tell him not to get too comfortable in that role." He stamped into the salon. "When Maxime returns, have him come pour me some wine."

Obediently, Isabeau relayed the message to Maxime. As the servant went to the salon, she hurried upstairs, knowing François would be enjoying his wine too much to wonder where she was. He never showed any curiosity over what she did while he was painting, or when he was absent, for that matter. When absorbed in creating, he was completely oblivious to everything. Indeed, she often thought the entire cottage and the studio could burn down, and he would sit amidst the conflagration, calmly applying paint to canvas for as long as humanly possible.

The second bedroom was at the back of the cottage, giving a good view of the lake. Standing beside the window where it would be difficult for anyone to see her, should he look in that direction, she watched the boys splashing and swimming.

Not the boys, she may as well admit it. Her attention was on Giovanni.

Lack of clothing brought with it a return to childhood. The young nobles played and dunked each other, had a water fight, sending sparkling waves reflecting rainbows of sunlight into the air. After much hesitation and continued urging, Giovanni joined in, if somewhat awkwardly, as if he had no idea how to play. Soon, however, he was making as much noise as they.

His yelp of laughter could be heard all the way to the cottage, as water splashed and the others dodged.

Isabeau gave them a negligible glance. She drank in the sight of his sun-bright body as she would a draught of sweet water, as he lingered on the bank before leaping into the water.

Compared to Giovanni, they were pale and sickly creatures. His thinness made him ethereal, so beautiful, even that disfigured rod becoming something exotic ... unearthly ... as he dived and burst from the lake's depth in an uprush of water. He was a young Poseidon, needing only a bevy of mermaids floating around him instead of a trio of very human young men.

Isabeau gloried in the way the water dripped from those tangled curls and slid down his shoulders as he climbed onto the bank and whirled with arms outstretched, slinging droplets onto the grass. She envied the young nobles being so close to him.

Eventually, she saw Maxime walking across the grass to them and hurried downstairs, fearing he might glance up and somehow see her.

"Come, young masters, supper will soon be ready. Then *Maître* Lascaux's coach will be here to take you back to the *château*."

Clothing clinging slightly to damp skin, they trudged toward the cottage, Aubert and Auguste rubbing their towels industriously over wet hair. Giovanni walked behind them, empty-handed. Immediately upon appearing, Maxime had confiscated his towel, practically snatching it from his hands.

François stood on the walkway. "Hurry, Your Lordship," he called to André. "Supper will soon be served, and when you taste it, you'll surely not want it to get cold."

"Why can't we sleep here tonight, sir?" Aubert asked. He tossed the damp towel at Maxime. His brothers did the same, and the servant caught all three, draping them over his arm, on top of Giovanni's. "It would certainly be more convenient than all this traveling we'll have to do."

"I'm afraid my humble cottage is too small," François replied smoothly, not by a twitch revealing how much he hated admitting that. "Alas, we have only two guest bedrooms."

"Ha!" André swatted at his little brother. "That means I'd get one and you two would have to share." He gestured at Auguste.

"I? Sleep with Aubert?" Auguste looked mock-horrified. "No, never. He snores like a pig."

"I do not!" Aubert replied, incensed. He looked as insulted as only a fifteen-year-old could.

"I'd much prefer to ride the distance every day, even in that jouncing old coach, than suffer that." Auguste snorted, looking away and biting his lip to keep from laughing.

"François." Isabeau appeared in the doorway. "Supper's waiting."

"See? What did I say?" He stepped aside so their young guests could enter.

The boys charged inside, speaking pleasantries to her. Giovanni followed.

As he started to enter, François put an arm across the entrance, blocking his way. "Not you. Get back where you belong." He waved a hand in the direction of the studio.

Giovanni ducked, dodging as if expecting to be struck.

"*Oui, maître.*" He turned and went back down the passage to the studio.

"Isabeau, see to him," François said.

She didn't speak, but obeyed. She found Giovanni waiting at the storage room door.

All he said was, "I was good," as he went inside.

* * *

WHEN THEY WERE SEATED in the dining room, however, André said, "There are only five places set. Where's one for Gio?"

"Giovanni's a servant," François replied, stiffly. "He eats in his room."

"That place where he was this morning?" André still had no idea of Giovanni's true status in the household. "Does he sleep there, too? Not in the house with your other servants?"

"As I said," there was a slight grating to François's voice, as if he might be gritting his teeth, "the cottage is small. It has no true servants' quarters."

To anyone who knew François, it would've been obvious he was annoyed that the boys kept asking questions. Fortunately, they were too naïve to sense this. Isabeau wondered if she should be glad of that or angered, also, that they expected him to have as grand a place as their own home.

"My cook and manservant sleep in what would've been the creamery. Since they are married, it's only proper that Giovanni have a separate room. He uses that one off my studio."

"You must bring him in, *maître*, I insist," André said. "We like him. Besides, if he's to be our fellow model and stand with us as your subjects, he shouldn't be confined in that no doubt dreary room while we enjoy your cook's fine repast, as I'm certain it will be." As he saw François about to argue, his young voice turned hard, the only sign Isabeau had seen so far of autocratic behavior from a noble-in-training. Apparently, there was a thin streak of steel forming beneath that as yet soft and youthful exterior. "You wouldn't wish our father to be told you'd been unaccommodating, would you?"

"Of course not, Your Lordship." Worry that a wrong word from him might cause an even worse one from André or his brothers to their father, François had no choice but to obey.

Isabeau found an odd sense of justice in seeing her bully of a husband so subdued.

Nevertheless, he tried to rationalize his actions. "It's simply that I didn't wish to foist his presence upon you, but, since he seems to have found your favor ..."

"He has, indeed," Aubert confirmed brightly.

Maxime was called. There was a murmured conversation. The butler looked surprised but nodded and left.

The dishes had already been brought in, the dinner plates filled with a portion from each, minus the meats. There was to be no elaborate entrance of Maxime and Mathilde carrying each platter to the table. François had ordered that so the boys wouldn't be reminded he had fewer servants than his father-in-law.

"In the meantime, I'll serve the meat." He indicated the platter of ham slices and highly seasoned sausages and held out his hand for André's plate. "What is your choice, Your Lordship?"

Maxime reappeared with Giovanni, who hesitated in the doorway, interrupting André's answer. He was now dressed in the smock and stocks François had re-consigned to the rag basket. Apparently, François had instructed Maxime to dress as well as to retrieve him.

"The young masters wish you to dine with them." François indicated the table and the chair opposite where the three sat, adding under his breath, "Be properly grateful."

Giovanni glanced toward Isabeau, seated at the far end of the table in the mistress's chair. She smiled slightly, and that seemed to hearten him.

"*Merci, maîtres.*" He bowed to each.

André said, "Sit, Gio." His manner was still as friendly as before, but the gesture he made was that of a noble graciously granting a privilege.

Seizing the chair, Giovanni pulled it from under the table and dropped into it, still looking apprehensive and uncomfortable. He kept his head down, seemingly staring at the table, though his eyes were turned in Isabeau's direction.

She nodded encouragement.

Ignoring him, François continued doling out ham slices and sausage links to Auguste, Aubert, then Isabeau, and lastly himself.

Maxime brought in another plate.

When, with the barest hesitation, he set it before Giovanni, however, the boy stared at its contents, lips turning down before he could stop as he realized what it held.

Isabeau tensed, remembering his initial reaction to cooked food. *If he spits a mouthful onto my white tablecloth, it won't be only François who's angry.*

Giovanni didn't say anything, however; didn't complain or protest, but simply looked around with what she interpreted as a resigned glance, accepting he'd have to eat what he considered an unappetizing meal, or the others would want to know why.

Without speaking, François pared a rind of fat off a ham slice and dropped it onto the plate with a movement so quick it looked as if he'd tossed it. Laying down the carving knife and fork, he sat, turning his head slightly so he didn't look in the boy's direction.

Giovanni started to pick up the pork rind. As the others lifted their forks and began to eat, however, his resignation turned to dismay. He jerked his hand back as if it had been slapped.

He glanced in Isabeau's direction. Picking up her own fork, she held it a little higher than necessary. Giovanni's gaze went from her fork to the one Maxime had supplied with the plate. He picked it up, awkwardly balanced between thumb and forefinger, his gaze holding the question, *This one?* She inclined her head in the slightest of nods and stabbed the tines into one of the little carrots on her plate. He did the same, perhaps a little too forcefully, for juice spattered, but when he lifted it, at least the carrot stayed on the fork. He thrust it into his mouth, scowling at the unfamiliar taste, chewed and, with an obvious effort, swallowed.

Isabeau did the same, without Giovanni's evident dislike. It was a wonderful meal, she thought. No doubt urged by François, Mathilde had outdone herself: glacéd carrots, creamed turnips in butter sauce, and vegetable marrows cooked with thick slices of salted pork, as well as the platter of ham slices and sausages. If the cook continued food preparation in this vein, Isabeau told herself she would sorely miss the meals when the boys returned home.

Maxime served the wine, beginning with the master and going clockwise around the table. When he reached Giovanni, he again hesitated. François didn't comment, patently ignoring the boy as he lifted his own goblet. Maxime poured a bare quarter cup of wine into the wine glass, then took up his position near the buffet upon which he set the wine bottle.

Giovanni stared at the goblet for a long time before lifting it. As he had with the wine cup at luncheon, he sniffed at its contents.

André looked up. "It does have a fine bouquet, doesn't it?" He raised his own goblet and copied the gesture. "Taste it and tell me what you think."

Giovanni again glanced at Isabeau.

Has he ever had wine before? She hadn't had a chance to warn him about the effect of strong drink. She had no way of knowing how he'd earlier been offered wine by André and prudently set it aside.

With great reservations, she nodded her permission. Very

carefully, he took a sip. His brow wrinkled, lips pursing as he swallowed.

"Well?" André demanded, eager for his opinion.

"It …" Giovanni took a deep breath. "Very good." He took a second swallow and another long exhalation, smacking his lips. "Make heart beat faster."

"Very observant," André agreed, smiling. "It's a delicious stimulant." He raised his goblet in Giovanni's direction, then drank.

Giovanni copied the gesture and sipped again.

After that, everyone applied themselves to the meal, and there was no further conversation.

* * *

WITH PERFECT TIMING, the coach arrived as they were finishing dessert, so there was no adjournment into the salon, no awkwardness as to Giovanni being admitted, to get in the way and irk his master with his presence while they shared more wine, or attempted conversation, as was the custom with guests. Isabeau was certain François would've protested allowing the boy to have even a taste of his prized brandy, given to him by the *marquis*.

"We will see you Monday morning, *maître*." André bowed to Isabeau and turned to step into the coach, where his brothers waited. Raising a hand in farewell, he nodded at Giovanni, who'd followed them outside.

Isabeau glanced at him anxiously. Though the wine in his goblet had barely been four swallows, he looked sleepy, standing docilely to one side, lifting one hand in answer to André's gesture, and accompanying it with a drowsy smile.

"Monday?" François spoke up. "Not tomorrow? My lord,

one can't pick and choose the days one wishes to pose for a painting."

"Tomorrow's the Sabbath. Did you forget?" André climbed into the coach, settling himself. "Would you have us forgo worship to stand on that platform?"

"Worship?" François did an immediate mental backstep. "Of course not, Your Lordship. I vow, wife." He glanced at Isabeau and laughed, though to her it was an obviously false and hasty sound. "I was so caught up in the excitement of painting, I let the day slip my mind." He looked back at André. "You're correct, Your Lordship. The painting can wait. Paying homage to Our Lord and hearing the good father's sermon is more important."

Gervais pushed the coach door shut and climbed to his seat. The coachman raised the reins, and they clattered away.

François lifted a hand in farewell. Under his breath, he muttered, "Thank God he didn't ask if I'd be there, too."

"You'd best have a good answer for Monday in case he asks you why you weren't," Isabeau reminded him.

He shot her a baleful glare.

Once the coach reached the entrance to the high road, François said, "Put him back in the storage room. *Now!*"

"What about his clothes?" she asked, and hid her smile as he allowed, with a grumble, "May as well let him keep them. I'm certain those three pests will demand he eat with us as long as they're here. You'd think, as a *marquis's* children, they'd have a better sense of the demarcation of classes."

If they did, she thought, *they wouldn't sit at the same table as you.* She didn't say that aloud.

Once again in the storeroom, Giovanni gave her a heavy-lidded stare, asking plaintively, "Did I do well, mistress?"

Isabeau was filled with a sense of pity. He looked distressingly hopeful, wanting to be assured he'd done nothing to warrant François's ire. Though her husband had successfully hidden his displeasure from his patron's sons, she knew François so well she could feel his anger. She was certain Giovanni had also sensed his vexation.

Didn't all canines have that heightened ability, able to perceive anger, fear, and other emotions even if they didn't show?

"Yes, Giovanni. You were as well-behaved as possible."

"Why is the master angry, then?"

"He's not angry ..."

"Mistress, don't lie." His reprimand was as soft as the sadness in those dark eyes. "He's furious. I smell it on him. He want to throw me out, hit me, but something stop him. Lord André, I think. He not want him to know how he feel. Why?"

"Yes, he was angry." With a sigh, she admitted it. No use lying. As she'd thought, Giovanni could sense not only hidden anger but lies as well. "But not at you," she explained. "It's because he was forced to do something he didn't want."

"Having me there?" he guessed. "But I not ..."

"The boys angered him, but he doesn't dare say so. They are nobles, and he has to do as they say, young as they are. That means he'll take his anger out on someone else."

"As long as it not you, mistress."

"Don't worry about me." He looked so earnest, so sweet in his caring, she wanted to sob but knew that might upset him more, especially when she couldn't explain why she cried. "You know, I think I like the name His Lordship gave you. Gio. I'm going to call you by that, too. Gio," she repeated, as if it should sound different when *she* spoke it.

There was a moment's silence. She wondered if her decision upset him, and that was his way of telling her.

Then, he said, slowly and shyly, not looking in her direction but with head bowed, "I like when you say it, mistress." As if uncertain he should have admitted that, he sighed loudly, placing a hand against his middle. "I thought that food make my belly hurt."

Thinking he was complaining, she said, "I'm sorry you had to eat cooked food tonight."

"It was good. Surprise me. Drink good, too. Burn a little at first, then make me sleepy." As if to point this out, he yawned widely, revealing those very sharp-looking incisors.

Or were they? Surely they weren't as wicked and fang-like as before.

"You must be careful when you drink wine," Isabeau cautioned. "It can do more than make you sleepy."

"Oh?" He looked curious. "What?"

"Never mind." She didn't have time to go into that now. François was waiting in the cottage, filling himself with more wine as he sat alone in the salon, congratulating himself on the success of the first day's session in spite of the things he'd had to allow against his will. She had to get back before he drank too much, for his drunkenness always brought on a surge of lust. "If you're offered any more, merely sip it, and never empty the cup. I have to go now."

"Wait, mistress." He leaned toward her.

For a terrifying, hoped-for moment, she thought he was going to kiss her.

Instead, he caught her hand, brushing his lips awkwardly across her fingers, then released them. Reluctantly, Isabeau pulled away. She went through the door, pressing that hand against her breast as if to keep the lingering sensation of his mouth upon it.

She found François relatively sober and decided to keep him that way, preventing him from drinking more by bringing up a subject she thought of as she watched Giovanni struggle through the meal.

"I suppose I should teach Giovanni how to act at table."

"Why?" He snorted, reaching for the wine decanter. Tonight, since it sat within easy reach on the table by his chair, he had decided to serve himself, for Maxime was nowhere in sight. "He certainly isn't going to eat at my table after les du Mauriers leave."

"I meant, so he'll have some purpose after your St. Jean is finally finished, of course."

"I think his fate's settled as far as that." His leer told her he hadn't forgotten what he said he'd do when Giovanni was no longer needed.

"Don't spin me that lie that you're going to kill him." She decided to say what she felt, to be forceful for a change, and call his bluff. "After the St. Jean is placed in the church, he'll be too recognizable." She threw in a little flattery. "This will truly be your masterpiece, François, and people will enquire after him, perhaps want to meet your St. Jean. What will you say when he's nowhere to be found?" She took a breath. "If something untoward should happen, I won't hesitate to tell the Watch."

"They won't believe you," he bluffed.

"Men have been arrested and convicted on little more than someone's testimony, with no other evidence," she replied.

"I don't doubt you would." His expression changed, showing he knew what she said was true. In some cases, all it took was one man accusing another for a guilty verdict to be rendered. "What's come over you, Isabeau? Showing these little sparks of rebellion? Has that creature bewitched you somehow?"

"Nonsense," she hurried on. No need to put that thought in his head. "I'm simply showing Christian concern for a fellow being."

There was nothing Christian about the emotion Giovanni engendered in her. It might be liberally described in the Bible, but it was to be deplored, for there was not a jot of holiness about it. Her emotion was purely profane. It was the desire the angels experienced when they looked on the daughters of Men, that burning lust, making them fall from Grace.

She desired the *loup-garou*, and that was all there was to it, even if she could never admit it lest she condemn herself and Giovanni with her. He might be an innocent, but he was a temptation as great as any apple plucked from the Tree. His broken French was as tantalizing as the knowledge whispered by the Serpent into Eve's ear, his undernourished body sensual in its gauntness. She wanted to hear him speak to her of forbidden acts, to feel his slim body writhing against hers.

Isabeau forced those thoughts from her mind, stifled the desires her thoughts brought to life, and said to her husband, "After your St. Jean is completed, surely you'll need him for other paintings."

"True, I can still use him as a model," he agreed and looked thoughtful. "I wouldn't have to pay him, so it'd save money."

"Otherwise, he'll make a good servant."

"Doing what?" He plainly thought Giovanni's usefulness didn't extend past the studio door.

"Doing the tasks Maxime can't—or won't."

"Such as?" François looked as if he'd never heard of Maxime shirking his duties.

"Caring for your horse." Isabeau didn't have to think about it. "Maxime is terrified of the creature. He cringes whenever it looks at him."

Unawares, she'd observed Maxime as he fed the horse. He'd actually poured the grain over the paddock fence onto the ground instead of going inside and putting it in the feed trough.

"Giovanni can also serve at table. Once the St. Jean is on display, patrons will come beating on our doors. We'll have more guests." She appealed to his vanity. "Won't it look better for you to have a butler *and* a footman?"

François looked thoughtful but didn't respond.

Isabeau kept talking, trying to give as many reasons as possible, not allowing him time to think of why he shouldn't allow Giovanni to survive past the moment François scribbled his signature in the corner of the painting.

He waited a full minute before he answered, then said, as if it were his own idea, "I admit he may be useful. Very well. Teach the wolf how to be a servant. A neat trick, if you're able. But do it between sittings."

He didn't see Isabeau's smile. She could be more in Giovanni's company without her husband protesting. She felt a twist deep inside, but it wasn't fear. This time it was anticipation.

Chapter Eighteen

THE DAYS FELL INTO A ROUTINE.

The boys would arrive and be shown to the studio by Isabeau, though by now they knew the way and could've found it themselves.

While proper etiquette as well as mere civility demanded that those of a noble status be escorted, Isabeau could've left that courtesy to Maxime. After all, in his capacity as butler, it was more his duty to do so. She liked being in the youngsters' company; however, even for that short time, so was always present in the foyer when they arrived, telling the servant she'd take them to the master, making it sound like a favor.

As it neared time for the coach to appear, François always made certain Giovanni was out of the storage room and in the studio, already posed in his animal hides on the platform.

André always greeted Giovanni joyfully, inquiring about his night, as if he might've been out carousing or at some *festivités*. The first time that happened, François gave the boy a sharp and anxious glare, but Giovanni answered that his night had passed well enough. From then on, that became his standard answer in one form or another.

After that, the day would go as usual.

François painted until noon, allowing them a respite during which they sat on the porch and chatted. He had fretted that Giovanni would say the wrong thing, though Isabeau assured him otherwise. After a brief talk with Giovanni during which he threatened the boy with a beating if he spoke out of turn, François had the audacity to eavesdrop on several of their conversations. At last, deciding Giovanni was sensible enough not to say anything he shouldn't, he relaxed slightly.

After Mathilde brought in the fruit, cheese, and bread for their midday repast, they resumed their poses until suppertime neared. With the session over for the day, it was a hasty dip in the pond, and all trooped into the dining room. By this time, Giovanni automatically followed the others without their having to prompt him or give his master pointed looks.

François silently suffered his model at his table, though the glares he gave the boy when the others weren't aware were murderous.

"It's intolerable," he complained to Isabeau one night as they sat in the salon. "Not only my having to allow his presence at my table, but he's getting fat."

It was true. Though he never gorged himself as the others did, and still let Isabeau see he didn't like eating cooked food, with each of Mathilde's meals he ingested, Giovanni's hollow cheeks were filling out. Now, even his thickening beard couldn't hide the fullness of his face. His ribs were no longer visible through the animal hide he wore when posing. With each mouthful he took, his beauty also became more evident.

"How will I ever be able to paint him as an emaciated zealot?" He struck the arm of the chair with his fist. "I must put a stop to this; tell His Lordship he can no longer eat with us." His voice rose.

"If you do that," Isabeau reminded him, "you'll have to

explain to Lord André why, and what will you say? 'I wish him to be thin for my masterpiece, so I'm locking him away with no food until I starve the fat off him?'"

"Hm. You're right. That won't do." He looked thoughtful. "There must be a way ..."

He fell into a thoughtful silence, and a little later, got to his feet and left the salon.

"Where are you going?" Isabeau asked.

"For a ride." His reply floated back to her.

"At this time of night?"

He didn't answer.

"François?"

The only sound she heard was the door to the walkway opening and closing. Later, the horse's hooves pounded the path to the highroad.

When François returned, Isabeau was asleep, not having waited for his return when the hour grew late. As he entered the bedchamber, she awoke, however, asking, "Where have you been?"

"Finding a solution to my problem." He dropped into a chair and kicked off his boots.

"What does that mean? A solution, how?" she demanded, his words sending a sting of fear through her.

"Don't be a scold, wife." His answer was short. "You'll find out soon enough."

* * *

It had become the custom for Giovanni to return to the dining room after Isabeau and François saw the boys to the coach and on their way. There, he would help Maxime clear the table, though the servant put as much distance between them as possible, so Giovanni did most of the work. Afterward, Isabeau had him reset one place at the table, explaining about the various plates and silverware, and the fundamentals of how to serve. She expected Maxime would stay and assist her, adding to her explanations with his own contributions on waiting at table. That thought died a quick death as the servant backed away, stating, "I'm not getting near that *bête* any more than I have to."

No use complaining to François, of course. After that, Isabeau taught Giovanni alone, each night going over what he'd been told, and making certain he'd memorized everything he must do, as well as when and how to serve certain dishes and wines.

Afterward, he'd return to the storeroom where Isabeau would have him review his letters and numbers.

* * *

WITH THE ABSENCE of young du Maurier voices, the cottage was quiet. Isabeau sat at her place at the table while Giovanni pretended to pour wine, using an empty wine bottle.

She was explaining the various sizes of wine glasses and when each was to be used, when François appeared in the doorway. "I would speak to you, wife."

"Wait here." She broke off her explanation, going into the hall. "What do you want, François?"

"When you put the wolf away for the night,"—he ignored the protesting shake of her head as he said that—"give him this." He held out a small phial holding powder. "Pour it into a cup of water and have him drink it."

"What is it?" Isabeau made no move to take the little container. "Is it to make him sleep? He's behaving and has been quiet at night. You don't need to do that."

"Nothing like that. It's only a compound I got from the

leech." His tone was careless. "That's where I went last night. To keep him healthy. I thought, after his ill-treatment ..." He left the rest of the sentence unsaid, thrusting the little bottle at her.

When she still didn't move, he caught her hand, slapping the phial onto her palm and closing her fingers around it.

"See that he drinks it all." He turned away, stalking into the salon. "Do as I say."

Isabeau held up the phial, studying its contents. The powder was pale yellow, looking like so much sawdust. *What is this? Surely it isn't a poison.*

After all his complaints, she thought François's concern for Giovanni's welfare odd. She might even call it suspicious, considering how he treated the boy. François had promised he wouldn't harm him. Nevertheless, a little voice deep inside whispered, *He's broken promises before.*

Clutching the bottle, she returned to the dining room where Giovanni waited.

"That's enough for tonight." She gestured and went out.

He followed, not speaking until they were inside his room.

"You're worried."

"No, I ..." She stopped. Why deny it? She should know by now that he could sense when she lied. "Yes, I am."

"What did the master say?"

Briefly, she was struck by how well he now spoke. His association with the young nobles was paying off in more ways than one. "He's still unhappy about you eating with us."

That was no lie. She hoped he didn't persist in asking more, that he couldn't sense a half-truth.

He accepted her answer, sitting down on the cot. The blanket was tossed carelessly across its foot. She wondered if he'd finally abandoned the floor in exchange for sleeping in that semblance of a real bed, a concession to being human.

"You handle the dinnerware easily," she said.

"Why shouldn't I?" He frowned. "Is it so unusual?"

"For a supposed *loup-garou*? Yes," she answered. "Don't you know silver is deadly to …" She wouldn't say 'to you.' "… someone of that ilk?"

His laugh was more of a snort. "I suppose no one told me. I must remember to act more afraid next time I pick up a spoon."

"Don't you dare." She couldn't tell if he jested or not.

"Did you ever think it might not be true?" She didn't answer. It had never occurred to her that the beliefs muttered about *loup-garou* might be false.

"As for being a 'supposed *loup-garou*?' I'd hope you never truly witness the truth." His eyes met hers. "I fear one day you may, mistress."

There was a silence. Isabeau's hand tightening around the phial reminded her of its presence. She asked, "Are you thirsty?"

"I'm always thirsty," he answered. "Cooked food does that."

"Mathilde does have a heavy hand with the seasonings, doesn't she?"

Glancing at the phial again, she told herself she had to believe whatever François planned, it wasn't to harm Giovanni. She also knew it wouldn't go well for her if she didn't use the powder. What would follow that, when Giovanni saw the result of her husband's anger at being disobeyed?

He'll attack François and probably kill him, and then …

She couldn't let that happen. Better to give Giovanni the powder and hope it didn't make him ill. She looked around for the water pitcher she insisted on keeping filled. It sat on the windowsill, the cup beside it.

She picked up the pitcher, pouring water into the cup. With her back to him, she uncorked the phial. Some caution made her shake only half its contents into the water. Briefly, the yellow grains floated on the surface, then sank to the bottom of the cup as they dissolved. Isabeau slid the little bottle into her pocket.

By the time she turned back to face Giovanni, the powder was well mixed with the water.

Still uneasy, she held out the cup. "Here."

He accepted it, raised the cup, then hesitated. Instead of drinking, he sniffed the water's surface.

"What is it?" Isabeau's heart sank. *Oh Lord, he can smell the powder*.

"Water smells different." He held out the cup. "I don't want it."

"Nonsense." She pushed the cup back to him. *What will I do if he refuses?* "Your nose is probably filled with the scent of all that garlic, pepper, and other spices Mathilde uses." She put more force into her voice. "*Drink*."

He held the cup a moment longer, then gulped down the water, handing it back to her. She marveled at his trust in her, that he'd drink something he was certain was unwholesome simply because she assured him otherwise. That made her feel even more traitorous.

"Get some sleep," she ordered, but this time made her tone softer and smiled. "Some of that uneventful sleep you've spoken of to Lord André."

"*Oui*." His stare was thoughtful as he asked, with a remarkably satirical twist to his lips, "What do you think Lord André do if I say to him, 'My night fretful, Your Lordship, I not like sleeping locked in storeroom any more than I like sleeping in gypsies' cage?'"

"Gio, you wouldn't." Isabeau gave him a shocked stare.

"No," he agreed. "But I sometimes wonder." His look was frank. "I know what *Maître* François would do. Don't want him to hit me again."

Gently, she touched his cheek, turning his head and examining his jaw. She was glad the bruises had faded into his beard so they were barely noticeable. Otherwise, the boys might've questioned them and caused François more embarrassment as he tried to think of a reasonable explanation.

"I wouldn't want that, either."

To her surprise, he shook his head.

"It not hurt all that much. Boamas hit harder, but"—he lowered his voice—"warn you, mistress, if *Maître* hit me again, I kill him."

"Giovanni!" Her hand went over his mouth. She looked around, making certain the walkway door was closed. "Be careful what you say. Someone might hear."

"No one hear," he assured her. "I never say that when anyone but you listen."

"I know you didn't mean that—"

"*Oui*, I do," he assured her. His expression was so earnest she believed he intended what he said. "I'd have killed Boamas any of those times he beat me—if I could."

"You're not thinking," she said. "Do you know what would happen to you if you harmed your master?"

He shrugged. Either he hadn't thought that far ahead or simply didn't care.

"What would you do afterward?" she persisted. "You couldn't run away. The Watch would hunt you down."

Something in his expression made her think he didn't fear the Watch. All he said was, "Would it make you sad if *Maître* François was hurt?"

Isabeau decided to tell the truth. "No, it wouldn't. What would make me sad is if *you* were hurt. Promise me you won't do anything foolish."

He didn't answer.

"Gio, promise me." Her voice became urgent, unconsciously letting him know something of how she felt. "I don't want you in danger."

"Then I'll not do it," he decided.

Isabeau realized she was still holding the cup. As she replaced it on the sill next to the pitcher, she began to tremble. Giovanni's words shook her. She truly believed if he got the chance, he would kill François without a qualm, and he'd not consider he'd done anything wrong, no more than someone who had no moral upbringing, someone raised as an animal, would.

As a wolf might.

He must've realized he'd frightened her, for he said, softly, "No worry, *maîtresse*. I ... ohhh ..."

A hand went to his belly. He went white, doubling over.

"What is it?" She fell to her knees beside him.

"Hurt." He clutched his stomach, wadding the tail of the shirt in his fist. "Belly burn ..."

She pressed a hand against his middle, feeling the skin under the shirt spasm into a cramp, tightening until it felt as taut as a piece of leather.

"Don't, mistress." His head came up, eyes wide and pain-filled. He swallowed loudly, and his free hand went to his mouth as the sound changed to a choking gasp.

"Oh no." Isabeau caught his arm. "Quick, get to the *puits de cess*."

Without giving him time to obey, she dragged him to his feet and through the door, bent over as he was. He stumbled along beside her, trying to straighten and walk faster, immediately crumpling again as another cramp struck. Abruptly, he gagged, a sound Isabeau recognized as a prelude to losing his supper.

He barely reached the *puits* before the upheaval began. With Isabeau's arm around his waist, he staggered to the pit's edge, leaning forward in time to aim the eruption of liquid and half-digested food into the foul-smelling hole.

"S-sorry, mistress," he managed.

"It's all right," she assured him.

Isabeau turned her head, not wanting to watch, feeling the

violent heaves of Giovanni's body transfer to her own as he raised his head, taking a deep breath. Another explosion followed, again and again, until they came so fast, he barely had time to catch a breath.

If this keeps up, he may stifle. What should I do? She wanted to call for François to summon the leech, but they were too far from the salon for him to hear. As for the servants, she doubted either would come even if they heard. She didn't dare leave Giovanni long enough to go to the back door and call for help. Ill as he was, he might tumble into the *puits* and drown in that awful mess.

She stayed, clinging to him, holding him upright, and making certain a powerful expulsion didn't make him lose his balance and cause them both to fall.

Eventually, it was over. He inhaled a long, desperate breath and fell against her. She staggered under his weight, then felt him attempt to pull away.

"Come, let's get back inside."

Together, they returned to the room, Giovanni leaning against her. She pushed him onto the cot, where he fell rather than sat, lying with his eyes closed. He was pale but breathing easily now.

Pulling her handkerchief from her sleeve, Isabeau poured water from the pitcher into it. She bathed his face, patting the damp fabric against his cheeks, wiping away the tears of illness staining them.

"I'm all right, mistress," he assured her, turning his head. His voice was raspier than usual, issuing from a scalded throat.

"Are you?" She pressed a hand to his forehead. It was cool and damp.

He swallowed. "Water. Throat hurts."

Going to the window, she lifted the pitcher, filling the cup and bringing it to him. He started to drink, then lowered it, staring into the cup.

"What is it?" Isabeau asked.

He didn't answer. Instead, he sniffed as he had before, then thrust a finger into the water, stirring it.

"What are you ...?" She took the cup from him, looking into it.

The bottom of the cup was stained yellow. Some of the grains of powder had discolored the metal.

"This cup needs washing." She tilted the cup, pouring the water out the window. Taking her handkerchief, she wiped the cup clean, removing the evidence of her guilt, then poured fresh water.

He refused to take it, leaving her standing with her arm outstretched, the cup in her hand.

"Why did you give me bad water, mistress?" His dark eyes were reproachful. "Have I done something wrong? Are you punishing me?"

"Of course not." She wanted to pat his cheek, convince him of her lie with her touch. She barely kept her hand from doing so. Instead, she slid it into her pocket, grasping the little bottle.

"Then why do you give me water, making me sick?"

"I'd never ..."

His look said otherwise.

She couldn't tolerate that accusing stare, the look of someone betrayed.

"If you think that ..." She raised the cup, taking a quick sip. "There." She lowered it and again offered him the cup. "If the water were bad, would I drink it? It's harmless." She hoped that was now the truth. "You're mistaken."

He studied the cup, then accepted it. She watched him drink. *I'm not giving him any more.* When she got back to the cottage, she'd pour out the rest of the powder.

He returned the cup. Rolling onto his side, he sighed and lay still, legs curled against his belly. She stayed with him a little longer to make certain he wasn't going to be sick again. When she realized he'd fallen asleep, she hurried out, locking the door behind her.

She nearly ran back to the salon, bursting into the room in such a rush that François gave a start, splashing his wine.

"Well. You've come back." He raised his goblet. "I thought perhaps you and Giovanni had decided to run away together."

"Don't make such a tasteless jest," Isabeau snapped, even more angry because she wished it were the truth.

"You're right," he agreed. "It is tasteless. If you were going to leave me, I hope it'd be for someone better than a *loup-garou*."

"Will you stop calling him that?" She spun, shouting before she realized it.

He lowered the goblet to stare at her. "What ails you, Isabeau? You come rushing in here as if the devil himself is chasing you. Now you yell at me. Lower your voice before the servants hear."

"What was in that powder?"

"What?" He looked at her as if he didn't know what she was talking about.

"You heard me. What was in that phial you gave me?" She stalked over to him, looking down at him with such a glare that he scowled in return. "I gave Gio that powder. He became terribly ill. It frightened me, François. I thought he was going to choke."

Briefly, he also looked alarmed. "He didn't, did he? I guess not, otherwise you'd be much more agitated. Frantic, probably."

Was that actual concern in his expression? He was so sarcastic she couldn't be certain.

"He's all right now?"

"He's sleeping. I swear he lost everything he ate tonight. What was in that powder?" she repeated.

"It was a harmless mixture," he hedged.

"Not too harmless." She realized she was gritting her teeth to keep from shouting at him. "What ... was ... it?"

"Only crushed mustard seed and red sea onion."

"Only ...? *Mon Dieu*, François, red sea onion is a poison. Did you wish to kill him?"

The look he gave her held something she could only describe as fear. That worried her as much as Giovanni's illness.

"It won't kill him," he said at last. "It's only to rid him of food." At the glare she gave him, he went on defensively, "The leech assured me he'd only vomit up what he'd just eaten. He prescribes it all the time for women who wish to become slim quickly, especially after childbirth."

Shaking her head, Isabeau looked away. In that moment, she didn't want to see her husband.

"I have to keep him from getting fat," he went on, speaking quickly as if to convince himself as much as her. "He's too healthy-looking to be my St. Jean."

"So you're making him ill, nearly killing him by having me give him that ... Oh!" Her hands went up, outstretched in anger. "How could you? You ... *you're* the beast ... no, you're much worse, a monster, to even think of such a thing."

"What else could I do?" He sounded as if he actually wanted an answer.

"Certainly not *that*." She pulled the bottle from her pocket, shaking it at him.

Within it, the remaining powder shifted. In a flurry of anger, she plucked out the cork, seized his goblet, and poured the rest of it into the wine.

"Here." She held it out to him. "Drink."

"What? No!" He actually cringed against the chair.

"Drink it." She shook the goblet, making the wine splash. "I want you to know how Giovanni felt. Perhaps when your own insides rebel and you think your bowels are going to come rushing out your mouth, you'll never do such a thing again!"

He flushed such a furious crimson she thought for a moment she'd gone too far, that he might retaliate with anger. Standing, he pulled the goblet from her hand and dashed the contents into the fire. The flames darkened, sizzling and sparkling, dying briefly, then flaring again. With a roar, they rushed up the chimney, expelling the poison's ashes.

François set the goblet on the chairside table. "I see now I was wrong to do that."

How it must have cost him to say that.

"It won't happen again."

"I'll make certain of that!" She spun to the fireplace, flinging the bottle into the fire, watching as the cork smoldered then flared.

She looked back at François.

"Starve him if you must, think of some excuse to give the boys as to why he isn't eating, but don't you ever do such a thing again!" She paused, breathing heavily, bosom heaving. When he didn't answer, she took a deep breath and said, a little quieter, "I think I'll go to bed now. This has upset me."

"What is happening to you, Isabeau?" There was wonder in his voice, not the surprise it held when before he asked a similar question, but as if he couldn't believe what he was saying. "You've changed. I don't know that I like it."

Giovanni has happened to me. She didn't answer his question, didn't dare, but whirled and stamped up the stairs, leaving him standing there.

When François later came to bed, she pretended to sleep so he wouldn't speak to her. She didn't trust what she might say.

Chapter Nineteen

FRANÇOIS TWISTED the tip of his brush into a point, swiped it through the smear of black on his palette, and wrote his name in the bottom right corner of the canvas.

"*Fini!*" He held the brush aloft with a flourish. "Now, my young gentlemen, you may look upon yourselves as portrayed on canvas."

He motioned them to the easel.

André hurried to it, bounding off the platform eagerly, his brothers following. Only Giovanni didn't move, continuing to kneel.

François stepped back. As they crowded around the easel, he picked up a large cloth rectangle caked with fresh paint and hardened from long-dried colors. Dunking the brush into an open jug of oil of turpentine, he began to rub it with the cloth, working the refined tree gum into the brush and removing the paint smeared on the bristles. The pungent scent of pine sap filled the work area.

"Is that how I look?" André was astonished. "*Maître*, you've given me the aspect of a king."

That made François smile quietly. *Not the aspect of a king,* he wanted to correct the boy, *but the face of hypocrisy*. With a few deft strokes of his brush and some subtle shading, he'd turned André's friendly post-adolescent countenance into a smirking leer of self-satisfaction, because he was the one wearing fine fabrics and stealing grapes from his brother while a starving man knelt only a few feet away.

"*Maître*," Auguste spoke in a reverent gasp. "You're a genius."

"Modesty prevents me from saying anything other than '*Merci*.'" François finished with the brush, dropped it into another open-mouthed jug to dry, and picked up a second.

"I think it's fabulous." Aubert was in evident awe. His hand hovered over his painted face.

"Be careful," François cautioned hastily. "Don't touch the paint."

Aubert's hand jerked away as if it had been slapped. "And Gio, look how he's been transformed." He glanced around, noting Giovanni was still on the platform. "Why aren't you here? Come, don't you want to see yourself?"

Giovanni glanced at François. As he nodded his permission with that usual flicker of irritation, the boy scrambled to his feet and joined the others. They parted, so he had a good view of the canvas. He studied it silently.

At last, he said, "That is me?" He gestured to the miserable, beseeching figure and glanced at François for confirmation. "Master?"

François nodded, breaking into an involuntary smile at his reaction.

Giovanni turned back to the painting. "Is that how I look?" He raised a hand as if to touch the figure of the beggar, then, remembering François's warning, touched his own face instead, as if that would confirm what he saw.

"Don't you know?" Auguste asked, thinking he had noted something odd in the way Giovanni worded his question.

"Never see before." He continued staring at the figure as if memorizing each feature. He brushed at his temple, fingers raking back the tangles. "My hair really look like a bramble-patch?" With both hands, he attempted to smooth the unruly curls.

"Here." André thrust a hand into the little purse at his belt. He brought out a rounded disk fashioned of tortoise shell, smaller than his palm. Into it, a little mirror had been fitted. He held it up. "See yourself, Gio."

Giovanni stared into the mirror. Hesitantly, he caught André's wrist, turning his hand so he could get a glimpse of his hair in the little glass. He laughed.

"I'm ugly. Look like wild man."

"Nonsense," the boy said, and dropped the mirror back into his purse. "You're the most handsome of us all. Put a comb to that hair and walk alongside us through town, and no woman would see anyone else."

Giovanni gave him a doubtful look as Auguste and Aubert agreed.

"Now then, my lords ..." François elbowed his way past Giovanni, picking up the cover cloth and carefully draping it over the painting. As if on cue, Maxime appeared with a tray on which rested a bottle of wine and four glasses. "Let us observe this moment."

Maxime poured wine, offering the glasses.

"Giovanni will have none," François said before André could ask. "One goblet with meals is all he's allowed."

Surprisingly, the boy accepted that.

"To your painting." François raised his goblet and they did also, and drank.

From outside came the squeak of harness and the thud of horses' hooves.

"I told the coachman to return early since I believed I would finish today." He glanced at the door. "Unless I'm mistaken, I hear the coach approaching."

It took some time to get the boys into the coach. Each was determined to make a farewell speech, most of which were aimed at Giovanni, after some gracious words to François.

"We shall miss you, Gio," Aubert said.

"Perhaps when *Maître* François comes to visit Papa, he'll bring you along," Auguste suggested. "Papa always travels with his servants."

Giovanni glanced at François, whose expression didn't betray what he was thinking.

That's never going to happen. Aloud, he replied, "Perhaps," and didn't say more.

One of the horses stamped his hooves, as if impatient to be off. Another snorted and shook his head, making the harness jingle. They'd seemed nervous since Giovanni came near the coach. Gervais pulled open the door. André prepared to step inside.

"I'm going to chide Papa for telling us such a tall tale, Gio. I'm going to tell him you are the most well-mannered *loup-garou* I've ever met."

He laughed. After a moment, François joined in, but Giovanni's laughter was the loudest of all. André climbed into the coach. His brothers followed. Gervaise shut the door and scrambled back to his perch. The coachman snapped the reins, and the coach drove away.

François didn't wait for it to be out of sight before he said, "Now then, wolf, there'll be no more sitting at my table. Tonight, you become the servant my wife insists you should be, and we'll see how well she's taught you. After that, it's back to the storeroom for you. Now, get inside!"

* * *

GIOVANNI ACQUITTED HIMSELF WELL, serving the meal while Maxime stood to the side and snapped orders authoritatively, making Isabeau bite her lip more than once since she thought the boy didn't deserve a single sharp word. As far as she could tell, his first attempt as a footman went perfectly. He set the platters and serving bowls where they should be. He placed the dinner plates properly before her and François. He poured the wine without spilling a drop upon the tablecloth.

Even François seemed surprised. He didn't make a single complaint.

She was quiet during the meal, even more so than usual, so François commented, "Why the woebegone look? Your husband has finished a painting that will reap him a goodly fee if young André has anything to say about it. That's going to add to my fame. What do you have to be sad about?"

"If you must know, I miss our guests."

It came to her in that moment that, except when they were abed, the only time she generally saw her husband was during meals, with the length of the table between them. Other than that, she was alone. Maxime and Mathilde didn't count. The young noblemen's presence had become a bright spot in her life.

"It was good to have young voices here." With a start, she realized she spoke of the boys as her mother might.

Why do I sound as if I'm so much older than they? André is only a few months my junior. Why don't I simply say I miss being around people, young women and men who are my peers? When did I become so much older?

François pondered that for a long moment before he spoke,

chewing thoughtfully and washing down his food with a swallow of wine.

He set the goblet beside his plate. "Don't blame me for that discrepancy, wife. If it weren't for the vagaries of your body, we might fill this cottage with young voices. It isn't for my lack of trying that you don't quicken."

Isabeau was shocked by his insensitivity. A glance in Giovanni's direction told her he also thought so. Though he didn't move, she saw his body tense, muscles in his jaw tightening. Fortunately, neither Maxime nor François noticed.

"I don't believe this is a subject to be spoken of in front of the servants," she said, stiffly.

"I suppose not." He threw down his kerchief, pushing back his chair and getting to his feet. "I think this meal is over. We'll finish this discussion in the salon."

Giovanni took a step in Isabeau's direction. She'd told him he was to pull back their chairs when they were ready to leave the dining hall. Since François was already on his feet, he started to assist her.

François stalked to her end of the table. Stepping in front of Giovanni in much the way he'd shouldered Gervais aside that night at the *château*, he seized her wrist. Pulling her from the chair, he pushed her through the door, calling out, "You and the wolf clear the table, Maxime."

Isabeau glanced over her shoulder. Giovanni had stopped, staring after her. With two fingers, Maxime gave his shoulder a light buffet.

"You heard the master. Get busy."

For a moment, she thought he was going to snarl at the servant. His lips curled back, teeth bared. Then, he relaxed and turned to take a large serving tray from the sideboard.

That was all she saw before she was pulled in the direction of the salon by François's grip.

In the salon, he slung her into a chair and turned to the mantel. Other than to rub her wrist, Isabeau didn't speak as she watched him select a decanter and pour a goblet of wine. François's grip had been tight. She hoped it didn't leave a bruise.

"Now then." He settled into his own chair, sipping at the wine, and continuing as if they'd been having a conversation about nothing more serious than the weather. "Let's talk about your ..." He paused with an obviously false delicacy. "... lack."

"What makes you think I'm the one lacking?" Her wrist began to throb, and the pain prompted Isabeau to reply sharply. "Look to yourself also, François. It takes two to make a child."

I don't care if he strikes me. I have to say it. I won't take the blame for this.

He didn't react as she expected but actually smiled, a smug *I-know-something-you-don't* expression. "Don't think to traduce my manhood. I have proof the fault doesn't lie with me."

"Oh?" She attempted to look skeptical and failed in the face of his apparent certainty. "How is that?"

"I've a bastard in Italy."

"Y-you never ..." She could only stutter an answer. "My father didn't mention ..."

"Do you think I'd tell my prospective father-in-law such a thing?" He didn't hide his contempt for both Pierre and her. "Yes, I've a son. His mother's a pretty little thing."

François laughed, a soft, satisfied sound deep in his throat. He took another swallow of wine, held up the goblet, and studied the liquid within it before continuing.

"Too bad she was only a serving maid. Otherwise, I might've married her."

"She'll never know how fortunate she is," Isabeau managed.

"My wife had to bring me status, which was what I thought I was getting when I married you. I've lately seen how mistaken I was." His answer was negligent, as if he didn't care how his words stung. François set the goblet on the chairside table, brushing his hands together as if dusting them. "You're becoming a bit of a shrew, Isabeau. Keep it up, and I may do something about it—legally, of course."

"You wouldn't." She had to swallow before she could speak.

"Wouldn't I?" He laughed, openly enjoying her dismay.

"You'd set me aside?" She couldn't believe it, but knew she should.

Would a man so hypocritical as to take money for painting religious themes but refusing to go to services, indeed stating privately he had no belief in such, follow *any* of the tenets of the Church? It came to her that she should be surprised he'd bothered to ask her father for her hand and hadn't forced himself upon her.

"Don't I have the best of grounds to dissolve my marriage?" he asked. "I've already mentioned my childless situation to *Pére* Ambroise. He was most sympathetic and would assist me in any way, I'm certain."

Isabeau fell silent.

Even before her marriage, she distrusted the priest. When attending services with her parents, she found him looking at her in a way that made her uneasy. She thought him a sensuous man thwarted by his vows. He and François spent many evenings closeted together, sharing goblets of wine while supposedly in disputation concerning his disbelief, but Isabeau felt he merely used her husband's recounting of his conquests to feed his own frustrated chastity. She was certain nothing good would come of that, and somehow, the one who might suffer would be she. Once, she even dared tell François her feelings. He'd laughed, of course, telling her she needn't think herself so alluring that she could attract a priest.

She realized her hands had tightened into fists and looked down at them.

"I'm certain you'd like to strike me." François saw the clenched hands and spoke with satisfaction. "Don't. I won't hesitate to protect myself from a hysterical woman ... and anyone hearing the tale I tell will accept that you're frenzied. I've made certain of that."

"What do you mean?"

"Merely that hints of your slightly erratic behavior have been finding their way through the village, as well as to your father's *château*." He smiled cruelly. "Seigneur Pierre was most upset upon learning how his daughter was comporting herself with indecent familiarity around any comely young man she met."

So that was the reason for her parents' restrained attitude the other night, for the anxious glances her mother kept giving her. Might it also be why he'd kept Gervais away from her, making it look as if he were putting himself between a servant and a woman apt to erupt into lewd violence?

Isabeau was momentarily stunned into silence.

"Now then, we will discuss this rationally. I've spoken to the leech of your problem."

"You've mentioned such an intimate thing with the leech?"

How dare he?

"He's a physician," he defended himself. "Who better to expound on the subject? He says there are potions able to counteract infertility. He doesn't have the herbs, but the apothecary does. He can write a recipe to be compounded. Taking them will guarantee you'll quicken."

"If I refuse?"

He shrugged. "I'm eight-and-thirty, Isabeau. I wish a child before I'm much older. Your father has assured me that if I give him a grandchild, whether boy or girl, he'll make me his heir, superseding your brothers. I'll get the *château* and the surrounding land, and they'll have what's left of the estate.

There'll be plenty of space for me to have a fine studio, where I can live in the style I wish while I paint, and I won't squander the remnant of the family fortune as he's tried to."

Isabeau didn't answer, thoughts thudding together in a panic. She struggled to bring order to her mind.

Perhaps it would be best simply to have a child. She'd always feared François would merely reproduce himself, but with the way he isolated while working and his many absences, she'd have much time alone with the babe. There might be a chance she could mold him into a decent, good man and counteract any bad habits he learned from his father. Besides, having an infant to tend would give her something to do and someone to associate with other than Maxime and Mathilde.

... and Giovanni ...

How will he react if I've a child? She didn't want to lose Giovanni's company.

She thought of the question he'd asked when she showed him *Madonna of the Grotto*.

You have babe? Why not?

A wave of longing swept over her, a wish that any child of hers would have Giovanni's curly locks and not François's stick-straight thatch, his eyes of that coppery-bronze and not the clear-glass blue of her husband's.

Dear Lord, what am I thinking? Isabeau shivered.

She was startled to feel all the fight, all the opposition, go out of her, as though someone had siphoned off her last ounce of free will.

As if it were someone else speaking, she heard herself say, "Very well, François."

From the hallway, there was a loud crash and a woman's scream, the sound of someone running. Behind the footsteps, the screams continued, high-pitched and terror-filled.

"Master, master!" Maxime burst into the salon, eyes wide, face white. "The creature ... he's gone mad!"

Chapter Twenty

Giovanni lay writhing on the floor, legs thrashing, heels drumming against the boards. A few feet away, Mathilde shrieked at the top of her lungs, hands clasped to her bosom, her screams beseeching the deity.

"Mistress." He raised his head, frantic eyes seeking Isabeau's. He held out a hand, then let it fall. It curled into claws, his fingers raking the floor.

Mathilde gave another wail.

"Stop that." Isabeau stamped across to the cook, delivering a teeth-jarring slap to her plump jowls, so violent it sent Mathilde reeling but effectively stopped her cries.

Whirling, she dropped to her knees and put an arm around Giovanni's shoulders. He jerked away, body shaking as if with ague.

He isn't mad. He isn't. There was no froth at his mouth. His eyes were clear, if frenzied. Only his body was affected.

"Gio, what is it?" She was afraid she knew.

Vaguely, she was aware of François's absence. She looked to the doorway. Maxime stood there, rooted to the spot. Her husband had disappeared.

He would, leaving me to handle this.

"Mistress ... I'm sorry ... the moon ... I didn't take notice ..." His head fell back as his body stiffened. One hand gripped her arm, fingers tightening.

"Help me get him to his feet," she said to Maxime.

"*Non.*" He actually took several steps backward, moving into the corridor. "I'm not coming near that—"

"Do as I say, you coward." Her tone told him not to argue. "Or get out of my house."

He hurried to obey. As they got Giovanni upright, half-dragging him through the door, François again appeared.

"You'll need this." He placed a small bottle in Isabeau's free hand. The elixir of valerian. Then, he went back down the hallway, taking refuge in the salon.

Coward. Isabeau's moment of gratitude that he'd thought of the soporific faded.

Together, she and the reluctant Maxime got Giovanni through the house to the walkway. They carried him more than he walked, however, for his legs kept giving way, knees buckling as if they couldn't hold his weight. They looked twisted, somehow, elongated in the wrong places as if ...

... as if they're being re-shaped.

Throughout the incident, he muttered apologies, blaming himself for not being more observant.

As they entered the walkway, Isabeau could see the moon was indeed full, so bright above the trees that it lit the walkway. Inside the studio, however, it was dark, and Maxime muttered, "I should've brought a lantern."

"No, it's better this way." She didn't want to see how Giovanni was changing ... if he *was* changing, if the misshapen twist to his legs wasn't merely a trick of shadow and her imagination. She certainly didn't want Maxime to see.

In the storeroom, the cot was barely visible.

"Put him there." She released her hold, leaving Maxime to totter to the cot and deposit Giovanni upon it.

He dropped the boy and fairly leaped backward.

The chain and collar were still attached to the window bars. She dragged the chain to the cot, fastening the collar around Giovanni's neck as he struggled to sit up. When she turned back to the window and the pitcher and cup sitting on the sill, she heard Maxime's footsteps clatter through the door. Having done as she ordered, the servant took himself back to the safety of the cottage at a run.

Isabeau's anger flared. *Gutless varlet. Like master, like servant.*

She didn't allow herself time for further recrimination. Pouring the drops of valerian into the water, she thrust the cup at Giovanni.

He took it without protest, gulping it down. She caught it as it fell from his hand. The drug worked fast, but then, she'd given him a double dose.

"Go ..." came out as a sleepy slur as he fell unconscious.

Isabeau pulled the shutters closed, latching them and blotting out the moonlight. There was no sound from the cot but a harsh, husky breathing and an occasional sound like the snarl of a sleeping hound. Hurrying out, she locked the storeroom door, then the studio.

It was as she walked back to the cottage, her haste now gone, that she realized her forearm stung. Stepping to the edge of the porch, she thrust it into the moonlight.

Blood oozed from five marks cut into her skin. Giovanni had gripped her so tightly he'd scratched her. They weren't the little crescents of nail marks, however, but deep gouges, as if made by claws.

"Is it subdued?" François stepped from the shadows near

the door. He saw the marks and smirked. "Do you still think you can make him into a man?"

* * *

THE NEXT DAY, Giovanni was himself again and repentant.

"Never mind," Isabeau told him as he served their breakfast, Maxime directing him from as far away as possible while still being in the same room. "It was everyone's fault. We must all be diligent from now on."

Giovanni carried the bowl of *pommes cuites*, seasoned with cinnamon, honey-butter, and cloves, to Isabeau's place. Bowing, he presented the stewed fruit. As she lifted the serving spoon, depositing a generous helping of apples upon her plate, he whispered, "How are you, mistress? Are you well?"

He knows he scratched me.

She was careful that the bandage around her forearm was tucked inside her sleeve and not visible. She'd bathed the scratches in witch hazel water, then dabbed wine over them, wincing at the sting of alcohol into the open wounds while praying the pain meant any taint from Giovanni's nails was being purged. The cuts still ached slightly but had already formed scabs, so she thought they were healing well.

"I'm fine." Her answer was also whispered. She didn't want to speak loudly and remind François of his own wound. It had healed, not even leaving a scar, but she was surprised he hadn't mentioned it when he saw she'd been scratched, reminding her how Giovanni had attacked him.

The full moon has no influence over François, so neither will this wound affect me. Giovanni can touch silver unharmed. What other lies about loup-garou *have we been told?*

"Mistress, I swear—"

"Yes, yes, we know you're sorry," François spoke from the other end of the table. "Grovel some other time." In spite of their whispers, he'd heard their conversation, looking up as Giovanni straightened. "Obviously, you're forgiven, but from now on, you'd best be more alert as to the dates," he went on. "*I'm* not wasting my time watching the calendar. I've more important things to do."

He dismissed Giovanni with a wave of his hand, sending him into the corridor to await Maxime's call, for Mathilde had already declared he wasn't coming into her kitchen, except for the brief time it took to pick up and return the dinnerware, and François had decreed he wouldn't stand in waiting in the dining room as a footman should. Isabeau decided he didn't want the boy near enough to hear any disparaging remarks aimed at her.

"Why do you care for this creature, Isabeau? I vow if I'd known he was going to be so much trouble, I'd have left him with the gypsies and lowered my standards to seek a lesser St. Jean. You've made him into a pet."

"If that's so"—Isabeau stifled a quake of anger—"at least I provide and care for my pets ... unlike some."

François's answer was a shrug as he reached for another helping of stewed apples.

Isabeau reached for her own fork, pulling her sleeve back into place.

* * *

Finished with their meal, she and François vacated the dining room. Giovanni began to clear the table while Maxime hurried to the kitchen, carrying the serving bowls set on the sideboard. Pausing in the doorway, Isabeau watched for a moment, noting that the boy was performing his chores perfectly.

Giovanni stood at François's place, carefully stacking plate, goblet, and utensils upon the tray. Lifting it, he walked to Isabeau's end of the table and did the same with her knife, fork, and spoon. He reached for her plate. It still held several slices of *pommes cuites*. She'd barely eaten any. He picked up the plate, studying it, then ...

To her surprise, instead of placing her plate atop François's, he scooped the apples off it, stuffing them into his mouth. He didn't bother chewing, simply swallowed, then swiped a finger through the remains of the sauce, licking off the spiced honey-soaked juice. Raising the plate, he lapped the sticky remnants until the plate was clean.

It was so like the way her uncle's servants set down dinner plates for his dogs to lick, Isabeau was appalled.

Giovanni sighed. It was a satisfied sound; one she'd often heard the hounds make after a good meal. *Poor thing. He's hungry.* Her heart shook with pity. *François is so cruel to starve him.* A second condemnation thundered after that one. *So am I, for allowing it.*

She must eat less, leaving him more morsels to scavenge.

His beard was sticky, a golden smear of honey clinging to the dark hair. Picking up her table kerchief, he wiped his mouth and chin until all traces had been removed, placing the napkin on the tray, also. He set the remaining serving bowls on the tray and lifted it, turning to the door.

Seeing Isabeau standing there, he stopped. He didn't look guilty, so she decided he didn't realize she'd seen. She came back into the room.

"How are you, mistress? Really?" He replaced the tray on the table.

"I'm fine," she answered, then added, "as I said." She was trying to sound impersonal, reminding him of their previous conversation.

"Are you?" Before she could reply to that, he caught her

arm. Pushing back her sleeve, he pulled away the bandage, dropping it to the floor.

The scratches were revealed in all their inflamed glory.

"Oh, mistress." His whisper was a lament as well as an apology.

Before she could speak, telling him it looked worse than it felt, he bent over her wrist.

Isabeau closed her eyes. *I must pull away. I can't bear the touch of his mouth. If he kisses me ...*

She started to speak.

The words were never uttered. Giovanni's lips touched the underside of her wrist, but he didn't kiss it. Instead, he pressed his tongue to the first of the scabbed gouges, licking each wound. She stifled her gasp, enjoying that damp caress, still tinged with the honey's healing smoothness, holding her breath as the gentle laps bathed each of the cuts.

Abruptly, he raised his head. Releasing her arm, he stepped back.

"Mistress." With a bow, he lifted the tray and walked past her, disappearing down the corridor to the kitchen.

Stooping to retrieve the bandage, Isabeau pulled her sleeve back into place. She got a good look at her wrist before she did so, and what she saw stopped her. The cuts in her flesh, redolent of spiced apple, were completely healed.

When she reached the salon, François asked, "What kept you?" though he sounded as if he really didn't care.

"Giovanni was a bit slow tonight in his serving," she lied. "I stopped to remind him he must be more prompt."

She was surprised when he accepted that feeble excuse.

Chapter Twenty-One

A WEEK LATER, Maxime announced, "Master, the *marquis* du Maurier's steward is here."

"Gerard?" François didn't hide his surprise. "Well, don't stand there, show him in!"

After the usual greetings, Gerard got directly to the reason for his visit.

"My master has sent me to inspect the painting you've done of his sons. They've been most effusive in their descriptions of it, *Monsieur* François, and he's eager to see it."

Though André said he would speak to his father, nobility was known for forgetting promises, especially to someone not a peer. That the boy had kept his word so flattered François, he ignored the steward's slight snub of calling him *Mister*.

Gerard held up a small bag. "If I consider it as good as they've said, I'm to buy it and take it back with me."

"Are you truly one to judge my work?" François allowed his ego to be ruffled at the thought that a mere steward might assess his talent.

"I've some skill in appraisal." Apparently, Gerard's own self-esteem didn't suffer from the artist's doubt. "It was through my advice that His Lordship acquired much of the artwork in the *château*."

His tone was calm, but François thought he detected a warning behind the quiet words, some nuance cautioning him not to question too strongly a man who could, with a word, declare his creation unworthy.

"*Désolé*." He affected a more conciliatory tone, smiling. "It's only that the paint is barely dry. To move the painting, indeed, even to uncover and view it just now, may smear it."

"I'm well aware of the length of time required for a painting to be considered safe to be moved, *Monsieur* François." Gerard's smile matched his own, letting him know he acknowledged François was allowed to make his protests, but, in the end, the *marquis* would be the one having *his* way. "As you know, my master is an impatient sort. He's so intrigued by Lord André's description, he can't wait to see." He finished with finality, "He wishes to see it *now*."

"Why didn't he come himself, then?" François skipped the expected ritual, saying with impertinence, "He could view the painting and later—"

"You've known His Lordship long enough to be aware he does things his own way," Gerard interrupted, cutting short any further argument. "May I see the painting?" He glanced at the front entrance. "The coach is waiting, and the horses impatient."

Show me now or I'll leave.

That left no room for further protest. With a bow, François led the way to his studio.

When he saw it, Gerard was astounded. He couldn't expound enough on the painting's beauty.

"Truly, this is a masterpiece. I could almost imagine my young masters standing before me. The colors are superb, and the perspective ... it's as if I might reach past them and touch those bundles ..."

His hand moved. Francois's did also, catching his wrist and gently pushing it away from the canvas's surface.

"And, as you see, the paint is nowhere near dry enough for the canvas to be moved."

Their eyes met. Gerard smiled. He held out the purse. "I'll have the footman and the coach driver put it into the coach very carefully." He had the audacity to pat the hand still clutching his wrist. "Don't worry, Master François, they've been fore-warned what will happen to them if so much as a single paint-stroke is harmed."

François saw he could make no further objections. Releasing the steward's wrist, he accepted the purse and spoke to Maxime, "Have the driver bring the coach around to the studio door."

He and Gerard went onto the walkway, waiting on the porch as the coach came around the corner of the cottage and the driver pulled to a stop in front of the studio.

As the driver and footman went inside, François asked, "Will it fit?"

"I believe so." The steward sounded unworried. "They'll place it flat, across the seats, so it won't slip."

"It's a large canvas. There won't be room for you—"

"I'll ride up top with the coachman." Gerard looked at him. "Be assured, Master François, the painting will be protected as if it were *le roi* himself. Once safe in the *château*, it will be hung in a place of honor and allowed to dry properly." He glanced at the bag of coins clutched in François's hand and allowed himself a bare smirk. "After all, it's no longer your worry, but the *marquis'*."

* * *

To François's way of thinking, things were going well. He'd received a missive from Alphonse acknowledging the arrival of *The Beggar and the Nobles*, echoing the steward's praise. Added to that was the *marquis's* promise that "I will be lauding your talent to all who will listen. Never fear, my dear François. Fortune shines upon you."

Thus assured, François settled in to await the results of Alphonse's promise. To Isabeau's surprise, he didn't spend the purchase price on more paints and supplies, but instead bought a smallish coffer, placing it on the chest of drawers in their bedchamber, and emptying the purse's contents into it.

"I've counted each piece," he informed the two servants and his wife. "I'll do so each night, so don't think if one goes missing, I won't know."

Though both Maxime and Mathilde looked disconcerted that he might think they'd steal from him, they didn't dare appear insulted. Isabeau was gratified that he let the servants know he didn't trust them. She didn't like being placed in the same category as a pilfering servant, however, but their expressions and the attempts to stifle those looks made her want to laugh aloud.

As if to point this out, she said, "Be assured *I* won't touch a piece of it, my dear husband. After all, you give me a generous household allowance, so why should I?"

She thought how she had to pinch each *sou* until it nearly shrieked in order to buy what was needed for the cottage.

Nevertheless, she was pleased with the way the painting and its sale turned out, hoping François's saving the money meant he might gather enough that he would soon become a bit more generous. The only thing she didn't like was the fact that he now stayed close to home, inflicting his presence upon her.

To her intense relief, that lasted only a few days before he declared himself bored with the humdrum of the cottage's daily routine.

"I vow it's no wonder you act so oddly sometimes, wife. Having to suffer the *ennui* of doing the same thing over and over day after day would drive me mad." Thus, to while away the time while he waited for his next commission, François went into the forests, sketching the mountains and the meadows, but always staying within calling distance.

At last, when he'd filled a sketchpad with renderings of the mountains, trees, and flowers surrounding the cottage, and felt there was nothing new to inspire him until the changing of the season brought different vistas and aspects, he decided to begin a new painting.

Another with Giovanni as the subject.

* * *

WHILE RENOVATING the barn into a studio, François had built at its back a full-length closet in which were kept pieces of furniture, drapes, and other accessories he used in his paintings. There were also garments donated by some of the more well-to-do townsfolk, flattered that even a piece of their clothing might be featured in one of *le artiste's* creations.

Searching through one of the wardrobes, François dressed Giovanni in a doublet and smocked shirt. He pushed him into an armed barrel-chair, producing a comb and handing it to the boy.

"Do something about that mess you call hair."

Giovanni accepted the comb but instead of running it through his hair, merely sat staring at it, turning it repeatedly in his hands.

"For the Good Lord's sake!" François grumbled. "Don't you know how to ...?" With a cry of impatience, he called for

Isabeau. "Take that comb and tame these wild locks into some semblance of order."

Giovanni's hair had been untended since his initial bath some weeks hence, though he had several immersions in the stream. It hadn't mattered for his role as the Beggar, but now ...

She took the comb from him, staring at the unruly tangles. She had no wish to comb those untamed dark curls, spoiling their wild beauty. She wanted to plunge her hands into the dark mass, feel its crispness between her fingers.

How can I touch him without revealing how I feel?

Isabeau took a deep breath.

As she dragged the comb through the unkempt curls, François explained his concept of the painting. It was to be a portrait of a young man holding a flower. She thought that was not an unusual device until he continued, "I'll call it *Young Man with a Sprig of Wolfsbane*," and laughed.

He thought it a great jest.

"Francois, you can't," Isabeau protested, pausing as the comb caught in a tangle, causing Giovanni to wince, though he didn't make a sound. "If someone sees it, they'll think—"

"Of course they're going to see it," he interrupted. "That's the purpose. To advertise my talent. Since it'll contain an herb, I'll give it to the leech or perhaps the apothecary to display in his shop. As for what they'll think?"

He snapped his fingers.

"Nothing! Why should they? Unless someone hints otherwise." He fixed her with such an intimidating gaze that she shivered. "Why are you so concerned with his welfare, Isabeau? Are you in love with this creature?"

As usual, François ignored the fact that the subject of his heavy-handed jest was sitting directly before him, hearing everything he said. Giovanni tensed. He didn't move otherwise, but his hands tightened on the chair's carved wooden arms.

"Of course not." It was to her credit that Isabeau didn't react guiltily. "I merely wish to—"

"Stop being so protective," François ordered. "He isn't a child. That reminds me, we never finished our conversation on that subject."

"That can wait." Isabeau spoke hastily as Giovanni turned a questioning gaze on her, asking without speaking aloud what François meant. She shook her head and tugged on the comb, causing him to give a slight grunt of pain from the force with which she pulled it through the tangle.

"No, it can't," François replied. "Therefore, we'll discuss it later tonight. Just now ..." He plucked the comb from her hand, tossing it onto the table. "Get out of here so I can begin work."

* * *

GIOVANNI QUIETLY ACCEPTED this new travail, by now recognizing François's lack of concern and cruelty in subjecting him to the one thing that not only caused him so much discomfort but also its mere nearness put him into a semi-trance. He understood that was exactly what his master wished.

During his rambles in the forest whiling away idle time, François returned to the grotto where the shorn plants had put out new growth, covering the fresh stalks with brilliant purple blossoms. He'd kept them hidden on a high shelf where they wouldn't be noticed, and now brought them down. Selecting a spray still fresh enough to be covered with both leaves and flowers, he thrust it into Giovanni's hand.

As with the draught of valerian Isabeau had given him, the effect was immediate. Obedient but drowsy, eyes heavy-lidded, Giovanni sat in the chair as directed, holding the spray.

Except for an occasional drooping of his head, after which he'd jerk slightly and blink as though waking from a brief slip into slumber, he was docile and quiet, exactly as François wished.

Isabeau protested. "How can you paint him when he's half asleep?"

"Easily." François was unconcerned, his shrug dismissing any problem. "It's no matter. When it comes time to paint his features, I'll take away the wolfsbane so he'll be alert."

It was then Isabeau remembered her conversation with the boy, when she'd explained to him about posing, and his reply.

Perhaps I sleep with eyes open so maître *not know.*

Giovanni was sleeping, all right, but his master was very much aware.

It was more evidence of François's cruelty that after sitting in a near-doze most of the day, he expected the boy to be alert enough to serve their meal that night.

When Giovanni staggered slightly and jostled the bowl of stew as he set it before his master, so it splashed onto the table-cloth, leaving a greasy smear, François reacted with exaggerated anger.

"Careful, *maladroit!*" As Giovanni released the bowl, he slapped the boy's wrist, a hard smack that sounded loud in the room's quiet.

"*Je suis désolé, maître.*" Giovanni's apology was so soft that Isabeau saw his lips move but didn't hear. It was to the wolfsbane's credit that he didn't carry out his previous threat to Isabeau then and there.

"You'd better be." Grumbling under his breath, François began to eat, slurping in the soup and pausing only long enough to order, "Stand over there by the sideboard. I don't want you near me lest you stumble again and make me sully my clothing with spilled stew."

Meekly, Giovanni positioned himself by the buffet. Through the rest of the meal, he made a valiant attempt to stay alert, offering servings and refilling François's wine glass often.

After supper that night, Isabeau came to the storage room under the pretense of replenishing Giovanni's water pitcher.

"How will you manage to stay attentive when you must have that herb in such close proximity?" she worried.

"I'll bathe my face," he answered. "Cold water will shock me awake."

She filled the tin cup, handing it to him. He accepted it and drank it all, handing it back. As Isabeau returned it to the windowsill, he continued, "The master said he had something to discuss with you. What did he mean?"

"It's nothing." She didn't look at him. "A household problem."

"Please, mistress." His sigh was such an approximation of François's own false patience that she scowled at him. "Don't lie." He then added softly, "You know I can tell."

"I know," she admitted, not looking at him. "But ..."

"What is it?"

A wave of concern so warm and gentle swept through Isabeau. He didn't touch her, didn't make a move toward her, but she felt as if he stood beside her, holding her hand in his own, comforting, calming her.

"François wishes a child. He ... the leech prescribed an herb he promises will help me conceive." She couldn't look at him and say that.

"That's good, isn't it?" His expression was at variance with his words. He looked as if he doubted the truth of what he said. His next statement underscored this. "I thought you want a little one. You aren't happy?"

She shook her head.

"You don't wish to have the master's child." It wasn't a question.

Isabeau's hand went to her mouth to stifle the sob. It didn't prevent the tears from rolling down her cheeks, however.

No, Giovanni, I don't want his child. I want yours. Oh, God, I'm the worst example of an unfaithful wife because you've no idea how you tempt me.

She didn't realize he was near until she felt his arms go around her. Isabeau went limp, leaning into Giovanni's embrace, pressing her forehead against his chest. His hand touched her head, stroking her hair through the cloth of her wimple.

"Oh, mistress, I wish I could make you happy." This time his sigh held none of the falsity it had before.

You could … if only you dared.

"Don't worry. When the babe is born, I'll protect him, too. I'll never leave either of you, mistress. I swear."

That made the tears come faster until she thought she might suffocate from the flood. Through it all, he continued holding her close, his warmth, the rough texture of his shirt, its dusty smell from the nights he'd lain on the floor, all blending into a miasma of comfort.

From now on, whenever I smell household dust, I'll think of this moment.

Abruptly, the gently caressing hand halted. He pushed her away. Giovanni's eyes held hers.

"Go. Your husband waits for you."

She told herself there was something in his gaze saying he wanted her to stay, however.

Chapter Twenty-Two

It was later in that same week when Maxime came to the studio with a startling announcement.

"Master, there's a footman at the door. He says he represents the *Comte* Duquesne, and his master wishes to speak with you."

"Duquesne?" François nearly dropped his brush. "Here?"

Like everyone in the province, he was aware of the stories circulating about the morally undisciplined Armand, *Comte* Duquesne, and the rumors of the scandalous *fêtes* held at his *château* in nearby Sainte-Louise Modeste, a most inappropriate name for the site of such questionable events. Duquesne's licentious behavior had more than once been cited from the pulpit as an example of the most profane of Man's nature, *Pére* Ambroise even making a complaint to the king, to no avail. The *Comte* apparently had friends in higher places than did the Church, for he was never brought to task by Louis XII, who was busier making war on Italy than worrying about the moral turpitude of one of his many nobles.

François wondered why such a man was calling upon *him*.

He placed the palette upon the worktable, laying the brush

aside, then hesitated, seemingly having an inner dialogue, before deciding. "I can't greet him like this."

His fingers plucked at the painter's smock, smeared with blobs of color.

"My shirt and stocks are passable, but I need a doublet." He pulled the smock over his head, tossing it to the floor. "Maxime, get the newest one." He started to the door.

"Master, what about …?" Maxime gestured to Giovanni, slumped in the chair.

"Leave him." François dismissed the boy with a negligible wave. "He's going nowhere."

As Maxime ran ahead to fetch the doublet, François made his way to the salon, skirting the hallway leading to the front entrance and the sight of the *comte's* footman. They met in the doorway. It took only a few moments to thrust his arms into the sleeves and hastily button the doublet's front, after which he nodded to the servant.

Maxime went out. He spoke to the footman waiting impatiently in the open front doorway, "My pardon for taking so long. My master would be pleased to welcome the *comte* into his home. Please, bid him alight and enter."

François rushed into the salon. He positioned himself near the hearth, one arm resting against the mantel, a nonchalant enough pose to receive a *comte*, he thought. Not too negligent, yet relaxed and dignified.

There was a clatter of footsteps going down the flagstones, the sound of movement as the footman opened the coach door and spoke to someone who ascended. A second set of footfalls came to the door, these firm and moving with purpose.

In a few moments, Maxime said, "Welcome, Your Lordship. May I take your chaperon and cape?"

There was a rustle of movement before the servant continued.

"My master is in his salon. Please come this way." Then he was at the salon door, announcing, "Master, His Lordship, *le Comte* Duquesne," and standing aside.

The count fairly sailed through the door, handsome, exuding fascination and at the same time repulsion, an elegant but malevolent peacock. Eyes of such an icy hue as to seem almost transparent were fixed upon François. He was extraordinarily fair, looking almost Nordic in appearance and not like a native Frenchman at all, with hair of such a pale shade of blond that an onlooker might wonder if it were his natural hue. Indeed, it was rumored the mingled white-gilt color was the result of a bleaching potion also applied to his armpits and nethers.

Everything about the man shrieked seducer, lecher, *debauchée*, from the sleek locks of his hair to the lustrous rose of his full lips to his well-shaped, stock-covered calves.

All François could think in that moment was that if he were to paint le *comte*, there wasn't a color on his palette matching that icy fairness ... and also that he'd like to try his hand at bringing that image to life on canvas.

"Your Lordship." He broke from his reverie, greeting him with a flourish of a bow, copied from Alphonse. "Welcome to my humble abode."

Duquesne's reply to that was an answering bow, equally elaborate. He straightened and looked around, taking in the furnishings and the various *objects d'art* before stating, with a tone saying François had passed some kind of test, "A comfortable-looking place, de Montaigne."

"You're too kind, sir." François stifled a simper. He'd heard tales that this man wasn't one to tolerate toadying. Duquesne liked plain talk, the franker, the better. "My servant said you wished to speak to me? How may I serve you?"

"I've come on business." Clearly, *le comte* wasn't going to indulge in idle chitchat.

At that statement, François's ears perked. *Business* meant only one thing.

Money.

Duquesne had plenty of that. It was said that this was one reason he was never censured for his behavior.

Le Comte might get directly to the point, but there were always niceties to attend, and François was determined to adhere to them first.

"Please, sir. Sit." He gestured to the chair where Isabeau usually settled, and as Duquesne dropped into it, he continued, "I was about to enjoy a goblet of wine. Will you join me?"

That was answered with a nod as His Lordship removed the gloves he hadn't relinquished to Maxime along with his cap and cape, dropping them onto a tabletop with a movement that might almost be considered *thrown*. His hands, like the rest of him, were finely shaped and so smooth as to appear he did nothing more strenuous than hold a horse's reins.

"Maxime, pour us some wine."

The servant was already there, hands fairly shaking in his eagerness to obey as he reached for one of the decanters on the mantel.

François made a slight sound, deep in his throat, nearly a cough. Maxime's hand stayed, releasing the decanter he'd chosen, moving to the second. The best of the three vintages, in fact. François gave an approving nod, and Maxime unstoppered the decanter and poured.

With the two goblets in hand, he turned. François took them from him, handing one to the *comte*, then seated himself in his chair. He allowed His Lordship to taste the wine, awaiting his opinion before he drank.

"This is a most interesting flavor." Duquesne's brows rose slightly. "A unique bouquet."

François beamed, ignoring the insinuation that his visitor was surprised he could afford such a fine vintage. "A red wine from Bordeaux. It was a gift from the *Marquis* du Maurier."

He was grateful for another chance to brag about his association with Alphonse.

Duquesne nodded. "I thought I recognized it." He raised the goblet, studying the wine through the glass. "Alphonse keeps a good cellar."

"You're acquainted with His Lordship?" François managed to hide his astonishment.

Duquesne smiled. "I dare say. He's my cousin." He paused, sipped, and said, "Second cousin, actually."

That was news to François. Alphonse had never spoken of being related to the notorious *Comte* Duquesne. Perhaps that was a kinship most would prefer to do without, much less have bandied about. He sipped his own wine, thinking of the implications.

As he was trying to decide how to respond, *le comte* said, "It was as I was visiting him recently that I had the pleasure of viewing the painting you did of his sons. Master François, that is truly a masterpiece."

Duquesne held his glass in one hand, the other moving gracefully, describing experienced emotion.

"The detail in those faces. It was as if the boys themselves stood before me. I felt if I placed my hand upon André's painted image, I would feel the actual strands of hair between my fingers."

Those fingers fluttered.

"You didn't touch it?" François asked, then momentarily winced at the anxiety in his tone. One didn't speak so to a noble, especially one so notorious.

"Of course not." Duquesne ignored his concern, smiled at it, in fact, indulgently, as if he understood an *artiste's* worry over his creations. "Alphonse warned me. Most vehemently, I might add ..." That expressive hand again waved. "... that the painting was still drying, but even if the outer layer appeared set, I was aware that inside it was still wet."

François relaxed.

"I found it magnificent, and therefore, I'm prompted to ask if you might be interested in accepting a little task from myself?" Finally, the patrician face turned toward him, those chilling eyes at last studying him as he continued, "For my winter *château*."

"Of a surety, Your Lordship." François didn't hesitate.

"You're certain?" Duquesne gave him an odd look.

At the haste of his answer, perhaps?

"My dear *comte*, of course." His expression made François wonder if he'd sounded too eager. He dared to ask, "Why should I not?"

"Well ..."

There was another movement of his hand, as if to say, *Isn't it obvious?* Though François saw nothing that would've made him hesitate. Yet.

Duquesne lowered his voice slightly. "Let us not bandy words. You're aware of my lifestyle ..."

Is that all? François relaxed.

"You've a certain reputation. Yes." His answer was cautious. Diplomatic, he thought.

"Please, let us speak frankly." His careful wording made Duquesne laugh. "I'm a libertine, de Montaigne. It's common knowledge, and I don't hide it. I believe in indulging the senses, *all* of them, and allowing the passions full play." He paused. "Does that repulse you? Make you wish not to sully your art by accepting my commission?"

"Your Lordship." François took a sip of his wine, fixing the nobleman with what he hoped was an empathetic expression, one inhabitant of a jaded world to another. "Obviously, you have an appreciation of the finer things in life. You recognize talent when you see it." He lowered his glass. "A man who has a taste for fine art can't be all bad."

Duquesne smiled. So did François. The *comte* liked his statement. Well and good. He didn't add that, for the right sum, he'd paint the portrait of the Devil himself—if he believed in Satan, that is—and Duquesne could be the model.

"My *château* in Sainte-Louise Modeste." The *comte* launched into an explanation. "Where I hide myself in winter when the snow shrouds everything and it's too cold to play outside ..." His mouth twitched slightly as if suppressing a smile at that phrase. "It's filled with sensual delights. All who come there are welcome to give free rein to their desires. I've traveled extensively, scouring my own country and others to furnish it with paintings, tapestries, and statuary reflecting this, but one wall stands empty."

Duquesne paused. Setting down his goblet, he turned in his chair so that he faced François. Again, those wintry eyes met his, as if in confrontation.

"After seeing my cousin's painting, I knew only a de Montaigne could fill that space."

"What are you interested in? A landscape? A still life?" Mentally, François began totting up the amount he might get for such a painting.

"Nothing of the sort." The *comte* shook his head, making the pale locks swing gracefully against his cheeks.

They gave off a faint whispering as they brushed his skin. Every movement the man made seemed designed to evoke sensuality.

"Something very special."

"A mural?" François guessed, leaning back in his chair.

"A painting," Duquesne confirmed. "A large one, around ten feet by eight. With a classical theme."

"Classical?" François thought quickly.

Knowing the *comte*, it would doubtless be an erotic one. Tales of the Roman and Greek gods and goddesses abounded with amorous adventures. Even with the war in the place of their origin, they were as popular as ever. Which one ...?

"One of the Greek myths, perhaps?" he guessed. "Something concerning ... Venus?"

"Exactly." Duquesne looked pleased. "I can see we're of a similar frame of mind. I thought ... Venus and Adonis?"

"That's a most popular story," François said. Immediately, his mind's eye began arranging the scene. "It should be easy to create."

"Do we have a bargain, then?" Duquesne held out his glass.

"My dear *comte*, I shall be honored to create a painting especially for you, with any theme you wish. Venus and Adonis, it is."

He raised his glass. Duquesne touched the rim of his own against it, making the two crystals give off a brittle tinkling. The two men drank, sealing the deal.

"*Bon.*" Duquesne set down the glass. "I give you free rein to do it however you wish. However, there are only three criteria I must insist upon."

"What are they?" François could feel the excitement, the eagerness, of beginning a new painting, already coursing through him.

"The subjects must be nude and the privates well displayed, Adonis's *organe d'amour* so engorged that upon seeing the scene the viewer will be stimulated to his own arousal."

"You're offering quite a challenge." François looked thoughtful.

Just thinking of creating such a scene made his *organe* twitch. *Yes, I can do it.* He'd hire Lisette to be Venus. *And after each session, Venus and I will have our own little* tête-à-tête. With such a goal, he'd imbue the painting with his burgeoning passion.

"Can you do it?" The *comte* mistook his silence for hesitation.

"Without a doubt," François assured him. "What is the third criteria?"

"I wish the Beggar from my cousin's painting to be Adonis."

Giovanni? Francois didn't answer. Without meaning to, he grimaced.

"Do I sense hesitation?" Duquesne misinterpreted his change in expression. "He's available, isn't he?"

"Oh yes, he lives here, in fact. A servant."

"Is there some problem with his posing?"

"No, of course not," François answered quickly, to dispel any doubt. "But may I ask, why Giovanni? That's his name. An Italian refugee," he said by way of explanation as the *comte* frowned. "Surely that lowly creature in your cousin's painting inspires lust in no one."

"I agree, but your skill turned that mean creature into something wondrous."

François managed to hide his surprise. He'd always said he had the ability to paint a sow's ear and make people think it was a silken purse, if only they saw it with the proper perspective, but to actually hear someone say so ...

"When I looked at him, I saw something beautiful but unearthly, almost divine."

You saw something else, too, if I'm not mistaken. François's cynicism crept in.

Once clean and clothed, Giovanni's sensuality, so appreciated by Isabeau, was readily obvious to someone attuned to physical beauty, such as an *artiste*. François had noted the boy's comeliness immediately.

You beheld a possible petit amour, *a new bedmate*. His mind swept into scenarios where he might exploit the *comte's* interest in his captive wolf. *You think to delve into the boy, to possess his body in your bed as well as his image upon your wall.*

This was confirmed when the *comte* asked, "May I meet him? It would be best to see him … in the flesh. If I were face-to-face with the actual person, I may change my mind."

François thought he tried to sound unconcerned, merely curious, but he was certain he heard a barely concealed tremor of anticipation.

"Of course. He's in my studio. As a matter of fact, he's sitting for a painting now. Your arrival called me away." François got to his feet, gesturing to the door. "Come. I'll introduce you and you may decide."

He had no doubt what was going to happen. Once Duquesne actually met Giovanni, he'd definitely want the boy. In more ways than one.

Do I dare let him? How much more can I charge if I allow him to groan with the wolf? I'll have to make certain there's plenty of wolfsbane around.

That Giovanni might object to having his body abused in such a way never crossed his mind. After the gypsies' treatment, why should he? Hadn't Boamas hinted as much?

Outside in the corridor, they met Isabeau, who'd come downstairs. Stopped by Maxime from entering the salon because "the master has a distinguished guest," she'd lingered outside, eavesdropping.

"We have guests, François?" She made her voice gracious, ignoring her husband's exasperated expression.

"Your Lordship, my wife." François grudgingly introduced her. "Isabeau, this is the *Comte* Duquesne. He's come to discuss a commission." He frowned as her eyes widened upon hearing his visitor's name.

If you dare say the least thing causing me to lose this commission ...

Isabeau saw the threat in his expression and stifled her reaction.

"*Madame* François." Displaying the charm that drew both sexes to him, Duquesne bowed with a flourish, then lifted her hand, kissing it.

"Your Lordship." She forced herself to smile, managing not to jerk her hand from his.

"My studio is this way." François dismissed her by turning his back and walking away, gesturing to the back corridor. "It's in a converted barn behind the cottage."

He led the *comte* to the studio where Giovanni still dozed in the chair. The wolfsbane had slipped from his fingers and fallen to the floor. François kicked it under the chair as he shook the boy.

"Giovanni, wake up." To Duquesne, he said in a disparaging tone, "Lazy bastard. I give him shelter, and this is how he repays me. Leave him unsupervised for a moment, and he can sleep anywhere and does." He raised his voice as the boy came awake with a start. "There's someone here who wishes to speak to you."

"Master?" Giovanni's voice was groggy. "I was only resting my eyes ..."

"Never mind," François interrupted. "On your feet. Greet His Lordship, *le Comte* Duquesne."

Barely awake, Giovanni staggered upright. He swung around, seeing the nobleman. Regaining his balance, he bowed as Isabeau had taught him. "Your Lordship."

Duquesne stared. Briefly, he appeared speechless, eyes widening as if he gazed upon such a treasure that he couldn't utter a word.

At last, he managed, "His face is perfect, but the body …" His near-transparent gaze flicked over the doublet and stocks. "I must see it to be certain it is also acceptable. Have him undress."

"Certainly." François didn't hesitate. Turning to Giovanni, he ordered, "You heard. Strip."

"Sir?" Still in a slight stupor, Giovanni looked at François as if he didn't understand.

"You heard me," François's reply was brusque. "Take off your clothes."

For a moment, François thought the boy was going to refuse. He took a step toward him, so close the boy was forced to back away. As he did so, he stepped on the sprig of wolfsbane protruding from under the chair. It crackled ominously.

Giovanni relaxed, his eyes once more becoming slumberous. Without protest, he slid off the doublet, dropping it into the chair, then hesitated.

"The rest of it, too," Duquesne ordered, his eagerness barely hidden.

Giovanni's hands went to the neck of the shirt, pulling it over his head. It fell to the floor.

"The stocks, also," the *comte* prompted. "That's an old-fashioned pair, isn't it?"

François gestured. Giovanni slid his fingers inside the cross-tied top of the stocks. He pushed them past his hips. They joined the shirt on the floor. Hands at his sides, head bowed, and eyes averted, he stood naked.

Duquesne didn't speak. The silence was so heavy that François swore he could feel it pressing in on them.

"Well, Your Lordship?" he dared ask. "Is he satisfactory?"

The question was unnecessary. He'd known the boy would be, that he'd fulfill any lustful image the *comte* had. He could see it in Duquesne's expression, as well as in that long, indrawn breath, almost like a gasp. He simply wanted the pleasure of *hearing* the nobleman say so.

"He's a bit thin," Duquesne commented, attempting to be critical.

Giovanni's enforced starvation was becoming evident. His ribs showed slightly, but not as much as François wanted. The portions of food Isabeau left on her plate for him to secretly consume kept him from total emaciation.

"He doesn't eat much," François excused. "Doesn't like our good French cuisine, I think. Don't worry, he'll fatten up quick enough."

"The beard will have to go, but otherwise ... *Magnifique.*" Duquesne ran his tongue over his lower lip, making its pink tint gleam damply.

The boy shivered, as if more than that icy gaze touched him. Briefly, his hands twitched as though he wanted to raise them and cover himself. Otherwise, he didn't move.

The *comte's* gaze roved Giovanni's body, then moved lower.

"What's this?" His attention concentrated on the dark-furred groin. "His *organe d'amour ...*"

Giovanni flinched. His hands, half raised, shielding the organ, then dropped again in resignation.

"What happened? It's missing its foreskin." He gestured, eyes accusing. "De Montaigne, did you ..."

"He came to me that way," François explained. "He was stolen by gypsies. They did it. Who can say why?"

"The godless bastards." Duquesne looked murderous. "Ruining such a masterpiece of earthly beauty ..."

"I rescued him," François lied, ignoring the abrupt glare the boy gave him. He added quickly, "I can paint in the missing flesh. There'll be no problem."

Duquesne looked thoughtful, catching that full lower lip between his teeth, tapping his forefinger against it. At last, he said, "I think not. That bit of bare rod gives him an exotic air, don't you think?"

Staring at the naked organ, François pretended to consider. "As you say, sir," he agreed.

"It evokes something rare and forbidden." The *comte* struggled to tear his gaze from Giovanni, who hadn't moved. He looked at François. "Yes, de Montaigne, he'll do perfectly as Adonis. Paint him as he is. *Exactly* as he is."

François bowed.

"May I touch him?"

François gestured permission. With his commission assured, he didn't have to think about it.

Eagerly, Duquesne placed a hand on Giovanni's shoulder, sliding it across the nape of his neck under the dark curls. Following the ridge of his spine, he stroked a path down the boy's back, making little circles around the knob of each bit of backbone, nails pressing in just enough to scratch a minute striation in the skin.

Under his fingers, the boy's skin visibly quivered. Giovanni tensed, hands at his sides, clenching into fists. Duquesne looked back at François, eyes gleaming, lust moistening those cold depths like tears.

"Would you allow me some time alone with him?"

Giovanni's head came up, eyes staring into his master's. François looked away, concentrating on the *comte*. He'd seen a warning in that dark gaze, a warning of something dire. *Do as he says and someone will die ...*

"I'm afraid I must say no to that, Your Lordship." At Duquesne's *moue* of disappointment, his frantic thoughts scurried for an excuse that wouldn't lose him his commission. *What the hell can I say?* "You see ..."

"No explanation is necessary." Duquesne quite willingly accepted François's refusal. He waved away any excuse he might give. "Perhaps it's best to wait until after the painting is completed before any kind of, uh, consummation. Anticipation betters the experience."

François's bow could've meant anything. His thoughts were something else, wondering how much wolfsbane and elixir of valerian it would take to make the wolf accept the libertine's affection.

"I trust you'll allow me to attend some of the sittings?"

François nodded.

"Shall we adjourn to your salon and discuss price and such?"

They moved away, leaving Giovanni standing there.

François called over his shoulder, "Get dressed and go to your room."

Chapter Twenty-Three

Outside the studio, Isabeau watched in disbelief.

She had followed François and his guest, curious as to what someone of Duquesne's reputation could want with her husband. Hiding at the corner of the studio's outer wall, she peered through the window, listening in outrage as François ordered Giovanni to disrobe. When Duquesne touched him, she began to shake with fury. How dare that sodomite touch her Gio as if he were a prize bit of horseflesh her husband had on display?

It was all she could do not to shriek a protest. She wanted to rush inside and push the *comte* away, curse him, perhaps pick up the little tack hammer lying near François's paints and send it crashing against that handsome but lustful skull.

Her husband had even less scruples than she realized. She'd seen the look passing between him and Giovanni, the anger in the boy's eyes, the threat. Fear of the wolf springing to life was the only thing keeping François from turning him over to that monster.

As the two left the studio, she shrank around the corner of

the building out of sight, waiting until they were back inside the cottage before she went into the studio.

Giovanni was struggling with his stocks, attempting to pull them on. As Isabeau had shown him, he worked them up his legs, smoothing the fabric over his calves and thighs.

"Mistress." He looked from her to the door. A hand concealed his privates where they peeked over the top of the stocks. He gave the waistband a final wrench. "You saw."

It wasn't a question.

She nodded.

"He wanted to lie with me." His voice shook with an emotion she couldn't define—anger ... bitterness ... rage? "The master refused."

"Thank God for that." She studied his face, wondering if she actually saw a change in it or if it was her imagination. Were his cheekbones tighter, eyes narrower? They seemed to have changed color, as if a fire kindled in his brain and was shining through.

"Your God had nothing to do with it," he snapped, startling her by talking back and so irreverently. "If he'd agreed, I'd have killed them both and he knew it." He made a slashing motion with his hand. "Ripped out their throats."

"Gio, don't say such a thing." She glanced at the door, fearful that François would return with more mischief in mind.

"They deserve it." In that moment, he looked murderous. "*All* of them ..."

She imagined his teeth sinking into François's throat as easily as they cut through his sleeve and wrist, of a taloned hand slashing the *comte*'s jugular, the blond hair crimson with gore, blood everywhere, and Giovanni ...

"Please, don't speak like that," she begged, seizing him by the arm and shaking it. "I don't want anything hurting you. If you were to die, I couldn't bear it. I—"

She'd said more than she intended. He stared at the hand on his arm, then at her. She released him, whirled, preparing to escape through the door.

He caught her hand, spinning her around so violently, she fell into his arms. They stared at each other. He bent toward her.

Inside, Isabeau felt a pain so sharp it pierced her very heart. She wanted to scream out the emotion welling in her chest. She pulled away, and Giovanni let her go.

Outside, she composed herself before walking with a determined stride into the cottage.

The *comte* had gone. She heard the echo of the horses' hooves on the path as she stormed into the salon.

François congratulated himself on his commission by enjoying a glass of wine. On the table lay a stack of coins. He tossed one into the air, caught it, then tossed it again. It gleamed in the candlelight.

"How dare you let that man touch him? How could you allow it?"

"I allowed it because he wishes to be my patron." He didn't ask of whom she spoke, nor was surprised she knew. "Eavesdroppers never hear anything good, Isabeau."

"He's a libertine, a degenerate."

"A degenerate who's very influential—and rich. As are his friends."

"They're as evil as he ..."

"Who cares? As long as they desire my paintings. They can make my fortune."

"Do you want it made that way, François? Do you wish to be known as 'de Montaigne, creator of *pornographie*?'"

"If it makes me rich, yes!" He dropped the coin atop the others. "Come, Isabeau, why are you so incensed? I didn't allow it, did I? Although I admit I was tempted. But no, I refused to let him violate the boy."

"For that, I thank you." She was more sarcastic than grateful, however.

"Don't get me wrong," François continued as if she hadn't spoken. "I don't care if Duquesne buries himself to the hilt in Giovanni's backside, but I fear such a bodily insult might so overcome the wolfsbane's spell it would awaken the beast and he'd kill the *comte*." He obviously didn't think Giovanni's revenge would extend to his master, either. "That wouldn't be good for business."

Isabeau stared. "You greedy man. You've no concern for Giovanni's welfare at all."

"So I refused," he went on, ignoring her interruption.

She relaxed visibly, and that didn't go unnoticed.

"You're growing overly fond of him, Isabeau," François said. "That's not good. Perhaps after I've finished with my St. Jean, I'll sell him to *le comte*—if he still wants him." He looked serious. "Yes. Adorn him with a necklet of wolfsbane and he'll be amenable to anything, I imagine."

"Giovanni's a pure, simple soul, and to let that corrupt, licentious ..."

"Pure? Simple? Stop your protests, Isabeau." François's laugh mocked her. "It isn't anything he hasn't done before."

"How can you say that?"

"I can because Boamas told me so," he retorted. "When I broached the subject of buying the creature, he asked if I wished to be serviced by him, remember?"

"Surely ..."

"Yes. Surely." Her horrified look said he'd made his point. "Perhaps I should simply make the *comte* a gift after my St. Jean is finished. Then the pederast and the catamite can be happy together."

"François! You wouldn't. You promised."

"Promises are made to be broken," he stated flatly and changed the subject. "Let's not talk of that now. We've other matters to discuss."

"Like what? What could be more important than protecting Gio from ..."

"Our conversation of the other night, which was never finished," he reminded. "I think it's time you stopped being concerned with the *loup-garou's* welfare and turned your thoughts to more maternal pursuits."

"What do you mean?" She frowned, still thinking of Duquesne.

"I mean, of our having a child. Have you dismissed the subject from your mind so quickly?"

"This isn't the time to—" That was the last thing Isabeau wanted to think about just now.

"I believe it is. Why do you avoid the subject, Isabeau? Is it that you don't wish to have a child?"

"François ..."

"That's it, isn't it?" Though she shook her head, something in her look must have made him think otherwise, for he went on, "I thought so. Thus, the day I spoke to the leech, I had him write out the recipe. I took it to the apothecary and got this."

He went directly to the mantel. On it lay a small open casque. Inside were little packets, wrapped in a physician's paper.

"What are those?"

"The remedy for your infertility, wife. I see no need to speak further on this, or to delay putting it into action. Cooperate, Isabeau, give me what I wish, and I promise the boy will be protected."

"How can I trust you?" she reminded him. "Didn't you just say promises are made to be broken?"

"This one I'll keep. I swear it on my eyes."

That shook Isabeau. An artist who couldn't see wasn't of much use. If something happened to François's eyes ... That convinced her he was serious.

If it keeps Giovanni safe. Grudgingly, she nodded.

"Good." Opening one packet, he shook its contents into a glass, poured wine over it, and handed it to her.

"What if I had refused?" She reluctantly accepted it.

"I was determined you'd take it tonight if I had to pour it into you." He made it a threat. "Drink it."

Isabeau stared at the contents for a long time, watching the grains on the surface make narrow black threads through the red wine as they dissolved. At last, she took two sips, then held it out to François. He shook his head.

"All of it."

She swallowed the rest. Whatever the apothecary had compounded gave the wine a bitter aftertaste. She handed back the glass.

He returned it to the mantel and poured a second glass. Into it, he sprinkled what the other packet held. This time, the powder turned the wine a murky green.

"Must I drink a second one also?" She was dismayed. "The taste of the other was revolting."

"You aren't the only one who must endure vile tastes to achieve this goal. I also have to suffer the leech's potions." He tossed it down in one gulp, set the glass upon the mantel, and turned to look at her. "You're flushed."

Isabeau put a hand to her head. As if prompted by François's words, she felt dizzy, her forehead hot and feverish. Heat spread down her shoulders, through her body, settling in her nethers. She looked up at François. His cheeks were also red, a fiery stain splotching his forehead.

"The leech said it would be so. That means it's working."

He glanced down at his codpiece, where a noticeable bulge was forming. He seized her wrist, pulling her from the chair. "Come, wife, let's not waste the opportunity."

With that, he hauled Isabeau from the room, dragging her through the doorway.

"I-I can't walk," she protested. Indeed, she stumbled and swayed against him, her legs feeling as if the strength in them trickled away.

"No matter." He pulled her toward him. "I'll carry you."

He swung her into his arms. She didn't fight, knew it wasn't any use, but went limp as he climbed the stairs. She felt languid, weak, her will melting away.

Inside the bedchamber, he slung her onto the bed. He was fully aroused now, rod straining against the fabric of his codpiece, a damp ring soaking through. François pulled loose the ties, and the rectangle of cloth fell, letting his erection spring free. As Isabeau struggled to sit up, he threw himself upon her, pushing up her skirts. She had time for one bare protest before he was inside her.

As far as Isabeau was concerned, the herbal concoction did nothing for her. Other than that monumental weakness, she felt not a bit different. If anything had changed, it was that her hatred for her husband had multiplied. François, however, was so affected that they coupled three times before he collapsed into a sleep resembling one of his wine-induced stupors, making her wonder how much soporific had been in his potion. Surely it wasn't the same mixture she had swallowed, for she felt none of the lust he'd displayed nor any sleepiness.

Listening to her husband's snores, she wondered if the potion worked, while dreading that it had.

Chapter Twenty-Four

THE NEXT DAY was a flurry of movement and excitement—for François, at least. He awoke filled with the enthusiasm he always assumed when beginning a new project. For everyone else, it was a mere inconvenience and confusion.

Rushing through the usual morning routine, he bolted his breakfast, leaving the table after only one slice of bread, a single pork cutlet, and half a portion of coddled eggs.

"There's something I was reminded of last night."

That surprised Isabeau, who'd have sworn he had nothing on his mind the night before but tupping her mercilessly until he fell asleep from exhaustion.

Calling to Maxime, he left the room, going down the corridor.

Uninvited, Isabeau trailed behind, thinking she'd best stay close. It always seemed better to be nearby when François did anything unexpected.

He went to the back entrance, onto the covered walkway to the studio, unlocked it, and walked directly to Giovanni's door.

"It's not locked." It was an accusation.

"You didn't tell anyone to lock it," she said quietly. She

wasn't about to admit she hadn't thought to lock Giovanni in when she left him the night before. "You were too eager to—"

"No matter. At least the creature took himself to bed like a good servant."

He pushed open the door.

It swung slowly, revealing the cot and the figure lying upon it, silhouetted by the sun coming through the unshuttered window.

"Master?" Giovanni's voice was heavy with sleep. He raised a hand, rubbing his eyes.

"Get up," François ordered. "Come out here where I may see you."

Giovanni obeyed, not with the hasty scramble of a servant eager to please, however. More a languid rising from the cot, a saunter toward them. His footsteps made no sound as he approached the rectangle of light on the storage room door.

Isabeau was relieved to see he still wore his stocks, though he'd removed his shirt. The sight of his bare chest and the definition of his ribs nevertheless made a trembling inside her, thin as he was. It wasn't completely from pity.

"Mistress." He looked past François to Isabeau, his manner changing subtly. The walk was no longer a stalking glide but became a solid step. He stopped in the doorway, bowing, saying as he straightened, "Sir?"

"It's come to me how Greek youths are portrayed beardless. For the *comte's* painting, you must be clean-shaven. Have you skill with a razor?"

No." Giovanni didn't hesitate. There was a pause before he added, "Sir."

François looked surprised. "Did I not see you beardless after the mistress bathed you?" He sounded eager to catch the boy in a lie.

Isabeau shifted uneasily. *What is he saying?*

"Yes, master." Giovanni didn't move, except to nod. "But the mistress used the razor, not I. I watch Boamas shave, but he never let me touch anything sharp."

"Not surprising," François muttered. "So you don't know how to use one?"

Giovanni shook his head.

"Doubtless, he didn't trust you with a blade ... Nor do I, but you must be rid of that beard." François looked at the servant. "Maxime, from now on, each morning, you'll bring water and shaving articles and ..."

"Oh, master, you can't mean I'm to ..." Maxime's voice shook.

"Since you've suddenly been granted the ability to read my thoughts, that's exactly what I mean. Don't argue," François snapped as Maxime went white and started to do exactly that. "Each day, I'll begin my painting session with Giovanni newly shaven. Understand?"

Silently, Maxime hung his head and nodded.

"We'll begin now. Fetch everything. That beard belongs to Alphonse's beggar, not to Adonis. It must go." When the servant hurried back up the walkway, François turned to Isabeau. As if Giovanni no longer stood before him, he said, "Speak to him. The creature's sly. Tell him he must behave. I'll have no mishaps with either Maxime *or* the razor. Understand?"

"Yes, François." She was so startled, she spoke meekly.

"Good. Now then, I have to ride into town and get the frame and canvas." He looked again at Giovanni, patiently waiting to be dismissed. "You. Be prepared to sweat today. There's much to do."

He stamped out, leaving her standing there. At the door, however, he turned back.

"You'll stay away while Maxime's here. It's unseemly for you to be present for the creature's *toilette intime.*"

Isabeau didn't remind him she'd already seen Giovanni naked when she bathed him, that she'd protested that, and been ordered to proceed.

Without waiting for a reply, François walked away.

Isabeau looked back at Giovanni. "You heard him. Please behave, Gio."

"Mistress, what would I do?" He gave her an innocent look.

"Don't pretend. Maxime's afraid of you. You'd enjoy taking that razor from him and waving it in a threatening manner, even in jest." She could envision it as she spoke, Giovanni wresting the razor from the servant's unresisting hand, perhaps with a growl, Maxime cowering ...

"Do more than threaten," he confirmed, smiling in a way that made his overdeveloped incisors even more prominent. The thought of the absent Maxime's fear amused him. "Like to cut his throat and the master's, too."

He made a slicing movement with one hand.

"That's exactly what I mean," she exclaimed. "Don't even think such a thing, much less say it, and definitely *don't* try it."

"What if Maxime cut *me?*" He raised his head, gesturing at his throat. "Shaky hand ... razor slip ...?"

"I've watched him shave François. He won't do such a thing unless he's frightened."

Giovanni shrugged. "Then I not frighten him." He looked earnest. "I not want a bloodletting, mistress."

She relaxed.

"Unless it's not my blood," he added, and smiled again.

In that moment, she saw in his expression something completely inhuman, but as she watched, it changed to a winsome smile, a twinkle in the dark eyes.

He's teasing me. She managed not to smile.

"Just be good," she begged and added, because she realized it might make him act properly, "for my sake."

He sobered. "For you, mistress." He bowed.

"That's—"

Whatever she was going to say was interrupted by Maxime's arrival. The servant carried a tray on which rested a towel and a basin filled with water. On the towel lay a small bar of soap and one of François's razors, a discarded one, meaning the blade had gone dull and probably could no longer be well-honed.

Good enough for a *loup-garou* but not for an *artiste*.

"I'll go now," she finished.

"*Madame.*" Maxime looked alarmed. "You're not staying?"

"My husband has ordered me away," Isabeau replied stiffly.

Maxime didn't see Giovanni's grin. Isabeau ignored it.

"Do you think you need a chaperone, Maxime?" She glanced at Giovanni. "Remember your promise."

His answer was a slight bow.

"Let's get this over with," Maxime muttered.

Giovanni bowed again, making a gesture as if to usher the servant inside the storage room.

Maxime didn't move. "You go first."

The water in the basin began to slosh as the hands holding the tray trembled.

Later, Maxime came to the salon where Isabeau had taken refuge with her embroidery stand. During a stay with the *marquis*, François had seen pillowslips embellished with the du Maurier crest. Therefore, he must have some like them, though he deserved no heraldic device.

"How can I sew what you don't have?" she'd asked him.

His reply was to sketch a fanciful monogram, the letter "M" in a garland of leaves and stars. Isabeau admitted it was beautiful, if historically erroneous. She'd dutifully transferred the design to the white cotton slips and gathered her silk threads and needles.

"*Madame ...*"

"You survived, I see. Unscathed." She made her tone sarcastic, turning her attention back to the tiny stitches necessary to create one curlicued end of the "M." "How does Giovanni fare? As well, I hope?"

"The crea ... boy was well-behaved, *madame*." Maxime's tone equaled hers. He affected a thoughtful air. "I think he may be trusted with a blade and taught to shave himself, providing I stay to supervise."

"And the fact that you won't have to touch him would have no part in your opinion, would it?" Isabeau wasn't certain whether it would ever be a good idea to allow anything with a sharp edge in Giovanni's hands, not after what he'd said, but she wasn't about to tell that to a servant.

"Not at all." Maxime looked insulted, actually huffed his reply. "Anyway, that isn't why I'm here."

"Why are you here, then?" she answered. Twisting the thread into a knot, she tied it off by driving the needle through, then snipping it before giving him a weary look.

"That woman is here. Lisette." Maxime spoke with distaste. "She says the master left word at the tavern that he had work for her."

Lisette Camargue was a serving wench at one of Aux-la-Piémont's taverns, a bright-haired voluptuous creature, and a wanton where any man was concerned, modeling for François when she wasn't beguiling the young men of the town. Neither Isabeau nor Maxime had a liking for her, the one subject upon which they had mutual agreement, since each believed that a woman who posed naked was nothing more than a slut. Isabeau also secretly believed that if François bestowed as much affection upon her as he did the bar wench, their married life might be more compatible.

She didn't hesitate. "Tell her to go around the cottage and wait in the studio. I won't have that woman inside my house."

With a satisfied nod, Maxime went to refuse Lisette entry.

"Maxime, wait." Isabeau had a sudden thought.

He paused, looking back.

"Giovanni, where is he?"

"The master gave me no more instructions concerning *him*, so after I"—here Maxime's lips curled in even further distaste than when speaking of Lisette—"after I finished that chore, I took him to the kitchen where he's now washing last night's supper dishes. If he's only going to wait at table, he may as well do something useful with the rest of his time," he added defensively as if Isabeau had protested.

"Mathilde didn't argue about that?"

"I set the tub in a corner so he's out of her sight," he answered.

"Good." Isabeau returned to the subject of Lisette. "My husband intends to use that woman in this painting, along with Giovanni, but I don't want her associating with him any longer than she has to."

She had no doubt once Lisette saw Giovanni, she'd attempt to make him another conquest.

"No doubt that'll be enough," Maxime muttered, his opinion obviously the same.

"What did you say?"

"Very good, mistress." Maxime bowed. "She's waiting. I must get her off the doorstep." He turned away.

Lisette's only reply when he repeated Isabeau's message was a smirk, as if she knew how they felt and that François preferred her to his wife.

* * *

THE COTTAGE WAS quiet until François returned several hours

later, bringing with him the usual disruptions, though this time they were kept outside.

Accompanying him was the carpenter, driving his horse and cart. In the back of the cart were several solid but narrow, lath-like strips of oak hardwood to make the frame on which the canvas would be stretched. They were very long, so much longer than the cart that the tailgate was open, their ends trailing above the ground.

The carpenter stopped the cart in front of the studio door. François tied his reins to the corral fence, and they unloaded the laths, as well as a large quantity of coarse cloth, canvas purchased from the local weaver who prepared the fabric especially for François. Its light brown color and smoother texture indicated it was linen, more expensive than cotton, which was cheaper to buy but less finely woven. As with his paints, François didn't stint in purchasing the best canvases. It was rolled carefully into a large scroll to prevent creasing or wrinkling the weave.

François preferred his canvases unprimed, without the application of the coating necessary before painting began. He liked to do the priming himself, using rabbit skin glue, buying the pelts from the butcher, separating under-tissue from fur, and boiling and rendering it personally to make certain the application layers were the correct thickness. After adding the proper amounts of chalk and white paint to form an emulsion, he'd compound the mixture with linseed oil to form a coating that would be flexible and not become brittle as it dried. Generally, he stretched and framed several canvases at once, which Isabeau had said was a mercy since the preparation of the glue was a noxious and malodorous process.

As they carried the wood, which wasn't heavy but unwieldy because of its length, the carpenter looked up at the door, and commented, "Are you planning on constructing the frame inside, *Maître* François?"

"I usually do," François replied, guiding the wood through the door. He saw Lisette, half-reclining in the chair where Giovanni had posed, and smiled.

"In that case, you may have a problem."

"What do you mean?" Francois released his end of the wood, laying it upon one of the worktables where the tools needed to stretch the canvas—the small hammer, carpet tacks, canvas pliers, a carpenter's right angle, and matte knife—lay waiting.

Lisette got up from the chair, and he greeted her with a hug.

"*Bonjour, chérie.* I see you got my message."

She replied by kissing his cheek. "Hugo at the tavern said you needed me?" She paused, then added with a simper, "To model, I mean?"

"Your studio door is only eighty-four inches high," the carpenter said, drawing François's attention back to him. "Two of these laths are eight feet long, two ten feet. If you assemble them inside the studio, you'll never get the painting out in one piece."

"Are you certain?" François had never thought about the height of the door. When rebuilding the barn, he'd simply taken the original frame of the side door and reused it. Being a little taller than most men in the village, if he could walk through a door without striking his head, he didn't worry about its actual height.

Now, however ...

"Positive."

As if to confirm this, the carpenter dug into the pouch slung over one shoulder and extracted a small dowel on which was wound a length of starched cloth marked in quarter, half, and inch-long increments. Pressing the end against the bottom of the doorframe, he unwound the fabric, pushing it up its side.

"Here." He handed the roll to François. "You're taller than I am. Check it."

Accepting the roll, François continued unwinding the cloth until his outstretched arm pushed it into the corner where the side frame met the crosspiece. He glanced at the marking on the cloth.

"Eighty-four inches," he read. "Damn."

Ignoring Lisette, who pouted prettily, he dropped the tape measure, leaving the carpenter to re-roll it.

"I've never done a painting so large before. I didn't think of that." He glanced around as if seeking a solution, then brightened. "The windows, we'll take them out ... no, they're single panes and won't open. Confound it!" He struck the table in vexation, making the wood bounce. "I can't paint outside and certainly couldn't leave the canvas there. What if it rains? What if someone were tempted to steal it?"

Returning the tape to his bag, the carpenter shrugged. He'd already been paid for the wood, as the weaver had for the canvas, so he wasn't really concerned, unless ...

"You aren't going to return the wood, are you?" His tone indicated he hoped not. No one else in the town would have use for laths of that size and length.

"Of course not," François snapped, as if the idea were absurd. "I've already been paid a partial commission for the painting. I simply have to figure out how to ..."

At that moment, Maxime appeared, escorting the *Comte* Duquesne down the walkway.

"Your Lordship?" François looked a little perturbed that the *comte* had appeared in the midst of this problem. "What are you ...?"

"You said I might sit in on your sessions," the *comte*

reminded him. "I apologize for being so early, but I confess I could hardly wait." He looked at the wood strips and the roll of cloth lying on the table beside François's hammers and tacks. "What is this?"

"Be assured, you're welcome, my lord," François back-tracked hastily, forcing aside his concern and assuming a welcoming air. "This?" He also studied the wood. "A minor problem."

"Oh?"

"I'm afraid the canvas is going to be too large to go through my studio door, and I'm currently trying to find a solution."

"That's right, noble sir," the carpenter put in his two *centimes'* worth.

"My dear *artiste*." Duquesne laughed. "There's no problem at all."

"No?" François frowned. "I'm glad you think so, Your Lordship." He affected a rueful tone to hide his irritation at what he considered the noble's cavalier attitude toward this complication. "For I see it as a great stumbling block to my fulfilling your wishes."

Duquesne put a hand on his shoulder, gesturing toward the cottage and by inference, through it to where his coach waited. "The rooms in my *château* are vast, and their doors taller than average. Indeed, some are so huge that one might think they were fashioned for giants. You'll simply come to the *château*, assemble your canvas there, and paint in the room where the picture will hang. Thus, one obstacle is surmounted, and I won't have to worry about transporting the painting after it's finished." He waved both hands and beamed. "Problem solved."

He made it sound so simple.

"Part of it, at least," François agreed. Nevertheless, he was always one to look ahead for snags and loopholes. "I'm afraid it's quite far to travel there and back each day, however."

How far was it by horseback? Four hours? Six? He wasn't certain where the *château* was located, except that it was in Sainte-Louise Modeste, which was next to La Chapelle.

"Why do such a commute?" Duquesne asked. "There are over a hundred rooms. You can take yourself, your models, paints, and whatever other equipment you need, and stay until the work is done." He paused, then added, in case there was any misunderstanding, "As my guest."

Stay at the *chateau*? Live there for however long it took to paint the picture? Perhaps be invited to partake of whatever forbidden pleasures were offered after work was done each day? François was momentarily wordless, in the next instant delighted, until he remembered one thing preventing him from accepting.

The full moon occurring in the middle of the coming month.

"Oh, Your Lordship, I couldn't impose ..." he began.

"No imposition," the *comte* denied.

If anything, he looked eager to have guests, thinking of Giovanni ensconced in one of those bedrooms, no doubt.

"In fact, it would be my pleasure to offer you the hospitality of *Château de l'Esroc Pâle*."

House of the Pale Rogue? Briefly, François was intrigued by the name. It so obviously referred to the *comte* himself. Nevertheless, if the wolf were in residence ...

He shook his head, setting himself back on a practical and safer track.

"The preparation of the canvases—it's a slow and filthy process, taking several hours. The glue making up the gesso has a smell."

"I have servants ready to clean any spills and mess. You can prepare the glue outside, using one of the laundry washpots and an open fire. If it must be done inside," he continued as François started to speak, "the windows can be opened to eliminate odors. If the smell lingers, we'll burn incense, and I have scented candles."

It seemed the *comte* had an answer for everything.

"Painting may take several months. My wife, I couldn't leave her that long."

"Why?" Duquesne asked bluntly. "Does she have a roving eye?"

The idea of Isabeau being unfaithful almost made François laugh, but he knew better than to do so aloud, for that would make it appear he had belittled the *comte's* question.

"Nothing like that," he denied, and glanced around.

The carpenter was waiting, a little impatiently, to see if François was going to return the wood, or, since he'd been paid to help assemble the frame as he'd done so many times before, if he could begin doing so. Lisette had dropped back into the chair, looking bored since she wasn't currently the center of attention, while Maxime hovered at the periphery, making certain he wasn't too close that he might be tainted by either her proximity or the *comte's*.

The prude. François managed a contemptuous glance in the servant's direction.

"I won't suggest bringing her with you." Duquesne didn't look the least apologetic as he said this. "A spouse will only be in the way of any after-hours relaxation."

"Actually ..." François took a step away, beckoning the *comte* closer. His Lordship leaned forward as he lowered his voice. "It's a delicate matter. *Intime*, as a matter of fact."

That brought a raising of one blond brow.

"We're trying for a child." He waved his hands ineffectually. "That requires my being at home every night, you see ..."

"Say no more." Duquesne waved away further explanation. "The wish for an heir. I understand fully. One can't sire a child long-distance. I went through the same thing before my son was born," he admitted, and looked sympathetic. "I was forced to reside in the same place as my wife for nearly seven months."

There was an expressive roll of the blue eyes as if such proximity had been a severe strain.

"You … you have a son, sir?" François had to admit that fact was most surprising. He saw nothing paternal about this man. At all.

Duquesne nodded. "He's with my wife in Paris. As soon as it was confirmed I had an heir, my duty was done, so I see them once a year and the rest of the time, I'm free." He clapped François on the shoulder. "So, each morning, my coach will bring you to the *château* where you'll work on my painting, and each evening, it will carry you back to your wife and your husbandly duty."

The icy eyes glowed with glacial brilliance.

"In between, you're invited to sample some of my little pleasure palace's delights. We get up a little earlier and retire a little later, eh? What do you say?"

"I say"—for a moment, François's voice trembled with anticipation—"I say, we must be on our way. We've wasted too much time talking."

"Good enough." Duquesne looked around. "Will it take long to prepare the canvas, do you think?"

"Not long at all," François assured him.

"Now, then." Duquesne's icy gaze lit on Lisette as if just seeing her. "Where's that beautiful boy? And who's this lovely creature sitting so dolefully in that chair?"

"This is Lisette Camargue, Your Lordship." François held out his hand, and she placed her own in it to be drawn out of the chair. "She'll be your Venus." He glanced at Maxime. "Get him."

The servant disappeared through the door.

"*My* Venus, most assuredly." The *comte* accepted her hand, bowing over it. "*Mademoiselle* Lisette, *enchanté*."

Lisette simpered prettily, fingers fluttering against her bosom and drawing the count's gaze there.

"Perhaps you'll accept my hospitality, also, when you aren't posing for *Maître* François?"

"Are any of those hundred rooms bedchambers, my lord?" Lisette let it be known she'd been actively eavesdropping.

"At least three-quarters of them," the *comte* replied. "One could sleep in a new room each night for nearly three months."

Lisette made a little moue of astonishment, mouth a round "O". "What about the other twenty-five?"

"I'll personally show them to you." Duquesne spun to look at François. "Gather what you need and let's be on our way." He squeezed Lisette's hand and released it. "The sooner we start, the sooner I shall give you the grand tour, *chérie*."

By now, Maxime was back with Giovanni. Upon seeing the *comte*, the boy hesitated, but when the noble merely looked at him and made no untoward movement, he came cautiously into the studio. He was likewise stared at by Lisette.

"You wanted me, sir?" He spoke slowly, drawling the words, giving François such a slack-mouthed look he appeared slightly addled.

That made his master frown. *Playing the dimwit? Do you think that'll make His Lordship shy away from wanting you?* He didn't say that aloud, however. If the wolf wished to attempt a bit of trickery, let him. They would see who was the best at that game. François had a feeling the *comte* would win, hands down.

"A problem with the canvas demands we go to his lordship's *château*. I'll paint there," he explained tersely. "Lisette and I will ride in the coach with his lordship."

Lisette smiled and fluttered her lashes at Duquesne, who grinned broadly.

"Maxime, you will ride atop with the driver." He glanced at the servant.

"I'm to go, too, sir?" Maxime blanched at the thought of entering such a hall of iniquity.

"Didn't I just say so? Are you deaf?" To the *comte*, he said, "Forgive the stupidity of my servants, sir."

Duquesne merely nodded, his attention alternating between Giovanni and Lisette, who was also studying the boy with a speculative look.

"The carpenter will follow us with the supplies, and you'll ride with him," he told Giovanni. "Help dismantle my easels ... yes, both of them ..." he snapped as Giovanni started to say something. "While I pack my paints."

With a bow, the boy skirted around the *comte*, moving to the table where the carpenter was already fitting a small wrench to one of the bolts holding an easel's crossbeams in place. Each was about five feet high, H-frames, with two horizontal posts and a crossbar that could be raised or lowered to accommodate the canvas's size.

"The carpenter's cart should hold everything," François told Duquesne. "Once the canvas is primed, I should have time to do some preliminary sketches while it dries."

With Giovanni and Maxime helping, the carpenter dismantled the two easels, stacking the pieces together and tying them in a bundle. While they carried them to the cart, François packed his paints into a leather valise. Inside the bag were pockets into which he placed the little pots of paint, turpentine, and linseed oil, tucking palette, tools, brushes, and palette knives into the bottom.

* * *

Isabeau was more than a little astonished when her husband appeared with his pack, informing her he was off to the *comte's château*.

"His *château*? *Non*. You're not taking Giovanni into that place," she stated adamantly.

"I not only am, but he's going every day until the painting is finished," François declared. "Don't worry about your little wolf in lamb's clothing, wife. I promise he'll return every evening, as will I."

He didn't miss the downcast expression that part of his statement caused.

Chapter Twenty-Five

EXCEPT FOR A FEW moments when the carpenter's horse balked as Giovanni climbed into the cart, the journey to Duquesne's *château* was without incident.

The *comte* must have had an invisible sentry system in place. Even before the coach turned onto the cobbled drive leading to the *château*, a row of servants assembled on the walk at the porticoed entrance. Accompanied by Duquesne's *maître d'hôtel*, twenty footmen and twenty serving maids stood on either side.

As soon as the coach pulled to a halt and the footman jumped down to open the door so the *comte* could alight, the butler was there, asking him his wishes.

"Guillaime!" He was greeted happily by His Lordship, who nodded to the others. "Efficient as usual."

There was a hurried conversation in which the words *"hall de classique"* were spoken. Guillaime called out a few commands, clapping his hands. The footmen sprang into action, hurrying to the cart and the coach where they unloaded François's equipment with efficient dispatch while the maids vanished back into the *château*.

"Come, my dear." The *comte* assisted Lisette from the coach. "*Maître* François, welcome to my home."

With that, he led them inside.

L'Esroc Pâle was vast, the illusion aided by gold-framed floor-to-ceiling mirrors strategically placed throughout the corridors. Each reflected the others, so there seemed corridors within corridors, mirrors within mirrors, stretching into infinity. White-painted doors trimmed in gilt opened into the halls, giving glimpses of rooms in which more treasures adorned walls or perched on pedestals.

Somewhere among them, the *comte* mentioned, with casual vagueness, was a formal and informal dining hall as well as his salon, a ballroom, and the kitchens. The rest were ... and here he paused and smiled, a most sly and secretive smile: "My playrooms." Before François could ask about those, he was given a quick, "Later, my dear *artiste*," with a sideways glance and a wink at Lisette, who kissed the air near his cheek in reply.

The corridors were of Carrera marble, white with gold-flecked veins: "Imported from Italy but no need to tell the king since we've a current war with that country." A narrow path of hand-woven carpeting from Persia formed a walkway down it. The walls alternated combinations of fabric in which gold leaf overlaid the silken threads with painted plastering in deep jewel tones of wine and maroon, and paneled mellow oak framed in gilt.

Above it all hung chandeliers of polished maple and brass, secured by chains attached to wall brackets for lowering and raising the lights. Hundreds of candle flames reflected in faceted crystal drops, lighting the hallway and shining upon its occupants as well as its treasures.

While the footmen trudged past them carrying easel parts, the laths for the canvas, and other items, Duquesne strolled leisurely down the magnificent hall, pointing out various bronzes, marbles, and paintings adorning its walls.

"That sculpture is an Escoffier, purchased when he was almost a beggar, selling plaster-cast figurines under an awning in the Paris marketplace. I acquired that painting from a family in Montpelier with whom La Rochelle stayed shortly before he journeyed to Italy. They were destitute, sold it for a pittance to save their home. That landscape with the three nudes? It was a gift from a dear little *duc* with whom I spent a most interesting week in Marseilles ..." And so on.

François and Lisette made appropriately impressed sounds, Maxime looked on disapprovingly, and Giovanni merely stared.

The paintings were all large and lavish, evidence of skill and talent, a good many early creations of artists later becoming well-known, Duquesne having the ability to detect budding talent and purchase their work for much less than the paintings were now worth. All the subjects were nude, of course—their colors flesh-bright—they were deliberately provocative, and so lifelike as to invite touch. None of the male statues wore the abbreviated fig leaf good taste required, but sported well-endowed members in a semi-aroused state, while the female figures had ample breasts and deeply chiseled mounds. A good many of the paintings were unsigned, however, as if the artists had no wish for their names to be associated with these beautiful if lascivious works.

Isabeau's question came to mind, and François's thoughts replied, *but not mine. My name will be upon my canvas, and whoever sees it will be in awe that I created something to stir even the basest passions.*

Maxime bypassed all these treasures with the faintest of sneers, kept well-hidden if the *comte* looked his way, but Giovanni was plainly awe-struck, though whether at the audacity of the subject matter, or their sheer beauty. Once, when he lagged behind, staring at a more than life-size rendering of a trident-wielding Poseidon surrounded by several mermen rising from a marble-composed wave, the *comte* stopped also, abandoning Lisette briefly to go to the boy's side.

"A magnificent sculpture, is it not?"

The statue had the usual fish's tail, a monumentally majestic sweep of fins and scales, though just below the waist, it also possessed a phallus worthy of any land mammal.

"Who is he?" Giovanni asked. His voice held what the nobleman interpreted as awe.

"Poseidon," the *comte* explained. "King of all the oceans of the world. In Italy, he was called Neptune."

Giovanni didn't answer, staring at the statue.

"You like him, my Adonis?" Duquesne purred, voice sinking to a near-whisper intended as a prompt to suggestive conversation.

Giovanni shook his head. He looked from the statue to the nobleman and said, with the outspokenness of a child, "He has a beard. Why did I have to shave mine for your painting?"

"Giovanni! Such impertinence!" François rushed over; hand raised to chastise his rude-tongued servant.

"No, no, *artiste.*" Duquesne's arm blocked François's, pushing it down. "The boy deserves an answer."

He gave him a speculative look because Giovanni didn't flinch but bared his teeth slightly at François.

"Only the older gods wore beards, my Adonis. Zeus, Poseidon, Hephaestus ... all the rest were considered too callow."

Giovanni considered that. He looked again at the statue, then back to Duquesne. François tensed as he started to speak.

"My name is Giovanni, not Adonis. Giovanni di Casalupo." Dipping his head in an abrupt bow, he added, "Your Lordship."

Duquesne laughed. "I vow, *Maître* François, this one is pert, isn't he? What a facile tongue."

François relaxed.

The *comte* leaned closer. "What else can that tongue do?" Without waiting for an answer, he again caught Lisette's hand, replacing it on his arm. "Come, the room we wish is on the uppermost floor and we've much walking to reach it."

With that, he continued down the hall, not looking to see who followed.

With a hiss at Giovanni, "Behave and watch what you say," François hurried after them.

On the third and uppermost floors, the rooms were themed, each with paintings and statuary based on the myths of various countries. Gold plaques set into the wall by each oversized door explained what was housed inside: *Mythes de l'Inde ... Légendes de Cathay ...* There was even one room marked *Mythologies de Noveau Monde*, Myths of the New World.

Duquesne steered them to the last one at the end of the hall, where an assortment of chairs, couches, and tables was gathered in the corridor outside the open double doors, some stacked atop each other helter-skelter.

As they entered, and François glanced at the doors, the *comte* said, "You see how tall? Surely this place was built for the giants who display their talents here."

Inside, the room was as vast as the size of the doors suggested. The footmen were busily reassembling the easels using the tools in François's valise. Someone had already opened it and was carefully retrieving the paint pots and other items from inside, placing them and the brushes, as well as his painting smock, upon a nearby table.

The maids were laying down muslin sheets, their corners overlapping so they covered the floor from the vast hearth at one end to the wall.

"To protect the marble from your paints," the *comte* explained. "I expect there will be numerous *spills*." He smiled as he emphasized that last word with a leer, making even François flush slightly.

"I certainly hope so," Lisette murmured, glancing back at Govanni, who was looking around with the curiosity of a child. She made a kissing *moue* at the *comte*, who laughed.

Behind them, Maxime gave a strangled, disapproving sound at which François scowled. The servant ducked his head.

Ignoring that, the *comte* continued, "As you can see, I've ordered a wash kettle confiscated from the laundress for you to prepare your priming."

He gestured at the fireplace where two footmen were starting a fire, one using flint and steel while the other worked a small hand bellows. On the hearth sat a large black iron washpot, several wooden buckets holding water beside it.

Once the fire was going, the two men set a brazier over the flames, settled the kettle upon it, and emptied two of the buckets into it.

"The water should be hot soon. In the meantime, you can stretch the canvas and do whatever is necessary to get it ready." There was a gesture to the table where the tools and canvas roll lay alongside the wood.

The carpenter was nowhere in sight.

"Where …?" François started to ask.

"I saw no need to keep him here since my men can help in whatever you need, as well as your own servant," Duquesne explained. "I sent him on his way with a few coins for his inconvenience at this unexpected journey."

"In that case, I'd best get to work." François allowed his eagerness to show.

The *comte* bowed in agreement. "The furniture will stay in the hall until you've had time to look it over and see if any can be used. Feel free to go through the other rooms and appropriate anything striking your fancy."

"*Merci*, Your Lordship." François bowed in return. His gaze swept the room, over the moving servants, the blazing fire, the high windows with their crimson draperies, and the peaked glass ceiling letting in the barely noonday sunlight.

The room was long but rather narrow. Though there were no paintings above the hearth, and only two pedestals, one holding a bronze of a very muscular Cupid on one side and a voluptuous Psyche on the other, the side walls held two paintings each, so large they might at first have been mistaken for murals.

As the room suggested, the paintings carried classical Greek themes. The first showed a naked woman lying on a couch, an enormous white swan between her splayed legs. Its wings were widespread as if beating frantically, a very human-looking penis protruding from between its webbed feet. At the end of the swan's long, delicate neck, a man's bearded face pressed against her breasts.

"*Leda and the Swan*," Duquesne said unnecessarily. "One of the few depictions escaping the Church's condemnation. I paid a pretty franc for it."

"After seeing this one"—François's laugh held unaccustomed embarrassment—"I can understand why they made this a forbidden subject. It is very ... vigorous ... but beautifully done," he added, lest His Lordship think him censorious.

Giovanni stopped before the painting, scowling.

"Zeus, King of the Gods, appeared to Leda in the shape of a swan and seduced her," Duquesne explained.

Giovanni didn't answer. He studied Zeus's face atop that slender neck.

Duquesne noticed the boy's frown. "The subjects bother you?" He sounded as if he sincerely wished to know.

"That one." Giovanni gestured to the swan. "He has a handsome face. Why does he pretend to be a bird to make love to woman?"

"The lady had a husband. Zeus didn't want him to know." The *comte's* expression said he thought he'd summarized the reason well. He was surprised when Giovanni laughed somewhat scornfully.

"Hah! He thinks bird fucking woman not be noticed?" He gestured to the other painting. "What is this one?"

"*Danaë and the Shower of Gold.*"

The painting showed an overblown beauty of a woman in the throes of apparent ecstasy. Swirling around her in a sinuous blur, a golden whirlwind molded itself to her body.

"Danaë's father locked her away. The easiest way for Zeus to get to her was as a shower of golden rain."

There was another laugh, this one even more derisive. "You say this Zeus King of Gods, but he has to disguise himself to get women?" Giovanni shook his head. "Why? They should beg him to make love to them. Something not right."

"Your Lordship." François decided it was time to step in. "Forgive the boy. He's ignorant ..."

"No, François. He has a point." The *comte* was clearly intrigued. He nodded at the next picture. "What do you think of these two?"

One showed a satyr lying on his back, hairy goatish legs spread, one hooved foot digging into the soil while the other kicked the air. On the ground lay a set of reed pipes. He was surrounded by three naked nymphs. One caressed his face, another kissed his chest, while between her fingers, the third manipulated a member twice the size of an ordinary human's. The satyr appeared on the edge of a physical climax, eyes squeezed shut, mouth open, as if preparing to bellow his satisfaction.

The second picture was of a centaur, rising on hind hoof-tips as if about to leap, its plumy tail raised. Head thrown back, his flowing mane tossed around a handsome human face. A woman clung to his chest, arms around his neck, while her legs gripped his waist where his human body joined his equine one.

"I daresay the Church would order these burned also, if they knew they existed."

Giovanni studied both very seriously before he answered, and then only after a long silence. "What are these creatures?"

"This one is a faun—half man and half goat," the *comte* explained. "They lived mainly to make music enchanting for females. See the little pipes lying on the ground where he dropped them?" He indicated the panpipes near the hoof, touching the dirt, then looked at the centaur. "And this one is ... well, I suppose it's obvious. He's called a centaur."

"Is it acceptable for such creatures, half man, half animal, to lie with women?" That appeared to be what was confusing the boy.

"I suppose some people might not think so."

"But these Greeks did?" Giovanni persisted. "And those from *my* country ... they, also?"

"My boy." Duquesne dared to lay a hand on Giovanni's shoulder. Surprisingly, it wasn't shrugged away. "In antiquity, anything was permissible."

"What *you* think?" Giovanni persisted. He waved a hand at the two paintings. "Man-animal, woman-human is per-permissible?" He stumbled over the unfamiliar word.

The *comte* thought about that. "Coupling with an animal is one desire I've never had," he admitted. "However, I'm not one to quell others' inclinations. If one wishes it, it's allowed, in my philosophy."

"Even if woman have husband?"

"Even so." Duquesne glanced at François. "And vice versa, also."

Giovanni's expression changed. It now held an emotion, making the *comte* stare, as if unable to interpret what he saw. He studied Giovanni's face for a moment longer, then, with the caution one might employ if seeing some danger heretofore hidden, he dropped his hand from the boy's shoulder and took a single step backward. Turning away, he bestowed a hasty smile upon François.

"And now, being superfluous at this point, I'll take myself out of your way. If you need food or drink or require a call of nature, simply tell one of the footmen your wishes and he'll fetch it or show you the way." He reached for Lisette's hand again. "Come, *ma belle*, let me give you that tour I promised. I think I've a few sights you may find interesting."

With that, he led the girl away, pausing at the door to call over his shoulder, "We'll return later, after your canvas is prepared. A pleasant day, *artiste*."

Chapter Twenty-Six

"You'd best open the windows. This is going to smell."

With his smock protecting his clothing, François found the ingredients for the gesso taken from his valise and placed them on the table with his paints. He added the proper amounts of chalk and white pigment to the kettle, then unbound the butcher's rabbit skins, denuded of their pelts so only the raw under-the-hide connective tissue remained. Tossing them into the pot, he set Giovanni to stirring the mixture with a large wooden spoon, ensuring it didn't scorch as it thickened.

As the liquid bubbled, a pungent, malodorous scent floated from it, wafting into the room. Hands to their noses, several of the maids hastened to do as François asked, unlatching and folding back the six windows.

Ordering two of the footmen, Alexandre and Henri—both handsome, robust lads, he imagined were no doubt chosen for their good looks—to place the easels side by side and raise the bottom crossbeams so each was even in height with the other, he and Maxime put together the frame and stretched the canvas. Despite its size, this was accomplished in a surprisingly short time, Maxime and his master being old hands at that sort of work.

Afterward, they hoisted the canvas, placing it upon both easels.

Taking the spoon from Giovanni, François inspected the gesso, studying the thick, paste-like blob in its bowl. "It's ready."

At his gesture, Alexandre and Henri donned thick leather gauntlets. Lifting the wash pot from the fire, they carried it to the canvas. A serving maid folded one of the innumerable muslin sheets, placing it on the floor. They set the iron pot upon it and backed away.

Taking a large paintbrush the length and width of his hand from those lying on the table, François dipped it into the kettle. He brought it out dripping with the thick paste-like mixture and skimmed it across the canvas, making a white swathe on the light-brown fabric. Splotches of gesso fell from the brush, spotting the protective muslin upon the floor as he continued swiping the brush back and forth until the canvas was thoroughly covered.

"Now then, while that dries ..." He looked to the fire where Giovanni still knelt, watching. "Get up and quit dawdling. Come." He went through the double doors into the hall where the furniture waited.

Giovanni followed.

There were more couches than chairs, and François asked the obvious question.

"For convenience, sir," Alexandre answered. When François raised a brow, he continued, "One enters, looks at the paintings." He gestured back through the doorway at *Leda and the Swan*. "And once aroused, simply selects a couch and a partner, and"—he shrugged—"follows Nature."

"His lordship seems to have thought of everything." François considered that. He gestured, "That one. I can use it."

He'd chosen one of the larger couches, a chaise almost the size of a bed. Thinking of the legendary strength of a *loup-garou*, supposedly three times that of a normal man, he ordered Giovanni to bring it inside. He didn't doubt the boy could handle it on his own, but as he lifted the chaise so easily, he realized his mistake, that this might immediately warn the others that he was different. Luckily, the chaise was oversized, making it unwieldy, and it wavered and tilted, one end striking the floor.

"Here, you two, help him," he called to the two footmen. "Can't you see he's not strong enough to do this by himself?"

As the footmen leaped to obey, Giovanni shot his master a glance. A sardonic smile twisted his mouth.

They carried the chaise into the studio, moving it twice before it was placed to François's satisfaction, in front of the wall where it would hang, struck by sunlight from not only the windows but also through the glass roof.

François studied it. The chaise was perfect, but ... He stroked his chin, thinking. "It needs something ... a surrounding, an enclosure ..."

"Like a pavilion?" suggested Alexandre.

"Exactly," François answered. "A kind of arbor, with the chaise inside."

He could see it, draped in the color of passion, adorned with the flowers of love. He looked at the other items: chairs, tables, more chaises, nothing he could use to approximate what his imagination now supplied.

He remembered what the *comte* had said about the other rooms. "I don't suppose any of them have a small summerhouse or gazebo?"

"Of a surety, we have gazebos, sir," Henri said. "But not inside."

"Eh? Where?"

He pointed to one of the wall-to-ceiling windows set

between the paintings, which the maids had opened to the summer air. With the gesso no longer bubbling, the scent of boiled rabbit skin and chalk was rapidly lessening.

François walked over, peering out. The windows were constructed like the doors for a giant. He had to stand on his toes to look outside, the bottom sill even with his chin.

Behind the *château* was a formal garden, a near acre of greenery, hedges cut into maze shapes with benches and little flower-covered alcoves. Torches, unlit because it was still daylight, were placed through the flagstoned paths, leading to six pavilions. They were covered by red running roses and ivy entwined with grapelike clusters of deep lavender wisteria.

"Yes. That one." He pointed. "That's exactly what I want, but unfortunately, as you say, it's outside."

"They can easily be dismantled," Alexandre said.

"We often do so and move them to various locations about the grounds," Henri added.

"Will His Lordship mind having one brought inside?"

"He's given orders you're to be accommodated in every way, sir," Alexandre reminded him.

"Then do so. Immediately."

With bows, the two men exited the room. In a short time, he saw them running through the maze to the pavilion he'd selected, followed by four more footmen, all six pushing wheelbarrows. While two used small handsaws to sever the vines and plants woven throughout the roof's latticework, the others began disassembling the little building. In a short time, the open dome of the roof, as well as the wrought-iron sides, had been placed upon the carts.

They pushed them toward the *château*.

Inside, with efficiency, they reassembled the gazebo around the chaise.

"There, sir," Alexandre said, with a flourish. "Is it as you wished?"

"It needs color," François answered. He'd envisioned the interior draped in red. "Are there any unused drapes? Crimson ones?"

Alexandre's answer was to point again to the windows and the red velvet curtains, drawn back to let in the sun. "How many do you need, sir?"

As they removed the draperies and affixed them to the inside of the gazebo, François told himself he could become quite accustomed to having a patron who was so accommodating.

The scene was now set.

He had them move the easels back a little, turning them slightly. They placed the table with his supplies so it was closer to hand. He retrieved his sketchpad and rummaged in the valise for his box of charcoals. He also checked the canvas. Thanks to the heat coming through the open windows, combined with the special formula he used, the gesso was nearly dry. While it finished setting, he'd do a few preliminary sketches ...

He paused.

Lisette. He needed her here, and she was who-knew-where, with the *comte*. Did he dare send one of the footmen to disturb whatever they were doing—François had a pretty good idea what that was—and order her to return? Was His Lordship so accommodating that he'd allow her to be pulled from his bed?

"It looks as if we've arrived just in time."

François looked to the doorway, relaxing. Duquesne had solved his problem for him.

"Your Lordship, I was about to begin my sketches."

"Not without me, I hope?" Lisette pulled away from the *comte* and sauntered to his side, looking up at the gazebo and then at the chaise. "An interesting arrangement, François." She took a deep breath, breasts threatening the neckline of her gown, then exhaled gustily. "Roses and wisteria—the scent is heavenly, so sensual." She gave the *comte* a heavy-lidded gaze. "So ... suggestive."

"I want you on this chaise," François told her.

"Of course you do," she murmured.

He ignored the innuendo, continuing, "Get out of that gown."

Giovanni was standing at the side of the gazebo, studying the little building with an expression of wonder. As François spoke, he jerked around, looking from his master to Lisette, mouth dropping open as the girl dropped into the one chair in the room. Pulling aside her skirts, she kicked off her slippers. She untied her garters, slid down her stockings, and dropped them over the arm of the chair.

Standing, she called to one of the maids, "Assist me."

The girl hurried forward, unlacing the back of her gown. Lisette slid it off her shoulders, letting it drop to the floor. Her kirtle and chemise followed. Stepping out of everything, she walked back to François and stood there with hands on hips as the maid picked up the garments and placed them in the chair.

Despite her nakedness, only the *comte* and Maxime reacted, His Lordship with a soft sigh, the servant by turning his head. Giovanni stared as if startled into immobility while the servants went about their chores as if a woman standing among them in total nudity was a commonplace thing.

At *Château de l'Esroc Pâle*, it undoubtedly was.

"On the couch." François became as businesslike as she, saying, as she sat upon the chaise, then swung her legs onto its velvet surface, "You're Venus, goddess of love. I want you lying back, reclining."

Resting on one elbow, Lisette arranged the cushions under

her, then leaned back. She ran her fingers through her hair, fanning it out upon the pillows.

"That's right, your hair is in amorous disarray. Your lover, Adonis, is about to possess you, *cherie*, look lost in *extase* ..."

She tilted her head, mouth open slightly, eyes closed. Pressing the back of one hand against her cheek, she let the other fall over the side of the chaise, as if abandoned in passion.

"Now your legs." As if he were doing no more than moving a chair or any other piece of furniture, François slid his hand under Lisette's left leg, pushing it until the knee bent. Equally impersonally, he pushed the other aside so it hung off the chaise negligently, as if it had fallen away from her body and she hadn't the strength to move it back. That made her open and visible, lady-nest pink and glistening, moist with juices he was certain weren't all her own.

He felt a surge of lust. The Church didn't call a female's privates the Gates of Hell for nothing, did they? He considered her body his private garden to delve, and now ...

Faithless bitch. He might be outwardly acting with disinterest, but inwardly, François suffered more than a stab of jealousy. *How many times did he possess you while I toiled over creating this scene?*

He forced the feelings away. The *comte* was a self-confessed libertine. François reluctantly acknowledged no one had a claim on Lisette. Hadn't he always ignored the reputation she had among the tavern's customers? Besides, for what he was being paid, he'd readily have let Duquesne bed Isabeau ...

... if he'd want that shrew.

So why not the model on whom he had no true claim?

He glanced back at the *comte*, receiving a second jolt momentarily making him silent.

Duquesne's hand lay against his codpiece, the flat of his

palm moving slowly back and forth over the hardening ridge beneath it.

He'd never thought he'd be shocked by another's actions, but for a moment, François couldn't speak.

He was the only one in the room affected, it seemed. The servants were doubtless accustomed to observing their master engaged in self-abuse and his guests as well.

He swallowed, managing to ask with a degree of nonchalance, "Do you agree with this pose, Your Lordship?"

"*Oui*, definitely." The words came out breathlessly. The hand didn't stop moving. "*Parfait*."

Damn. François turned his attention back to Lisette. While painting, he always kept his lust in check, waiting until a session was over before bedding the girl, but with his model so blatantly displaying her privates, and the presence of a man openly fondling himself, he wasn't certain he would be able to control his own passions. As if to agree, his nethers quivered.

To cover his momentary lack of control, he looked at Giovanni, still standing where he'd been after the chaise was brought in.

"You. Get over here. Get out of those clothes."

The boy jumped, staring from François to Lisette. He started to speak, then apparently thought better of it. With a haste that might under other circumstances have been comical, he pulled his shirt over his head, dropping it to the floor. It wasn't eagerness, however, for his expression was anything but enthusiastic. His hands went to the top of his stocks, and then he hesitated.

"Yes," François snapped. "Those off, too."

The boy pushed them down; stepped out of them. He moved to the chaise and stopped.

"Here. Over here." Refusing to touch him, François gestured.

The boy came around the chaise, dropping onto its end, in a spot that placed him between Lisette's splayed legs. He glanced down at the damp female nest, his face expressionless.

Dieu, how will such close proximity to a naked female affect him? François had no idea. *A fine time to think of that now.* Too late, he realized he hadn't packed the wolfbane.

"What must I do, master?"

The question sounded so bewildered that it made François smile, as well as relax.

"Is it like with Mariah?" Giovanni stuck out his tongue, the tip as wet and pink as Lisette's nethers. "Should I ...?"

"No!"

He didn't mean to react so. To have the boy mouth-service Lisette, even in pretense, might evoke the wrong response in the creature, awaken it while it obviously now slept. François didn't believe Giovanni was half as civilized as his wife insisted, nor as naïve.

"Don't move. I'll pose you."

That meant he had to touch the creature. As quickly as possible, he pushed Giovanni closer to Lisette. He caught her bent leg, placing it on the boy's shoulder, her heel resting between his shoulder blades. Catching Giovanni's right hand, he pulled him forward, placing it on the girl's left breast. Giovanni's fingers stiffened, reacting to the touch of her soft flesh as if he had been burned. He tried to pull away.

"Keep your hand on her teat." François put his own over the boy's, pressing it down. "Take her nipple in your fingers and tweak it."

"Like this?" Giovanni caught the pink bud between thumb and forefinger as if plucking a berry from a vine.

His hand shook. François could feel the tremor transferring itself to his own hand. He relaxed his grip.

"Perfect."

From behind them, Duquesne prompted, "And the other hand ...?"

"Clasp your rod," François ordered.

This time, the boy didn't hesitate, though his movements were more resigned than anything, as if he realized a protest would do no good. Thrusting his free hand between his legs, he lifted balls and rod, letting them rest against his thighs. He cradled his member in his hand, then gripped it tightly and began to work his fist.

"No."

The movement stopped. Giovanni looked up at him, brow wrinkled in a question.

"Don't get yourself hard yet. That will come when I actually paint that part of your anatomy."

Giovanni relaxed his grip, expression clearing slightly.

During all this, Lisette remained silent, though she raised her head, staring frankly and intently at the boy's groin. She frowned, looked as if she wanted to speak, but didn't.

"Now then." François backed away from the chaise to where the *comte* stood. He didn't look at the noble, forcing himself to say conversationally, "What do you think, Your Lordship? Will this do?"

"It's as if you've seen into my mind, *maître*. It's exactly what I wished."

Duquesne removed his hand from his crotch. François saw the expected damp spot leaking through the codpiece's fabric, now stretched outward in a peaked tent, the shape of the organ inside plainly visible. The *comte* followed his gaze and smiled ruefully.

"Too much of what I wished. Get on with your sketches while I solve this problem."

He looked around, beckoning to a nearby maid.

"You. Come with me."

Obediently, the girl stepped to his side. He caught her arm, pulling her into the hall.

"I feel the need for a visit to *l'Egypte*."

They disappeared into the room marked *Contes de l'Egypte Antique*, the giant double doors slamming behind them.

Forcing himself to ignore the sounds issuing through those doors, François reached for his charcoal and picked up his sketch pad.

"Don't move," he told Giovanni.

As if the boy needed to be reminded. He truly looked as if he were frozen into that pose, staring down with what François could only describe as dismay at the exposed and open female nest.

If I didn't know better, I'd think Maxime had gotten to the boy with his prudish ideas.

He made four sketches, each from a different angle. Remarkably, Giovanni didn't move the entire time. Lisette, veteran that she was, appeared at ease with the entire episode, almost bored. At one time, it seemed she actually napped.

At some point while he sketched, the servants slipped away. Maxime now sat by the fire in a half-doze, as if closing his eyes divorced him from what he no doubt considered total depravity. From where he stood, François could feel the servant's disapproval like a visible wave.

He won't be coming here again, he decided, *not even to help dismantle the easels when I leave. But I swear if he says one word or looks down his nose one more time ...*

He studied the drawings, deciding which one he liked best when he heard the doors to the Egyptian room open.

"You've finished, François?"

"And have you, *comte*?" François dared to give Duquesne a leer as he looked around.

The serving maid dawdled behind her master. Her cap was missing, her hair mussed.

"Quite satisfactorily." There was a nod of that pale head. No insinuation fazed His Lordship. "May I see your sketches?"

Looking at him, François was astounded that there was no sign he'd been out of his clothing, lying naked with the maid on a couch. Unlike the maid, his blond hair was perfect, not a strand out of place. His doublet was smooth and buttoned, stocks and codpiece neat ... Wait, there was no dampened spot. He'd changed into another pair.

"I like this one." Duquesne was all business now.

"My choice also."

"Will you begin now?"

"The light's going, I think." François glanced upward through the glass ceiling. "It would be best to start fresh tomorrow."

"Perfect timing. My cook has sent word that supper awaits." Duquesne gestured. "Come. We'll dine and then I'll offer you the promised hospitality of my little pleasure palace. As for the beautiful Lisette ..." He clapped his hands. "Up, my dear. Get dressed."

Lisette sat up, swinging her leg off Giovanni's shoulder and to the floor. She reached to the chair for her dress. Only Giovanni didn't move, hand still outstretched, fingers clutching empty air as that pink nipple slid from his grasp.

"That means you, too," François called. "Let go of your rod and put on your clothes."

Giovanni struggled into his stocks even faster than he'd gotten out of them. Amazing how quickly the boy moved. Perhaps not so amazing. François still remembered that quick lunge, those teeth sinking into his wrist.

Duquesne took François's arm. "Your servants are also welcome to join in our revelries." He glanced at Maxime, who opened his eyes when he heard voices. The *comte* gestured to the maid. "Take that one to the kitchen, and afterward keep him company."

"Thank you, sir, but no." Maxime stood, showing as much indignation as he dared. "I won't profane myself with one of your whores."

"Well." Duquesne's pale brows rose. "You certainly have outspoken servants, François." He didn't look insulted, however. "Very well, take him to the kitchen. Make certain he's fed, then let him stay there. Alone. And the boy ..."

"He isn't to be fed," François said quickly. "That's his punishment for being disobedient."

"Very well." The lift of the blond brows said plainly the *comte* wondered when Giovanni had not followed orders, but he didn't argue. "Coming, Lisette?" he prompted, holding out a hand.

Chapter Twenty-Seven

LISETTE DIDN'T STAY absent long.

An hour later, she reappeared in the doorway, carrying a single candle. Not speaking, she walked over to where the boy sat on the couch, stopping before him, holding the candlestick high so the light shone on his face.

"Won't you be missed?" Giovanni greeted her.

"His Lordship is showing *Maître* François a love manual brought from Cathay. Since I can't read, it didn't interest me."

"Why have you come back?" Something in his tone told her he knew the answer.

"His Lordship reminded me you were invited to the revels, too, even if you can't dine with us."

The scent of wine wafted toward him as she spoke. Giovanni turned his head.

"I thought to escort you to one of his playrooms and keep you company."

"I'm not interested." He didn't look at her.

"Are you like that pietist Maxime? Or is it something else?" She shifted the candle to her other hand. Touching his shoulder, she slid her hand up his neck, grasping a handful of curls, raking her fingers through them, once, then again. "I saw what's been done to your *organe*."

"You didn't mention it." He looked at her then. "My 'horrible mutilation.'"

"That's because I don't think it's a mutilation." She shrugged. "I thought perhaps you're Jewish. I know they follow that practice." She smiled. "I had a Jewish lover once. His bare rod caused the most exquisite lovemaking. I thought perhaps you and I, we could have such fun ... play Venus and Adonis for true, no?"

She placed her hand on his crotch, grasping.

"Don't, *damoiselle*." Giovanni dodged, sliding further away.

"*Pourquoi pas?*" She jerked her hand back as if he'd struck it. "You don't want a warm *corps femelle* against yours? Don't you like women? Do you prefer boys?"

He didn't answer, merely looked away impatiently.

"I saw how you shied away from His Lordship, so I don't think that's it."

"I like women. I want one." He looked back at her. "But not you."

"I see. That puts me in my place, doesn't it?" Like the *comte*, she didn't look insulted, however, but more amused. "So. You've a sweetheart, and you've promised to be true?"

"*Oui.*" His answer was so low it was a whisper. He darted a glance at the open doorway, his manner revealing this was a confession torn from his heart. "Please, don't tell my master."

"Why not?" Lisette asked. "It's nothing to be ashamed of." Seeing the forlorn shake of his head, however, she patted his cheek, saying, "Don't worry, *mon joli*. I won't tell." She sighed. "This is a disappointment, you know. Such a waste."

"I'm sure you'll survive." Giovanni gave her a sardonic look worthy of Duquesne himself.

"Indeed." With that, she left him and returned to the *comte*.

Chapter Twenty-Eight

"Why are you sitting in the dark?"

The fire was dying. The room darkened as the light outside died. The halls had been silent for a long time, only an occasional laugh or raised voice drifting up the stairs from the main floor.

Giovanni glanced toward the still-open doors. Duquesne stood there.

"I wasn't given permission to light a candle."

"I'll remedy that." The *comte* went to the hearth. Taking a taper from the mantel, he thrust it into the dying fire and lit the seven-candle holder sitting there. "*Let there be light—*"

He brought it to where the boy sat. A pinpoint gleamed in the darkness, sending candle glow back at him. Duquesne stopped.

"What is it?" Giovanni asked.

"Nothing," the *comte* denied. "For a moment, I thought ..." He held the candles higher. "But no, it couldn't be. Here, I brought you these."

In his other hand, he held an apple and a pear.

Without a word, Giovanni snatched the fruit from his hand, biting first into the pear, then the apple with the eagerness of the famished.

"It's good," he said, through the mouthful, sending a spray of juice spattering his shirt front.

Duquesne set the candelabrum upon the floor and sat beside Giovanni on the chaise. The boy continued his rapid devouring of the fruit, alternating a bite from each.

"Why did your master say you weren't to be fed?" His expression was bemused. "You've done nothing wrong as far as I can see."

"A painting he wants to do." Giovanni stopped eating long enough to answer. Juice dribbled down his chin. His tongue licked some of it back into his mouth. "Some saint or other. He wants me thin for it."

"Doesn't he know if you don't eat, he may be painting a corpse?"

"He doesn't care." He took two bites out of the pear, sucking loudly at the mellow flesh. "Aren't you afraid you'll anger him by feeding me?'

"My dear boy. This is my *château*. I can do whatever I want, and he'll not dare speak a word." Duquesne's eyes twinkled. He leaned toward Giovanni slightly, voice dropping to a whisper. "That doesn't mean either of us has to tell him, though. You've juice on your chin."

He pulled a handkerchief from his sleeve, catching the boy's chin in his hand. Gently, he dabbed at the sticky splotches.

"You are so beautiful, my Adonis."

"My name is Giovanni," the boy answered. There was something to his tone, making it sound as if he were doing something other than correcting the *comte's* misuse of his name.

The handkerchief's movement stopped.

"So it is—and always will be, I fear." With a sigh, Duquesne let his hand fall to his side. With meticulous care, he folded the handkerchief and returned it to his sleeve. He got to his feet.

"I'll leave you to enjoy your meal. Toss the cores into the fireplace when you're done. Tomorrow, I'll bring you more. You won't starve in *my* house."

He walked out.

"I prefer meat," Giovanni called after him. "Red meat with the blood still in it."

* * *

As with the carpenter's horse, the coach horses reacted to Giovanni's presence. When the boy climbed up to sit next to the footman's perch, the lead horses neighed and reared, almost jerking the reins from the driver's hands. They danced and trembled with frantic little neighs and snorts. It took him several moments to control them.

"I'm sorry, *maître*. I don't know what's gotten into them," he apologized. "They're spirited creatures but usually easily controlled."

With a brusque nod, Duquesne waved away the apology. "Perhaps it's the lateness of the hour."

François entered the coach and settled himself beside Lisette. The footman closed the door and reclaimed his seat next to Giovanni.

When the coach arrived back at the cottage, Isabeau was at the door before the horses halted.

The footman opened the coach, and François emerged. Maxime climbed down from his perch beside the driver.

"Where is he?" Raising the lantern she held, her gaze darted from one end of the coach to the other. "Where is Giovanni?"

"Relax, my dear." François gave her an infuriatingly patronizing smile.

Remembering the lie he'd told her parents, she forced herself to remain calm while the footman climbed back onto the coach and the driver drove past the cottage, turning around and heading back to the highroad.

Maxime hurried inside.

"He's unharmed," François answered her question. "I had the coach stop and let him out so he could go around the cottage to his room."

"Alone?"

"I think by now I can trust him, can't I?" He waved a hand in the direction of the studio. "Go, see for yourself if you don't believe me."

"Mathilde saved your supper." She made it a reproach.

"I don't need it. I dined with the *comte*. I'll do that from now on." He walked to the cottage, leaving her standing there, then looked back. "Well? Aren't you going to check on your precious wolf? Make certain he returned intact?"

Gathering her skirts, Isabeau rushed past him.

* * *

From the room's darkness, she heard the splash of water.

"Gio? What are you doing?"

The floor felt damp under her feet. In the lantern's light, she saw the pitcher in his hand, water gleaming on his bare shoulders and chest, and the ends of his hair.

In the absence of the tub, he had poured the water over himself. There was a sodden mass of cloth on the floor at his feet. How many times had he done that, then mopped up the betraying water with his blanket?

"I wanted to wash away the feel of that place. He lets me have water to shave. Why can't I have more to bathe?"

"Why should he do anything to accommodate you?" She pulled her handkerchief from her sleeve, using it to pat his face dry. "I wasn't able to save you any food tonight. I'm sorry."

"The *comte* fed me. An apple and a pear." He took the handkerchief from her and swiped it along his neck and arms.

"I worried about you."

"You needn't." He handed back the little square of fabric. "It's an evil place, but it didn't harm me."

"The *comte*. He didn't bother you?" She couldn't bring herself to ask more plainly.

He shook his head. "We reached an understanding, I think. That woman, though, the pretty one the master sent for ..."

"You think she's pretty?" She didn't like that.

"The *comte* and the master do."

That wasn't really an answer. She scowled.

"What about her?"

"She wanted me." He said it in such a way that it didn't sound as if he were boasting, however.

"And?" Isabeau tensed. *If she's touched him, I'll kill her.*

"I don't want her."

His gaze caught the light of the lantern, eyes gleaming. The flickering flame made his expression say something other than his words.

"The count explained some of his art to me." Giovanni looked thoughtful. "He said some things I must think on." Again, his eyes sought hers. "Important things."

Without knowing why, Isabeau shivered. She also felt her legs go weak with relief.

"I must get back." She forced herself to move. "François is waiting. I'll make certain you have a basin and washcloth when you return tomorrow night," she promised as she hurried to the door.

She didn't look back, didn't want to see Giovanni receding into the darkness. François was waiting, all right, with his apothecary's potion and another night of her being ridden into the mattress. She wished he'd die from the exertion.

Chapter Twenty-Nine

IN WHAT WAS to become the routine, the next morning, before the sun was barely risen, the coach arrived to convey them to the *château*. Giovanni now rode with the footman. Maxime, as François promised himself, was left behind, much to the servant's relief.

François painted through the noon meal, not stopping until the light went, at which time he and the *comte* enjoyed supper and afterward the pleasures the *château* offered. Sometime during the evening, the *comte* would always appear with food for Giovanni.

The second night, he brought a generous cut of beef. Giovanni accepted it eagerly, then paused as he realized what he held was uncooked. His hesitation lasted only a moment before he tore at the meat with his teeth, gulping it down.

"Thank you." It was a garbled mouthful.

"You ate it all." Duquesne watched in quiet fascination.

"It was good." He wiped his bloody mouth with an equally red-stained hand.

"Aren't you going to ask why it wasn't cooked?"

"Should I?"

"You said you preferred meat, but you didn't say you wished it raw. I guessed, because you wanted blood in it." Duquesne held out a table kerchief.

"You were right." Giovanni accepted the kerchief, wiping his mouth and hands. He folded the cloth carefully, making certain the bloodstains were hidden from sight. "Why are you being so kind? What do you want?"

The *comte* accepted back the kerchief. "I thought I wanted *you*. I think you are the most beautiful *homme* I've ever seen. The sight of you stirs my soul and arouses my body. I'd give a good portion of my fortune to possess you, but now ... I hesitate."

"I'm unwilling, my lord. And I don't think you're a man who'd force me."

"Never," Duquesne assured him. "It would only be with your consent." His voice was earnest.

"You don't want me, my lord." Giovanni spoke into the darkness, not looking at him.

"No? Not even for a little while?"

"You say you'd give your fortune. Would lying with me be worth giving your life?"

"Perhaps." Duquesne didn't hesitate. "To feel your passion ..."

"I think not," Giovanni said. "Sometimes that which passion arouses isn't what a man expects. Or wants."

"Would that be what you would give me?" The *comte's* question was thoughtful, almost fearful. "Something I don't want?"

Giovanni didn't answer. He simply turned his head in the *comte's* direction. Their gazes met. Duquesne stared into those dark depths, his own eyes widening.

"I was right," he whispered. "Your eyes *do* reflect the light. What are you, boy?"

"I think you know."

"The Lord have mercy." Duquesne crossed himself.

"The Lord didn't show any mercy to me." Giovanni's words were bitter.

"There can be nothing between us, can there?"

"Not for your safety's sake, my lord."

"My poor boy." There was such sadness in the *comte's* voice; none of his peers would've recognized it. "How did this happen to you?"

"I'm told my parents committed sin, but I received their curse." Giovanni shrugged. "Who can say for certain?"

"If it's a curse from God, there's nothing to be done, then," Duquesne muttered. "I'm sorry, Giovanni." He sounded as if he truly meant it.

"*Merci*, my lord." Giovanni nodded. "You are only one of two people to ever say that. It means a great deal."

"Who was the other?" the *comte* asked, voice barely above a whisper.

"The woman I love." Giovanni's voice was just as soft.

Duquesne placed a hand on his shoulder, but this time his touch was more consoling, a kindly, gentle pat and not the sensual caress he'd made in François's studio.

"If I can't be your lover ... will you count me as a friend?"

Giovanni didn't answer, but when he looked up, his expression held gratitude.

The *comte* got to his feet. He hesitated, as if not wishing to leave but unable to think of a reason to stay. Finally, he said, "Would it be dangerous for me to ask for a single kiss?"

Giovanni made an acquiescent gesture.

He caught the boy's face in his hands, pressing his lips gently to Giovanni's, then raised his head, staring into the boy's eyes again.

"Thank you for the food," Giovanni said. "It was kind of you."

"You are most welcome," the *comte* whispered. A tear rolled down his cheek. He looked shaken. "God bless you."

"He hasn't so far." Giovanni's answer was barely audible.

After that, a servant was sent with the food, and the *comte* was never alone with him again.

Chapter Thirty

FOR MOST OF the current session, Giovanni was restless, fidgeting and moving on the chaise in unsettled agitation. Even the sprigs of wolfsbane François had remembered to bring with him didn't help. Several times, François raised his voice, ordering him to be still. The boy obeyed, but it was with an obvious effort. As expected, his discomfort transferred itself to Lisette, who also became uneasy.

"What is it?" she hissed at him.

Her whisper didn't reach François. Since that first night, she treated the boy with studied indifference bordering on coldness, tolerating him because their occupations forced them together. His rebuff had wounded her pride, and she didn't speak to him unless it couldn't be avoided.

François, lost now in the fervor of creation, didn't notice.

Giovanni didn't answer. He simply closed his eyes, taking a deep breath. Both hands abruptly clenched. His fingers tightened on the nipple he was supposed to caress, and she gave a quick gasp.

"Careful! That's living tissue, you know."

He looked at her apologetically. "*Je suis désolé.*" His grip loosened. "Is that better?"

"Much." Her answer was sharp. "Listen, you. Neither of us is happy about this arrangement, but it can't be helped. I need the money, and you ..." She shrugged. "Well, I know what you need, though you don't want it from me, so you may as well relax. Think of your sweetheart. Pretend it's her little tit you're fondling." She raised her head, glancing down. "And for goodness's sake, don't grip your rod so tightly. I don't want you spilling on me."

With a mumbled apology, Giovanni relaxed the grasp of his other hand.

"That's better." Lisette leaned back upon the crimson cushions, her features again assuming Venus's feigned ecstasy.

"Silence, you two." François let them know he'd seen them talking, even if he hadn't heard their words.

It wasn't long, however, before Giovanni was fitful again. This time, Lisette merely gave a long-suffering sigh and closed her own eyes.

A single exhortation of "Be still" came through gritted teeth.

Later, when they were ready to leave, François waited until after Lisette was inside the coach before seizing the boy's arm and pulling him aside. Tonight, the horses were even more skittish at his nearness, causing the driver to struggle in bringing them under control.

"What ails you today?" François shook him roughly. "All day, you've squirmed like a worm thrown into hot ashes."

"Look to the sky, master. There's your answer." Giovanni's whisper was so soft that not even the coach driver heard. "Did you forget?"

François looked up, seeing the nearly full silver globe. "*Dieu.* So soon?"

He released the boy who climbed onto the bench at the back of the coach.

Once at the cottage, he sent Giovanni to his room immediately.

"Tomorrow's the full moon," he told Isabeau, who met him at the door, pitcher of water in one hand, basin in the other. "Prepare the valerian and give it to him now, and another tomorrow night."

He went up the stairs but was back so quickly she had time to get no further than a few feet down the corridor.

"The door to one of the guest chambers is open. Why?" He looked as if he already knew the answer.

"It's my time," she said and gave no other explanation.

"So, you've failed me." He didn't hide his disappointment. "No matter, I can be patient. There's always next month." Spinning on his heel, he walked away. "See that he's chained tonight."

For once, she obeyed without argument.

* * *

In the morning, when the *comte's* coach arrived, François told them Giovanni was ill and there would be no painting that day.

"My master won't like this," the coachman said. It was obvious he expected François to relent at that bit of information.

"That's too bad." François managed a bit of bluster, showing he didn't let a mere servant dictate to him. "By the morrow, he should be recovered. You might also stop and inform *Damosel* Lisette. Or take her to His Lordship as a distraction for today." With a flick of a hand, as if shooing the coach and driver on their way, he went back inside, saying over his shoulder, "Give my apologies to your master, and return in the morning."

The following day, they were back at work again. The *comte* inquired about Giovanni's health.

"I'm fine," the boy assured him.

"It was doubtless one of those summer fevers children get." François made excuses. "One that is here today and gone on the morrow."

The *comte* didn't comment but looked thoughtful.

"There was a lovely full moon last night, wasn't there?" His pale gaze met Giovanni's before he looked away. "Too bad you can't incorporate that into your painting, François."

* * *

The next month, François proved he had been watching the calendar. On the day of the full moon, he said to Isabeau as he climbed into the coach, "Go to the grotto and pick more wolfsbane. That I have is so dried as to be useless."

When they returned that night, he hustled Giovanni from the coach, not even bidding the coachman farewell. Without ordering Isabeau to do so, he hurried him to the storeroom, scattered the newly cut herb around, then fastened the collar around the boy's neck, attaching the chain to the window bars. Pouring the valerian and handing him the cup, he latched the shutters, keeping out the moon's rays, then went away, locking both doors behind him.

Giovanni's howls and barks were audible to Isabeau, once again ensconced in one of the guest chambers. Francois attempted a failing patience as he went to his bed alone while his wife slept a relieved slumber that she still wasn't with child.

The following day, François turned away the coach with the same excuse as before.

Upon their return to the *château*, the *comte* asked François if Giovanni's fevers were of a contagious kind, and was assured they were not. As he left, he gave the boy an anxious glance, but for whom he was anxious wasn't as plain.

The next month, when François spoke to the coachman before he drove away, telling him the usual tale, Giovanni dared say, "*Vraiment*, master? A fever for three months in a row? His Lordship is no fool. He knows."

"What does he know?" François demanded.

"The truth." That was all Giovanni said.

François slammed the door and locked it, stamping away.

This time, the *comte* didn't bother asking Giovanni how he fared. He merely looked sad. Putting a hand into the neck of his doublet, he drew out the beads of a rosary and kissed the cross hanging from it, then tucked it away again before anyone other than the boy saw. He crossed himself, pressing his fingers to his lips and blowing a kiss.

Giovanni bowed his head, muttering so low no one but Duquesne heard, "Thank you, my lord."

At last, the day came when François laid down his brush, declaring the painting completed. It wasn't as noisy a finish as it had been with the du Mauriers. While Giovanni and Lisette were given permission to dress, he and Duquesne studied the finished creation, staring at it in silent admiration.

The *comte* ventured in an awed whisper that it was a masterpiece of erotic imagery. François agreed, while trying to appear modest and completely failing. It was true. He'd outdone himself in creating the scene His Lordship asked for. Why shouldn't he let his pride show?

Duquesne still lauded it as the painting was hung upon the wall, so it would dry.

With an efficiency bordering on haste, though he was in no hurry to leave, François cleaned his brushes and packed everything away. In truth, he found himself admitting he would miss the lavish nightly feasts with their abundance of wines, and especially the availability of the *comte's* serving women. He managed to hide his reluctance as he supervised the disassembling of the easels with the assistance of the carpenter, fetched from Aux-le-Piémont, and their packing everything into the back of his cart.

Afterward, while one of the serving maids entertained the carpenter in the creamery, there was a celebratory feast with more of that very good wine, roast goose, and many side dishes. On instructions from the *comte*, a platter consisting of a drumstick and two wings, cut from one of the geese before it was prepared, was carried to Giovanni.

Duquesne made a great ceremony of saying farewell to Lisette, promising to visit her at the tavern as well as inviting her back to the *château*.

"I'll send my coach for you, *chérie*."

Lisette listened to that with a patronizing expression, as much to say she'd heard such promises before and would believe them when the coach actually appeared, though she accepted with apparent great enjoyment Duquesne's caresses as he kissed her hand, her wrist, and elbow before pressing a last against her mouth.

As he escorted François to the coach, with Giovanni trailing a respectful distance behind, the *artiste* said, "About the boy, Your Lordship ..."

"What about him?" Duquesne immediately looked guarded.

"You've had no time with him, and I know you're disappointed. I'm of a mind to sell him to you—if you wish him, that is." He thought he sensed a sudden cooling of Duquesne's attitude but hoped he merely imagined it.

"Sell him?" The *comte's* expressive brows shot upward.

"I don't like it known." François lowered his voice. "The only way I could rescue him from those heathen gypsies was to buy him," he rationalized in apology. "Surely I need a little compensation for that."

"It's most kind of you to offer." Duquesne glanced back at the boy as he spoke, giving Giovanni a look holding not the extreme regret François imagined but instead concern. "But ... no. I don't think it would be proper for me to take him away from you. Don't you need him for another painting, a very special one?"

"I can always find another model, I suppose." François didn't ask how the *comte* had learned of his St. Jean. Perhaps he'd mentioned it while in his cups? That the notorious "Pale Rogue" might consider anything improper, however, was close to being a shock.

"You are too kind," Duquesne replied. "I must decline, however." He then changed the subject. "Be assured, once the painting is ready to be viewed, I'll urge anyone who sees it to seriously consider commissioning you."

Realizing transfer of Giovanni's ownership was effectively dismissed, François could only bow in gratitude and wonder what had caused His Lordship's change of mind. The prospect of Duquesne's peers securing his services was enough to distract him from further thought on that subject.

Chapter Thirty-One

"THE COMTE HAS PROMISED to refer his friends to me," François told Isabeau when he returned home. "I'm not going to sit idle while I wait, however. When patrons come to my door, they'll find me busy. Tomorrow, I begin my *St. Jean*."

"Is *he* ready?" Isabeau spoke before she thought, realizing it was a mistake as soon as the words left her mouth.

"Ready? What do you think?" François snapped. He waved a hand in Giovanni's direction. The boy glanced back at him guiltily, as if being accused of disobedience. "No, he's not ready, as you very well know."

"What do you mean?" Isabeau's gaze said she saw nothing wrong with Giovanni's appearance. It was a moment before she realized *that* was the problem—there was *nothing* wrong with the way the boy looked.

"Look at those rounded cheeks," François ordered.

With a sinking heart, she studied the smooth contours of the boy's face. As pleasing as they were, she realized his gaunt look, brought on by François's enforced starvation, had completely disappeared.

"I know you've been sneaking him food under the pretense of bringing him water at night."

"I assure you, François—" She began an earnest denial.

"Don't lie." He didn't let her finish. "Who else could it be? I'm certain Mathilde isn't secretly feeding him."

Isabeau shook her head. That seemed to anger him, and he caught her by the wrist. There was a low sound from Giovanni, a snarl, his muscles tensing. Isabeau glanced at him, raising her free hand as if to stop him.

François's other hand swung back. Isabeau flinched.

"It was the *comte*."

"What?" François looked at Giovanni, the words staying his hand.

"Every night while you ate his food and drank his wine and pleasured yourself with his whores, he sent a servant with a meal for me," the boy confessed.

"He did that?" François looked as if he didn't believe it. "After I told him ... Why?"

"It's his *château* and he'll do in it as he pleases." Glibly, Giovanni repeated what Duquesne said to him. "He ordered me to eat."

"So you obeyed him rather than your master." François looked as if he couldn't believe the boy would dare. "What did you do in exchange for food?" he asked, face grimacing with suspicion. "Is that why he didn't wish to buy you? Because he'd already had you?"

"I did nothing and neither did he," Giovanni answered. "He acted out of pity."

"Duquesne hasn't a pity-filled bone in his lecherous body," François denied.

"He has more than you," Giovanni dared say. "Don't you know if he hadn't fed me by now, I'd be dead?"

"You little *bâtard*!"

François backhanded him so violently, Giovanni was knocked off his feet. He fell with a crash, blood spattering as his cheek struck the floor.

"Deal with him," François ordered and stamped out.

Isabeau rushed to the boy's side, pulling a square of linen from her sleeve.

Another of my handkerchiefs ruined. She hated herself even as she thought it.

* * *

When Isabeau returned to the cottage, François was waiting for her just inside the walkway door.

"I see the guest chamber's open," he accused. "You've failed me. Again."

She didn't answer. There wasn't anything to say.

"It'll be the last time," he went on. "My patience is at an end, Isabeau. If you don't quicken by next month, I go to *Pére* Ambroise."

She had no doubt he'd carry out his threat. *Pére* Ambroise held François in such admiration, he would help him dissolve his marriage and somehow arrange it so he could take another wife.

While I'll be disgraced. No decent man will ever look at me again.

The only future for her would be to hide herself away in a nunnery, expiating her sterility through permanent chastity and prayer.

I'd never see Giovanni again.

She was certain he had something disastrous planned for Giovanni, also.

The only way either of us will escape François is if we die.

It wasn't a comforting thought.

Chapter Thirty-Two

"Where is Mathilde?" François demanded as Giovanni transferred little pots of jam and preserves from tray to table. "Why hasn't she brought my breakfast?"

Isabeau noticed he didn't say "our breakfasts," though she was sitting in her usual place in plain sight.

Halting steps sounded in the corridor, followed by a very audible puffing. In a moment, Mathilde appeared, red-faced and breathing heavily. Maxime was behind her, a hand on her arm as if assisting her in walking. On the other hand, he balanced a platter holding a single loaf of bread.

"Well?" François glared at her, waiting for an answer.

"I fear breakfast may be a bit late, master," Mathilde apologized.

Maxime released her and she bobbed a curtsey, nearly losing her balance. Maxime hastily set the platter on the table next to the jam pot. His hand went to her elbow again, steadied her, then once more let go.

"What do you mean?" François scowled, his expression accompanied by a low belly-growl.

"That boy Robert," she went on. "He looked a little peaky

when he came by the other day. Had a bit of a cough, he did. He didn't show up this morn so I expected he's come down with something."

"Does that mean we've no fresh eggs today?" Isabeau spoke up in alarm.

She didn't care for herself. She could have eggs for breakfast or do without, but François never faced a morning without a full platter, and from his expression, never intended to. That wouldn't do his temper any good.

"Maxime walked over," Mathilde answered, "to discover the cause."

"And a far trudge it is, too," Maxime put in, looking vexed.

"He found young Robert abed with a fever and his *pére* as well. Jean-Henri's good wife is taking care of both of them but coughing herself." She glanced at Maxime. "He brought back eggs but they're a day old, so I won't vouch for their flavor. She hadn't time to gather today's."

"Never mind." François dismissed Jean-Henri's plight and that of his son. "Just get them cooked. I'm hungry. Fry up some ham slices, also."

"I'd be glad to do that, sir," she answered hastily. "But when I walked to town, the butcher was complaining of a cough, too, and didn't really give me the best cuts. Wheezing like a bellows he was, the whole time. The ham is mostly *dos de graisse* with a bit of loin."

Mathilde looked distressed, a hand unconsciously wrapping in her apron and twisting it. She'd never before had to tell her master such a thing and was unsure of his reaction.

"I fear he simply hacked whatever was nearest off the carcass. I thought to score part of the fat and boil it with some pulses. We've a good supply of peas and beans."

"Don't tell me about it, just do it!" François ordered, but as the cook bobbed a second curtsey and began a retreating shuffle, he held up a hand. "No, wait. Doesn't it take lentils a long time to cook?"

"Aye, sir. A good four hours if they're dried as these are."

"Serve that for the evening meal, then. For now, I suppose breakfast is a total loss." François's lower lip thrust out like a pouting child's.

Isabeau didn't even marvel at his lack of sympathy.

"It's not my fault, sir." Mathilde's voice went into a whine as she laid the blame at everyone else's door. "It's Jean-Henri's, and that lazy son of his, and the butcher's. For being sick. Though I'm not feeling too spry myself." She emphasized this by coughing and huffing slightly. "Can't seem to catch my breath."

"Perhaps if you didn't sample so much of your own cooking, you might be able to breathe better," Isabeau said ungraciously, not feeling the least guilty for directing François's attention, and therefore his anger, on the cook and away from herself.

"Can I help it if I'm such a good cook?" Mathilde defended herself.

"Nevertheless, refrain from the basted eggs for a few days and see how much your breathing improves. For now, get to the kitchen and see what you can scavenge for your master's breakfast."

"Make it as quick as possible." François seconded Isabeau's order. "I'm anxious to begin my St. Jean. It's going to take all my energy, so I need nourishment."

At that, Giovanni stirred slightly, making Isabeau glance his way. He immediately stilled, but his expression held nothing of his master's eagerness. Rather, he looked as if he were dreading having to pose.

"Your standing here isn't making my belly any less hungry. Don't feed me excuses. I want food!"

"Yes, master." The cook went out, more slowly than she

came in, pausing to sneeze as if underscoring her own weakened condition.

Maxime followed after her, leaving Giovanni standing by the sideboard.

"I suppose I'll have some bread and jam in the meantime." François reached for the platter holding the loaf of bread.

Shortly thereafter, there was a loud crash from the kitchen.

Maxime's panicked bellows of "Master! Mistress!" brought them running, with Giovanni trailing behind.

Amid a deluge of water, Mathilde lay on the floor, the source an overturned pail near her hand. Her cap was askew, hair spread out on the floor in damp curls, her apron sodden. On a griddle in the hearth, cakes sizzled and scorched. Maxime knelt by her side, shaking her.

"She was carrying water to the hearth when of a sudden, she gasped, choked, and swooned," he reported as Isabeau knelt beside them.

"Mathilde, wake up." A vigorous slapping of the plump jowls brought the cook around.

"Mistress, why do you beat me?" Immediately, she began to cry in long, loud wails. "I'm doing my best!"

"I'm not beating you, you silly cow. You swooned. Oh, do shut up!" Catching the cook's arm, she tugged uselessly. Mathilde was too heavy for her to lift alone, and she was too weak to get up by herself. She shot the butler an exasperated look. "Here, Maxime, help me get her up."

She glanced at the door. As expected, François was nowhere in sight. She remembered him pausing as he saw Mathilde's unconscious body, though she had no memory of him entering the kitchen.

"Giovanni, help us." Struggling under the heavy weight, she called to the boy.

As he came toward them, however, Mathilde cringed and

again began to weep. "Not him ...oh no ..." She made a vague waving of arms that might've been an attempt to cross herself, nearly striking Isabeau in the process.

Isabeau dodged, holding up a hand.

Giovanni stopped. She waved him back into the corridor.

At her instructions, she and Maxime somehow lugged Mathilde to her feet, then half-walked, half-carried her to their bedchamber. They got the cook into her night-rail and put her to bed. Isabeau pressed the back of her hand to the cook's cheek. It was hot and dry.

"It's obvious she needs the leech."

She swiped her forearm across her own forehead. It had been a struggle getting Mathilde upright, and sweat seeped under the edge of her wimple. Her arms ached from the strain of heaving the cook's heavy weight.

"Maxime, you must fetch him."

"The leech lives on the other side of Aux-le-Piémont," Maxime protested. "I should stay here and tend Mathilde. Send that creature." He gestured vaguely in the direction of the kitchen.

"Giovanni is a stranger to the town." She wasn't about to loose the boy among the townsfolk with no one to protect him ... or them. "He'd never find the leech's house."

"I can't walk that far."

"Take the horse, dolt." She didn't remind him he'd nearly run it the day she'd fallen in the forest. Of course, that day, he'd had François's ire urging him on.

"Me? Ride that animal?" Maxime visibly cringed.

"Without treatment, whatever is wrong could worsen, and Mathilde may die." She doubted it, but it wouldn't hurt to exaggerate. "Which do you prefer—becoming a widower or riding the horse?"

Maxime blanched, gulped, and dashed for the walkway door.

Isabeau satisfied herself that Mathilde was merely sleeping and not in another swoon and left the little room. On the way through the kitchen, she took the griddle from the fire lest the cakes on it burn further, placing it on the worktable.

She found François pacing in the hallway before the salon.

"Well?"

"She has a fever. I've sent Maxime for the leech."

"So that's why he rushed past me like a bat out of hell and didn't answer when I called to him? No breakfast then, I suppose." He brightened hopefully. "Unless you wish to cook it?"

"François, don't you ever think of anyone but yourself? Our cook is ill. Our neighbors are also, and all you want is to fill your belly."

He didn't answer, merely shrugged.

"There are griddle cakes in the kitchen. Add some glacéd fruit and be done with it." She turned away. Truly, in that moment, she couldn't bear looking at him. "I need to check on Mathilde."

* * *

When the leech arrived, he was wearing a mask. Isabeau didn't like the looks of that.

She had a vague memory of hearing her parents speak of such a thing long ago, when she was a child, during an epidemic sweeping through towns to the north. Aux-le- Piémont was miraculously spared, as was La Chapelle, but larger, more populated places were devastated, some nearly wiped out.

Carts had gone through town, their drivers ringing bells and crying, "Bring out your dead." Corpses were burned by the hundreds, their ashes thrown into pits and buried, her father had said.

Isabeau thought the mask ludicrous, its long beak of a nose making him resemble a marsh crane. Elongated and pointed as a bird's beak, it was fastened around his head by a leather strap, the pointed end filled with herbs and spices, sun-dried flower petals and other aromatic substances whose fragrances were carried by straws inserted into the nostrils, their scent supposedly filling the physician's lungs and preventing the invasion of illness's deadly stench.

His cassock-like outer robe added a final, bizarre likeness to a Hell-escaped demon.

Isabeau wondered how many patients had died of fright upon seeing the doctor, rather than being carried away by illness.

As he moved, the doctor's robe swayed with the crackling of a sail touched by the wind. It was fashioned of leather, painted over with melted wax, as were his leggings and gloves. It rattled and billowed, the overpowering fragrances of mint, camphor, roses, and sweet shrub floating around him in a sweetly ambiguous aura.

"Your man says you've someone ill?" His voice came hollowly through the tunnel of the beak on the mask. As he spoke, he dropped the black leather knapsack he carried to the lamp table.

"Our cook. She swooned and is too weak to work. I put her to bed." She wished he'd remove the mask. She wanted to see the man's face as he spoke. It was vexatious speaking to that bizarre head-covering.

"You're fortunate your servant arrived when he did. I was about to leave and make the rounds of my patients." Without an expression accompanying those words, they sounded accusing.

"There are others ill?" That thought diverted Isabeau from

the doctor's appearance. Other than the shepherd, his son, and the butcher?

"Two dozen so far. It's been going on for at least a month now. I think it's the war. A miasma was probably sweeping up from Italy, the wind blowing illness into our country from those left dead on the battlefields. War always breeds illness."

He pulled the covering with its crystal-shielded eye sockets from his head, the hand holding it falling to his side.

The movement soothed Isabeau somewhat, for it meant he didn't consider that he was personally endangered by his surroundings. The next moment, she reacted angrily,

Dolt. Do you think wearing wax-smeared leather and sniffing camphor and vinegar will protect you? Doctors die of the same things as their patients. All the time. That was how the leech had obtained his position. Aux-le-Piémont's former physician succumbed during that long-ago illness of which Isabeau's parents still spoke.

"Thus far, only those on the outskirts of town have been affected. So far, I've treated the shepherd and his son, two of the butcher's children, four of the vegetable farmers, two of the fruit farmers, and some of the priests."

All of whom had gone into town and mingled with others. Isabeau was appalled.

"François is your friend." Briefly, resentment flared, also. *Aye, so much a friend, you counsel him on the most intimate part of our lives, and write the recipes for potions interfering with the natural order of things.* "If you were aware of this, why didn't you warn us?"

"I thought your cottage far enough removed from town to be affected," he defended himself. "The wind was blowing north-east. I suppose it changed course at some time."

"What's the nature of this illness?" Isabeau asked. "Tell me so I may watch for symptoms among the rest of us."

I shouldn't have to beg for information. He should tell me forthwith. Again, it was driven home to her how little worth she had in her own home ... correction, her husband's *home*.

"It's a coughing sickness," the leech explained. He laid the mask on the lamp table as he spoke. "The miasma fills the lungs, constricts the breath, causing nausea and fevers."

Approaching the bed, he studied Mathilde's face, carefully pressing the back of a forefinger to her forehead, as if fearing to touch her any more than necessary. Using the same finger and his thumb, he peeled back an eyelid. Twitching slightly, the cook's sleeping eye stared dully at him. He studied it, then let the lid slide back into place.

Her breath, harsh and wheezing, rippled the air.

Nodding, he stepped back from the bed.

"Is it fatal?"

"Not yet."

That wasn't much solace. *Not yet*. Inferring it soon might be?

"The coughing and nausea make the victim *think* he's going to die." He said that almost jovially, as if the idea amused him. "The sickness is prolonged, and that's the worst part."

Isabeau felt dismay rush through her. *Prolonged*. That meant she'd have to take the cook's place in the kitchen until she was well again. Who knew how long that might be?

"How do *you* feel?"

"I?" Isabeau looked surprised at the change of subject. "I feel fine. Why do you ask?"

"The illness acts quickly on those exposed. I'm amazed you aren't also showing symptoms." He studied her so intently that Isabeau became uneasy. "Wait, when you were much younger, didn't you have *croup de la gorge*?"

"You should know," she answered. "You treated me for it." She managed a rueful laugh as she remembered a much younger leech minus the mask and waxed cassock, coming into her bedroom and speaking kindly to a wheezing, frightened child. "I don't know how much of that terrible-tasting elixir of wintergreen I drank. I still don't understand how anything smelling so good could taste so vile. Is having that illness of import?"

"It's come to my attention that those who've suffered from *croup de la gorge* have an immunity to this present malady." His smile was genuine this time. "I believe, *Madame* François, you won't have to worry about becoming ill."

"That's a blessing then," she replied. "If everyone else may."

He rummaged in the knapsack, bringing out several small squares of parchment, thrusting them at her. "I've run out of my own remedies, so I've written recipes. It'll save time if you go directly to the apothecary rather than wait for me to replenish my herbals."

Isabeau took them, staring at the near-illegible words scribbled upon them. She managed to decipher a few: chamomile and borage to break the fever, horehound and goldenseal expectorant to clear the throat and lungs, fennel and mint for nausea.

"Now, I must go. I've other more seriously sick patients to treat."

With that, he retrieved his mask and put it back on, shouldered the knapsack, then left, saying, in what he considered a comforting tone, "You've caught this soon. Most wait until they're well into the disease before summoning me. That's in your cook's favor. I don't doubt she'll recover well, providing no one else gets ill."

* * *

ISABEAU HURRIED TO THE KITCHEN, fetching a basin and several torn squares from the rag basket. She went to look for Maxime.

She found him sitting in the creamery, leaning against the wall. When she called to him, his reaction immediately drove home the leech's parting words. His cheeks were now flushed, his eyes heavy-lidded as if he might at any moment fall asleep.

"How is Mathilde?" he asked, anxiety showing through his torpor, accompanied by a short, sharp cough.

In that moment, Isabeau didn't doubt he truly cared for the slovenly cook. That was ironic. She thought how handsome François was and how she despised him. If he were to become ill ...

She didn't let that idea go any further. One couldn't account for how the heart felt, could one?

She hoped no one else was stricken. She'd never seen François ill but was certain he'd be a difficult patient.

"The leech assured me the sickness has been caught before it can do harm."

She ordered him to the bedchamber. He followed her sluggishly, with the words, "My apologies, mistress. I ran a good part of the way. I haven't yet caught my breath."

Fearing it was something more than that, Isabeau placed a basin by the bed and left him sitting there, telling him to periodically bathe his wife's face with cool water.

Isabeau went looking for François.

She found him in the studio, sketching as if nothing out of the ordinary had occurred. Giovanni stood on the platform, wrapped in those filthy hides. Arms partially raised, as if he were about to take flight, he stared upward, eyes fixed on a spot on the ceiling. He didn't move as Isabeau came into the studio, didn't even glance in her direction.

"What is it?" François didn't look at her, either; simply aimed the curt question in her direction.

"The leech has come and gone."

"And?" He applied more charcoal to the sketch page, bold

lines and a firm hand forming Giovanni's slender though now well-fed figure.

"There's a miasma in the village. Many are ill. It isn't fatal but long-lasting. He's given me recipes to take to the apothecary. I have to go to the village." She took a deep breath before saying, not as a request, "I need Giovanni to accompany me."

On the platform, Giovanni lowered his head to look at her. Surprise ... or eagerness?

"Be still, damn it!" The sketching hand jerked, making a dusty smear upon the sheet. "Didn't I say, don't move?"

François reached for a bit of *gomme indienne*, pressing the gummy little blob to the sheet, erasing the charcoal's mistake. Nodding in satisfaction, he tossed it back onto the table. A swipe of the charcoal stick narrowed Giovanni's waist, accenting his ribs into prominence. Already, the figure no longer resembled the boy standing before them.

"I need him here. Can't you see I'm working? Take Maxime."

"Maxime's ill also." Another man might've volunteered himself, offering to help his wife. Isabeau knew better than to expect that from François, so she didn't bother saying it.

François accepted that statement with a scowl. "Take the horse. You'll get there faster."

"The leech said some of the farmers are also ill." She knew she sounded as though she was making excuses, though every word was true. "If this is truly an epidemic, food may become scarce, so I thought to buy extra supplies. I can't take baskets on a horse." They had no cart, and a saddle mount couldn't pull a wagon, anyway. "I must walk."

"Come back after I stop for the day. Then you can take the wolf."

She was surprised he'd give even that concession.

"François, that'll be long into the evening. The market will be closed by then. Besides, I'd have to walk the road in the dark."

She dared lay a hand on his arm, impeding its movement and causing him to press the charcoal into the sheet. It crumbled, leaving another smeared line. He grimaced and again reached for the Indian gum.

"If there's illness about, why should I expose the wolf to it?"

But you'd let me be? Isabeau took a deep breath. "If he's a *loup-garou* as you insist, will a mere miasma harm him? Surely the unnatural can't be threatened by malady afflicting mere mortals."

He didn't have an answer for that, so he merely scowled, irritated that she'd momentarily bested him.

"For once, think of someone other than yourself." She decided to appeal to him in the only way possible, through his still-empty belly. "If the farmers are ill, they won't be bringing their produce to market. I must replenish our stores if I'm to have anything to cook until Mathilde is well again. I need Giovanni's help in carrying the baskets." She decided to beg. A little. "Please, François. You can continue painting tomorrow. On a full stomach."

"Very well." He laid down the charcoal, studying the sketch for a moment.

It was rudimentary, but the force of the future painting was there, even in the few lines slashing their way across the paper's pale expanse. Giovanni was slowly disappearing into François's vision of him.

"Well?" He looked at Giovanni. "You heard the mistress. Go with her."

Probably the promise of the forthcoming meals was the only thing making him agree.

Chapter Thirty-Three

"When I meet these townspeople of yours, how must I act, mistress?" Giovanni said.

For François's benefit, he pretended reluctance to go with Isabeau until the moment the cottage was lost to sight. Then his eagerness showed itself.

"What must I say?"

Isabeau realized she hadn't thought about how to explain Giovanni to others.

She wasn't even aware how many people knew of the boy's existence. To how many had François spoken of his new "servant"? Had that wanton Lisette told anyone of him? Did Robert, or that loose-lipped Mathilde?

"We'll fall back on the lie François told *le comte*," she decided. "You're a refugee from Italy. Come here because of the war."

"*Oui*, the war. A terrible thing." Giovanni spoke with overdone solemnity as if quoting someone, face twisted into a mournful grimace. "I came to beautiful France to hide from it." He shook his head mournfully.

"Don't say too much," she cautioned, frowning as she

thought she saw a glint of mischief behind his words. "In fact, don't speak unless spoken to, and then, only say as much as is necessary. Let me do the talking."

"As you say, mistress." He nodded and fell silent.

They walked on for several minutes before he spoke again.

"I don't like this posing."

"You didn't complain before," she reminded him.

"Before, I had Lord André and his brothers with me, and at *le comte*'s ..."

He hesitated, not wanting to tell her how he'd spent hours staring at Lisette's exposed privates, and was inflamed, not with lust but rather curiosity, wondering if all women's intimate areas looked that way. The only other he'd seen was Mariah's fiery curls. The females in the paintings surrounding him were all hairless and bare. That led him to a forbidden question about Isabeau herself. Abruptly, the tips of his ears glowed pinkly.

As if she might sense his thoughts, he finished lamely, "It was interesting. But this standing alone, my arms raised, staring at the ceiling. My neck gets stiff, my hands numb. The master yells at me if I move an inch. He says I should look *enraptured*. By what? A former hayloft? It makes me want to ..."

He stopped, as if not certain what rebellious act he might commit. As if there were so many to choose from.

"You won't do anything, will you?" Her question was anxious. She'd never heard the boy so verbal. "Don't, Gio. Please."

"Don't worry, mistress," he reassured her. If his hands hadn't been filled with basket handles, he might've dared touch hers, patting it gently. As it was, he merely nodded and kept walking.

Ahead, the limits of Aux-le-Piémont beckoned.

There were people about, though not as many as the last

time Isabeau had been to town. Granted, that was over a year before, but ...

Several shops were closed, with signs nailed to their doors, words scribbled in thick black ink on sheets of cheap pressed rag. Giovanni stopped before one, studying the scrawl.

"Closed ... because of ... illness ..." He looked up, surveying the row of doors before them. "Do all those notices carry the same words, do you think?"

"I suppose they must. It's the custom to warn people away from a place where a miasma has caused illness."

She was surprised and pleased he remembered enough of his tutoring to read the words. Whoever had written the notice had a terrible scrawl, and that, combined with it being in a foreign language, should've made it most difficult.

"I remember my parents saying they heard that entire towns were quarantined during that other great illness."

"This has happened before?" He scowled. "Often?"

"I don't know about that. The only one I've heard of is the one my parents mentioned."

"Was this town of yours attacked by that miasma?" As he spoke, he wandered down the row, glancing at each notice.

"No. It somehow was bypassed." Isabeau didn't follow but remained where she stood, thinking the leech was greatly mistaken in his estimate of how many had already been stricken.

"Perhaps this one is making up for that." He paused, gesturing at a notice. One nail had come loose, the corner fluttering in the wind. Giovanni pressed a finger to it, holding it against the wood. "*Le propriétaire est mort ...*"

The owner has died.

"Died ..." Isabeau started to him, then stopped. "Don't get any closer," she cautioned, forgetting how she'd suggested Giovanni was immune to human disease. "In fact, come away.

Let's get these errands done and go home as quickly as possible."

She hurried away, Giovani following, to the marketplace.

A good many of the stalls were empty, their canopies buffeted gently by the wind. The few that were occupied had weary-looking men standing by them, several of whom were coughing and sneezing. Compared to the few shoppers about, there was a great deal of produce.

"Where is everyone?" Isabeau asked as she stopped at a stall with a wagon, its tailgate down. She was afraid of the answer.

"No doubt at home in their beds, struck down with this illness."

The farmer was Renaud, owner of a fine apple orchard south of town. She remembered that Mathilde purchased fruit from him often. He grew the biggest, reddest apples in all Aux-le-Piémont.

"Are you wishing to buy?" He selected one of the apples, abruptly sneezed, then rubbed it against the chest of his blouse before offering it to her. "I've only three dozen left, and once they're sold, I'm for home also."

Apples could be prepared in several ways. Isabeau tried to remember how many were still in that basket in the pantry, but couldn't. She bought them all.

Noticing how Giovanni studied the fruit as he stuffed them into his knapsack, she said, "Eat one if you wish. Or two. The Good Lord knows you won't get anything once we're back home."

She was surprised when he shook his head.

"If I don't lose this good fat the *comte* kindly put on me, the master will be angry. As much as I'd like to eat half a dozen of these apples, I mustn't."

"I won't be able to leave you food. Not now."

"It doesn't matter, mistress." As she started to protest that it did, indeed, matter, he added, "Don't worry."

Isabeau paid the farmer. Nodding, he touched his forehead deferentially, slammed the tailgate into place, and went to slide the bit back into his horse's mouth.

They watched him drive away.

"How can you survive?" Isabeau worried. "That paltry amount the *comte* and I have given you isn't enough to keep a mouse alive."

"Perhaps not, but a mouse can keep *me* alive. The master doesn't know I share my room with them, or that they nibble on some of his older canvases."

"But ..." Why did the thought of him catching a mouse unnerve her? "I've seen no bones or blood."

"That's because I don't leave either."

That made Isabeau shudder and hurry on to the next stall.

The only vegetables available were beans, which Isabeau didn't buy, remembering how Mathilde said they already had a great many, and marrows, turnips, cowcumbers, cabbage, slender green spears of sparrowgrass tied in bunches, and morels, which she did.

As each farmer's wares were depleted, he drove away as quickly as possible. Soon, the marketplace was empty, leaving only a few shoppers behind. A slight breeze blew through the square, ruffling the cloth canopies, raising a faint dust.

Tightening his hold on his baskets, now much heavier when filled, Giovanni asked, "Where must we go next?"

"The apothecary's shop. I must have him mix these recipes for me."

* * *

THE APOTHECARY'S shop smelled of mint and lavender, sage and thyme, and a myriad of other scents. Herbs hung in bunches before the open windows, drying in the breezes blowing inside and wafting out again, taking the herbs' savory fragrances with them. The interior of the shop was filled with shelves lining the walls. Jars holding powders, elixirs, crushed and whole minerals, and dried flower petals and roots sat row upon row.

Giovanni paused just inside the doorway, setting down his baskets. He looked around, nostrils wrinkling slightly.

The apothecary greeted them genially, as if he were glad to see someone not coughing and sneezing. Though he wore a robe much like the leech's, it was pale blue in color, making him look less severe and in no way frightening. Wiping his hands on the full-length apron covering it, he took the recipes from Isabeau.

He glanced at the leech's script and announced, "My supplies are running low. I've sent messages to La Chapelle and Sainte-Louise Modeste, asking the herbalists there to share their supplies. As yet, I've received no answer, so I fear they are also besieged by this complaint and have none to spare."

"What must I do?" Isabeau felt dismay sweep through her. "I need these recipes filled. My cook and butler are ill. There may be herbs in the woods, but I've not the knowledge to recognize them."

"I didn't say I had no herbs," he corrected her. "Only that they are low. You're lucky you've come just now before they are completely gone. I shouldn't do it, but I'll double the recipes. That should be enough if you, your servant there, or *le artiste* are afflicted. Just don't tell anyone."

With that, he walked around the shop, selecting various jars. He made the mixtures and compounds in a surprisingly short time, shaking the dried compounds into little bags and pouring the elixirs into pottery jugs.

Giovanni helped Isabeau tuck them into her knapsack.

As they left, Isabeau saw him place a small sign in the window.

I have no more feverfew, calendula, or goldenseal. Come back tomorrow.

She had a bare moment's guilt that they'd gotten the last of the goldenseal before rationalizing, *if it was someone else and I the unlucky one, would they care?*

At the butcher's, they were greeted affably enough by his brother, Bernard, bluff and big, looking so huge and healthy he could probably wrestle a grown ox to the ground with one hand. Kicking up sawdust from the floor, he came from the back of his shop, from the room where the carcasses were prepared. In one hand, he held a cleaver, its blade glistening redly as he tossed it onto the counter.

Unlike the apothecary, he was dressed in hosen and shirt, an ill-smelling brown leather apron overall, discolored with many spatters and stains, some fresh and red, some faded and dark brown.

"Mistress François. It's been quite a while since you've graced my brother's shop."

Giovanni inhaled sharply. He glanced toward the cutting room door, taking a long, deep breath, seeming to hold more than a little satisfaction. Isabeau wondered if he smelled the raw meat beyond the door. She envisioned bloody carcasses hanging from iron hooks, the boy wandering among them, sniffing and nipping, a bite here, a nibble there ...

"I heard your brother was stricken," Isabeau said. "How is he?"

"Doing well." Bernard nodded. "I don't doubt in a day or two he'll be back here as hard at work as ever, and I can go back to farming again."

"That's good to hear. You look well."

"Aye, the farming life's kept me strong and fit. No miasma would dare attack me." Bernard laughed.

"I don't doubt it." Isabeau didn't remind him that many of the farmers who usually came to the market were absent because of illness. She studied the man. He hadn't sneezed or coughed once since they entered the shop, and she took that as a good sign.

"Who's this strapping lad?" Bernard went on. "He doesn't look as if this pesty illness has bothered him."

"Master Bernard, this is Giovanni," Isabeau began.

She wrinkled her nose slightly. In spite of his obvious well-being, a stomach-turning odor exuded from the butcher's apron, of fresh blood, and older, dried fluids. It was all she could do to keep from putting her hand over her mouth.

"Giovanni, eh?" He didn't give her a chance to finish. "An Italian? What's he doing here?"

"I'm a refugee from the war," Giovanni spoke up before Isabeau could respond. "It's a terrible thing, and I ran away from it to France's safety."

"Smart of you," Bernard spoke approvingly. "You definitely look to be a sharp lad. Strong and handsome, too." His gaze lingered a bit longer on Giovanni's face before he looked at Isabeau. "I've just received carcasses this morning, Mistress François, so fresh they haven't yet been prepared."

"You know what Mathilde usually buys." Digging into her pocket, she handed over the coins.

He glanced at Giovanni, and his eyes narrowed in some kind of speculation. "Come into the cutting room while I select the portions. You can help me pack them in that knapsack you carry." He picked up his cleaver and gestured to the closed door.

Setting down the baskets, Giovanni followed the butcher.

They were gone for quite some time.

Isabeau busied herself looking around the shop. As Bernard said, it had been a long time since she'd been to town or done any shopping. Mathilde had been given that responsibility when she arrived at the cottage, and though she complained mightily, she jealously guarded the task as her responsibility. Whenever Isabeau went to town, it was merely to visit.

She was just beginning to realize how truly useless she was.

I'm merely a figurehead, le artiste's *wife, superfluous at running his household, good for only one thing ... and I only fulfill half that duty.* She was surprised the merchants remembered her name, then realized none had actually called her by it. She was merely "Mistress François." *Another woman could take my place and they'd call her the same thing.*

That was unsettling.

She listened to the murmur of their voices wafting through the closed door, mostly a drowsy drone, punctuated now and then by the sharp *thwack* of the butcher's cleaver and the liquid squeak of a knife as he hacked and sliced. Abruptly, the door swung open.

Giovanni returned, trailed by Bernard. The knapsack dipped in his hands, much heavier now with its contents. One bottom corner was darkened slightly, an improperly wrapped slab leaking through. A drop of blood fell to the floor, soaked up immediately by the sawdust.

"Goodness, I hope you didn't give me all the meat," she said, eyeing the sack, trying to make a joke to cover her uneasiness as she thought it didn't look too full.

"As good as you can get, for what I was paid, *madame*." The butcher looked at Giovanni as he spoke.

Hefting the knapsack, Giovanni stalked past him. Bernard spoke to him in an undertone.

"Think about it," sounded like what he said.

"Do we have other stops?" Giovanni placed himself so that Isabeau was between him and the butcher. He kept his head down, looking at neither. When she shook her head, he said, "Let's go, mistress."

He was equally quiet as they left town.

Chapter Thirty-Four

"WHAT IS IT?" Isabeau waited until the sounds and sight of Aux-le-Piémont were left behind before she asked.

"What is what?" He still didn't look at her.

"What's wrong?"

"Nothing is wrong." He heaved a deep sigh as if irritated. "Why should there be?"

"I'm going to tell you what you told me." She made her voice stern. "Don't lie to me, Giovanni. I know that's what you're doing."

He stopped, set down the baskets quickly, almost dropping them, and spun to face her. His expression was so dark that Isabeau flinched.

"That butcher ... He wants me."

"What?"

"Must I repeat that?" He looked away, staring up at the sky as if seeking a reply in the clouds.

"You mean ..."

He nodded.

"You must be mistaken," she protested. "He has a wife and four children."

"And hides his perversion behind them while he lusts after young men." He waved a hand in the general direction of town and the butcher shop.

"He said, 'Think it over.'" Isabeau remembered that half-muttered phrase. "Think over what?"

"In that back room, he told me he thought I was a well-put-together lad, and if I'd offer him my backside, lay myself out like one of those carcasses for him to delve," in his anger, he fairly spat the words, "he'd make certain you got the best cuts of meat."

"You didn't agree, did you?" She thought of the sounds she'd heard. None of them seemed like a coupling of any sort.

"Did you want me to?" His look begged she would say she didn't. "If you do, next time we come to that place, I'll bow to him as much as he desires."

"Of course I don't." Now, it was she who was angry. "How can you even think I'd barter your body for mere food?"

"Then accept you got the meanest portions there are. Mostly fatback and some tripe, I think, with a couple of scrawny birds that might be crows for all I know, because I refused him and told him if he ever laid a hand on me, he'd lose it." He sucked in a deep breath, which sounded suspiciously like a sob.

"Gio, no matter that you've done it before, I'd never ask that of you."

"What do you mean?" He shrank away from her, as if she'd struck him. "I've never ..."

"Don't worry. I don't think less of you," she assured him, touching his arm. "François told me, you see ..."

He shook his head as if to stop what she was saying.

"Of how the gypsy offered to have you service him. As you did that girl."

His face flamed.

"Mistress, I swear. I've never touched a man. All were too

afraid to accept Boamas's offer. Feared I'd bite off their rods, I suppose," He sneered. "As for Mariah, that was play-acting. I put my head between her legs and slavered a bit, that's all. Boamas would never let me—she's his daughter."

"Oh, Gio ..." She dared touch his cheek. Inside, anger flared, followed by shame. "I'm sorry I believed him."

He turned away, shaking his head.

Something in the woods moved. Leaves crackled. A rabbit scampered across the road, disappearing into the woods on the other side.

"Shall I catch it, mistress?" He seized the opportunity to change the subject. "If we're to be deprived of good meat, rabbit stew is tasty. Squirrel, too."

Isabeau let him distract her. She had eaten both rabbit and squirrel before, and each could be made into quite edible dishes. She almost told him to go ahead, then remembered him chasing the squirrel at the grotto, its cries, and afterward the awful crunching.

"You'll do that as a last resort." She hurried down the road, sending the baskets she carried swinging in her haste. "Come along, the sun's nearly overhead. I've much to do when we get back. So do you."

Chapter Thirty-Five

François greeted them at the entrance, drunk and not trying to hide his anger.

"You finally decided to come back? Did you dawdle over every fruit and vegetable in sight? Maxime is taken ill. Too sick to even pour my wine. I've had to serve myself. I—"

He broke off as Isabeau rushed past him.

"Put the baskets in the pantry," she called to Giovanni, setting down her own so quickly it was as if she tossed them.

Vegetables and apples jostled against each other. She slid the knapsack from her shoulders, letting it fall to the floor.

"Nay, you'll get yourself to the studio," François said. "I have to make up for lost time."

She didn't hear Giovanni's answer as she rushed down the hall to the room beyond the kitchen.

* * *

Maxime still sat in the chair. Mathilde now lay on her side. One arm hung over the side of the bed, suspended above the floor, as if she'd negligently tossed it away. Between them on the floor sat the chamber pot. It was half-filled, floating evidence of illness. Maxime's stained clothing, as well as his awkward posture, slumped over the arm of the chair, suggested he had contributed to the mess.

He roused as Isabeau came into the room. "I'm sorry, mistress, I—" He tried to stand and nearly fell.

Isabeau caught him, staggering under his weight, for he was nearly as big and brawny as Francois. She was certain she would drop him when Giovanni appeared, catching the butler's arm and hauling him upright.

"We must get him to bed," she said.

Maxime had removed his doublet. It lay across the back of the chair. She pulled at the tie at the neck of his shirt.

He feebly pushed her hand away, "Mistress, it's not right ..." then he was sick again.

Isabeau held the chamber pot while Giovanni kept him upright. As soon as the upheaval was over, she asked, "Do you still insist on modesty, Maxime? Where's your nightshirt?"

He flapped a hand at the door, swallowing loudly. "On the back."

With Giovanni's help, she got the butler stripped, redressed in the smock-like garment, and tucked into bed beside his wife. Isabeau tugged Mathilde onto her back. The cook was breathing heavily, a sharp wheeze accompanying each inhalation.

She pushed pillows under each of them so they were slightly upright.

"The medicine. I must get it." She rushed to the door. "Watch them."

In the kitchen, she found the baskets. Giovanni had brought them inside, setting her knapsack upon the worktable. Wondering what he'd said to François and where her husband had gone, she pulled it open, taking out the packets and jugs, jumbled together as she dropped them. The apothecary had written the name of each mixture on a small square of paper tied to the neck of the jugs; instructions scrawled on the packets. The ink had run into the weave and blurred, but she was still able to decipher it.

Hastily, she scanned the packets, wondering which to use first. She selected one.

Chamomile. *Onne spoonefulle in a fulle cuppe of boylynge watter. Cool. Drinke. Reepeate in two houres.*

The packet of borage held the same inscription. She spooned chamomile and borage into two cups. It took only a few moments to put water in a kettle and set it over the brazier in the fireplace. Though low, the fire was still lit. She added a couple of logs and waited impatiently for the water to boil.

While that was happening, she put away the vegetables and fruit, transferring each to its proper bins in the pantry. As she was doing that, Giovanni appeared.

"I told you to—"

"They're both sleeping." He cut off whatever she was about to say. "The master's in the studio, calling for me. He can wait. You need my help."

The last thing she wanted was to anger François, but there seemed no way around that. Truthfully, she needed Giovanni's help.

"Very well. The meat must be put away." She nodded at his knapsack, its bottom now sodden, sitting in a puddle soaking into the boards of the kitchen floor.

He picked it up. Blood dripped. She saw his nostrils work, the way his chest expanded as he took a deep breath of blood-laden air. For a fraction of a second, she thought she saw a feral glow lighting his face.

It disappeared as he asked, "Where?"

Briefly, she didn't understand, caught by that look she told herself she'd imagined.

"In the pantry ... there's a trapdoor in the floor."

Hefting the knapsack, he carried it into the pantry. Other than the rustle as he set down the sack, no sound issued from inside. She wondered if he was staring at the trapdoor in the floor, with its heavy iron ring.

"Pull the ring," she called. "There's a well."

The pantry was built over another part of the stream running behind the cottage, where it formed a second spring. Mathilde used the well to float baskets of eggs, keep meat, and other perishables cool.

There was the creak of wood, a clank of metal. She imagined Giovanni staring at that round opening into damp darkness.

"Be careful and don't fall in."

"There's a rope tied to the underside of the door," he called. "What must I do with it?"

"Pull it up," she answered.

The following noisy movements told her he'd discovered the net bag on the end of the rope, and the tightly closed jar under it. In a moment, there was the sound of the trapdoor falling shut. Giovanni reappeared.

"I put the eggs in the net bag," he reported. "There were some ropes with hooks. I hung the meat from them and lowered them into the water, too, except for a smoked ham. I hung that from one of the hooks in the ceiling. There's also a wrapped packet of butter in the well."

"Oh, good," Isabeau said. "I didn't think of butter." Her voice went up in a sarcastic lilt. "Francois can't go without his buttered bread for breakfast."

"He did today," Giovanni said, with grim satisfaction.

"What's that on your mouth?" She thought she saw a red spot at the corner of his lower lip.

"Nothing." He stuck out his tongue. The spot disappeared.

She wondered if he'd taken a bite out of the meat before lowering it into the well.

"I touched none of it." He anticipated her question, making her leave it unsaid. "I won't go against the master's orders, mistress, though I do hunger. The beef bled. I *tasted* it."

The way he said that sent a shiver through Isabeau. She envisioned him licking a bloodied haunch.

"The master opened a bottle of wine to celebrate completing *The Beggar and the Nobles*. He and the *comte* feasted, also. Does the master celebrate every time he finishes a painting?"

"Always. Why do you ask?" She thought that an odd question, wondering what it had to do with anything.

A sudden, very wicked smile lit his face. "Perhaps after he finishes this St. Jean, *I'll* celebrate." He paused slightly, and his expression took on a definite lupine cast. "Perhaps I'll eat *him*."

He said it so quietly that Isabeau felt a shiver judder down her spine.

A metal clanging jolted the air, a lightning bolt of sound. Giovanni looked around, stiffening against attack. "What's that?"

"François ringing for Maxime. See?" She pointed to a series of bells affixed to brackets on the wall beside the chimney. One jangled again. "Would you see what he wants?"

"Probably another glass of wine he can't be bothered to get up and pour." He raced out.

The water was boiling now, bubbling noisily. Isabeau found a pot mitt, stuck her hand inside, and hauled the heavy kettle from the fire. She splashed water atop the herbs, setting the kettle on the tabletop, and stirred the powder vigorously. It mixed somewhat, small bits of herbs floating atop the water.

"What must I do now, mistress?" Giovanni was back.

"Did you tend to your master?"

"Not as I wished," he retorted, speaking more freely than she'd ever heard. "Do you have any of that potion that makes one sleep? I'll slip it into his next goblet."

"Don't say that." She told herself she should be shocked by how firmly he showed his contempt for François, that she should threaten him with punishment. She couldn't. He was only saying what she often thought. This sickness had liberated Giovanni somewhat.

Picking up the cups, she hurried out the door. He followed.

* * *

Giovanni held Maxime, propped against his shoulder, while she got the man to drink.

"Come, Maxime. This will help you get well."

He swallowed, choked, gulped, gagged, and eventually got the entire cupful down. Mathilde was surprisingly much easier, though still unconscious. She drank as if her body was parched, for indeed, with the fever, it might be.

"Stay with them," Isabeau ordered. She pointed to the basin and cloths on the table. "Use those. Bathe their faces."

Another jangle of bells cut the air.

"They're in here, too?" Giovanni sounded dismayed.

"The master must be able to summon his servants no matter the time of day or night." Isabeau pointed to the single bell above the door. "Go."

She didn't wait to see if Giovanni obeyed, hurrying back to the kitchen and the rest of the herbs she'd left sitting on the worktable. *Fennel and mint, for nausea.* She'd wait on using that, since both were sleeping and not throwing up at present. *Horehound and goldenseal,* the expectorants. She didn't know how chamomile and borage would react to those two. Best to space

380

them apart. She lined the jugs in a row on the tabletop, the packets in front of them.

Giovanni came rushing in.

"The master wants to paint. I must go, mistress. I'm sorry."

She didn't answer, pushing past him into the corridor. François was nowhere in sight. Remembering his impatience, she was surprised he'd waited this long before ordering Giovanni to the studio. She went down the walkway, found François before the easel, re-opening the paint pots.

"How dare you call Giovanni away. I need him—"

"Not as much as I do, wife. He is, after all, my possession, bought for only one purpose, and that purpose is to pose for my St. Jean."

"Fine, but know this." She was in no mood to argue but wasn't going to back down, not with so much weighing on her. "I've two sick people to care for and the duties of the cook to take over. If you wish food filling that ever-empty belly of yours, you'd best be prepared to let him go whenever I call, for if I have to give all my time to caring for the sick, something will go lacking, and it'll be your dinner!"

With that, she stamped out and didn't see François's mouth drop open in astonishment.

Without speaking, she passed Giovanni on the walkway.

* * *

Supper was late. It consisted of stewed apples and creamed parsnips.

François complained. "Only two dishes?"

"We must conserve," Isabeau snapped. "The illness is in the town. One of the shopkeepers has died. We should stay away as long as possible."

That didn't stop his complaints. A belly missing breakfast

and luncheon joined in with growls. "No meat? Didn't you stop at the butcher's?"

Oh yes, I stopped at the butcher's, she wanted to say to him. *Bernard wanted to barter Giovanni's body for the best side of beef.* She was certain she knew Francois's response to that: *Why didn't you agree?*

He'd send Giovanni back to the butcher shop posthaste.

"Of course, I stopped there. He had very little left," she lied. *I hate you. Hate you, you selfish pig.*

Giovanni, in footman mode, served. François took most of the two dishes, leaving a single bare serving of each for her. When the boy brought the bowl to her end of the table, she waved him away.

"Mistress, you must eat," he whispered. "You have to keep up your strength."

Bolstered by his concern, she accepted the remnants of the meal, forcing it down. It felt as if it might come back up. For a harrowing moment, she feared she was also coming down with sickness, in spite of the leech's assurance. After a few rapid swallows, her stomach steadied, and she realized it was simply anxiety plucking at her innards.

Because of fewer dishes, the meal ended quicker than usual. François took himself to the salon, where he bellowed for Giovanni to pour his wine, taking the boy away from assisting Isabeau in clearing the table.

That was the first night of the Little Plague of 1499. The only good thing coming of it was that François didn't bother Isabeau that night when they were abed.

Chapter Thirty-Six

THE DAYS FORMED themselves into a routine—lengthy, filled with complaints of inconvenience from François, sickened mutterings from Maxime and Mathilde interspersed with frequent upchucking, silent resentment from Giovanni, and occasional open rebellion from Isabeau. The latter brought a mixture of glowering silences and threats from François, with no follow-through, sullen stares directed at him by Giovanni (but only when he wasn't looking), inert sleep from the two servants, and the fervent wish by Isabeau that the day might soon end but the next one never begin.

Each morning she greeted the day as the sun came up, staggering into the kitchen muzzy with sleep from awakening during the night to check on the servants, making certain neither had choked on some unspewed vomit lodging in the windpipe or flooded the bed because a full bladder had gone unnoticed. If that happened, the bedclothes would have to be changed as well as nightshirts, meaning Giovanni would have to be rousted from bed. It also meant there would be sheets to be laundered.

Giovanni always seemed awake, waiting for her call, ready to help.

Without complaint, he did whatever was necessary, anything she asked. He carried Maxime and Mathilde from bed to chambers, neither complaining of modesty as he held the pot under Maxime's trembling organ or flipped up Mathilde's night-rail and set her sagging buttocks upon it, steadying her shoulders so she didn't tip and fall. He set the butler in his chair, held Mathilde in his arms while Isabeau changed the bed sheets, the cook's weight not a burden at all. If nightshirts needed to be laundered, he calmly whisked them off, wrapping each in a blanket and back to bed until the garments had dried on the line behind the cottage and were ready to be worn again.

Isabeau had to cook twice for each meal served, one for her patients, the other for François. Preparations for Maxime and Mathilde weren't so difficult. The water drained off vegetables, rice water, broth, or gruel ... easy to swallow yet full of nutrition. François's meals were more complicated, not because of the recipes, but because she had to decide what to cook, preparing something that would keep him from complaining that she was starving him, while making their food supply last as long as possible.

She didn't want to go back into town any sooner than she had to. She feared what she might say to Bernard.

Except when called for meals, François was visibly absent, though audibly very present, taking refuge in his studio where he kept Giovanni posing when he wasn't called away to help Isabeau.

The only time he ventured into the house was to eat or sleep. He ordered Isabeau to keep their bedchamber door as tightly closed as he did the studio door, preventing the malady from seeping inside.

François ate what was put before him, sparse as it was, no

longer complaining. Isabeau noticed he was losing weight. Often, she heard his stomach grumble and hoped that made him think about how poor Giovanni felt.

She wondered if the mouse population in the storeroom had been decimated yet.

Of her own situation, that her lack of appetite might be detrimental to her health, she gave no thought. She merely ate enough to keep going, and that was all.

After supper, François supplemented his meager meal with copious goblets of wine, so much that Isabeau dared venture their small wine cellar might soon be depleted. His answer was that when it happened, he'd send Giovanni to her father's, asking for more vintages.

Isabeau wished she had recourse to something to make her forget what she faced each day. There was only one good thing: after the first night, François banished her to the best guestroom, making his fear of contagion evident.

"It's not good for my health, having you in such close proximity after being in the presence of pestilence all day."

She didn't remind him that he ate the food she prepared after being in the presence of that same pestilence. Instead, she expressed in a single mutter, "From adversity, some good may always come. *Merci, Dieu.*"

Mentioning her father's wine cellar reminded her she'd heard nothing from her parents, neither to assure her of their welfare nor enquire after her own. She thought of that, then dismissed it. If they were ill, she could do nothing. She certainly wouldn't abandon everyone to go to her parents' aid, for whether she liked it or not, her family was now those in the cottage. Besides, they were on the far skirts of town, closer to La Chapelle, and had both the leech from there or from Aux-le-Piémont to minister to them.

Putting her parents from her mind, she concentrated on the

immediate, listening and watching for any cough, sneeze, or wheeze suggesting either Giovanni or François was also about to succumb. Once or twice, Giovanni coughed while serving, and that sent her nerves skittering so she was certain her hair might be standing on end.

"Dust," he explained. "That fat cook isn't much of a housekeeper."

That was true, so Isabeau let it go. She also hadn't done any dusting or mopping of floors since taking over the chores. Dividing her time between nursing and cooking was enough.

On the fourth day, there was a knock at the front door. To her surprise, Isabeau found a child standing there, a little girl of about ten. She clutched a basket tightly.

"Don't come too close, child." Isabeau immediately fended her away. "There's illness here."

"Please, *madame*." Her voice was thin and quavery as if she were terribly frightened. "I'm Charlotte, Jean-Henri's daughter. My papa's still ill as is Robert, but I'm well now, so *Maman* sent me with eggs." She hesitated. "The hens kept laying while everyone was sick, and we need to be rid of them. We also need money to pay the leech."

Eggs. A welcome change to François's diet.

Retreating from the door, Isabeau told the child to place the basket on the stoop, then move away. As Charlotte obeyed, she pulled the basket inside, tossed money on the steps, and closed the door, calling out, "*Merci*." She heard the child scamper to the stoop, scoop up the coins, and run away.

That night, when François displayed his delight at the bowl of butter-basted eggs and actually paid her a compliment, all she felt was fatigue.

By now, François was painting during each waking moment not spent eating and drinking. His bouts with the wine bottles were becoming less frequent as the fervor for bringing his creation into being increased. As usual, he forbade Isabeau's entrance to the studio. She suspected it was more to prevent access to Giovanni than for any other reason, for after the fifth day, François stopped allowing him to assist her at meals, as well as the chores or helping with the servants. She could handle the household tasks, and since the servants were more or less unconscious, they were no problem, he said.

Thus, during mealtimes, while Giovanni sat in his room in the studio, Isabeau brought the dishes to the table herself and afterward cleared them away.

By now, she was so tired, her mind so centered on the two tasks of meals and care, she stopped worrying about Giovanni, telling herself he couldn't be touched by whatever evil the wind had brought to Aux-le-Piémont. From the moment she woke, all she wished was to get through the day and into bed again.

It was on the eighth day, or it might've been the tenth or the twelfth or perhaps even half a month later, for by now the days blended together with frightening speed. One sunrise led to a sunset leading to a sunrise to a sunset and so on. In between each was the same set of events: cooking, washing soiled bedlinens, emptying chamber pots full of matter she didn't want to think about ... It all ground to a shattering halt on that specific day, whenever it was.

Giovanni became ill.

* * *

SHE WAS IN THE KITCHEN, up to her elbows in hot soapy water, thinking of nothing more than the next chore she had to do and how tired she was, when François stamped through the door.

"You bitch!"

She didn't see his fist descend. There was a moment's blackness, the plate flew from her hand, splintering into shards against the wall, and Isabeau found herself lying in suds, blood pouring onto the bosom of her gown from her nose.

"Why?" she mumbled, voice muted in shock. Her nose was numb. She cupped a hand to the blood. "Why did you strike me?"

"Because you lied, you stupid bitch," he gritted. "The wolf is stricken."

* * *

Chapter Thirty-Seven

Giovanni lay on his cot. His hands twisted into fists, clawing the hides on his chest in attempts to pull them loose as he struggled to breathe.

"How long has he been like this?" Isabeau asked.

To her eyes, becoming accomplished in surveying the disease, he didn't look like someone just succumbing, but more like someone halfway through the worst of the malady.

Nevertheless, hearing his struggling inhalations and their accompanying wheezes, she was stricken with conscience. While she was hurrying about her chores, worrying about all she had to do, he'd been seized by the pestilence. As she ran about the cottage, letting her thoughts be filled with making certain François was fed and Maxime and Mathilde didn't choke on their broth, mixing the elixirs and potions the leech prescribed, Giovanni was burning with fever, forced to stand in that beseeching pose for François.

"Three days, a week." That was accompanied by a negligent shrug. "I didn't notice until he collapsed—"

"A week? You *bâtard*!"

She flew at him, fists pounding his chest. He grunted, more

in surprise than pain. Isabeau's attack was as unexpected as his own had been.

"You let my Gio sicken and didn't tell me? Why?"

"How can I paint him if he's abed with illness?" He caught her wrists. Briefly, they struggled against each other before he shoved her away. "My painting is more important than his being ill."

"So that was why you forbade me coming to the studio." She realized she was ranting and tried to calm herself, but anger spurred her on. "You knew I'd see and stop you. You ..."

"It's your fault, you know," he accused. His hand tightened on her wrist lest she attack again. "You said the miasma wouldn't harm him. Well, it has, as you see."

"All the other things we've been told about *loup-garou* have turned out to be false; why not this also?" she snarled at him. "Yet you blame me?"

A mutter from Giovanni made her wrench herself from François's grasp and rush back to the cot.

"Gio?" She bent over him.

"Mama?" He opened his eyes. They were bright with fever, specks of molten copper splashed with bronze darkness. "Mama, Papa ... *nonio lasci qui ...*"

"What did he say?" She spun, head flicking in François's direction with the swiftness of a snake, her gaze so deadly he took a step backward. "Is it Italian?"

"He asked his parents not to leave him." He looked as if that poignant statement meant nothing.

Isabeau was shaken. In his delirium, Giovanni thought he was again at that moment when he was abandoned to Boamas, the illness bringing back a fragment of his native language.

"Water ..." He spoke again, this time in a whisper so dry she swore she heard his tongue crackle against his teeth like leaves breaking against each other.

She hurried to the window where the pitcher sat. It was empty.

"You've let him go without water? *Imbécile.*" She slammed the pitcher back into its place so violently it was a wonder it didn't crack. She didn't care that her anger made her disrespectful to her husband, giving him just cause to retaliate with a beating. "How do you expect him to quench a fever if there's no water in his body?"

"I couldn't have him interrupting his pose every hour or so rushing to the *puits de cess*, could I?" He ignored her insult.

It was all she could do to make her fists relax. Instead, she put an arm around Giovanni's shoulders, hauling him upright. Head lolling onto his chest, he lay lax in her arms.

"Help me get him up." He was too heavy for her to lift further.

"Get him up?" François didn't move. "Why?"

"Because I'm taking him to one of the guest bedrooms. He can have the one I've been sleeping in. I barely use it, anyway."

"Oh, no." He backed away, shaking his head. "I'll not have this creature sleeping in a bed meant for a guest. He might leave fleas."

"You don't have any say about it," she snapped, glaring at him. "I'm the one tending the ill. I'm the one sitting up with them at night. When you decide to do that, then you can say who sleeps where." She added, defiantly, "The hangings are made of taffeta. That repels fleas."

When he still didn't move, she forced her voice into a calmer tone.

"I want everyone together, so I won't have to be running all over the house treating them. Now get over here and help me, or shall I carry him myself?"

"You can't carry him," he said matter-of-factly, as if it were his decision, and pulled him from the bed, though it was probably more his surprise that she dared speak to him so, making him submissive, than any other reason.

Tossing Giovanni over his shoulder as he would a rolled-up rug or bundle of rags, he followed Isabeau out of the studio and up the stairs to the guest room.

* * *

Ignoring Giovanni's nudity, Isabeau tore the hides from his body, flinging them to the floor.

"Take those away." She kicked at one of the hides with enough force to send the odorous garment landing at François's feet.

"They stink." Swallowing loudly, he coughed.

"Stink, do they?" That made her angrier. "Think of being forced to wear them."

He turned his head, grimacing. "What must I do with them?"

"Burn them." She pressed a hand to Giovanni's forehead. It was so hot. "I don't care."

"If I do that, what will he wear as he poses?"

Why is he being so stupid?

"Oh, for the Lord's sake, François!" Isabeau's stretched nerves snapped. She didn't look at him, her attention on Giovanni, who had begun to mutter again. "I don't care. Just take them away."

"Very well." With obvious reluctance and great distaste, he gathered them, holding them at arm's length. He started out, then looked back. "You won't need me for anything else, I trust?"

"Just get out of here." She hurried to the pitcher sitting on the commode near the window, lifting it. Also empty. It wasn't filled unless they had a guest. Clutching its handle, she gave François an impatient glare.

With a final disgruntled stare, he disappeared into the hallway. As if in rebuke, a sneeze drifted back to her, followed by a violent hawking.

She hoped he didn't spit on the floor.

Isabeau waited only long enough for his footsteps to die away before she took the pitcher to the kitchen, filling it from one of the buckets of water she'd brought in for washing the dishes. Some of the dishwater, spilled when she fell to the floor, had dried into sticky puddles. A good deal of the floor about the worktable was still wet. The broken dish lay in shatters on the floor.

Later. I'll clean up later.

Seizing a cup from the worktable and a handful of cloth from the rag bag, she hurried back upstairs.

She could hear Giovanni's wheezes as she neared the door. He hadn't moved. Pouring water into the cup, she slid an arm under his shoulders, raising him enough to put it to his lips.

"Drink, Gio."

He obeyed, swallowed, and coughed, spraying water. Hand dripping, Isabeau pulled the cup away. He reached out blindly, caught her wrist and pulled the cup to him again, drinking in loud, hasty gulps until it was empty. With a sigh, he fell back upon the pillows.

She set down the cup. Bringing the basin to the bedside table, she poured water into it and wet one of the cloths she'd brought from the kitchen. With it, she bathed Giovanni's face and neck, hesitated, then tossed back the blankets. She patted the dampened cloth down his chest, holding her own breath in pity and anger at the sunken indentations of his ribs, the concavity in his belly.

Obviously, mice weren't filling.

"Oh, Gio, if I'd had any idea, I never would've taken you with me. I'd have lugged those baskets myself if I had to make a dozen trips to town and back."

No use worrying about that now. It was done and past. What she had to do was make certain he didn't die.

I can't bear it if I lose you, Giovanni.

"I love you," she said aloud, then glanced guiltily at the open door.

I shouldn't have said that. What if François lingered somewhere nearby? What if he heard?

She hoped he'd again taken refuge in the studio, far from the sound of her voice. That made her wonder what else she might've said in unguarded anger. Had she blurted anything incriminating while in Giovanni's room, any word alerting her husband to how she felt? She couldn't remember. She hoped not, but, if she had, prayed that he was so diverted by her behavior that he ignored it.

Carefully, she tucked the blankets around Giovanni. Assuring herself he was stable for the moment, she hurried back to the kitchen to mix the leech's powders. She had no idea if any of the herbs might harm the animal portion of his nature. Hoped since he was in human form, that part of him would be stronger and accept the leech's mixtures.

He's been so long without medicating. Days longer than Maxime or Mathilde.

In desperation, she mixed all the powders together, dumping horehound, chamomile, goldenseal, fennel, mint, and borage in a full cup of tepid water. She stirred it frantically with a spoon, grimacing at the lumpy mass floating on the water's surface while other clods sank to the bottom and burst, dissolving. Hand over the top of the cup to prevent it from splashing out, she hurried back to the bedchamber.

He drank it with surprising ease in spite of its near-solid

contents, with no choking or coughing. He didn't open his eyes, however, or speak, but lay still the moment she released him to the pillow again. Isabeau hurried away to check on the cook and butler, finding them sleeping easily, breathing raspy, although nothing was causing alarm, but ...

What is that smell?

Isabeau sniffed. Something smoky. Like ... scorch.

It was then she remembered the cookpot she'd filled with lentils and water and hung over the fire to cook while she washed the dishes. She hurried back to the kitchen to see smoke pouring from the cookpot and filling the room.

The water had boiled out, splashing over the fire and half-dousing it. A bare flame guttered and sparked. With no liquid in the pot, the beans had burned. They were now blackened and sticking to the sides and bottom. Wrapping her hand in her skirt, she swung it from the fire, lifting it from the hook and setting it to one side while swatting the smoke away with her other hand.

Let it cool. She'd clean the pot later. Now, she had to find something else to cook.

I should serve it to François, she thought maliciously. *Let him see how not telling me earlier that Gio was ill has ruined his supper.*

With a heavy sigh, she went into the pantry. There were still some apples and pears, three heads of cabbage, and a few other vegetables. That package of butter had been a large one. The near-whole smoked ham hung from its hook. She decided she'd save the meat, and instead would chop a few apples and pears, shred some cabbage, and make a *salade* with a butter sauce spiced with mustard seed and honey. Quick. Easy.

If he doesn't like that, he can take that dagger of his and find himself a rabbit or two in the woods.

It was already getting toward evening. Where had the hours gone? It seemed only moments before that François had stormed into the kitchen and struck her to the floor. As if remembering that, her cheek began to ache. A glance in a mirror told her a large black bruise was forming just under her eye, making her look as if someone had taken one of François's charcoals and drawn a swathe with it across her cheek.

I'll bathe it in witch hazel water. Later.

Her mouth was ringed in red, the top of her kirtle spotted where her nose had bled. She'd soak it in cold water tonight. She didn't remember trying to staunch the blood or when it stopped. The stain on her lips reminded her of Giovanni's blood-smeared mouth after he killed the squirrel. She shuddered the thought away.

She'd prepare the *salade*, then go in search of François.

He was in the studio, lounging in a chair, consoling himself with a bottle of wine.

How many do we have left now?

"Well? Will he live?" He roused, giving her a baleful look. His voice was husky. He coughed and cleared his throat as he spoke, spitting a splotch of something onto the floor.

Isabeau ignored it. *I'll not clean that.*

"That's up to *le bon Dieu*." It was a struggle speaking civilly to him. "I think so, though he's coming to treatment later than anyone else, no thanks to you." She had to add that. "Your supper's ready."

She walked out, not waiting to see if he followed.

* * *

Two hours after eating, François was ill, losing the *salade* in a malodorous splatter on the foyer floor.

"Bitch," he accused, between heaves. "You've poisoned me."

"Don't be foolish," Isabeau said coldly. "You've caught the illness." Probably from Giovanni, but she didn't say that.

Briefly, she wondered what would happen if a man died of poison while ill. Would sickness be blamed for his death? Would anyone think of any other cause? She brushed the thought away.

"Here, let me get you to bed."

The routine was so well ingrained now, she did it automatically—getting him to bed, bathing his face and neck, mixing the powders and administering them, returning to the dining room to clean the floor. She marveled at how she offered help to someone she so despised that she'd think about him dying while giving him herbals to make him live.

Placing a chamber pot within easy reach and telling him so, repeating the words several times to make certain he understood, she listened to his mumbled acknowledgment and left the room, leaving the door open.

In case.

Going back to the chamber where she'd left Giovanni, she was surprised to hear him breathing normally, his wheezing less distinct. His skin was still warm, but hadn't his flesh always had more heat than a normal human's? She thought back to the times she'd touched his hands or face.

That sent a shiver through her that was startling because it was all sensuality, holding no true fear for his welfare.

Isabeau settled herself in a chair by the bed.

Giovanni was restless, moving about, turning his head from side to side. He continued his mutterings, mostly in a half-audible whisper. Occasionally, he said a word or two in Italian, or so she thought. Mostly his mumbles were too garbled for her to understand.

Twice more, she wiped his face, neck, and chest with the damp cloth. Then, she settled again into the chair, leaning her cheek upon her hand. She dozed slightly, ready to leap to wakefulness if she was needed.

Around midnight, his murmuring awoke her.

She blundered to her feet, staggering to the bed. Touching a hand to his forehead, she peered at his sleeping face.

The lamp she had set by the bed shed little light. The room felt close and airless. Hurrying to the window, she pushed open the shutters.

I'll risk letting in a little fresh air. She thrust a hand through the opening. *There's no wind. Surely no floating miasmas will invade if I leave the shutters open a short while.*

She peered through the window. The little clearing behind the cottage was clearly outlined in light, the stream reflecting the full moon in glimmering silver swirls ...

... the moon ...

A sound behind her made Isabeau turn from the window.

Chapter Thirty-Eight

"Water ..." Giovanni struggled to sit up.

She hurried to the table, getting the cup. He opened his eyes, reaching for it, gulping it down. He handed it back to her.

"Thank you, Isabeau." His voice was so calm, so lucid, it shook her.

"You're ..." She touched his cheek. She'd swear it now felt no warmer than anyone else's. "You're all right?"

His mouth quirked in a crooked smile. "Didn't you say a puny miasma couldn't harm me?"

"I thought it had," she answered. "You looked so ill."

"I *was* ill, make no mistake." His answer was rueful.

"I was frightened." She thought of how he'd called for his parents, of bathing him, wiping the wet cloth over his body.

"I'm sorry if you were." His smile became oddly shy. He looked away. "Your hands felt good on me, Isabeau."

Oh God, he can read my thoughts. She didn't answer.

"Where am I?" For the first time, he realized he was no longer in the storage room. "How did I get *here*?"

"I had François bring you into the cottage. One of the guest rooms. He didn't want to." Why did she add that?

"Where's the master now?" He didn't seem to notice her discomfort.

"He's ill, also."

"Badly?" He sounded hopeful.

"It would seem so." She thought of how violently François had lost his supper.

"I can't say I'm sorry."

Isabeau swore his expression held the thoughtful, calculating look of someone hoping for the death of a lifelong enemy. It gave her the most uncomfortable feeling. In spite of the things Giovanni had said about wishing François dead, it hadn't hit home as it did now, when there might be a possibility of her husband actually dying.

"I gave him the medicines and put him to bed."

"We're alone?" His tone changed.

"As alone as one can be in a house filled with sick people." She ignored his tone. Her unease was growing, becoming a near-tangible presence.

"It wasn't only the pestilence making me ill."

"What do you mean?" Something about the way he said that sent a prickle up her back, sharp as needles stabbing into her spine.

"Did you forget?" He nodded at the window.

Moonbeams played on the sill, sparkling light dancing there as if silently asking permission to enter.

The shutters. I should close them. Keep the moon out. I must get myself out of here and lock the door. She didn't move.

"Isabeau ..."

"That's the third time you've spoken my name."

"You don't like it? If so, I'll never speak it again ... *maitresse*." His smile said he lied. He intended to continue speaking to her that way, no matter what she said.

"Just be careful of when you say it." Her expression told

him she liked the way he said her name, the foreign intonation of that sibilant second syllable a caress to her ears. Not 'mistress,' but 'Isabeau,' as if they were equals. The barrier between them was broken and could never be repaired.

"There's something I must tell you." He pushed back the blankets, swinging his legs over the edge of the bed. "And something I have to do."

"It can wait." She forced herself to ignore his nakedness.

"No, it can't." There was another glance at the window, at the moonbeams gathering like puddled silver on the sill. "Because of *that*."

It wasn't a warning. He made it a matter-of-fact statement.

He caught her hands. She let them lie lax in his grasp, started to speak. He released her long enough to press fingers against her lips.

"Listen to me, Isabeau, I haven't much time. When I was at the *comte's château*, I saw paintings of fabulous creatures. Half horse ... half goat ... part human ..." His words came quickly, with barely a breath between, hastily as if he couldn't speak them fast enough. When his eyes met hers, she was unable to look away, that dark but fiery gaze pinning her immobile.

He pulled her closer as he spoke. She wanted to resist, keeping her distance, felt her feet move until her knees touched his.

"What does that have to do with you?"

"The paintings showed them loving mortals. He said it was accepted. It made me think ... if a half-horse could love a human woman, why can't a half-wolf? It means what I feel for you isn't wrong or wicked or ..."

"Wh-what do you feel for me, Giovanni?"

Can it be? Is it actually going to happen?

"I love you, Isabeau."

He didn't say that. I imagined it.

She wanted to repeat it back to him. Didn't dare, couldn't, because her heart began pounding so fast, the pulse rose into her throat, and if she dared try to speak, the sheer joy might stifle her. Momentarily, she couldn't breathe, felt darkness swoop and surround her, making her want to throw herself into his arms, lest she swoon to the floor.

In the next reason returned.

Get out of here. Before the moonlight floods the room. Love or not, if he transforms ...

She took a step back, spun to go. He caught her wrist, pulled her back to him so roughly her body struck his. He kissed her.

He was awkward but possessed a passion as shocking as it was unexpected. For a moment, she was rendered motionless. The thought sprang into her mind to fight, wrench herself from him, and run before the moonlight acted.

That lasted only a moment.

If I die now, so be it. Once, just once, I must *know true love.*

Isabeau relaxed against him. His arms went around her. She caught his head in her hands, deepening the kiss, brushing her tongue against his lips. She felt his own lips shy away at her touch, then return the caress with abandon.

She was pulled closer, his legs encircling her own, imprisoning her within their clasp as his arms confined her body. His hands roved her back, cupping her buttocks, lifting her off her feet. Somehow, sometime, her gown found its way to the floor, kirtle and chemise with it. The kerchief she tied around her head was gone, her hair flowing freely. He pulled her onto the bed, rolling her into the goose down mattress, crushing her deep into its softness as he kissed her again.

The moonbeams tumbled over the sill, spilling onto the floor, creeping noiselessly toward the bed.

He looked that way.

"I need more time ..." A hand flicked the switch of the lamp, killing the flame and sending the room into darkness except for the inexorable flow of moonbeams across the floor.

She felt warm breath on her throat, kisses nibbling down her breast, an equally warm tongue laving a nipple, suckling gently, then with more force.

Isabeau gasped a voiceless cry.

She flung her arms wide, pressing them into the goose down. His hands encircled hers, entwining their fingers, grip tightening painfully, pinning them to the bed. His body stiffened, a husky groan forcing itself from between gritted teeth.

Moonlight touched the edge of the bed, crawled across the mattress, bathed their fingertips ... no ... *her* fingertips, his, a taloned paw ...

Did I really see that?

His body jerked, went rigid, and a low groan burst from him, of pain and relief. His weight ... too heavy for someone so starved ... the girth too wide for Giovanni's slender frame ...

She embraced him, her grasp tightening. The shape of his body was wrong, the conformation distorted, shoulders too wide, too thick under her hands ...

He began to pant, alternating with little growls fading into deep whines that might be equally pain or pleasure.

"Perhaps it's better this way," came as a guttural rumble from deep in a throat not meant to form human words.

He wrapped his arms, suddenly muscular and hairy, around her and thrust.

Isabeau felt a moment of mortal terror. She tried to cry out, but when the sound came, it was a mere sigh as a wave of passion flowed over her, so fierce she thought her heart might stop its beating then and there. Her body flooded with a satisfaction she'd never before experienced, like a wave of warm blood pouring over her ...

... soothing as it nourished.

Why did I think that? A heavy head rested against her shoulder, shaggy hair tickling her skin, harsh, damp breathing in her ear.

The moonlight stopped its progress across the bed, just short of revealing to her the creature looming above her, now possessing her.

"Isabeau," rumbled into the darkness.

He began to move within her, and she responded, crying out with the joy of it all.

If I must die, if he kills me, let it be now.

Powerful muscles bunched in rhythmic thrusts. She clasped narrow hips, legs encircling them, the hair on his flanks sending the sharp sting of tiny thorns grazing the insides of her thighs.

"Gio ... Gio ..." She moaned his name in the cadence of a hymn, over and over, in rhythm to the rush of his breath and the pounding of their hearts.

Abruptly, he pushed himself upright, thrust a single time, and froze, head thrown back, a deep rumbling torn from his throat, half-strangled into a howl dying to a human groan of release. He thrust again, then collapsed upon her, momentarily stopping her breath.

He panted damply against her neck, long and deep. She clasped coarsely bristled shoulders heaving with spent passion as his breathing slowly subsided into regular inhalations. Moonlight swirled around the bed, blending with the medicinal scent of herbs and a feral mingling of dry animal musk and human sweat, heated by the warmth of those deep breaths.

Isabeau touched his head, felt the point of an ear, and caressed fur instead of Giovanni's crisp curls.

She wouldn't turn on the lamp, didn't want to see the face of the creature who had possessed her, giving her more passion than she'd ever experienced, showing her how love really felt.

Instead, she simply hugged him tighter, pressing a kiss against a hairy cheek.

The moon disappeared behind a cloud. The moonlight became a silver patch upon the floor, then vanished, and they were in total darkness.

"Isabeau," was whispered against her ear. His breath tickled.

Head cradled against her shoulder, the creature slept in her arms.

Chapter Thirty-Nine

IN THE MORNING, Isabeau was afraid to open her eyes. She felt a body beside hers. Her exploring fingers touched warm flesh, but it was bare, with no coarse, wiry fur. The hand gripping hers had fingers, not claws.

She turned her head, forcing herself to look.

Giovanni lay beside her, dark curls tousled about his face. Impulsively, she kissed him. His eyes opened, delight in their dark depths.

"*Bonjour, chérie.*" He kissed her back, arms encircling and holding her tight. "You are not afraid to lie beside me?"

"How could I be? You didn't harm me last night. Anyway, the full moon's gone. For now."

The blankets had gotten pushed back, their nakedness in full view. Even if no one was there to see, she felt uneasy. Catching at the bedclothes, she pulled them up.

"*Non.*" He pushed the sheet and blanket aside. "I want to look at you as I make love to you."

"But I must get up ..." Her protests died away as he loomed over her, nuzzling her neck.

The blankets were kicked further away as he again possessed her.

Afterward, she was held in a gentle embrace, her cheek resting against his chest, his chin touching the top of her head.

"Did I please you last night?"

His voice echoed through his chest, directly into her ear, a quiet rumbling, reminding her of the wolf's growls. It made her shiver, but in a delicious way.

"Please me?" Never had François asked her that. He hadn't considered her feelings at all. "You did more than please me." She didn't have to think about it. "You showed me how it can be. What I've missed all these years."

He leaned back, eyes serious. "I'd never loved a woman, Isabeau, so I …" He glanced away. "I feared I might be awkward. I'm glad I pleased you, for I hope to keep doing so."

She tried not to show she was surprised by his confession, wondering if it shamed him to admit he'd been untouched.

"But not now." She wanted Giovanni to love her again and again, would've liked nothing more than to stay in that bed with him for the rest of the day and night, but …

Isabeau's sense of responsibility drove a wedge between desire and duty. Gently, she pushed him away. "I've chores to attend, patients to care for."

"That fat cook and the frightened servant?" His lip curled in scorn.

She wanted to kiss away that trace of contempt.

"Let them wait." He held her closer.

She laughed, reveling in the brush of his chest against her nipples, marveling at the way his hair, so soft, not stiff and bristly at all, could make them bloom and harden.

"Your master, too."

"Him?" He snorted. "He can die. I don't care. Do you?"

"Hush." She kissed him to prevent his saying more, not

wanting thoughts of François intruding. "One must think only charitable thoughts of the ill."

"Who says so?" he asked. "Is that one of your Christian concepts?"

A dark brow arched. She found it intriguing, touching a finger to the curve, following it with the tip of a nail.

"I'm not certain. I suppose so."

"Then it doesn't apply to me." Her touch must've tickled. He shook his head the way a dog might if a fly landed on its ear. "I'm well outside your God's boundaries."

"Gio, don't say that." Neither did she want religion raising its dogmatic head into the peace she felt. "*Le bon Dieu* ..."

"... abandoned me at my birth. Let's not speak of that, Isabeau." He didn't want disruption, either. "If you *must* get up" —he made a gesture of acquiescence—"do so."

He let her go, lay watching as she dressed. She swore she felt the brush of his gaze upon her naked skin, making her flesh warm. *Almost* embarrassing, but not quite, for she enjoyed it. It was a new sensation, so daring. She wanted him to touch her, though she knew if he did, she'd never leave the room that day. She moved away so he couldn't, picked up the chemise and slid it over her head, then put on the rest of her clothing.

Only then did he sit up, silently relacing the back of her gown. She liked the way his fingers felt as they tightened the little strings. That was another thing François had never done, though he was very skilled at getting her out of her clothes, even without her cooperation.

"There's blood on the neck of your kirtle." He saw it as soon as she faced him. "What happened?"

"It's nothing." She looked away. She'd forgotten about the stain; should've changed while he slept.

Too late now.

"Just as that bruise is nothing?" A finger under her chin

turned her back. His fingers hovered over the black shadowing her cheek, now fully visible in the sunlight. "What happened? Why did the master strike you?"

"He was angry because you were ill," she admitted. "He blamed me, and ..."

He looked at the door. "Let me smother him while he sleeps."

"Gio, no!"

"No one will be the wiser. Breathing problems come with this illness."

She didn't answer, simply shook her head.

He gave a sigh, exasperation in its heaviness, but equally agreeing to her wishes.

"Forget François," she said. "If you're as well as you say ..."

"Do you doubt it?"

"Not after last night. So, as the only other here in good health, you must help me."

"Gladly." He pushed back the blankets, then did an exaggerated glance at the floor with a gigantically bewildered shrug. "But what am I to wear? My clothes ..."

"... are in the studio," she told him with mock severity. "Get them."

"*Madame*, you would have me walk naked through the cottage?" He pretended shock.

"Why not?" A giggle trickled out, and she let it burst into a delighted laugh. She wanted to see him walk away from her, watch the muscles in his hips glide beneath his skin as he went down the stairs. "There's no one to see, is there? Other than I?"

While Giovanni dressed, Isabeau checked on her husband.

Sometime during the night, François had awakened. Vomit in the doorway bore silent, vile-smelling witness to the fact he'd gotten out of bed, if only briefly.

Isabeau felt a cold stab of fear. Had he heard them, reveling in their love so close by? Did he come to the door, peer in and witness their abandon, their naked bodies entwined? If so, would he remember?

She'd worry about that later. If François spoke of it, she'd convince him he imagined it in the throes of a fever dream. As for now ...?

He still slept, though breathing heavily with a distinct wheeze. She thought of what Giovanni said, wondered if she should watch him and make certain he didn't carry out his threat.

No, her Gio wouldn't harm François, not after she told him not to.

She pressed a hand against François's cheek. Still feverish. Another dose of medication was in order. Some chamomile and borage, also.

"He's very ill, isn't he?" Giovanni spoke from the doorway. He stepped over the spatters on the doorsill and came into the room.

Isabeau sighed. "More to clean."

"Not yet." He caught her hand, pulling her to him and kissing her. He cupped a breast, brushing his lips across the fabric of her bodice.

"Gio, not here ..." She began a protest, glancing at François, fearing he might abruptly awaken, miraculously healed, to behold his wife being fondled by his servant.

"Hush." Giovanni kissed her again, then looked past her to the man lying in the bed. "I can still finish him, Isabeau. Shall I?"

When she gave a frightened glance from him to François, he laughed.

"*Non, chérie*, I tease. I won't harm him. *This* is a much better revenge." With that, he sneered at the sleeping man. "*Oui, maître*, I kiss your wife, I've done more than that, to be truthful, and will keep doing it, because she loves me, and not you ... you drunken bully."

With that he kissed her a third time.

When he was gone, Isabeau changed her kirtle, consigning the stained one to the rag bag.

* * *

While Giovanni mopped the floor, Isabeau looked in on Maxime and Mathilde. Their fevers had broken, and both now experienced fitful bouts of lucidity and consciousness. They were still too weak to sit up or move about without assistance, however. Mathilde didn't complain as Giovanni hoisted her from the bed and guided her to the chamber pot. Giving him a heavy-lidded glance, she simply closed her eyes again and allowed herself to be placed upon the pot.

"She's not as heavy as before," he commented.

The cook had lost much weight through an enforced diet of broth, which, though laden with nutrition, did nothing to keep the fat on her bones. Sardonically, Isabeau wondered how long it would take to replace it once Mathilde began eating her own cooking again.

Maxime was even less of a burden. Giovanni lifted him as if he were a child.

"One might think he had bird bones," he said. He studied the butler critically. "Neither would be much of a meal now."

Isabeau shivered. She told herself it was merely a sudden chill in the air; Giovanni had developed a morbid sense of teasing her, and he said such things merely because he realized how they affected her.

After bathing their faces and hands and retucking each into bed, Isabeau left him emptying the chamber pots into the *puits de cess* while she again checked on François. He was sleeping soundly, if stentoriously, snoring loudly. She hoped that didn't mean his throat was obstructed. She did nothing to check, however. Telling herself he didn't *sound* as if he were choking, she hurried to the kitchen to mix the morning's medicines and prepare meals.

Their food supply was getting smaller. She didn't dare go into town and leave them untended. Nor would she leave Giovanni watching over them while she was gone.

Not that she didn't trust him, but ... perhaps she didn't, *a little*, but surely he wouldn't do anything to harm any of them, especially Francois, however much he might wish it.

Isabeau forced herself not to think further along those lines. She calculated that if Mathilde and Maxime both recovered soon, with only François for her to tend, the victuals would last to the end of the week. At that time, she would be able to place Maxime in charge while she and Giovanni went to town and saw how much damage the pestilence had wrought in the populace.

If not, she wondered how much of a squirrel and rabbit population there was around the cottage and if Giovanni could catch them all.

* * *

GIOVANNI WORKED AS CONSCIENTIOUSLY and strenuously as before, even more so since François wasn't there to bully him and take him away with demands that he posed. He mopped the floors, washing away any evidence of illness. He helped Isabeau feed Maxime and Mathilde, tending to their other needs, too. He even assisted her in treating François, though she could see he did that reluctantly.

"I don't care if he dies," he declared. "Unless it would cause you problems, Isabeau."

"Didn't I say be careful when you speak my name?" she cautioned. "Maxime and Mathilde are more alert now. What if they heard? A servant speaking to his mistress so intimately?"

"But I love your name. I wish everyone to hear me say it." He threw his arms wide, declaring loudly, "Isabeau ... *Isabeau* ... ISABEAU!"

His voice echoed down the hallway. Isabeau made shushing sounds.

"Don't worry. I won't say it when anyone is around who could hear." He grinned his assurance. "As for speaking to you intimately ..." His smile made her kiss him, and that led to more kisses, and then it was a short walk to the guest chamber ...

Having now been exposed to the true passion of the marital act, even if not by her husband, Isabeau was fulfilled, transformed. It was glorious. If she was changed, so was Giovanni. Once fully cognizant of female carnality and also of the woman he loved, he wanted more of both.

Seeking further knowledge of each other, they had little trysts like courting lovers—in the hallways, pausing in the shadows of a corridor for kisses and caresses.

Isabeau might find herself waylaid on the stairs, lying full-length with her skirts about her waist. Giovanni would lift her off her feet, pressing her against the wall as his eager rod slid into her. She might be standing at the kitchen worktable, only to suddenly lie upon it, pots and pans swept to the floor, while the heat of the fire warmed the backs of her calves as well as Giovanni's bare flanks as he showed her how much he cared.

He was always ready to make love to her, whenever and wherever they were, and delighted in taking what she considered unwarranted risks. Showing contempt for his master, he pulled her away as she administered his medication. Taking the herb-filled goblet from her hands, he placed it on the table, set her on the end of the bed, and laughed as he cuckolded François while he lay unconscious a few feet away.

And always, he whispered, "I can't get enough of you, *amour*."

Isabeau loved every wonderful, ecstatic, adulterous moment of it.

At night, they slept together in the bed in the guest chamber, locked in each other's arms. For a short time, Giovanni, the *loup-garou*, the accursed, was master of the cottage with Isabeau, the downtrodden wife, its mistress, in a life they pretended should have been.

*** * ***

GENERALLY, both avoided the studio. There was too much to do in the cottage; they had no reason to go there. Besides, that was François's domain, and neither wanted to be reminded of him, other than as that unresponsive lump in the master bedroom. Likewise, now free to sleep in a *real* bedchamber, Giovanni didn't wish to think of his imprisonment in the storage room.

One day, however, curiosity spurred Isabeau to the studio to look at the painting abandoned by sickness. She was astounded at what lay on the canvas. It was Giovanni, but not the Giovanni she knew, the man who lay next to her and filled her with his passion and made her tremble with desire.

On François's canvas, he truly became St. Jean, wanderer in the wilderness, preacher of salvation, a man in whose eyes burned the love of God and the desire to have others see that love for themselves. It might have been the intensity of fever François had depicted, but to Isabeau, it was the same fervor burning in Giovanni's eyes when he made love to her. Could it be the saint's passion and that of the *loup-garou* were in some way the same? Could both a holy man and an unnatural creature experience the same ardor for a woman as for God?

All she knew was that François had this time truly created a masterpiece, no matter that others called every painting such. *St. Jean dans la Région Sauvage* was the greatest thing he had done, and her Giovanni was the reason.

When she spoke to him of it—"You should see it, Gio"—he shook his head.

He wanted nothing to do with the painting. "It's bad enough I had to pose for the thing and will again, once the master's recovered. I don't wish to look upon the cause of my suffering any sooner than I must."

He refused to enter the studio.

"I'll go back there soon enough."

* * *

BRIEFLY, they had their own little Eden, but even Paradise can only last so long.

Eventually, the winds blew the pestilence away from Aux-le-Piémont and life returned to normal, as it had to, as it must.

The dead were buried, masses said, candles lit, prayers begged for their souls. Surviving merchants re-opened their doors, and farmers' carts reappeared in the marketplace. Robert again came to the cottage door with his eggs and butter. Maxime and Mathilde tottered from their sickbeds and reclaimed their assigned tasks.

And François recovered and awoke.

Chapter Forty

As soon as he was able to walk without support, François tottered to the studio and resumed painting. Giovanni again became the servant, not speaking unless spoken to, while Isabeau was once more ignored. Neither earned even a *"merci"* for the care they'd given him. Both tolerated this ungrateful treatment in well-hidden but seething silence, yearning for the freedom they'd had.

When François again ordered Isabeau back to his bed and once more began mixing the potions given him by the leech, Isabeau, now having experienced the freedom of *actual* love, fretted even more at submitting to him.

"Don't worry," Giovanni soothed. "While you were busy tending that ungrateful lout, I soaked his remaining packets in elixir of valerian. He'll sleep before he can act, and while he does, you'll come to *me, chérie.*"

Thus, while François snored in drugged bliss, she spent her nights in her lover's arms. In the morning, she assured her husband he'd performed his duty, and complained as she always did of the rough and inconsiderate way he'd treated her, and he was none the wiser.

He did remark on Isabeau's improved appetite, however, and that she appeared to have gained some weight, to which she replied she was merely enjoying eating food cooked by someone else, and appreciating that Mathilde had once again taken over the preparation of their meals. Shortly thereafter, she was a bit peaky on several mornings and bilious, causing Giovanni anxiety he managed to hide while François merely looked inconvenienced, and Isabeau silently decided the leech had been misinformed that *croup de la gorge* produced immunity to this particular pestilence.

Mathilde grumblingly mixed the remnants of the fennel and mint and brought them to her. Isabeau drank the potion and soon was on the mend, causing François to declare he was grateful she'd had only the mildest case of whatever had attacked the countryside, so the household routine wouldn't be further disrupted by another person falling ill.

The lovers now took their pleasure sparingly, during the continued shopping trips to town, Isabeau telling both the cook and the butler they were still too weak to endure the strenuous walk. The servants were only too glad to be relieved of that task while they performed the household duties. Besides, Isabeau declared, she enjoyed the walks and exhilaration of the fresh air. It made her feel better whenever a twinge of her recent illness flared.

That wasn't the only excitement she enjoyed. Always, on the way back, Giovanni would make a detour, pulling her off the highroad and into the woods where, abandoning baskets and packs, he'd find a tree's low-hanging branch, set her on it, and make love to her.

When they returned, François always remarked how cheerful and energetic Isabeau looked after such a long and difficult walk.

The winds had not only blown away the illness but also

brought something else to Aux-le-Piémont. While everyone was suffering, dying, or recovering, the seasons were changing. Now the nights were cooler, the air crisp in the mornings. Even the sun didn't warm until midday, and then quickly became chill as it crept toward the horizon. Leaves turned crimson and orange and began falling. The pines covered the ground with stiff brown needles. Shepherds moved their flocks to the meadows where the grass stayed greener long into winter. Flowers and herbs began to dry and fade.

"No more wolfsbane until spring," Giovanni whispered to Isabeau.

Now, when they went to market, they bought extra supplies to put aside through the winter. Mathilde's meals were still full of flavor, but she also cut back on how much she cooked since many of the farmers had lost crops due to their illnesses, and as a result, there wasn't as much selection at the market, and therefore, less to buy.

The sickness had prevented those patrons, Alphonse and *le comte* promised, from seeking out François. Slowly, they now made their appearances, only to be told they might have to wait until spring before he could speak to them of commissions, for his *St. Jean*, now begun, then interrupted, must be finished before all else.

Nevertheless, it was pleasant, their secret keeping them satisfied, and able to bear the unpleasantness of François's presence.

Things might've gone on forever like that, but then the full moon came again, and Giovanni had to be locked away. Hiding her tears, thinking of the injustice of it all, Isabeau herself put the chain around his neck and gave him valerian to drink. With François watching, she locked the door and walked with him back to the cottage, where she drank her own potion and wished it held something to make her forget what was to come.

This time, François's packet was a fresh one, unlaced with valerian. He'd gone earlier to the leech's to replace the last of the drugged packets.

She could hear the howls coming from the studio above her husband's rutting grunts.

Later, as she lay in the darkness beside a snoring François, she told herself she was glad her time would soon be upon her and she could again lie in the room where Giovanni had loved her, and think of what they'd done there, even if he wasn't beside her.

That was when the thought struck her with the force of a blow to her chest, leaving her breathless. *Oh, mon Dieu, no ...* Two months had passed since her last flow, that one while François was employed by the *comte*. Her courses had always been regular, but she'd ignored their absence because of the chaos of illness and work forced upon her, and then the joy of Giovanni's love. Now, it was borne home the cause of those bouts of nausea striking her in the mornings, the increase in appetite ...

I'm with child.

Chapter Forty-One

She had to tell Giovanni when she was certain no one would hear. The only time to do that would be as they went to town for more supplies. She fretted through the long, frustrating week, agonizing over how to phrase it, going over the words again and again in her mind until they were perfect. When the time came, she didn't speak until they were on the return trip.

Stopping on the highroad, she set down her baskets. "I've something to tell you."

He stopped also, waiting.

Every word she'd practiced deserted her. She wouldn't, *couldn't* say them. After two false starts during which he scowled at her struggle, she simply said, "I'm with child."

The way he stared at her ... he couldn't have looked more shocked if she'd thrown herself upon him in a vicious attack, scratching and clawing. Momentarily, he staggered. The baskets fell from his hands, spilling vegetables from the impact, and his shoulders sagged before he recovered, and his body settled into lines of resignation.

"Master François will be pleased his potions worked, though I see you are not. Cheer up, mistress. You've done your duty.

You'll give him the son he wants. Has he been told of the happy event?"

Though he spoke with forced calmness, he managed to inject bitterness into that last statement, expression impassive but at the same time so *hurt*, as if she'd betrayed him somehow. It made Isabeau want to scream at him.

Instead, she slapped his arm with a gesture of impatience and anger that in the next moment she regretted, thankful no one was there to see.

"How dare you say that to me?" She let her anger at his assumption show. "No, François doesn't know, and I wish there were some way to keep him from learning. This child isn't his, Giovanni. It's *yours*."

At that point, her resolve failed, and she burst into tears.

"Mine?" His expression underwent such a transformation, she might've laughed had she not been so upset. He took a step toward her, then stopped as if wondering if he dared touch her.

After all, they were on the public highroad where someone might chance along at any moment.

Instead, he asked quietly, "Are you certain?" then added, lest she misunderstand, "He *did* lie with you before his illness."

"But not after my last courses. Not at all until this week, and I'm at least two months breeding." She stifled her sobs, a sad smile touching her mouth. "You and I were afflicted at the same time, *cher*. I count my time by the full moon also. Being nurse, cook, and maidservant distracted me from the fact I've suffered nothing since the miasma struck our home, but now ..." Her mouth twisted ironically. "Oh yes. I'm certain."

"Oh, Isabeau." He touched her cheek, palm warm against her skin.

"Giovanni, what will I do?" She dared lean against him, again weeping, but this time, it was a despairing trickle of tears and not a frightened flood.

"You'll tell the master," he said, touching her shoulders gently, hands stroking and soothing. "You'll have the child and call it his."

"What if it looks like you?" she persisted. "François is fair and you're ... Gio, what if it inherits your nature?" One hand went to her mouth, muffling the scream she could feel building in her throat. "He'll kill my baby and he'll kill you and leave me to suffer for my sin."

"Isabeau." He let his hand drop.

"I won't live if that happens, I swear."

"You won't do that," he said. "Do you want *my* child?"

The look he gave her begged her to reassure him that her fear was not merely because she carried a babe, but because it was *his* babe.

"How can you ask that? I want no child but yours." She pushed away from him, looking around as if she'd run but saw nowhere to go. "If I lose either of you, I'll kill myself and join you in Hell."

"And for me to stay silent while he raises my son as his own would be Hell on earth. I admit it." He took a step toward her, again catching her hand. "There's only one thing to do ..."

She waited, silent, hoping he wasn't going to say they must commit murder.

Instead, what he said was almost as shocking.

"And that's to run away."

"Run away?" she repeated, stupidly, as if she didn't understand the meaning of the words. "You mean ... you'll desert me?"

He shook her gently. "Didn't I say I'd never leave you? I mean, *we'll* run away. Go where we're not known." He spoke as if he'd been thinking of this very thing for some time and waiting only for the chance to say it aloud. "Tonight."

"Tonight?" The thought of leaving the cottage, of the town

that had been her home all her life, frightened her. But escaping François? Forever? *That* filled her with elation.

"What better time? No one will expect it." He touched her mouth, stifling whatever else she might say. "After everyone is asleep, meet me at the studio. We'll take the horse. By the time the master awakens, we'll be gone."

She didn't argue, simply nodded. *We'll run away. We'll have a life somewhere else. Together. We'll be happy.*

She let herself believe it could happen.

Chapter Forty-Two

Isabeau went through the rest of the day in a haze of agonized anticipation.

This is the last time I'll do this ... That was the continuous thought in her brain as she did those odious chores Mathilde should have been doing. As she tucked in the sheets and fluffed the pillows on the bed. *This is the last time I'll make up this bed.* When she sat in the salon, sewing a rip in one of François's blouses. *The last time I'll patch his shirts.* As she peeped through a studio window, watching Giovanni with arms upraised, beseechingly. *The last time Giovanni will stand in one spot for hours.*

The day seemed endless, as if Time itself stretched and the hours doubled and tripled in length.

She glanced at the clock so many times that François, rummaging around in the rag bag for a scrap on which to wipe his brushes, finally asked, "Why do you keep doing that, Isabeau? Do you have an engagement somewhere?"

Flushing, she focused her attention on the shirt. "My apologies, husband. For some reason, I'm hungry. I was wondering how long it is until the supper hour."

"I've noticed your appetite has improved lately," he said. He extracted a swathe of fabric, studied it, and nodded. "This'll do. Best watch it, wife. You're beginning to put on weight. If you aren't careful, you'll be vying with Mathilde in heft."

Once well and back cooking again, Mathilde rapidly regained the weight she'd lost to illness and added even more.

Isabeau didn't answer, shocked and cold by the fact that her girth was increasing so quickly that François noticed. *That shouldn't be happening yet. Does a* loup-garou's *child develop faster than a human one?*

She decided it was a good thing she and Giovanni were leaving that night.

* * *

Supper was such a tense affair on her part; she was ready to scream. Isabeau picked at her food, anxiety chasing away her appetite.

When François said impatiently, "Don't let what I said earlier put you off your food. Eat, for God's sake!" she obediently stuffed a forkful of cabbage and butter sauce into her mouth, chewed and swallowed but the moment he concentrated on his own food again, she went back to merely moving the other morsels around the plate.

At last, the meal was over. Maxime began to clear the sideboard. Giovanni stacked the plates, giving Isabeau a meaningful glance as François stalked out as usual.

She started to get up. Immediately, Giovanni was there, pulling back her chair.

"The master looks tired," he whispered, mouth close to her ear. "I think he needs a good sleep tonight."

He extended a hand. Isabeau placed her own in it, and he helped her rise from the chair. She felt something brush her palm. He transferred something from his hand to hers as he released her fingers.

She inclined her head in bare acknowledgment, fingers closing around the valerian phial. "Thank you, Giovanni, for assisting me." She then followed François to the salon.

He'd already consumed a goblet of wine by the time she arrived. As soon as she was inside, he was out of his chair, reaching for the packets on the mantel, unadulterated by the sleeping elixir.

That might've been a problem. If she didn't have that little phial in her hand. If she could get it into the wine without François noticing.

Isabeau got to the hearth first. "Let me," she said, plucking his empty goblet from his hand. "I may not like taking the leech's concoctions, but I suppose I should do my part in mixing a few. You've done it long enough."

With a bemused expression, he gestured agreement and sat back in his chair.

She had uncorked the phial while in the hallway. Now, she filled François's goblet, and, hiding the phial behind the packet of herbs, turned away slightly, emptying both into his wine.

"Here." She held it out to him.

He accepted, raising it to his mouth as she turned back to mix her own. He didn't even glance at the discoloration in the wine. The valerian barely changed the color of the liquid at all. The powders took care of that. When she looked back, he was setting it beside the vase of daisies and lupine flowers on the end table. As Isabeau finished drinking her wine, he yawned.

"We'd best go to bed now, else I may fall asleep before we finish our coupling." There was another yawn, wide and cavernous. He shook his head. "Don't know why I'm so weary."

"You've been slaving over that painting." She set down her own glass. She made her voice slightly waspish so he wouldn't

think she was showing concern. That would be too out of char-
acter. "What do you expect?"

There were a few drops of wine on the table, a single splash
of red on the petals of one of the daisies in the vase.

"Really, François, must you be so clumsy? Look, you
splashed wine on the flowers when you set down your glass."

"Eh?" He glanced down, put a hand over the spot, smearing
it across the tabletop.

"If you're so tired you spill your wine, you shouldn't have
drunk it."

"This is no time to discuss wine." With that, he swept her
off the floor and carried her out of the room.

His gait was so unsteady, Isabeau clung to him, hoping he
wouldn't stumble on the stairs and fall with her in his arms. He
was walking a little straighter as he got to the bed.

This is the last time I'll have to submit, she thought, as his
heavy weight fell upon her. *The last time ...*

* * *

She waited until she was certain François was asleep,
listening to a quarter hour of pig-like snorts and snores before
she moved.

Raising the blankets and sliding from the bed, she gathered
her clothes and silently put them on. She didn't put on her slippers but held them in one hand as she tiptoed to the chest where
the little coffer holding the partial payment for the *St. Jean* was
kept.

Carefully, Isabeau raised the lid. The coins were heaped
atop each other. Putting her hand into her pocket, she brought
out the little purse holding her household money, laying it
beside the coffer.

She selected two coins. They clinked together as she

dropped them into the purse. From the bed came a sudden snort, then a cessation of sound.

Isabeau hesitated, hand poised over the coffer. After a moment, François's snoring resumed, noisier than before. It drowned out the faint clashing of metal against itself as she carefully transferred all the coins to the purse. She closed the coffer's lid, then picked up the purse.

Pausing long enough to make certain François was still asleep, she quietly opened the door and hastened out.

In the hall, a lit lamp sat on a table. Sliding on her slippers, she lifted it, continuing her silent way to the stairs.

Chapter Forty-Three

THE STUDIO DOOR WAS OPEN. Giovanni had to have done that, a last defiance. François would never leave the door ajar.

She hoped he hadn't done anything else, such as splashing the canvases with paint or slashing any of them.

"Giovanni?" She went inside, her whisper loud in the silence.

There was no answer.

The storage room was open, also. Setting the lamp upon the table near the door, she peered inside. The room was empty. The cot, with its blanket half hanging onto the floor, gave a forlorn semblance of abandonment in the dimness.

A sound behind her made her look to the entrance.

Giovanni was tying the horse to one of the walkway's roof supports. It shook its head, sending the bits jingling as it made an anxious little *wuffling*, a milder display of fright than the coach horses had at Giovanni's nearness. After all, he was the one who tended the animal, and it had learned against its nature not to fear him.

Patting the horse's neck, he left it and came inside.

"*Amour.*" Taking Isabeau's hand, he pulled her against him

and kissed her forehead. As he released her, he smiled. "Come. Let's quit this place."

He was so changed, so sure of himself and what he was doing.

Still holding her hand, he led her to the horse, but as he went to lift her onto the animal's back, there was a movement in the shadows near the door leading into the cottage.

"Did I give you permission to take my horse for a ride?"

"François!" Hand to her mouth, Isabeau cowered against Giovanni, who straightened protectively.

"We're leaving, and we're taking the horse." He turned so that Isabeau was behind him, his body hiding her from her husband's sight.

"Are you, now?" Surprisingly, François didn't sound angry. Rather, he seemed amused. He walked from the shadows to where he could be plainly seen. "Isabeau, can it be you truly love this *loup-garou*?"

He sounded disbelieving.

"More than I've ever loved you," she found the courage to say.

"Truly, wife, I question your taste in men." With a derisive chuckle, François leaned against one of the roof supports.

"Don't laugh." Isabeau felt herself on the verge of tears, and she knew that wouldn't do. She mustn't show weakness now. "Stop it, François. Stop!"

"I'm sorry, my dear. I can't. This is too ironic." He laughed again, a cruel, ugly sound.

Giovanni caught Isabeau's hand. "Come, Isabeau."

"You're going nowhere." François's voice changed, rising with threat. "Except back into that room where I'll put that collar around your neck and this time it'll stay there." He directed his next words at Isabeau. "And you, my dear wife, will get yourself back to our bedchamber."

Neither moved. François raised his right hand. In it, he held a weapon Isabeau had only ever seen one of the Town Watch brandish.

"Inside. Now."

"You think a pistolet will stop me?" Giovanni actually smiled, but it wasn't with amusement. In that moment, his expression was as cruel as François's own. "Silver won't harm me, you know."

"Silver may not harm you, but I imagine a lead bullet will do some damage." François raised the pistolet higher, aiming it at him. He gestured with it to the studio door. "Inside."

Giovanni didn't move. "I'm not going in there."

"Then perhaps I'll simply shoot you here and now. You're eloping with my wife. I've good reason."

"François," Isabeau spoke up. "You won't get away with that."

"Idiot wife." He looked at her but kept the gun trained on Giovanni. "Do you think the Watch will arrest me? After *Pére* Ambroise tells them how I've suffered with your hysteria and your flirtations with my servant?"

"There's no way you could know ..." Isabeau stopped as she realized she'd just incriminated herself.

"I'm not deaf, nor am I blind." François's voice dropped menacingly, so low, it became a near growl. "I've seen how you look at him, heard your whispers. I got out of my sick bed, saw you together ... It was all I could do not to denounce you then and there, but I wished to see just where it would go. That little courtesy tonight—mixing my wine for me. Do you think I'm stupid? When did you ever do such a thoughtful thing? I poured it into the vase when your back was turned. Then, when you left my bed, I waited a few moments, followed you ... and what did I find?" His eyes widened in mock surprise. "My lustful servant and my adulterous spouse eloping. He attacked me ... I was forced to kill him ...”

“No one will believe you,” Isabeau cried. “I’ll tell the Watch!”

“You won’t tell anyone anything,” François snapped. “You tried to stop us, and I accidentally shot you, too.”

“You won’t harm Giovanni!” Isabeau screamed. She didn’t care about her own safety, but he mustn’t hurt Gio. “I won’t let you.” She sprang at her husband, striking out.

Francois dodged. One hand struck his cheek, gouging a rivulet of nail marks.

“You bitch!” Catching her by the wrist with his free hand, he swung Isabeau around, slamming her against the door. With a cry, she collapsed, and he let her go, rubbing at his wounded cheek.

A snarl behind him made him spin. Baring his teeth, Giovanni leaped at him. The pistolet roared, the shot going wild. It struck the lamp, shattering the globe. The flame continued to burn, flickering in the darkness, reflecting in gleaming splinters off the broken glass.

Briefly, the two men grappled before François hurled Giovanni against the table. It tilted, spilling paints and jars to the floor with a crash and taking the lamp with it. The smell of turpentine and linseed rose into the air, along with the scent of lamp fuel as the contents of the overturned lamp splashed onto the floor. The open flame flickered toward the liquid beneath it. It caught and flared, bursting into a running fire, skimming along the line of spilled fuel trickling across the floor into the storage room.

With a growl, Giovanni recovered. Body hunched, he took two steps toward François, dropped to a lope, then flung himself into the air.

“Holy God!” Seeing what sprang at him, François jumped

backward, trying to avoid the *loup-garou's* attack. He aimed the pistolet and fired again. There was a hurt-dog yelp as the heavy body crashed into him.

Recovering, Isabeau rolled over, seized the door handle, and pulled herself to her feet as creature and human fell to the floor. Hands to her mouth, she watched in silent terror.

Silhouetted against the flames, they rolled about on the floor, somehow missing the stream of fire and the broken glass and oils. François's hand rose and fell. Now that the pistolet's bullets had been spent, he used the weapon as a bludgeon, striking again and again at Giovanni's head and shoulders.

It was no use.

Driven by anger and the months of mistreatment, the *loup-garou* ignored the blows. Straining against François, he snapped and snarled, fangs aimed for his master's unprotected throat.

"Giovanni, don't kill him!" Isabeau didn't know if he had heard or not. She simply knew he mustn't murder her husband.

He lunged forward. There was a loud *snap*! François screamed as Giovanni's teeth met the arm wielding the pistolet. The gun flew from his grasp, landing on the floor at Isabeau's feet.

A claw-like hand, talons extended, rose and fell. She heard the dull, meaty thud as it collided with François's temple.

François stopped struggling. Both men lay still. Isabeau didn't dare move. She couldn't tell if either was breathing.

There was a long, drawn-in inhalation.

Giovanni pushed himself off François's body and got to his feet. His smock was torn. There was blood on his shoulder, his face bruised where he'd been struck with the gun barrel. Panting, he looked at her through a tangle of hair. Briefly, she thought a stranger—a deadly stranger—stared out of his copper eyes. A growl, low and menacing, rolled from his throat.

"Gio?" She took a step toward him, hand touching the blood-soaked spot. "Are you hurt?"

She knew the answer immediately. The wound had already healed, leaving only bloodstains behind.

He shook his head as if recovering his senses, catching her hand. "Let's go."

"François ..." She held back. "You didn't kill him?"

He glanced back into the studio. "Let the fire do that. Come, Isabeau. We must leave before someone sees the flames."

She didn't move. "You can't leave him here to die."

"We owe him nothing." His reply was sullen and impatient, filled with the eagerness to leave, the anxiety that they might be stopped again.

"I don't want him to die." She caught his arm, shaking it. "Please. Let's not start our life together with a death."

He didn't argue, simply released her and dashed to where François lay. Catching his wrists, he dragged him across the floor to the door and hauled him outside, dropping his body in the grass before the studio.

Without speaking, he ran to the horse, reaching for the tied reins.

"Mistress, what's happened? Why is the studio on fire?"

Maxime's question came from the shadows so unexpectedly that Isabeau cried out. Giovanni whirled, once more placing himself between her and the two servants.

Think fast.

"The master"—Isabeau assumed her usual exasperated air, the one the servants were accustomed to hearing—"drank too much wine. He knocked over a lamp and ..." She gestured. "You see the result."

I have to act normally. Mustn't make them suspicious. She felt Giovanni's gaze on her, knew he was poised to attack if Maxime made a threatening move.

"Where's the master now?"

"Giovanni got him to safety, but we can't rouse him." She moved aside so Maxime might see François's body. *I must distract Maxime so we can get away.*

"Giovanni," Maxime called. "Help me move the paintings."

Giovanni whirled, staring from Maxime to Isabeau. She could feel his question. *Should I delay our escape to rescue his paintings?* She nodded. With a shrug, he glanced at the butler, then gestured and started back into the studio.

The fire in the storage room was raging now. The legs of the cot were ablaze, the blanket beginning to smolder. It flared in a bright burst, setting the rest of the cot afire. The flames leaped upward, igniting cobwebs hanging from the ceiling. It shot across to the canvases stacked against the wall, licking at the wooden frames. Fabric and paint burst into flame, sending it leaping to another, then another.

Fire billowed out of the storage room door into the studio. Mathilde gave a squeak of fright. "Maxime ... hurry!"

Isabeau anxiously watched the door.

Giovanni stumbled onto the porch. He'd picked up the *St. Jean* by one end, attempting to drag it through the door. One corner of the unwieldy canvas was smoldering, bright sparks and little flames spitting and flaring as patches of paint ignited. He was halfway through when the frame slipped from his grasp, wedging itself in the doorway.

Face smudged with smoke, Maxime reappeared. Clutching the end of the frame, he helped Giovanni wrench the painting free. With a loud ripping, the wood cracked as it was pulled through the doorway. Together, they staggered off the porch, dropping the painting in the grass, then stood there, breathing heavily.

A groan made everyone turn to where François lay. He rolled over and sat up, one hand going to his head.

"François." Isabeau ran to him. "You're all right."

"All right?" He was staring at the burning building. "How can you say that? When you and that ..." He looked around, saw Giovanni, and clambered to his feet. "My paintings. They're burning!"

Clambering to his feet, François staggered toward the studio. "Help me. I must save my paintings."

"Stop." Giovanni caught his shoulder, spinning him around. "It's madness to go into that. You'll—"

"Get out of my way!" With a violent heave, François pushed him aside.

"Master, don't," Maxime called.

Before he could move, François leaped onto the porch. Arms wrapped protectively around his head, he dashed into the studio. Briefly, his figure was silhouetted against the flames as he ran through the storage room door.

"François, come back!"

Isabeau's cry was lost in the roar of burning timbers.

The flames flicked out, licking at his body like the tongue of a giant snake, enveloping him. His body glowed incandescent as the fire swirled around him ... and the roof gave way.

She had time for one scream before Giovanni spun her around and away from the sight of the burning timbers engulfing François's body.

"Oh, Gio, I didn't want him to die ..." She began to sob, burrowing her forehead into his shoulder.

"Mistress de Montaigne, what has happened?"

The question brought her upright and out of Giovanni's arms. Robert the shepherd stopped his cart, his son on the seat beside him. Behind them were men on foot and others on horseback, Captain Aristides and the members of the Night Watch.

Without waiting for an answer, Robert climbed out of the

cart. He pulled two wooden buckets from the back. The others had also brought pails. They and the watchmen rushed behind the house, forming a brigade from the well to the side of the storage room, drawing water, passing buckets, and splashing them on the fire. Maxime and Giovanni joined in, while Mathilde and Isabeau watched silently.

By now, the building was an inferno no amount of water was going to douse. Realizing this, they simply stopped, watching as the fire burned itself out. When the wind began blowing the smoke away, they could see that the studio itself was gone. Only a part of the floor remained, with the flame-blackened furrow where the lamp oil had flowed into the storage room.

While Isabeau watched, stony-eyed, and Mathilde sobbed softly, a couple of Aristides's men ventured into the ruin, their leather boots protecting them from the smoldering ashes. Using a stick to poke at the blackened timbers, they pushed aside glowing bits of frames with shreds of scorched canvas clinging to them.

One stopped, kneeling, to shove aside the remains of a now unrecognizable piece of wood that crumbled in his hands. The other dropped beside him, reached out to something, then turned his head and violently threw up onto a pile of ash that had been a recently commissioned portrait.

Silently, they carried out the twisted travesty that had been François. While the others gathered around, they laid it in the grass next to the *St. Jean*. Maxime fetched a blanket, and they covered it as Isabeau rushed to them.

"No, mistress. You don't want to see." Robert put out a hand, stopping her.

"Mistress Isabeau, I'm sorry—" Captain Aristides began his customary expression of sympathy for such an occasion, and that was when Mathilde, eyes streaming, pushed through the crowd.

"She killed him!" she declared, stabbing a finger at Isabeau. "She and that creature. They killed the master and set the fire. To make it look like an accident."

That brought an uproar of exclamations, of disbelief and shock. Everyone began talking at once, while the captain tried to silence them.

Behind her, Isabeau felt Giovanni stiffen. Fearing he would react further, she spoke quickly.

"Mathilde, what are you saying?" She looked up at Aristides, shaking her head in pity. "Captain, you must forgive my cook. She was very fond of my husband, and his death has affected her ... She's obviously hysterical."

Thinking her own voice too calm, she took a deep breath and finished with a choking sob.

"Of course, *Madame*." Aristides was understanding, giving Mathilde a look that quelled her momentarily. "It's to be expected."

Isabeau relaxed. There might be an investigation into the fire, but she could weather that. The captain would believe what she said. She'd have to pretend to mourn for a while before they could leave.

Maxime reached Mathilde, put his arm around her, and whispered something. She glared at him and shrugged off his embrace. Shaking her head, she cried, "They killed him, I tell you. That one ... He's a *loup-garou*!" She stabbed a finger at Giovanni. "He bit the master! Drew blood."

Giovanni took a step toward her, a growl coiling low in his throat. Isabeau's hand on his arm drew him back. There was a muttering from some of the men. Again, she spoke to the captain, raising her voice to distract them.

"*Loup-garou*? Mathilde, what are you saying?" Forcing

shock into her voice, she directed her next words to the captain. "Giovanni is our servant, as are Maxime and Mathilde. He's a refugee from Italy, but that's no reason to accuse him of being a beast."

Italy? From the war? The muttering increased.

"Can anyone confirm that?" Aristides asked.

"My husband spoke to his patron, *le Marquise* de Maurier, about him. Also, the *Comte* Duquesne was aware." Isabeau answered confidently. "They both met Giovanni."

"I'm afraid neither is present at the moment, *Madame.*" Aristides frowned at the mention of the *comte.* His voice changed, holding what sounded like a note of suspicion.

Isabeau felt her heart tremble. Perhaps it hadn't been such a good idea to mention Duquesne.

"I will have to send someone to their *châteaux* to speak to them. Is there anyone from Aux-le-Piémont who can verify this?"

"Perhaps those with whom my husband shared a tankard at the tavern?" Isabeau forced her tone to remain calm. "I'm certain François spoke to some of them about his new servant, and Giovanni went with me to town many times—to the apothecary's, the butcher's ..."

Aristides looked around. "Is there anyone here who knows this to be true?"

From the crowd, someone said, "*Madame* François told me this on one of her trips to my brother's shop. The Italian was with her."

Bernard took a step forward, and the crowd parted for him.

"He said he'd come to France to escape the war," he continued.

Aristides nodded as if convinced, and Isabeau relaxed. Then, Bernard gave Giovanni a hard stare, a look the others interpreted as a man realizing he'd been lied to, but which

Isabeau and Giovanni saw as that of a man whose advances had been rejected.

"But I thought there was something odd about him. I spied on him as he packed the meat into his knapsack, saw him slaver and lick the blood dripping from it." He pointed at Giovanni, finger jabbing like a knife. "As they left, he helped her with her baskets and touched her too familiarly, like a lover more than a servant."

"*Madame?*" Aristides looked down at Isabeau. "Can you explain—"

He got no further. Everyone began talking at once, drowning out his question, and everything fell apart.

Someone shouted a question. Above it all rose Mathilde's shrill, "Why do you stand here talking? Seize the beast. Arrest the slut who killed my master."

Snarling, Giovanni lunged at her, escaping Isabeau's detaining hand. Mathilde leaped back, screaming. Maxime put up an arm to ward him away.

"Here now, none of that." Immediately, Aristides called out, "Seize him."

That quickly, everyone turned against them. Though he'd moments before worked with them in putting out the fire, now they surrounded Giovanni.

He snarled and whirled, raising hands curled into claws. All shrank back, cowering as a loud growl broke the air. As one, they froze, seeing what they would've pursued ...

... and for the first time, Isabeau beheld her lover in his other body.

It was Giovanni, but at the same time not Giovanni. A nightmare creature, wolf-like but still human, a monster in man's clothing. Tufted ears lay back, lips raised in a snarl, fangs gleaming in a still-recognizable face. As they hesitated, cringing, he rushed to the horse. It reared in fright, but the creature scrambled onto the saddle, sending it lunging through them.

They scattered before it, watchmen and townsfolk alike, to keep from being trampled under its hooves, then watched as it vanished into the highroad's dark.

"Go after him!" Aristides shouted, and to others, "Secure the woman."

Two of his men mounted their horses, aiming them in pursuit. A small group of townspeople followed on foot, shaking their fists and shouting. In the turmoil, Isabeau was seized. Someone brought ropes from Robert's cart and bound her wrists, even as she cried out and protested her innocence.

As calm was restored, Aristides spoke the unbelievable words, "Isabeau de Montaigne, in the name of Louis *Douze*, *le roi*, I arrest you for the murder of François de Montaigne."

Chapter Forty-Four

THE SKY WAS dark as *Pére* Ambroise hurried up the hill toward the stone tower. Dusk was settling into evening, and the night braced itself for the horror of the coming day. In preparation, clouds obscured the sky and, in the distance, thunder rumbled amid brief flashes of light on the horizon.

In his white robes and black scapular and cowl, he looked an eerie and sepulchral figure floating between the darkened trees, a ghost well in keeping with this night of nights: October 31, *Veille de la Mort de Sainte*, Eve of the Holy Dead.

A sudden, sharp breeze swooped, skittering under the skirts of the friar's cassock. The bite of the wind stung like the snap of a whip, flicking sharp fingers against his bare legs before immediately rising again.

It's as if le bon Dieu *himself is angry*, he thought, *but why?*

At the fact of the coming execution? That perhaps an innocent woman was to die on the morrow—Ambroise had no doubt Isabeau was guilty through circumstance alone, and he'd done nothing to prove otherwise—or because her death couldn't come soon enough? Perhaps because the judges, meaning he, Lord Alphonse, and her father, for *Comte* Duquesne, had protested loudly enough, had ruled it should be carried out on the day of the Holy Saints?

What better way to worship God than to make a murderer pay for her crime on a holy day?

During the day following the trial, Ambroise thought often of Isabeau, perhaps more than he'd thought about her all her life, or that part of it when she became old enough for him to notice. He'd always felt uneasy around her. From the moment of her adolescence, she'd been a budding temptress, inspiring lustful thoughts in him, thoughts for which he often prayed long into the night. Though his Order didn't practice self-punishment, he occasionally scourged himself to drive out those vile feelings. Now, he told himself, it was well she should die for her sins ... the sins of murder and adultery, as well as that of making a priest briefly have such profane imaginings whenever he looked at her, of making him think like a *man* and not a representative of God.

A pity such a beautiful woman had to die, but it was to the glory of God that she would no longer lead others to sin.

Immediately, he crossed himself, looking around fearfully as if someone could hear his thoughts, as if perhaps by doubting what he, along with the other judges, decreed, he committed blasphemy. Shifting the weight of the items he carried, he pulled his cowl more snugly over his head.

At the top of the hill, the door of the tower loomed before him. Jean, the guard appointed by the magistrates, stood to one side. Armored in chain with a metal breastplate under a short tabard, he was armed with a matchlock *mousquet* and sword. Since such firearms were still relatively rare among the private populace, Jean was proud of being given such a weapon and styled himself a *mousquetaire*.

He looked up, starting slightly, raising the *mousquet*, then relaxed as he recognized the priest, dropping the weapon to his side again.

"Ah, *Pére*, you gave me a scare. I thought a spirit had come to free our prisoner." His laugh was hollow. "What brings you here with the weather threatening so?" Before Ambroise could answer, he went on, "You aren't going to try again to get that bitch to confess?"

"Watch your language," the priest said. It was his habit to reprimand men using such words about the weaker sex, though as soon as he said it, he wondered if he should've. "*Madame* Montaigne—"

"—is an adulterous bitch who lay with a *loup-garou* and murdered her husband," the guard interrupted. "That's the truth. Why shouldn't I say so?"

"Nevertheless, she's a gentlewoman and deserves the proper respect."

"She'll get no respect from me, Father. Not for what she did."

Jean wrapped a gloved hand around the bar set across the door to keep it shut, giving it an upward jerk. There was a jangle of metal as his mailed fingers dug into the wood. There was only one way to enter the tower, by seizing the leather tied to the bar inserted through a hole in the door.

"She's a convicted murderess who'll go to her very just reward in a few hours." He stepped back, gesturing Ambroise inside. "Before you say it, I'll speak ill of the dead, too, when she's lying in the quicklime pit next to the bones of her fellow murderers."

The first drops of rain spattered on the dirt outside the door. They struck Jean's sleeve, splashing off the chain.

"Damn."

He didn't apologize for that either, shaking his arm so the drops were slung in *Pére* Ambroise's direction, striking his face. Jean didn't notice. The priest turned his head, hastily wiping away the moisture lest it be mistaken for tears.

Truly, ambiguously, he felt like weeping because of what was to happen ... or was it conscience, somehow telling him he and the others had made a mistake?

"Starting to rain. Get in, Father. Quickly. Don't want to get that parchment wet. Is it real or paper, by the way?" Jean was well aware that both parchment paper and dried sheep hide were extremely expensive. "Don't know why you'd risk something so valuable for someone so worthless."

Ambroise didn't answer. Instead, he hurried inside, looking around at the interior.

The tower hadn't changed since the last time he'd seen it on the day he and Jean escorted Isabeau de Montaigne back after the sentence was passed.

The rounded main floor of the tower was lit by torches held in metal brackets affixed to the walls. Even their light did nothing to dispel the gloom or dismal ambience. Two cells faced him, empty, their doors open. They'd been recently cleaned, and fresh straw put on the floor.

Mucked out as if they're stables instead of a place where humans are held, he thought sadly.

The guard followed the priest. He propped his spear against the wall, fumbling at his belt for the ring of keys hanging there. Holding them close to his face, for even with the torches, the area was dim, he sorted through them until he found the one he sought.

"After you, Father." He motioned to the stairs lining the walls.

They were made of stone also, built out from the wall itself, circling to the next floor. Pulling a torch from its bracket, he held it aloft, walking with ease up the steps into the darkness. Ambroise followed behind, treading carefully.

There was no light from the narrow windows above, and the higher one went, the less light filtered from below. There were also no railings or banisters on the stairs. The guard might walk them with familiarity, but the priest wasn't so certain where his feet stepped in the dark. One movement too far to the right, and he'd plunge back to the floor beneath them. By the time they reached the next story, they were in almost total darkness, the guard's body a dark bulk above him, shielding the torch from his sight.

The steps ended on a small landing before a single cell. The condemned cell, set apart from the others for those few committing a capital offense, as they would be separated from their fellow humans even after their deaths.

Ambroise stopped before the door, hesitating. He was certain he'd come on a fool's errand. She was no more likely to be amenable to confession tonight than she had been since her trial, but he had to try. For the salvation of her soul, murderous creature that she was, it was his duty.

The cell door was of thick wood, rough-hewn and roughly planed. Its edges were iron-bound, the hinges holding it in place also metal. There was a small Judas window set in the top center, a square peephole which, when opened, allowed one to peer into the cell. The window was barred, but was of so small a size that nothing larger than a rat could've escaped through it.

The little door was partially opened. Whoever had used it last to spy on the prisoner hadn't shut it properly. A faint light seeped through. There was no sound from inside. *No, wait …*

Ambroise thought he heard a slight susurrus as if someone whispered.

Clutching against his chest the sheaf of parchment he'd taken from the church library and tightening his hold on the quill and inkpot in his hand, he waited while the guard held the torch toward the door. Thrusting the key into the lock, he turned it.

The click was loud in the quiet.

Inside, the whispering stopped.

"I'll have to lock the door behind you, Father," Jean apologized.

Ambroise knew that. It had happened the other times he'd visited the prisoner. He nodded. For some reason, he found it difficult to speak.

"When you're ready to leave, call out. I'll be listening." Jean pushed the door open.

The hinges screamed their protest. They were long-rusted, further evidence of the rare use of this particular room. Even being currently occupied, no one had bothered to oil the hinges.

The priest walked inside. Jean pulled the door shut to another objection from the hinges and locked it.

Through the half-open peephole, Ambroise watched after him as best he could, craning his neck as he studied the light of the torch throwing the shadow of Jean's body and helmet against the wall, making them into a dancing horned demon. Outside, the wind whistled through one of the open windows, as narrow as arrow-slits. It changed to a moan appropriate for the shadow's grotesque gesticulations as the flames flickered.

The priest shivered. Not a good thought for a night like this.

The light disappeared. He heard the metal clang as the torch was returned to the bracket, the sound of Jean retrieving his spear, and settling himself by the door. The patter of rain became louder. Wind swept up the stairway.

Taking a deep breath, he turned to face the prisoner.

Surrounded on three sides by stone, Isabeau de Montaigne sat on a bare box of a cot tucked into a niche in the wall. It had no linens, pillow, or mattress, only a single threadbare blanket.

"Why are you here?" After a hasty glance at the slit of a window, she cringed visibly against the wall. "It isn't yet dawn."

"Isabeau ..."

She didn't look like a murderess, the priest thought.

Her gown had been taken away, exchanged for a prisoner's shift of gray, drab, as plain as a penitent's robe. Reaching to her ankles, the sleeves immodestly above her wrists, it was barely long enough to be considered a garment covering her properly.

Ambroise thought of the lovely gowns he'd seen her wear.

Now, to be forced to be garbed in this ... The magistrates saw no need to allow a prisoner the comfort of familiar or well-made clothing.

And her hair ... It was blonde, gloriously so, like ripened wheat. She'd always worn it tucked inside a wimple, curls hanging down her back under a veil. Now, it hung in a lank braid between her shoulder blades.

He was reminded of how she'd looked as a child, when she'd attended catechism classes in order to be confirmed and welcomed into the congregation of God's beloved. On the heels of that thought was how she'd lured him to think such wicked thoughts.

He looked around the room. Before that narrow window, there was a small table and stool. A candle flickered, blown by the wind trickling through the window. The candle had burned long; it was only a few inches before guttering out.

Once that happens, she'll be left in the dark, waiting for that eternal darkness.

He also saw the rosary lying as if tossed carelessly, its pink quartz beads reflecting the candle flame.

"You've abandoned your rosary?" It was a reprimand. "Shouldn't you pray for the Holy Mother to intercede for you?"

"Why should I ask for intercession?" Her answer came back harsh and remarkably strong. "God has abandoned me. So I've abandoned Him."

"You must pray, Isabeau."

"I've done enough praying. All my life I've prayed. I prayed for someone to prevent my marriage to François and it didn't happen. I prayed for the judges to believe I spoke the truth, but they preferred to believe what others said. Whatever I have to say to God, I'll do it in person when I get to Heaven."

"I doubt you'll be going to that blessed place."

"Do you?" She dared to smirk. "We'll see."

Her attitude shook him.

"What's that you have clutched to your chest?" She'd seen the parchment and quill. "Writing utensils? Surely you haven't come to again ask me to confess?"

"Isabeau, you must." As before, he gave his reply as if it were learned by rote. After all these years, it was automatic. "You'll be turned away from entering the realm of glory if you don't ..."

"I won't confess to something that isn't true. I won't lie. God will see the truth when I stand before Him, or"—her voice trembled—"I'll go gladly to that other place and leave Him to His hypocrisies."

"If you won't admit to your crime, at least let *me* hear your confession," Ambroise pleaded, but his words held the ring of defeat. By now, he wondered who he was trying to save—Isabeau or his own conscience. "That will guarantee your way to forgiveness."

She didn't answer.

He tried one last attempt. "At least denounce that evil creature. Say he seduced you into this wickedness. Say he killed François."

There had been some doubt as to who actually did the deed, but since Isabeau was the one they held and the *loup-garou* was still at large ...

Though he hadn't had time to get far from the village, the guards couldn't find him anywhere. They'd even searched the houses one by one, much to the inhabitants' chagrin. Some shepherds swore they'd seen a lupine hulk lurking near their flocks, but the *gendarmerie* discovered nothing despite beating the meadows.

The gypsies camped near the river also claimed not to know anything, but they couldn't be trusted. They'd swear it was midnight when it was plainly noontide. Besides, di Casalupo had once been one of them. Perhaps they thought they owed him loyalty?

Ambroise began to speak quickly, as if he could feel Time creeping up on them. "If you do, I'll do everything in my power to have your sentence commuted. The judges will spare your life, have you consigned to a nunnery, and hunt down that foul beast and bring him to judgment."

"Father, if I'm guilty of anything, it's of loving a man other than my husband, but neither of us killed him, and I won't say we did. I won't turn on Giovanni, either."

"How can you defend him? He abandoned you, Isabeau. Left you for the Watch to seize and condemn."

It had taken all Ambroise's skill at persuasive rhetoric to convince them not to torture her to extract what they wanted to hear, and to only accuse her of murder and not of lying with a demon. That would have been a burning offense instead of a hanging one.

"He hasn't deserted me." To his horror, Isabeau continued defending her lover. She smiled. "He'll come for me soon."

She's completely besotted. She can't see how evil that creature is. Ambroise's heart sank.

"There's nothing I can say to make you change your mind?" His tone held defeat.

"Nothing." She didn't hesitate. "Now, please leave."

"I'll go." He glanced at the window. "But I'll be back soon enough."

He made the sign of the Cross. Isabeau turned her head.

"May God have mercy on you, my child."

"Don't call me that," she snapped. "I'm not your child. I'm no one's child." Earlier, she'd denounced her father, also.

"Then you'll be daughter to no one soon enough." Shaking his head, *Pére* Ambroise turned to the door, calling, "Jean?"

He heard the clomp of the guard's boots on the stairs. There was a clatter of keys, and the door swung open. This time, the hinges' squeal seemed muted, as if they also had given up. Ambroise looked back at Isabeau. Her defiant gaze met his. He thought that sparkle in her eyes, caught by the candlelight, was tears.

"I'll leave these." He placed the parchment, inkpot, and quill on the table. "In case you change your mind."

"I won't."

"Nevertheless ..." He didn't finish, simply turned away and hurried through the door, head bowed, dejection in the stoop of his shoulders.

I've failed in my charge to God. Heavenly Father, I've lost one of your flock. Lord, forgive me.

As Jean pulled the door shut, he said, "Didn't I say you were wasting your time?"

Ambroise didn't answer. Shrugging, Jean led the way down the stairs.

* * *

MEN HAVE BEEN ARRESTED *and convicted on little more than someone's testimony, with no other evidence. In some cases, all it takes is one man accusing another for a guilty verdict to be rendered.*

Hadn't she said that very thing to François, once? In a time that now seemed so very long ago?

Isabeau had consigned herself to death. She accepted there was no way Giovanni could rescue her, though she was certain he'd try if he could. She hoped he didn't make some futile but brave attempt and get himself captured, that he was far away and safe.

I'll never see him again in this life, but I'll see him in Heaven. The good God will take away Giovanni's curse and bring us both there, for he knows we're innocent.

When that time came, she'd be held in his arms, protected. He'd look at her with those odd copper-colored eyes, and the love in them would chase away the chill with which the grave would permanently encase her bones.

It was quiet now, except for the grumble of thunder and the occasional patter of rain striking the tower's stones. Wind blew through the window, ruffling the parchment. That drew her attention.

It took her a moment more to make a decision.

Getting up, she went to the table, pulling out the little stool and dropping onto it. The light was dim, but she was still able to see. She selected a sheet of parchment, smoothing it upon the tabletop, marveling at its thick feel, and that Father Ambroise dared bring so many sheets of the costly writing material to her. It took a moment's struggle to pull the cork from the inkpot and drop it to the table, where it made a bluish smear of a circle upon the wood. Dipping the quill into the ink, she shook off the excess, pressed the point against the parchment, and began to write.

I, Isabeau Charlotte Catherine Lescaux de Montaigne, have stood before men and been judged guilty; when I stand before God, He will know my innocence. Thus do I now, and for this reason only, make my confession: I and my lover, the so-called loup-garou, *are innocent of the crime of murder ...*

Chapter Forty-Five

Signing her name at the bottom of the page, Isabeau lay down the quill.

It was done. Like it or not, she'd told the truth, and they could burn her "confession" or hide it away in the Watch's archives or nail it to the church door for all to see; she didn't care.

A brief wave of nausea swept over her. She didn't know if it was merely fear or the child trying to communicate, protesting perhaps the fact she hadn't made its presence known to her accusers. Pleading her belly would've saved her life, for a few months more, at least.

Fear of what would happen to the child after she was gone kept her from speaking. Who would care for it? Her parents? After disavowing her? She couldn't bear the thought of her child being mistreated, constantly reminded of its mother's crime, abused because it was the child of a *loup-garou*.

"Better you die with me," she whispered, cradling the soft mound of her belly, rapidly becoming a noticeable bulge. "Better—"

A sound from outside the door interrupted her thoughts.

There seemed to be a disturbance downstairs, men's voices, one raised in protest, the sounds of a scuffle, then ... silence.

There came a slap of footsteps on the stairs, fast, as if their owner were running up them, perhaps taking two at a time.

Keys rattled, the lock clicked as it was turned. The door swung open.

Heart clutching, Isabeau sprang from the stool so quickly that it overturned. She glanced at the window. It was still dark outside.

A man came through the door. He wore a split-tailed riding coat whose hood hid his face. He took two steps inside, pushing back the hood.

"I'm sorry I couldn't get here sooner."

No dramatic declarations, simply that straightforward statement, but it was enough.

"Gio!" She threw herself into his arms, "Gio ... Gio ..." and began to sob softly.

"Here, now." He gave her a quick but loving kiss, then pushed her away. "Time for that later. Come, let's go."

He pulled her from the room. Isabeau stumbled with him, as if she couldn't believe it was happening.

"Walk carefully." He started down the steps, still holding her hand. "These stairs are treacherous."

"Wait." She held back. "The guard ..."

"He'll be no trouble," he assured her.

"You didn't kill ..."

"No, but he'll sleep for quite a while."

"Where have you been?" she whispered. "The Watch couldn't find you. I was certain you'd left the province."

"I went to the *comte*," he answered. His voice echoed down the stairwell, sounding ghostly in the darkness. "He hid me."

"Duquesne? He tried to testify on my behalf," Isabeau said. "They wouldn't let him."

"So he said. He was furious at that." He turned his attention to the stairs. "We can talk later, for now we must go."

They started downward again.

On the main floor, a bulky shape lay near the door. It moved slightly and moaned.

"See?" He gestured. "He isn't harmed, though he'll have a terrible headache when he awakens."

Seizing the latch's leather strap, he pushed open the door and led her outside.

The horse was tied to a nearby cottonwood. It nickered softly as they approached.

Giovanni patted its neck, quieting it.

"His Lordship has a fleet of ships at Marseilles. One is sailing in two days to the New World—New France, to be exact —and we are going to be on it."

Isabeau took a deep breath. She looked up at him. "Giovanni, it takes months to sail that far. What will you do when the moon is full?"

The thought of being at sea with a wolf on the prowl ...

Even in the darkness, she knew he'd smiled. As she'd sensed a change in him the night Francois died, now she realized the past weeks had brought about an even deeper transformation. This Giovanni was looking ahead and was self-assured enough to make the future happen.

"I'll say I'm an invalid and stay out of sight. Wolfsbane grows on the *comte's* estate, too. He had his servants pick all they could. With the plants in our cabin, it'll be easy to pretend to be ill. We'll take the seeds and grow more. His captain says New France has forests and plenty of land where I can be free." He tugged on her hand again. "We mustn't stand here talking."

"So our child will be born in the New World," she mused.

"A better one than this, I hope. For him," he caught her hand, kissing her fingers, "and for us."

With that, he lifted Isabeau, placing her on the pommel of the saddle. Gathering the reins, he swung up behind her. As he put his arms around her, she clasped his hands tightly.

"I thought I'd never see you again." As she looked up at him, she felt her fear, her desperation, sift away, like dust from a newly polished object.

"Didn't I say I'd never leave you, *amour?*" Tone chiding, he kissed her temple, the brush of his cheek warm against her own. Not waiting for her reply, he turned the horse's head toward the highroad leading to Marseilles.

Epilogue

Musée de Louvre
Paris, France
Present Day

IN ONE OF the rooms of the *Musée de Louvre*, housing lesser-known mid-Renaissance artists, hangs a single painting.

The frame appears to have been broken and repaired, with the right lower corner missing, and a space between canvas and frame. The canvas is scorched, and it is obvious the missing part was burned away. The painting is unfinished, part of the background and lower half of the picture still blank. The subject is St. Jean le Baptiste. It's a powerfully stirring piece, evocative of great emotion, and it has been said that the visual intensity is such that looking at the painting for a long time burns the image into the viewer's brain.

The card accompanying this painting explains: *Though there are other works attributed to this artist, the painting,* St. Jean dans le Sauvage (St. John in the Wilderness), *is the only actually authenticated work of François de Montaigne (1461-1499). The subject is believed to be his servant, Giovanni di*

Casalupo, an Italian refugee. The painting was damaged in a fire reportedly set by the artist's wife and her lover, di Casalupo, in which de Montaigne died. The two were arrested, tried, and convicted of his murder and condemned, but before sentences could be carried out, they escaped. They were never apprehended and were never heard from again.

Join Our Newsletter

To make sure you don't miss a new release from Tony-Paul de Vissage, subscribe to our newsletter at www.epic-publishing.com/subscribe.

Author's Notes

Legend of the Loup-Garou

A popular facet in European folklore as well as of contemporary horror movies, werewolves are mentioned by the Classical Romans, Classical Greeks, as well as in ancient Asia and the Native Americans of the New World. Besides the witch trials of the 15th through 18th centuries, many were accused and persecuted for having the ability to change from human into wolf.

According to the mythology, the most common causes of werewolfism are: being born on Christmas Day; drinking water out of a wolf's pawprint; having the full moon shine on a sleeper's face; or as part of a pact with the Devil—and, as those familiar with the dicta the "horror" cinema sets forth (as in *The Werewolf of London* and *The Wolfman*)—a werewolf's bite.

According to the cinematic belief, which point of reference for vampires as well as werewolves has become the popular criteria, a werewolf is recognized by having hair on its palms, eyebrows that meet, overdeveloped canine teeth, and, of course, transforming when the moon is full.

Today, the actual diagnosis for anyone believing he can

become a wolf is that of *lycanthropy*. Other theories are that supposed werewolves might've also been stricken with rabies or *hypertrichosis*, which causes an overabundance of hair growth. Called "malignant down," this condition is either congenital or can be acquired through cancers, eating disorders, or the use of certain drugs. In 1642, Petrus Gonsalvus ("so-called The Man of the Woods", 1537-1618) of the Canary Islands was the first person documented as having hypertrichosis.

Unfortunately, there seems to be no cures for werewolfism, since the most popular—the use of wolfsbane or shooting with a silver bullet—are fatal to the victim.

On the feline side of the coin, there is also a condition in cats, similar to hypertrichosis, causing them to be called "were-wolf cats."

For those interested, more complete information may be found at the following sources:

https://en.wikipedia.org/wiki/Werewolf

The Book of Were-Wolves by Sabine Baring-Gould, Causeway Books, New York, 1973.

Leda and the Swan

This well-known classical theme, of the love affair between Zeus and Leda producing Helen (the cause of the downfall of Troy) and her brother, Pollux (the heavenly twin of Gemini), was a fairly forbidden one during the Renaissance. In spite of many artists daring to paint it, most of their artwork ended up being destroyed.

Both Leonardo da Vinci in 1504, and Michaelangelo in 1529, attempted studies of the subject. Though there are records of their paintings being at *Château* de Fontainebleau in 1625 and 1536, respectively, both paintings eventually disappeared, probably destroyed by later owners who considered the subject immoral.

Further information on Leda and the Swan in art can be found at:

https://en.wikipedia.org/wiki/Leda_and_the_Swan

The New Century Classical Handbook by Catherine B. Avery, Ed., Appleton-Century-Crofts, New York, 1962

Bulfinch's Mythology, Gramercy Books, New York, 1979.

About the Author

A Southerner of French Huguenot extraction, one of Tony-Paul de Vissage's first movie memory is of being six years old, viewing the old Universal horror flick, *Dracula's Daughter*, on television and being scared sleepless.

That may explain his lifelong interest in vampires and why he's now paying back his too-permissive parents by writing about those who walk the night.

A voracious reader whose personal library has survived following their owner more than 3,000 miles across country, Tony-Paul has read hundreds of vampire tales and viewed more than as many movies.

Readers may discover more about this author at his Facebook page: www.facebook.com/tonypaul.devissage or on Twitter: @tpvissage.

Except from The Nightman's
Odyssey
Tony-Paul de Vissage

*"Hail, Mary, full of Grace, the Lord is with thee . . . Holy Mother,
Pray for us now and at the time of our deaths . . ."*

Even as he muttered the prayer, Damién cursed himself as a
hypocrite and a liar.

*The priests teach Man is a Sinner from his first breath, cursed
by our Primal Parents and born into willful disobedience against
the Lord, and therefore should welcome death and its reward of
heaven with open arms.*

Damién suffered the double guilt of his disbelief and of
keeping that doubt secret.

To him, Death was the end, not a beginning or even a
continuation, and he was sorely afraid he would be confronting
that ending very soon.

It was a reasonable fear, he told himself. Everyone feared
death, though some might accept it more readily than others.

He tried to rationalize his terror. His life was too valuable;
his death would leave the Domaine de La Croix without an
heir, but that was a mere shading of the truth.

Damién didn't care who died as long as it wasn't himself. As far as he was concerned, Heaven was a lie fed to ignorant peasants to hide a stark reality discovered only too late . . . that death was Oblivion . . . a fall into bottomless darkness with no resurrection in sight, a snuffing of breath, heartbeat, and thought.

Damién didn't want that oblivion, he wanted to continue his existence . . . to be with his Antoinette . . . to live and love with her . . . not become food for some hungry worm waiting even now to grub in his grave.

He was a child of his Time, pampered and spoiled, accustomed to getting what he wanted. At this particular moment, what he wished most was to live to enjoy the woman he loved. Nevertheless, in this instance, what he desired was being cruelly withheld.

This time, Damién wasn't going to get his way.

His traitorous mouth continued praying as he'd been taught, spewing words more and more desperate . . . *Sweet Jesu, don't let us die* . . . Protect us from this scourge...I call upon St. Jude Libraeus, *Saint of the Impossible, Patron of Desperate Situations, have mercy, and bring about this miracle, I beg you* . . . *St Christopher, have mercy, I invoke your protection against this plague . . . Dear Lord, Holy Savior help me!*

Desperation and panic mingled with unmanly tears, streaming down his clean-shaven cheeks.

St. Damién, Patron of Physicians, and my namesake, steal the power from this plague, prevent it from infecting us so my Antoinette and I may survive . . . oh God, I don't want to die . . .

For over a year, the *Great Mortality* had been in France—a year and fifteen days, to be exact—and in Limousin less than a month. If ever a Scourge from God had been placed upon Mankind, this was it.

Nevertheless, no one dared question. All accepted as something deserved, for being human, if for no other reason. Sinners condemned by the mere fact of their existence to suffer and die.

And be swept away into nothingness. If Damién's doubts had previously hovered secretly in his mind, the falling of this pestilence upon the people of Limousin—*his* people—confirmed them with a vengeance.

Doctors attempted treatment, and he asked himself, *Why? If we are already condemned, why bother? Why go through such useless motions?*

And if a few survived? Did that mean those were so saintly as to be allowed to live, or were they simply now doubly condemned, and the dead to be envied as destined for that much-touted salvation?

He was well aware such thoughts were heretical and could consign him to flames much worse than the plague fires should he dare speak them aloud, so he held his own counsel and his ever-growing anger.

Who would he speak them to, anyway? His friend Armand? His betrothed Antoinette? Neither was allowed near his father's estate, as he was forbidden theirs. Some nonsense about isolation making one safer.

He doubted that.

If the pestilence is miasma-borne on the wind as the physicians think, how can hiding ourselves away protect us? The wind was everywhere; even if a man climbed the highest peak or sank himself into the deepest well, that ebbing and flowing stream of air would find him.

All seclusion did was prevent his having the solace of friendship or love.

His desperate supplication ended, he got to his feet.

Now for something more important. Going to his Antoinette.

Crossing himself once more, he returned his rosary to his belt-purse and started down the aisle to the entrance only to stop as the doors swung open. A body blocked his path, a bulky silhouette against the late evening sun.

"*Père* Gervais?" Damién put up a hand, shading his eyes from the direct glare. Under its shield, he could make out the priest's features . . . eyes reddened, face pale and streaked . . . with tears?

Thinking the Father was manifesting some new phase of the plague, he took a step backward as Gervais came toward him.

Damn it, if he's infected, I'll kill him before I let him touch me, priest or not.

"Damién . . . my son . . ." The words were muffled by a filled throat, so low he barely heard. One hand extended, clutching something inside.

A folded piece of vellum. A letter.

"Wh-what is it?" Damién's own hand went to his side, remembering too late he'd left his sword and belt-dagger hanging from his saddle, obeying the priest's command not to bring weapons into the Lord's House. He stepped back, holding up his hands, warding him away.

The priest stopped. Lowering the upraised hand, he took a deep breath and collected himself.

"I'm sorry, my son. Truly I am." A tear trickled down his cheek, making a new track across the others.

"What do you mean?"

"I've just come from *Château de Chevigny . . .*"

"*Non.*" If the priest was called, that meant only one thing.

Gervais said nothing else, merely held out the letter. When Damién snatched it from him, he let his hand drop to his side, like a dead thing, like those in the *château* would soon be. He stood without speaking, watching the young man rip away the seal and unfold the single sheet, closing his eyes as Damién's frantic ones scanned the words placing a death sentence on all his hopes.

Damién, ma cher.

I am stricken. In spite of your prayers, the Scourge is visited upon me. My maman has already been taken and I fear I will be next. As I breathe my last, I will think of you and of the life we might have had.

I pray we meet again in Heaven.

Toujours je t'aime,
Your Antoinette.

"It can't be. I saw her just yesterday." He didn't add it had been through the bars of the *château's* gates. He waved the sheet. "This letter is a lie!"

"'Tis no lie, my lord." Gervais dared come close enough to place a hopefully calming hand on his shoulder. "I was called to the *château* early this morning. I gave Lady Antoinette her Last Rites and she, in turn, asked me to deliver that letter to you."

With the swiftness the Plague carried away its victims, it had become the custom to call in the priest as soon as symptoms manifested.

Silently, he accepted Gervais' words. His Antoinette was going to die. Instead of coming a blushing bride to his marriage bed, she would be consigned—a rotting, blood-weeping corpse— to the plague fires.

Nevertheless, he said again, "Lies," as if repeating it would make it so. "Just as everything else is a lie . . . even the Scriptures we've been taught all our lives."

"Lord Damién!" Gervais staggered as if he'd been struck. Clutching the rosary around his neck, he sucked in the strength to say, "Listen to yourself. You speak blasphemy." He looked upward, clasping the length of beads. "Father, forgive him. 'Tis his grief speaking."

"Grief? Aye, I've grief. A great one. I'm losing the woman I love, damn it! And I can't even tell her goodbye. I have to receive her last words in a *letter*." He spoke the word as if it also held pestilence.

He wouldn't even be allowed to attend the funeral, for there would be none, only the plague wagon, coming with its tolling bell. Come to carry his Antonette to the fire.

"She'll be placed in the de Chevigny crypt. She won't be burned."

He hadn't realized he spoke aloud until Gervais said that.

"It doesn't matter. She'll still be dead. Dead—and not my wife." Damién flung the letter to the floor. Turning away so the priest might not see, he allowed tears to flow.

Grief mixed with his anger. Crying because God had failed him, tears for someone lost before she was gained.

"Why is it happening, Father? I prayed . . . most devoutly . . . every day since the Plague came to La Croix. Why didn't the Heavenly Father answer my prayers?" He began to sob in earnest, hands pressed to his face.

"Perhaps . . ." Gervais was at a loss for words. He left that single one fade into silence.

"Perhaps . . . *what?*"

Damién's expression startled the priest. Briefly, he appeared furious rather than grief-stricken.

"Perhaps God was too busy? Perhaps he doesn't care? *Perhaps he doesn't really exist?*" He spat the sentence viciously. "Why not tell the truth for once, Father?"

He was raving now, fury building with each word.

"That all this—" Waving his arms to take in the now-empty pews. "—is a farce . . . a falsehood to make us accept dying without a struggle. Those of us fool enough to believe such deceits."

The priest didn't answer.

* * *

To get your copy of *The Nightman's Odyssey*, visit your favorite bookstore or go to our online book catalog at www.epic-publishing.com/books.

www.ingramcontent.com/pod-product-compliance
Lightning Source LLC
Chambersburg PA
CBHW010646100726
47901CB00009B/2453